10 Minutes 38 Seconds
in This Strange World

10 Minutes 38 Seconds in This Strange World

ELIF SHAFAK

BLOOMSBURY PUBLISHING

NEW YORK · LONDON · OXFORD · NEW DELHI · SYDNEY

To the women of Istanbul
and to the city of Istanbul, which is, and has always been, a she-city

BLOOMSBURY PUBLISHING
Bloomsbury Publishing Inc.
1385 Broadway, New York, NY 10018, USA

BLOOMSBURY, BLOOMSBURY PUBLISHING, and the Diana logo are trademarks of
Bloomsbury Publishing Plc

First published in 2019 in Great Britain by Penguin Random House UK
First published in the United States 2019

ISBN: HB: 978-1-63557-447-0; eBook: 978-1-63557-448-7

Library of Congress Cataloging-in-Publication Data is available.

2   4   6   8   10   9   7   5   3   1

Printed and bound in the U.S.A. by Berryville Graphics Inc., Berryville, Virginia

To find out more about our authors and books visit www.bloomsbury.com and
sign up for our newsletters.

Bloomsbury books may be purchased for business or promotional use. For information on
bulk purchases please contact Macmillan Corporate and Premium Sales Department at
specialmarkets@macmillan.com.

Now he has again preceded me a little in parting from this strange world. This has no importance. For people like us who believe in physics, the separation between past, present and future has only the importance of an admittedly tenacious illusion.

Albert Einstein upon the death of his
closest friend, Michele Besso

1. Bosphorus Bridge
2. The street of brothels
3. Galata Tower
4. A synagogue
5. Saint Antoine Church
6. Istiklal Avenue
7. Taksim Square
8. The Intercontinental Hotel
9. The Street of Cauldron Makers
10. Golden Horn
11. Cemetery of the Companionless
12. Mevlevi/ Sufi dervish lodge

The End

Her name was Leila.

Tequila Leila, as she was known to her friends and her clients. Tequila Leila as she was called at home and at work, in that rosewood-coloured house on a cobblestoned cul-de-sac down by the wharf, nestled between a church and a synagogue, among lamp shops and kebab shops – the street that harboured the oldest licensed brothels in Istanbul.

Still, if she were to hear you put it like that, she might take offence and playfully hurl a shoe – one of her high-heeled stilettos.

'*Is*, darling, not *was* . . . My name *is* Tequila Leila.'

Never in a thousand years would she agree to be spoken of in the past tense. The very thought of it would make her feel small and defeated, and the last thing she wanted in this world was to feel that way. No, she would insist on the present tense – even though she now realized with a sinking feeling that her heart had just stopped beating, and her breathing had abruptly ceased, and whichever way she looked at her situation there was no denying that she was dead.

None of her friends knew it yet. This early in the morning they would be fast asleep, each trying to find the way out of their own labyrinth of dreams. Leila wished she were at home too, enveloped in the warmth of bed covers with her cat curled at her feet, purring in drowsy contentment. Her cat was stone deaf and black – except for a patch of snow on one paw. She had named him Mr Chaplin, after Charlie Chaplin, for, just like the heroes of early cinema, he lived in a silent world of his own.

Tequila Leila would have given anything to be in her apartment now. Instead she was here, somewhere on the outskirts of Istanbul, across from a dark, damp football field, inside a metal rubbish bin with rusty handles and flaking paint. It was a wheelie bin; at least four feet high and half as wide. Leila herself was five foot seven – plus the eight inches of her purple slingback stilettos, still on her feet.

There was so much she wanted to know. In her mind she kept replaying the last moments of her life, asking herself where things had gone wrong – a futile exercise since time could not be unravelled as though it were a ball of yarn. Her skin was already turning greyish-white, even though her cells were still abuzz with activity. She could not help but notice that there was a great deal happening inside her organs and limbs. People always assumed that a corpse was no more alive than a fallen tree or a hollow stump, devoid of consciousness. But given half a chance, Leila would have testified that, on the contrary, a corpse was brimming with life.

She could not believe that her mortal existence was over and done with. Only the day before she had crossed the neighbourhood of Pera, her shadow gliding along streets named after military leaders and national heroes, streets named after men. Just that week her laughter had echoed in the low-ceilinged taverns of Galata and Kurtulush, and the small, stuffy dens of Tophane, none of which ever appeared in travel guides or on tourist maps. The Istanbul that Leila had known was not the Istanbul that the Ministry of Tourism would have wanted foreigners to see.

Last night she had left her fingerprints on a whisky glass, and a trace of her perfume – Paloma Picasso, a birthday present from her friends – on the silk scarf she had tossed aside on the bed of a stranger, in the top-floor suite of a luxury hotel. In the sky high above, a sliver of yesterday's moon was visible, bright and unreachable, like the vestige of a happy memory. She was still part of this world, and there was still life inside her, so how could she be gone? How could she be no more, as though she were a dream that fades at the first hint of daylight? Only a few hours ago she was singing, smoking, swearing, thinking . . . well, even now she was thinking. It was remarkable that her mind was working at full tilt – though who knew for how long. She wished she could go back and tell everyone that the dead did not die instantly, that they could, in fact, continue to reflect on things, including their own demise. People would be scared if they learned this, she reckoned. She certainly would have been when she was alive. But she felt it was important that they knew.

It seemed to Leila that human beings exhibited a profound impatience with the milestones of their existence. For one thing, they assumed that you automatically became a wife or a husband the moment you said, 'I do!' But the truth was, it took years to learn how to be married. Similarly, society expected maternal – or paternal – instincts to kick in as soon as one had a child. In fact, it could take quite a while to figure out how to be a parent – or a grandparent, for that matter. Ditto with retirement and old age. How could you possibly change gears the moment you walked out of an office where you had spent half your life and squandered most of your dreams? Not that easy. Leila had known retired teachers who woke up at seven, showered and dressed neatly, just to slump at the breakfast table, only then remembering they no longer had a job. They were still adjusting.

Perhaps it was not that different when it came to death. People thought you changed into a corpse the instant you exhaled your last breath. But things were not clear-cut like that. Just as there were countless shades between jet black and brilliant white, so there were multiple stages of this thing called 'eternal rest'. If a border existed between the Realm of Life and the Realm of Afterlife, Leila decided, it must be as permeable as sandstone.

She was waiting for the sun to rise. Surely then someone would find her and get her out of this filthy bin. She did not expect the authorities to take long to figure out who she was. All they had to do was locate her file. Throughout the years, she had been searched, photographed, fingerprinted and kept in custody more often than she cared to admit. Those back-street police stations, they had a distinctive smell to them: ashtrays piled high with yesterday's cigarette butts, dregs of coffee in chipped cups, sour breath, wet rags, and a sharp stench from the urinals that no amount of bleach could ever suppress. Officers and offenders shared cramped rooms. Leila had always found it fascinating that the cops and the criminals shed their dead skin cells on the same floor, and the same dust mites gobbled them up, without favour or partiality. At some level invisible to the human eye, opposites blended in the most unexpected ways.

Once the authorities had identified her, she supposed they would inform her family. Her parents lived in the historic city of Van – a thousand miles away. But she did not expect them to come and fetch her dead body, considering they had rejected her long ago.

You've brought us shame. Everyone is talking behind our backs.

So the police would have to go to her friends instead. The five of them: Sabotage Sinan, Nostalgia Nalan, Jameelah, Zaynab122 and Hollywood Humeyra.

Tequila Leila had no doubt that her friends would come as fast as they could. She could almost see them sprinting towards her, their footsteps hurried and yet hesitant, their eyes wide with shock and a sorrow still incipient, a raw grief that had not sunk in, not just yet. She felt awful for having to put them through what was clearly going to be a painful ordeal. But it was a relief to know that they would give her a brilliant funeral. Camphor and frankincense. Music and flowers – particularly, roses. Burning red, bright yellow, deep burgundy . . . Classic, timeless, unbeatable. Tulips were too imperial, daffodils too delicate, and lilies made her sneeze, but roses were perfect, a mixture of sultry glamour and sharp thorns.

Slowly, dawn was breaking. Streaks of colour – peach bellinis, orange martinis, strawberry margaritas, frozen negronis – streamed above the horizon, east to west. Within a matter of seconds, calls to prayer from the surrounding mosques reverberated around her, none of them synchronized. Far in the distance, the Bosphorus, waking from its turquoise sleep, yawned with force. A fishing boat headed back to port, its engine coughing smoke. A heavy swell rolled languidly towards the waterfront. The area had once been graced with olive groves and fig orchards, all of which were bulldozed to make way for more buildings and car parks. Somewhere in the semi-darkness a dog was barking, more out of a sense of duty than excitement. Nearby a bird chirped, bold and loud, and another one trilled in return, though not as jovially. A dawn chorus. Leila could now hear a delivery truck rumble on the pockmarked road, hitting one pothole after another. Soon the hum of early morning traffic would become deafening. Life at full blast.

Back when she was alive, Tequila Leila had always been somewhat surprised, unsettled even, by people who derived satisfaction from speculating obsessively about the end of the world. How could seemingly sane minds be so consumed with all those crazy scenarios of asteroids, fireballs and comets wreaking havoc on the planet? As far as she was concerned, the apocalypse was not the worst thing that could happen. The possibility of an immediate and wholesale decimation of civilization was not half as frightening as the simple realization that our individual passing had no impact on the order of things, and life would go on just the same with or without us. Now *that*, she had always thought, was terrifying.

The breeze shifted direction, whipping across the football field. Then she saw them. Four adolescent boys. Scavengers out early to sift through rubbish. Two of them were pushing a cart packed with plastic bottles and crushed cans. Another, with slouched shoulders and buckled knees, tagged along behind, carrying a grimy sack containing something of great weight. The fourth, clearly their leader, was walking ahead with a distinctive swagger, his bony chest puffed out like a cockerel in a fight. They were making their way towards her, joking among themselves.

Keep walking.

They stopped by a waste container across the street and started rummaging through it. Shampoo bottles, juice cartons, yogurt tubs, egg boxes . . . each treasure was plucked and piled on to the cart. Their movements were deft, expert. One of them found an old leather hat. Laughing, he put it on and walked with an exaggerated, uppity strut, hands tucked into his back pockets, mimicking some gangster he must have seen in a film. Instantly, the leader snatched the hat away and placed it on his own head. Nobody objected. Having picked the rubbish clean, they were ready to go. To Leila's dismay they seemed to be turning back, headed in the opposite direction.

Hey, I'm over here!

Slowly, as though he had heard Leila's plea, the leader lifted his chin and squinted into the rising sun. Under the shifting light, he scanned the horizon, his gaze wandering until he caught sight of her. His eyebrows shot up, his lips trembling slightly.

Please, don't run away.

He didn't. Instead he said something inaudible to the others, and now they too were staring at her with the same stunned expression. She realized how young they were. They were still children, mere striplings, these boys pretending to be men.

The leader took the smallest step forward. And another. He walked towards her the way a mouse approached a fallen apple – timid and uneasy, but equally determined and fast. His face darkened as he drew closer and saw the state she was in.

Don't be afraid.

He was by her side now, so close she could see the whites of his eyes, bloodshot and flecked with yellow. She could tell he had been sniffing glue, this boy who was no older than fifteen, whom Istanbul would pretend to welcome and accommodate, and, when he least expected it, throw aside like an old rag doll.

Call the police, son. Call the police so they can inform my friends.

He glanced left and right, making sure there was no one watching, no surveillance cameras nearby. Lurching forward he reached for Leila's necklace – a golden locket with a tiny emerald in the centre. Gingerly, as if afraid it might explode in the palm of his hand, he touched the pendant, feeling the comforting chill of the metal. He opened the locket. There was a photo inside. He took out the photo and inspected it for a moment. He recognized the woman, a younger version of her – and a man with green eyes, a gentle smile and long hair, combed in a style from another era. They seemed happy together, in love.

On the back of the photo there was an inscription: *D/Ali and I . . . Spring 1976.*

Swiftly, the leader yanked off the pendant and stuffed his prize into his pocket. If the others, standing quietly behind him, were aware of what he had just done, they chose to ignore it. They might be young but they had enough experience in this city to know when to act smart and when to play dumb.

Only one of them took a step forward and dared to ask, his voice merely a whisper, 'Is she . . . is she alive?'

'Don't be ridiculous,' said the leader. 'She's as dead as a cooked duck.'

'Poor woman. Who is she?'

Cocking his head to the side, the leader studied Leila, as though noticing her for the first time. He looked her up and down, a smile spreading on his face like ink spilled across a page. 'Can't you see, you moron? She's a whore.'

'You think so?' the other boy asked with earnestness – too shy, too innocent to repeat the word.

'I know so, idiot.' The leader now turned halfway towards the group, and said, loudly and emphatically, 'It'll be all over the papers. And TV channels! We're going to be famous! When journalists get here, let me do the talking, okay?'

In the distance a car revved its engine and roared up the road towards the motorway, skidding as it turned. The smell of exhaust mingled with the sting of salt in the wind. Even at so early an hour, sunlight just beginning to brush the minarets, the rooftops and the uppermost branches of the Judas trees, people were already rushing in this city, already late for somewhere else.

PART ONE

The Mind

One Minute

In the first minute following her death, Tequila Leila's consciousness began to ebb, slowly and steadily, like a tide receding from the shore. Her brain cells, having run out of blood, were now completely deprived of oxygen. But they did not shut down. Not right away. One last reserve of energy activated countless neurons, connecting them as though for the first time. Although her heart had stopped beating, her brain was resisting, a fighter till the end. It entered into a state of heightened awareness, observing the demise of the body but not ready to accept its own end. Her memory surged forth, eager and diligent, collecting pieces of a life that was speeding to a close. She recalled things she did not even know she was capable of remembering, things she had believed to be lost forever. Time became fluid, a fast flow of recollections seeping into one another, the past and the present inseparable.

The first memory that came to her mind was about salt – the feel of it on her skin and the taste of it on her tongue.

She saw herself as a baby – naked, slick and red. Only a few seconds earlier she had left her mother's womb and slid through a wet, slippery passage, gripped by a fear wholly new to her, and here she was now in a room full of sounds and colours and things unknown. Sunlight through the stained-glass windows dappled the quilt on the bed and reflected off the water in a porcelain basin, despite it being a chilly day in January. Into that same water an elderly woman dressed in shades of autumn leaves – the midwife – dipped a towel and wrung it out, blood trickling down her forearm.

'*Mashallah, mashallah*. It's a girl.'

The midwife took a piece of flint, which she had tucked away in her bra, and cut the umbilical cord. She never used a knife or a pair of scissors for this purpose, finding their cold efficiency unsuitable to the messy task of welcoming a baby into this world. The old woman was widely respected in the neighbourhood, and considered, for all her eccentricities and reclusiveness, to be one of the uncanny ones – those who had two sides to their personality, one earthly, one unearthly, and who, like a coin tossed into the air, could at any time reveal either face.

'A girl,' echoed the young mother lying in the wrought-iron four-poster bed, her honey-brown hair matted with sweat, her mouth dry as sand.

She had been worried that this might be so. Earlier in the month she had taken a walk in the garden looking for spiderwebs in the branches overhead, and, when she had found one, she had gently pushed her finger through it. For several days afterwards she had checked the site. If the spider had repaired the hole it would mean that the baby was a boy. But the web had remained torn.

The young woman's name was Binnaz – 'One Thousand Bland-ishments'. She was nineteen years of age, though this year she felt much older. She had full, generous lips, a dainty, upturned nose that was considered a rarity in this part of the country, a long face with a pointed chin, and large, dark eyes speckled with blue flecks like a starling's eggs. She had always been slender and of delicate build but now looked even more so in her fawn-coloured linen nightgown. There were a few faint smallpox scars on her cheeks; her mother had once said they were a sign that she had been caressed by moonlight in her sleep. She missed her mother and her father and her nine siblings, all of whom lived in a village several hours away. Her family were very poor – a fact she had often been reminded of ever since she had entered this house as a new bride:

Be thankful. When you came here, you had nothing.

She still had nothing, Binnaz often thought; all her possessions were as ephemeral and rootless as dandelion seeds. One stiff breeze, one torrential downpour, and they would be gone, just like that. It weighed heavily on her mind that she could be thrown out of this house at any time, and if that happened where would she go? Her father would never agree to take her back, not with so many mouths to feed. She would have to marry again – but there was no guarantee that her next marriage would be any happier or a new husband more to her liking, and who would want her anyway, a divorcee, a *used woman*? Burdened with these suspicions, she moved around the house, around her bedroom, around her own head, like an uninvited guest. That is, until now. Everything would be different with the birth of this baby, she assured herself. She would no longer feel ill at ease, no longer insecure.

Almost against her will, Binnaz glanced towards the doorway. There, with one hand on her hip, another on the door handle – as if debating whether to stay or leave – stood a sturdy-looking, square-jawed woman. Although she was in her early forties, the age spots on her hands and the creases around her blade-thin mouth made her appear older. Across her forehead there were deep lines, uneven and magnified, like a ploughed field. Her wrinkles came mostly from frowning and smoking. All day long she puffed away on tobacco smuggled in from Iran and sipped tea smuggled in from Syria. Her brick-red hair – thanks to generous applications of Egyptian henna – was parted in the middle and formed into a perfect plait that almost reached her waist. Her hazel eyes she had carefully lined with the darkest kohl. She was Binnaz's husband's other wife, the first one – Suzan.

For an instant, the two women locked gazes. The air around them felt thick and slightly yeasty, like rising dough. They had been sharing the same room for more than twelve hours and yet now they were thrust into separate worlds. They both knew that with the birth of this child their positions in the family would shift forever. The second wife, despite her youth and recent arrival, would be promoted to the top.

Suzan averted her eyes, but not for long. When she looked back, there was a hardness in her face that hadn't been there before. She nodded towards the baby. 'Why doesn't she make a sound?'

Binnaz turned ashen. 'Yes. Is there something wrong?'

'Nothing's wrong,' said the midwife, giving Suzan a cold glare. 'We just have to wait.'

The midwife rinsed the baby with holy water from the Zamzam well – courtesy of a pilgrim who had recently returned from the Hajj. The blood, the mucus, the vernix were all wiped away. The newborn squirmed uncomfortably and kept on squirming even after the washing, as though fighting with herself – all eight pounds three ounces of her.

'Can I hold her?' asked Binnaz, twirling her hair between her fingertips – an anxious habit she had picked up over the past year. 'She . . . she's not crying.'

'Oh, she *will* cry, this girl,' said the midwife in a decisive tone, and instantly bit her tongue, the statement echoing like a dark omen. Quickly, she spat on the floor three times and stepped on her left foot with her right one. That would prevent the premonition – if that's what it was – from travelling far.

An awkward silence ensued as everyone in the room – the first wife, the second wife, the midwife and two neighbours – stared at the baby with expectant eyes.

'What is it? Tell me the truth,' said Binnaz to no one in particular, her voice thinner than air.

Having had six miscarriages in only a few years, each more devastating than the last and harder to forget, she had been extremely careful throughout this pregnancy. She had not touched a single peach so the baby wouldn't be covered in fuzz; she had not used any spices or herbs in her cooking so the baby wouldn't have freckles or moles; she had not smelled roses so the baby wouldn't have port-wine birthmarks. Not even once had she cut her hair lest their luck also be cut short. She had refrained from hammering nails into the wall in case she mistakenly hit a sleeping ghoul on the head. After dark, knowing too well that the djinn held their weddings around toilets, she had stayed in her room, making do with a chamber pot. Rabbits, rats, cats, vultures, porcupines, stray dogs – she had managed to avoid looking at them all. Even when a roving musician had appeared on their street with a dancing bear in tow, and all the locals had flocked outside to watch the spectacle, she had refused to join them, fearing her baby would emerge covered in hair. And whenever she had run into a beggar or a leper, or seen a hearse, she had turned around and scurried off in the opposite direction. Every morning she had eaten a whole quince to give the baby dimples, and every night she had slept with a knife under her pillow to ward off evil spirits. And secretly, after every sunset, she had collected hairs from Suzan's hairbrush and burned them in the fireplace so as to reduce the power of her husband's first wife.

As soon as the birth pangs had started, Binnaz had bitten into a red apple, sweet and sun-softened. It now stood on the table by her bed, slowly browning. This same apple would later be sliced into several pieces and given to women in the neighbourhood who could not get pregnant, so they too might one day bear a child. She had also sipped pomegranate sherbet that had been poured into her husband's right shoe, scattered fennel seeds in four corners of the room and jumped over a broom placed on the floor, just by the door – a frontier to keep Sheitan away. As the cramps intensified, one by one, all the caged animals in the house were released to facilitate the labour. The canaries, the finches . . . The last to be freed was the betta fish in the glass bowl, proud and lonely. Now it must be swimming in a creek not far away, its long, flowing fins as blue as a fine sapphire. If the little fish reached the soda lake, for which this eastern Anatolian town was famous, it would not have much chance of survival in the salty, carbonated waters. But if it travelled the opposite way, it could reach the Great Zab, and, somewhere further down the journey, it might even join the Tigris, that legendary river issuing out of the Garden of Eden.

All of this for the baby to arrive safe and healthy.

'I want to see her. Can you bring me my daughter?'

No sooner had Binnaz asked this than a movement caught her attention. Quiet as a passing thought, Suzan had opened the door and slipped outside – no doubt to give the news to her husband – *their* husband. Binnaz's whole frame went rigid.

Haroun was a man of scintillating opposites. Remarkably generous and charitable one day, self-absorbed and distracted to the point of callousness the next. The oldest of three, he had raised his two siblings on his own after their parents had died in a car accident that had destroyed their world. The tragedy had shaped his personality, making him overprotective of his family and distrustful of outsiders. At times he recognized that something was broken inside him and he dearly wished he could mend it, but these thoughts never led him anywhere. He was fond of alcohol and fearful of religion in equal degree. Knocking back yet another glass of raqi, he would make hefty promises to his drinking buddies, and afterwards, when he sobered up, heavy with guilt, he would make even heftier promises to Allah. While his mouth may have been hard for him to control, his body proved a greater challenge still. Every time Binnaz had got pregnant, his belly, too, had swollen in tandem with hers, not much, but enough to make the neighbours snigger behind his back.

'The man is expecting again!' they said, rolling their eyes. 'Too bad he can't give birth himself.'

Haroun wanted a son more than anything in the world. Not just one. He told whoever cared to listen that he was going to have four sons, whom he was going to name Tarkan, Tolga, Tufan and Tarik.* His long years of marriage to Suzan had yielded no offspring. The elders in the family had then found Binnaz – a girl of barely sixteen. After weeks of negotiations between the families, Haroun and Binnaz had married in a religious ceremony. It was unofficial, and if anything were to go wrong in the future it would not be recognized by the secular courts, but that was a detail no one had cared to mention. The two of them had sat on the floor, in front of the witnesses, opposite the cross-eyed imam whose voice became more gravelly as he switched from Turkish to Arabic. Binnaz had kept her gaze on the carpet throughout, although she

* Meaning, respectively, 'Bold and Strong', 'War Helmet', 'Torrential Rain' and 'The Way to Reach God'.

could not help stealing glances at the imam's feet. His socks, pale brown like baked mud, were old and worn. Every time he shifted, one of his big toes threatened to push through the threadbare wool, looking for an escape.

Soon after the wedding Binnaz had got pregnant, but it had ended in a miscarriage that almost killed her. Late-night panic, hot shards of pain, a cold hand gripping her groin, the smell of blood, the need to hold on to something, as if she were falling, falling. It had been the same with each subsequent pregnancy, only worse. She could not tell anyone, but it seemed to her that with each baby lost, another part of the rope bridge linking her to the world at large had snapped and fallen away, until only the flimsiest thread kept her connected to that world, kept her sane.

After three years of waiting, the family elders had once again started pressuring Haroun. They reminded him that the Qur'an allows a man to have up to four wives, so long as he was fair to them, and they had no doubt that Haroun would treat all his wives equally. They urged him to look for a peasant woman this time, even a widow with children of her own. It, too, wouldn't be official but it could easily be done through another religious ceremony, just as quiet and quick as the previous one. Alternatively, he could divorce this useless young wife and then get remarried. So far, Haroun had turned down both suggestions. It was hard enough providing for two wives, he said; a third would ruin him financially, and he had no intention of leaving either Suzan or Binnaz, both of whom he had grown fond of, though for different reasons.

Now, as she propped herself up on the pillows, Binnaz tried to imagine what Haroun was doing. He must be lying on a sofa in the next room, one hand on his forehead, another on his stomach, expecting a baby's cry to pierce the air. Then she imagined Suzan walking towards him, her steps measured, controlled. She saw them together, whispering to each other; their gestures smooth and practised, shaped by years of sharing the same space, even if not the same bed. Unsettled by her own thoughts, Binnaz said, more to herself than to anyone else: 'Suzan is telling him.'

'That's all right,' said one of the neighbours soothingly.

So much was insinuated in this remark. *Let her be the one who delivers the news of the baby she herself could not deliver.* Unspoken words ran between the women of this town like washing lines strung between houses.

Binnaz nodded even as she felt something dark brewing inside her, an anger she had never let out. She glanced at the midwife and asked, 'Why has the baby still not made a sound?'

The midwife did not answer. A nub of unease had lodged deep in her gut. There was something peculiar about this baby and it was not just her unsettling silence. Leaning forward she sniffed the infant. Just as she had suspected – a powdery, musky scent that wasn't of this world.

Placing the newborn on her knees, the woman turned her over on to her tummy and slapped her bottom, once, twice. The small face registered the shock, the pain. Her hands clenched into fists, her mouth drew into a tight pucker and still no noise came.

'What's wrong?'

The midwife sighed. 'Nothing. It's just . . . I think she's still with *them*.'

'Who's them?' asked Binnaz but, not wanting to hear the answer, she added in haste, 'Then do something!'

The old woman considered. It was better if the baby found her own way at her own pace. Most newborns adapted instantly to their new environments, but a few chose to hang back, as though hesitating whether or not to join the rest of humanity – and who could blame them? In all her years, the midwife had seen plenty of babies who, either moments before or right after their births, were so intimidated by the force of life pressing in from all sides that they lost heart and quietly departed this world. '*Kader*', people called it – 'destiny' – and said no more, because people always gave simple names to the complex things that frightened them. But the midwife believed that some babies merely chose not to give life a try, as though they knew, and preferred to avoid, the hardships ahead. Were they cowards or were they as wise as the great Solomon himself? Who could tell?

'Bring me salt,' the midwife said to the neighbourhood women.

She could have used snow as well – had there been enough of it freshly piled outside. In the past, she had submerged many a newborn in a heap of pristine snow, pulling them out at just the right moment. The shock of the cold opened their lungs, made their blood flow, boosted their immunity. These infants had, without exception, grown up to be strong adults.

In a little while, the neighbours returned with a large plastic bowl and a bag of rock salt. The midwife affectionately placed the infant in the middle of the bowl and began to rub her skin with salt flakes. Once the baby stopped smelling like one of the angels, they would have to set her free. Outside in the upper branches of the poplar tree a bird trilled, a blue jay by the sound of it. A single crow cawed as it flew towards the sun. Everything spoke in its own language – the wind, the grass. Everything but this child.

'Maybe she is mute?' said Binnaz.

The midwife arched her eyebrows. 'Be patient.'

As though on cue the baby started to cough. A rattling, throaty sound. She must have swallowed a bit of salt, the taste sharp and unexpected. Flushing crimson, the infant smacked her lips and scrunched up her face but still refused to cry. How stubborn she was, how dangerously rebellious her soul. Simply rubbing her with salt was not going to be enough. That was when the midwife came to a decision. She would have to try a different approach.

'Bring me more salt.'

There being no more rock salt left in the house, table salt would have to do. The midwife made a hole in the pile, placed the baby in it and covered her fully with the white crystals; first her body, then her head.

'What if she suffocates?' asked Binnaz.

'Don't worry, babies can hold their breath longer than we can.'

'But how can you tell when to take her out?'

'Hush, listen,' said the old woman, placing a finger on her chapped lips.

Underneath the sheath of salt, the baby opened her eyes and stared into the milky nothingness. It felt lonely in here but she was used to loneliness. Curling into herself as she had done for months, she bided her time.

Her gut said, *Oh, I like it here; I'm not going up there again.*

Her heart protested, *Don't be silly. Why stay in a place where nothing ever happens? It's boring.*

Why leave a place where nothing ever happens? It's safe, her gut said.

Baffled by their quarrel, the baby waited. Another full minute passed. Emptiness swirled and splashed around her, lapping at her toes, at her fingertips.

Just because you think it's safe here, it doesn't mean this is the right place for you, her heart countered. *Sometimes where you feel most safe is where you least belong.*

At last, the baby reached a conclusion. She would listen to her heart – the same one that would prove to be quite a troublemaker. Keen to go out and discover the world, despite its dangers and difficulties, she opened her mouth, ready to release a sound – but almost at once salt poured down her throat, blocked her nose.

Immediately, the midwife, with movements deft and swift, thrust her hands into the bowl and pulled the baby out. A loud, terrified wail filled the room. All four women smiled with relief.

'Good girl,' said the midwife. 'What took you so long? Cry, my dear. Never be ashamed of your tears. Cry and everyone knows you're alive.'

The old woman wrapped the baby in a shawl and sniffed her again. That beguiling, other-worldly scent had evaporated, leaving only the slightest trace behind. In time that, too, would disappear – although she had known quite a few people who, even in old age, still carried with them a whiff of Paradise. But she felt no need to share this information. Lifting herself on to the balls of her feet, she laid the infant on the bed, beside her mother.

Binnaz broke into a smile, a flutter in her heart. She touched her daughter's toes through the silky fabric – perfect and beautiful, and frighteningly fragile. She tenderly held the baby's locks of hair between her hands as if she were carrying holy water in her palms. For a moment she felt happy, complete. 'No dimples,' she said, and giggled to herself.

'Shall we call your husband?' asked one of the neighbours.

This, too, was a sentence laden with unspoken words. By now Suzan must have told Haroun that the baby had arrived, so why hadn't he come running? Clearly, he had lingered to talk to his first wife and soothe her worries. That had been his priority.

A shadow passed over Binnaz's face. 'Yes, call him.'

There was no need. In a few seconds, Haroun walked in slouching, round-shouldered, moving out of the shadow into the sunlight. He had a shock of greying hair that gave him the look of a distracted thinker; an imperious nose with tight nostrils; a broad, smooth-shaven face and downturned dark brown eyes, shining with pride. Smiling, he approached the bed. He looked at the baby, at the second wife, at the midwife, at the first wife, and finally upwards to the heavens.

'Allah, I thank you, my Lord. You've accepted my prayers.'

'A girl,' said Binnaz softly, in case he was not yet aware.

'I know. The next one will be a boy. We'll name him Tarkan.' He ran his index finger across the baby's forehead, as smooth and warm to the touch as a favourite amulet rubbed too many times. 'She's healthy, that's what matters. I was praying this whole time. I said to the Almighty, if You let this baby live, I won't drink any more. Not a single drop! Allah has heard my plea, He is merciful. This baby is not mine, nor is she yours.'

Binnaz stared at him, a flicker of confusion in her eyes. Suddenly, she was seized by a feeling of foreboding, like a wild animal that senses – albeit too late – that it is about to walk into a trap. She glanced at Suzan, who was standing by the entrance, lips pursed so tight they were almost white; silent and motionless save for the impatient tapping of her foot. Something about her demeanour suggested that she was excited, overjoyed even.

'This baby belongs to God,' Haroun was now saying.

'All babies do,' murmured the midwife.

Oblivious, Haroun held his younger wife's hand and looked straight into her eyes. 'We'll give this baby to Suzan.'

'What are you talking about?' Binnaz rasped, her voice sounding to her ears wooden and distant, the voice of a stranger.

'Let Suzan raise her. She'll do an excellent job. You and I will make more children.'

'No!'

'You don't want to have more kids?'

'I'm not going to let that woman take my daughter.'

Haroun drew in a breath, then released it slowly. 'Don't be selfish. Allah won't approve. He gave you a baby, didn't He? Be grateful. You were barely scraping by when you came to this house.'

Binnaz shook her head, and kept doing so; whether it was because she was unable to stop herself or because it was the one small thing she could control, it was hard to tell. Haroun leaned over and held her by the shoulders, pulling her close to him. Only then did she become still, the light in her eyes dimmed.

'You're not being rational. We're all in the same house. You'll see your daughter every day. It's not like she'll be going away, for God's sake.'

If he had meant his words to be consoling, that was lost on her. Trembling to hold back the pain ripping through her chest, she covered her face with the flat of her palms. 'And who will my daughter call "Mummy"?'

'What difference does that make? Suzan can be *Mummy*. You'll be Auntie. We'll tell her the truth when she gets older, no need to confuse her little head now. When we have more kids, they'll all be brothers and sisters anyhow. They'll be running riot in the house, you'll see. You won't be able to tell who belongs to whom. We'll all be one big family.'

'Who is going to nurse the baby?' asked the midwife. 'The mummy or the auntie?'

Haroun glanced at the old woman, every muscle in his body strung taut. In his eyes, reverence and loathing formed a wild dance. He thrust his hand into his pocket and took out a jumble of items: a dented pack of cigarettes with a lighter tucked inside, crumpled banknotes, a piece of chalk he used for marking alterations on garments, a tablet for his upset stomach. The money, he handed to the midwife. 'For you – a token of our gratitude,' he said.

Tight-lipped, the old woman accepted her payment. In her experience, getting through life as unscathed as possible depended to a large extent on two fundamental principles: knowing the right time to arrive and knowing the right time to leave.

As the neighbours began to pack their things, and removed the blood-soaked sheets and towels, silence filled the room like water, seeping into every corner.

'We are off now,' said the midwife with quiet resolve. The two neighbours stood demurely on either side of her. 'We'll bury the placenta under a rosebush. And this –' She pointed a bony finger towards the umbilical cord that had been tossed on to a chair. 'If you'd like, we can throw it up on the school roof. Your daughter will be a teacher. Or we could take it to the hospital. She will be a nurse, who knows, even a doctor.'

Haroun considered the options. 'Try the school.'

After the women had left, Binnaz turned her head away from her husband, facing the apple on the bedside table. It was rotting; a soft, tranquil decay, achingly slow. Its browning colour reminded her of the socks of the imam who had married them, and how after the ceremony she had sat alone on this very bed, a shimmering veil covering her face, while in the next room her husband and the guests tucked into a banquet. Her mother had taught her absolutely nothing about what to expect on her wedding night, but an older aunt more sympathetic to her concerns had handed her a pill to pop under her tongue. *Take this and you won't feel a thing. It'll be over before you know it.* During the commotion of the day, Binnaz had lost the pill, which she suspected was just a pastille anyway. She had never seen a man naked, not even in pictures, and, though she had often bathed her younger brothers, she suspected it was a different type of body, the body of a grown man. The longer she had waited for her husband to come into the room, the higher her anxiety had soared. No sooner had she heard his footsteps than she had blacked out, collapsing to the floor. When she had opened her eyes, it was to the sight of neighbourhood women frantically rubbing her wrists, moistening her forehead, massaging her feet. There was a sharp smell in the air – of cologne and vinegar – and undertones of something else, something unfamiliar and unbidden, which she would later realize had come from a tube of lubricant.

Afterwards, when the two of them were alone, Haroun had given her a necklace made of a red ribbon and three gold coins – one for each of the virtues she would bring to this house: youth, docility, fertility. Seeing how nervous she was, he had spoken softly to her, his voice dissolving in the dark. He had been affectionate, but also acutely aware that people were waiting outside the door. He had hurriedly undressed her, perhaps fearing she might faint again. Binnaz had kept her eyes closed the whole time, sweat breaking out on her forehead. She had begun to count – *One, two, three . . . fifteen, sixteen, seventeen* – and carried on doing so even when he had told her to 'Stop that nonsense!'

Binnaz was illiterate and could not count beyond nineteen. Every time she had arrived at the last number, that unbreakable frontier, she had taken a breath and started all over again. After what felt like infinite nineteens, he had left the bed and marched out of the room, leaving the door open. Suzan had then rushed in and turned on the lights, paying no attention to her nakedness or to the smell of sweat and sex hanging in the air. The first wife had whisked off the bedsheet, inspected it and, clearly satisfied, disappeared without a word. Binnaz had spent the rest of the evening by herself, a fine layer of gloom settling on her shoulders like a dusting of snow. As she remembered it all now, an odd sound escaped her lips that could have been a laugh had it not been hiding so much hurt.

'Come on,' Haroun said. 'It's not –'

'This was her idea, wasn't it?' Binnaz interrupted him – something she had never done before. 'Did she just come up with this plan? Or have you two been plotting for months? Behind my back.'

'You don't mean that.' He sounded startled, though perhaps less by her words than by her tone. With his left hand, he stroked the hair on the back of his right hand, his eyes glazed and distracted. 'You are young. Suzan is getting old. She will never have a child of her own. Give her a gift.'

'And what about me? Who's going to give me a gift?'

'Allah, of course. He already has, can't you see? Don't be ungrateful.'

'Grateful, for this?' She made a little fluttering motion, a gesture so indistinct it could have referred to anything – this situation or perhaps this town, which now felt to her like just another backwater, on any old map.

'You're tired,' he said.

Binnaz started to cry. These were not tears of rage or resentment. They were tears of resignation, of the kind of defeat that is tantamount to a loss of greater faith. The air in her lungs felt heavy like lead. She had been a child when she had arrived in this house, and now that she had a child of her own, she was not allowed to raise her and grow up with her. She curled her arms around her knees and did not speak again for a long time. Thus the subject was closed, then and there – though, in truth, it would always remain open, this wound in the midst of their lives that would never heal.

Outside the window, pushing his cart up the street, a vendor cleared his throat and sang praise of his apricots – juicy and ripe. Inside the house, Binnaz thought, *How strange*, it not being the season for sweet apricots but the season of icy winds. She shivered as though the cold, of which the vendor seemed oblivious, had slipped through the walls and found her instead. She closed her eyes, but the darkness didn't help. She saw snowballs piled up in threatening pyramids. Now they were raining down on her, wet and hard with pebbles inside. One of the snowballs hit her on the nose, followed by others, flying thick and fast. Another landed on her bottom lip, splitting it. She opened her eyes, gasping. Was it real or was it just a dream? Tentatively she touched her nose. It was bleeding. There was also a dribble of blood on her chin. *How strange*, she thought once again. Could no one else see that she was in dreadful pain? And if they couldn't, did that mean that it was all in her head, all make-believe?

This wasn't her first encounter with mental illness, but it would remain her most vivid. Even years later, every time Binnaz wondered when and how her sanity had sneaked away, like a thief climbing out of the window in the dark, this was the moment she would always hark back to, the moment that she believed had debilitated her forever.

That same afternoon Haroun held the baby up in the air, turned towards Mecca and recited the *ezan*, the call to prayer, into her right ear.

'You, my daughter, you who, Allah willing, will be the first of many children under this roof, you with eyes dark as the night, I'll name you Leyla. But you won't be just any Leyla. I'll also give you my mother's names. Your *nine* was an honourable woman; she was very pious, as I am certain you'll be one day. I'll name you Afife – "Chaste, Untainted". And I'll name you Kamile – "Perfection". You'll be modest, respectable, pure as water . . .'

Haroun paused with the nagging thought that not all water was pure. He added, more loudly than he intended, just to make sure there was no celestial mix-up, no misunderstanding on the part of God, 'Spring water – clean, undefiled . . . All the mothers in Van will chide their daughters, "Why can't you be like Leyla?" And husbands will say to their wives, "Why couldn't you give birth to a girl like Leyla!"'

Meanwhile, the baby kept trying to jam her fist into her mouth, her lips twisting into a grimace each time she failed.

'You'll make me so proud,' Haroun carried on. 'True to your religion, true to your nation, true to your father.'

Frustrated with herself, and finally realizing that her clenched hand was simply too big, the baby broke into a wail, as though determined to make up for her early silence. Quickly, she was handed over to Binnaz, who, without a second of hesitation, began to nurse her, a sizzling pain drawing rings around her nipples like a marauding bird circling the skies.

Later on, when the baby had fallen asleep, Suzan, who had been waiting to one side, approached the bed, careful not to make a noise. Avoiding eye contact, she took the infant from her mother.

'I'll bring her back when she cries,' Suzan said, and swallowed. 'Don't worry. I'll take good care of her.'

Binnaz said nothing in return, her face as pale and worn as an old porcelain plate. Nothing emanated from her, except the sound of her breathing, faint but unmistakable. Her womb, her mind, this house . . . even the ancient lake where many a heartbroken lover was rumoured to have drowned, everything felt hollowed out and dried up. Everything but her sore, swollen breasts, leaking rivulets of milk.

Now alone in the room with her husband, Binnaz waited for him to speak. It was not an apology she wanted to hear as much as an admission of the injustice she faced and the enormous hurt it would do to her. But he, too, said nothing. And so it was that the baby girl, born to a family of one husband and two wives on 6 January 1947, in the city of Van – 'the Pearl of the East' – was named Leyla Afife Kamile. Such self-assured names, grandiose and unambiguous. Big mistakes, as it would turn out. For while it was true that she carried the night in her eyes, befitting the name

Leyla, it would soon become clear that her middle names were far from apt.

She wasn't flawless, even to begin with; her many shortcomings ran through her life like underground streams. In truth, she was a walking embodiment of imperfection – once she figured out how to walk, that is. And as for staying chaste, time would show how, for reasons not of her own doing, that would not exactly be her thing either.

She was to be Leyla Afife Kamile, full of virtue, high in merit. But years later, after she had turned up in Istanbul, alone and broke; after she had seen the sea for the first time, amazed at how that vast expanse of blue stretched to the horizon; after she had noticed that the curls in her hair turned to frizz in the humid air; after she had awoken one morning in a strange bed next to a man she had never seen before and her chest felt so heavy she thought she could never draw breath again; after she had been sold to a brothel where she was forced to have sex with ten to fifteen men each day in a room with a green plastic bucket on the floor, collecting the water that dripped from the ceiling every time it rained . . . long after all that, she would be known to her five dear friends, one eternal love and many clients as Tequila Leila.

When men asked – and they often did – why she insisted on spelling 'Leyla' as 'Leila', and whether by doing so she was trying to make herself seem Western or exotic, she would laugh and say that one day she went to the bazaar and traded the 'y' of 'yesterday' for the 'i' of 'infinity', and that was that.

In the end, none of this would make any difference to the newspapers that covered her murder. Most did not care to mention her by name, finding her initials sufficient. The same photo accompanied almost all the articles – one of Leila's unrecognizable old snaps, back from her secondary-school years. The editors could have chosen a more recent image, of course, even a headshot from the police archives, had they not worried that the sight of Leila's heavy make-up and conspicuous cleavage might offend the nation's sensitivities.

Her death was also covered on national TV on the evening of 29 November 1990. It followed a lengthy report on the United Nations Security Council Resolution to authorize military intervention in Iraq; the after-effects of the tearful resignation of the Iron Lady in Britain; the continuing tension between Greece and Turkey following the violence in Western Thrace and the looting of stores owned by ethnic Turks and the mutual expulsion of the Turkish Consul in Komotini and the Greek Consul in Istanbul; the merging of West Germany and East Germany's national football teams after the unification of the two countries; the repeal of the constitutional requirement for a married woman to get her husband's permission to work outside the home; and the smoking ban on Turkish Airlines flights, despite passionate protests from smokers nationwide.

Towards the end of the programme, a bright yellow band scrolled along the bottom of the screen: *Prostitute Found Slain in City Waste Bin: Fourth in a Month. Panic Spreads Among Istanbul's Sex Workers.*

Two Minutes

Two minutes after her heart had stopped beating, Leila's mind recalled two contrasting tastes: lemon and sugar.

June 1953. She saw herself as a six-year-old, a thicket of chestnut-brown curls surrounding her frail, wan face. No matter how remarkable her appetite, especially for pistachio baklava, sesame brittle and all things savoury, she was as thin as a reed. An only child. A lonely child. Restless and bouncy, and always a little bit distracted, she reeled through the days like a chess piece that had rolled on to the floor, consigned to building complex games for one.

Their house in Van was so large that even whispers echoed throughout. Shadows danced on the walls as if across cavernous space. A long, winding wooden staircase led from the living room to the first-floor landing. The entrance was adorned with tiles that featured a dizzying array of scenes: peacocks strutting their plumage; wheels of cheese and loaves of plaited bread next to goblets of wine; platters of open pomegranates with their ruby smiles; and sunflowers in fields, tilting their necks longingly towards a shifting sun, like lovers who knew they would never be loved the way they wished. Leila was fascinated by these images. Some of the tiles were cracked and chipped; others were partly covered in coarse plaster, though their patterns were still visible, bright with colour. The child suspected that together they told a story, an ancient one, but, hard as she tried, she could not fathom what it was.

Along the hallways, oil lamps, tallow candles, ceramic bowls and other decorative ephemera sat in gilded alcoves. Tasselled carpets ran the length of the floorboards – Afghan, Persian, Kurdish and Turkish carpets of every possible shade and pattern. Leila would wander idly from room to room, holding the objects close to her chest, feeling their surfaces – some prickly, some smooth – like a blind person reliant on touch. Parts of the house were excessively cluttered, but strangely even there she could sense an absence. A tall grandfather clock chimed in the main parlour, its brass pendulum swinging back and forth, its booming gong too loud, too cheerful. Often, Leila noticed a tickle in her throat and worried that she might have inhaled dust from long ago – even though she knew every item was cleaned, waxed and polished religiously. The housekeeper came each day, and once a week there was a 'big clean'. At the start and end of the seasons, there would be an even bigger clean. And if anything was overlooked, Auntie Binnaz was sure to spot it and scrub it with baking soda, fastidious as she was about what she called 'whiter than white'.

Mother had explained that the house used to belong to an Armenian doctor and his wife. They had six daughters, all of whom loved to sing, their voices ranging from low to very high. The doctor was a popular man who allowed his patients to come and stay with the family from time to time. Adamant in his belief that music could heal even the direst of wounds to the human soul, he had made each of his patients play an instrument, regardless of talent. While they played – and some did so pitifully – the daughters sang in unison and the house swayed like a raft in high seas. All of this was before the outbreak of the First World War. Not long after, they had disappeared, just like that, leaving everything behind. For some time Leila could not understand where they had gone and why they hadn't returned since. What had happened to them – the doctor and his family, and all those instruments that had once been trees, mighty and tall?

Haroun's grandfather Mahmoud, an influential Kurdish agha, had then moved in his own kin. The house was a reward from the Ottoman government for the role he had played in the deportation of Armenians in the area. Resolute, committed, he had followed the orders from Istanbul without a moment's hesitation. If the authorities decided that certain people were traitors and they had to be sent packing to the Desert of Der-Zor, where only a few could hope to survive, so they would be – even if they were good neighbours, old friends. Having thus proven his loyalty to the state, Mahmoud had become an important man; the locals admired the perfect symmetry of his moustache, the shine of his black leather boots, the grandiosity of his voice. They respected him the way cruel and powerful people have been respected since the dawn of time – with abundant fear, and not a speck of love.

Mahmoud had decreed that everything in the house be preserved, and so it was for a while. But rumour had it that, just before they left town, the Armenians, unable to carry their valuables with them, had hidden pots of coins and chests of rubies somewhere within reach. Soon Mahmoud and his relatives were digging – in the garden, the courtyard, the cellars . . . not an inch of ground was left unturned. Unable to find anything, they started to break through the walls, not once considering that, even if they hit on a treasure, it did not belong to them. By the time they gave up, the house had turned into a pile of rubble and had to be rebuilt from the inside out. Leila knew that her father, who as a boy had witnessed the frenzy, still believed there was a casket of gold somewhere, untold riches just a breath away. Some nights, as she closed her eyes and drifted off to sleep, she would dream of jewels, glowing in the distance like fireflies over a summer meadow.

Not that Leila had any interest in money at that tender age. She much preferred to have in her pocket a bar of hazelnut chocolate, or a piece of Zambo chewing gum, whose wrapper had the picture of a black woman with huge round earrings. Her father would order these delicacies to be sent to her all the way from Istanbul. Everything new and interesting was in Istanbul, the child felt with a twinge of envy – a city of wonders and curiosities. One day she would go there, she told herself – a self-made promise she kept hidden from everyone, the way an oyster conceals the pearl at its heart.

Leila delighted in serving tea to her dolls, watching the trout swimming in cold-water streams, and staring at the patterns in the rugs until the shapes came to life; but, most of all, she loved dancing. She longed to become a famous belly dancer one day. It was a fantasy that would have appalled her father, had he known how thoroughly she had envisaged the details: the sparkling sequins, the coin skirts, the clicking and clacking of finger cymbals; shimmying and rotating her hips to the rat-a-tat of the goblet drum – the *darbuka*; charming the audience into a steadily rising synchronized clap; turning and spinning to a thrilling finale. Even the thought of it made her heart beat faster. But Baba always said that dancing was one of Sheitan's myriad, time-honoured tactics to lead humans astray. With heady perfumes and shiny trinkets, the Devil seduced women first, weak and emotional as they were, and then, through the women, he lured the men into his trap.

As a much sought-after tailor, Baba made fashionable *alla franga* garments for ladies – swing dresses, sheath dresses, circle skirts, Peter Pan-collar blouses, halter-neck tops, Capri trousers. The wives of army officers, civil servants, border inspectors, railway engineers and spice merchants were among his regular customers. He also sold a large collection of hats, gloves and berets – stylish, silky creations that he would never allow his own family members to wear.

Because her father was opposed to dancing, so was her mother – although Leila noticed that she seemed to waver in her convictions when there was no one else around. Mother became a different person altogether when it was just the two of them. She allowed Leila to unbraid, comb and braid her henna-red hair, to slather vanishing cream on her wrinkled face, and to apply petroleum jelly mixed with coal dust to her eyelashes to darken them. She lavished her daughter with hugs and praise, made garish pompoms in a rainbow of colours, threaded conkers on to pieces of string and played cards – none of these things would she do in the presence of others. She was especially reserved when Auntie Binnaz was around.

'If your aunt sees us enjoying ourselves, she might feel bad,' Mother said. 'You shouldn't kiss me in front of her.'

33

'But why?'

'Well, she never had children. We don't want to break her heart, do we?'

'It's okay, Mummy. I can kiss you both.'

Mother drew on her cigarette. 'Don't forget, my soul. Your aunt is sick in the head – just like her mother, so I have heard. It is in their blood. Hereditary madness. Apparently they have it in every generation. We must be careful not to upset her.'

When Auntie got upset she had a tendency to hurt herself. She pulled out clumps of her hair, scratched her face, and picked at her skin so hard that it bled. Mother said that the day she had given birth to Leila, Auntie, waiting by the door, either out of envy or some other perverse motive, had punched herself in the face. When questioned why she would do such a thing, she had claimed that an apricot seller outside the street had been throwing snowballs at her through the open window. Apricots, in January! None of it had made any sense. They had all feared for her sanity. This story, and many others, which were told repeatedly, the child listened to with a petrified fascination.

Yet the damage Auntie inflicted upon herself did not always seem intentional. For one thing, she was as clumsy as a toddler taking her first steps. She burned her fingers on red-hot skillets, banged her knees on furniture, fell out of bed in her sleep, gashed her hands on broken glass. She had sad-looking bruises and inflamed, angry scars all over her body.

Auntie's emotions swung back and forth, like the pendulum of the grandfather clock. Some days, full of energy, she was indefatigable, scurrying from one task to another. She swept the carpets with a vengeance, ran a dust cloth over every surface, boiled the linens she had laundered only the night before, scrubbed the floors for hours on end and sprayed an ill-smelling disinfectant all over the house. Her hands were raw and cracked and did not get any softer, even though she regularly rubbed them with mutton fat. They would always be rough, washing them as she did dozens of times a day, convinced still that they were not clean enough.

Nothing was, really. At other times, she seemed so worn out she could hardly move. Even breathing became an effort.

There were also days when Auntie appeared to be without a care in the world. Relaxed and radiant, she spent hours playing with Leila in the garden. Together they dangled strips of fabric from apple boughs laden with blossom, calling them ballerinas, took their sweet time to weave little baskets out of willow or crowns out of daisies; tied ribbons around the horns of the ram waiting to be sacrificed next Eid. Once they secretly cut the rope that kept the animal fastened to the shed. But the ram did not break loose as they had planned. After meandering here and there in search of fresh grass, it returned to the same spot, finding the familiarity of captivity more reassuring than the strange call of freedom.

Auntie and Leila loved to fashion tablecloths into gowns and stare at the women in magazines, imitating their erect postures and confident smiles. Of all the models and actresses they studied closely, there was one they admired the most: Rita Hayworth. Her eyelashes were like arrows, her eyebrows like bows; her waist was thinner than a tea glass, her skin as smooth as spun silk. She might have been the answer to every Ottoman poet's quest, but for one tiny mistake: she was born at the wrong time, far away in America.

Curious as they were about Rita Hayworth's life, looking at her photos was all they could do since neither of them knew how to read. Leila had yet to start school; as for her aunt, she had never been to one. There was no school in the village where Auntie Binnaz had grown up, and her father had not allowed her to walk the rutted road to town and back every day, with her brothers. They didn't have enough pairs of shoes, and she had to take care of her younger siblings anyway.

Unlike Auntie, Mother was literate and proud of it. She could read recipes out of a cookbook, flip through the page-a-day wall calendar, and even follow articles in the newspapers. It was she who relayed the news of the world to them: in Egypt, a group of military officers declared the state a republic; in America, they executed a couple accused of being spies; in East Germany, thousands of people marched to protest the government's policies and were crushed by the Soviet occupiers; and in Turkey, far away in Istanbul, which sometimes felt like a different country altogether, a beauty contest was being held, young women posing on the catwalk in one-piece bathing suits. Religious groups were out on the streets denouncing the show as immoral, but the organizers were determined to go ahead. Nations became civilized in three fundamental ways, they said: science, education and beauty contests.

Whenever Suzan read such news aloud, Binnaz quickly averted her gaze. A vein pulsated in her left temple, a silent but steady signal of distress. Leila sympathized with her aunt, finding something recognizable, almost comforting, in the woman's vulnerability. But she also sensed that, on this matter, she could not be on Auntie's side for long. She was looking forward to starting school soon.

About three months earlier, behind a cedarwood cabinet at the top of the stairs, Leila had found a rickety door that opened on to the roof. Someone must have left it ajar, inviting in a cool, crisp breeze that carried the smell of the wild garlic growing down the road. Since then she had visited the roof almost every day.

Whenever she looked out upon the sprawling town and pricked her ears to catch the cry of a booted eagle soaring over the great glittering lake in the distance, or the honking of flamingos searching the shallows for food, or the chirping of swallows as they darted between the alders, she felt certain that, if only she tried, she, too, could fly. What would it take to grow wings and glide through the skies, carefree and light? The area was inhabited by herons, egrets, white-headed ducks, black-winged stilts, crimson-winged finches, reed warblers, white-throated kingfishers, and swamphens, which the locals called 'the sultanas'. A pair of storks had taken possession of the chimney and built an impressive nest, one tiny twig at a time. Now they were gone, but she knew they would come back one day. Her aunt said that storks – unlike humans – were loyal to their memories. Once they had made a place 'home', even if they found themselves miles away from it, they always returned.

After each visit to the roof, the child would tiptoe downstairs, careful not to be seen. She had no doubt that if her mother caught her she would be in big trouble.

But that afternoon in June 1953, Mother was too busy to pay any attention to her. The house was full of guests – all of them women. This happened without fail twice a month: on the day of Qur'an reading, and on the day of leg waxing. When it was the former, an elderly imam would come to deliver a sermon and read a passage from the holy book. The women of the neighbourhood would sit silently and respectfully, their knees pressed together, their heads covered, rapt in thought. If any of the children wandering around made so much as a peep, they were hushed immediately.

When it was waxing day, things were quite the opposite. With no men around, the women would wear the skimpiest of clothes. They would slouch on the sofa with their legs apart, their arms bare, their eyes glittering with repressed mischief. Chattering incessantly, they would pepper their remarks with curses that made the youngest among them blush like a damask rose. Leila couldn't believe that these wild creatures were the same people as the imam's riveted listeners.

Today it was waxing time again. Perched on the carpets, footstools and chairs, women covered every inch of space in the living room, plates of pastries and glasses of tea in their hands. A cloying smell wafted from the kitchen, where the wax bubbled on the stove. Lemon, sugar and water. When the mixture was ready they would all set to work, fast and serious, wincing as they pulled the sticky strips off their skin. But for now, the pain could wait; they were gossiping and feasting to their hearts' content.

Watching the women from the hallway, Leila was momentarily

transfixed, searching in their movements and interactions for clues as to her own future. She was convinced, back then, that when she grew up she would be like them. A toddler hanging on her leg, a baby in her arms, a husband to obey, a house to keep shipshape – this would be her life. Mother had told her that when she was born, the midwife had thrown her umbilical cord on the school roof so that she would become a teacher, but Baba was not keen for that to happen. Not any more. A while ago, he had met a sheikh who had explained to him that it was better for women to stay at home and to cover themselves on the rare occasions they needed to go out. Nobody wanted to buy tomatoes that had been touched, squeezed and sullied by other customers. Better if all the tomatoes in the market were carefully packaged and preserved. Same with women, the sheikh said. The hijab was their package, the armour that protected them from suggestive looks and unwanted touches.

Mother and Auntie had therefore started to cover their heads – unlike most of the women in the neighbourhood, who closely followed the fashion in the West, their hair combed into bob-shaped bouffants, permed into tight curls or pulled back into elegant buns, like Audrey Hepburn's. While Mother had settled on a black chador when she went out, Auntie had chosen bright chiffon scarves, firmly tied under her chin. Both took the utmost care not to show even a strand of hair. Leila was confident that someday soon she would follow in their footsteps. Mother had told her that when that day arrived they would go to the bazaar together and buy the prettiest headscarf and a matching long coat for her.

'Can I still wear my belly-dancing costume underneath?'

'You silly girl,' Mother had said, smiling.

Lost in her thoughts, Leila now tiptoed past the living room and headed to the kitchen. Mother had been toiling away there since early morning – baking börek, brewing tea and preparing the wax. Leila could not understand, for the life of her, why any-one would slather this sugary delicacy on to their hairy legs rather than eat it, as she happily did.

On entering the kitchen, she was surprised to find someone else there. Auntie Binnaz was standing alone by the worktop, her hand closed around a long, serrated knife that caught the light of the afternoon sun. Leila was worried she might hurt herself. Auntie had to be careful these days as she had just announced that she was expecting – again. No one talked about it, fearing *nazar* – the evil eye. Based on previous experiences, Leila reckoned that in the coming months, as Auntie's pregnancy became apparent, the adults around her would behave as if her growing bump was due to a hearty appetite or chronic bloating. That's what had happened each time so far: the bigger Auntie had got, the more invisible she had become to others. She might just as well be fading before their very eyes, like a photograph left on asphalt under an unforgiving sun.

Gingerly, Leila took a step forward and stood watching.

Her aunt, slightly stooping over what appeared to be a heap of salad, did not seem to have noticed her. She was staring at the newspaper laid across the worktop, her gimlet eyes burning against the paleness of her skin. With a sigh, she grabbed a handful of lettuce and started cutting the leaves rhythmically on a chopping board, the knife soon moving so rapidly it became a blur.

'Auntie?'

The hand stopped. 'Hmmmm.'

'What are you looking at?'

'The soldiers. I heard they were coming back.' She pointed to a photograph in the paper, and for a moment they both stood peering at the caption beneath it, trying to make sense of the black dots and swirls lined up like an infantry battalion.

'Oh, so your brother will be home soon.'

Auntie had a brother who was among the five thousand Turkish troops dispatched to Korea. They were helping the Americans, supporting the good Koreans in their fight against the bad Koreans. Given that the Turkish soldiers spoke neither English nor Korean, and the American soldiers were probably equally ignorant of anything but their own language, how on earth, the child wondered, did they communicate, all these men with their rifles and pistols, and if they could not communicate how did they manage to understand each other? But this was not the right moment to raise the question. Instead, she beamed a broad smile. 'You must be excited!'

Auntie's face closed. 'Why should I? Who knows when I will see him again – if ever? It's been so long. My parents, brothers and sisters . . . I haven't seen any of them. They have no money for travel and I cannot go to them. I miss my family.'

Leila didn't know how to respond. She had always assumed that *they* were Auntie's family. Being the accommodating child that she was, she found it wiser to change the subject: 'Are you preparing food for the guests?'

Even as she spoke, Leila studied the shredded lettuce piled up on the chopping board. Among the ribbons of green she noticed something that made her gasp: pink earthworms, some cut into pieces, others still wriggling.

'Eww, what is that?'

'It's for the babies. They love it.'

'Babies?' Leila felt her stomach sink.

Clearly Mother had been right all along: Auntie was sick in the head. The child's eyes slid down to the floor. She saw that Auntie wasn't wearing any shoes; that the soles of her feet were cracked and hard around the edges, as though she had trudged miles to get here. Leila lingered on that thought: maybe Auntie was a sleep-walker, disappearing into the rustling darkness each night before rushing back home at dawn, her breath clouding in the chill air. Maybe she slunk past the garden gate, climbed up the drainpipe, jumped over the balcony rail and sneaked into her bedroom, her eyes remaining closed all the while. What if one day she couldn't remember the way back?

If Auntie was in the habit of roaming the streets in her sleep, Baba would know about it. Sadly, Leila couldn't ask him. It would be one of the many subjects that were off-limits. It troubled the child that while she and her mother slept in the same room, her

40

father stayed with her aunt in another room upstairs. When she enquired about why that was, Mother had said that Auntie was scared to be alone because she fought demons in her sleep.

'Are you going to eat it?' Leila asked. 'It'll make you feel poorly.'

'Me, no! It's for the babies, I told you.' The look Binnaz gave the child was as unexpected as a ladybird landing on her finger, and just as gentle. 'Haven't you seen them? Up on the roof. I thought you were there all the time.'

Leila raised her eyebrows in surprise. She had never suspected that her aunt might be visiting her secret place. Even so, she wasn't worried. There was something ghost-like about Auntie: she didn't take possession of things, but merely floated through them. In any case, the child was sure there were no babies up there on the roof.

'You don't believe me, do you? You think I'm crazy. Everyone thinks I'm crazy.'

There was such hurt in the woman's voice, such sadness pooling in her beautiful eyes, that, for a moment, Leila was taken aback. Ashamed of her thoughts, she tried to make it up to her. 'That's not true. I always believe you!'

'You sure? It's a serious thing to believe in someone. You can't just say it like that. If you really mean it, you have to support them no matter what. Even when other people say awful things about that person. Are you capable of doing that?'

The child nodded, happy to accept the challenge.

Pleased, Auntie smiled. 'Then I'll let you into a secret, a big one. Do you promise not to tell anyone?'

'I promise,' Leila said instantly.

'Suzan is not your mother.'

Leila's eyes grew.

'Do you want to know who your real mother is?'

Silence.

'I am the one who gave birth to you. It was a cold day, but a man was selling sweet apricots on the street. Weird, eh? If they find out that I've told you, they'll send me back to the village – or maybe they'll lock me up in a mental hospital, and we'll never see each other again. Do you understand?'

The child nodded, her face inert.

'Good. Then keep your lips sealed.'

Auntie went back to work, humming to herself. The bubbling of the cauldron, the chit-chat of the women in the living room, the clinking of the teaspoons against the glasses . . . even the ram in the garden seemed eager to join the chorus, bleating a tune of his own.

'I've an idea,' said Auntie Binnaz all of a sudden. 'Next time we have guests over, let's put worms in their wax. Imagine all these women running from the house half-naked, worms clinging to their legs!'

She was laughing so hard there were tears in her eyes. She lurched backwards, stumbled on a basket and knocked it over, sending the potatoes inside rolling left and right.

Leila broke into a smile, despite herself. She tried to relax. It all had to be a joke. What else could it be? No one in the family took Auntie seriously – so why should she? Auntie's remarks were no more substantial than the drops of dew on the cool grass or the sighs of a butterfly.

Then and there, Leila resolved to forget what she had heard. Surely that would be the right thing to do. But a seed of doubt niggled at her mind. Part of her wanted to unveil a truth that the rest of her was not ready for, perhaps would never be. She couldn't help sensing that something remained unresolved between them, like a muddled message on a poorly transmitted radio wave, strings of words that, though conveyed, could not be formed into any-thing coherent.

About half an hour later, holding a spoon dolloped with wax, Leila sat in her usual spot on the roof, her legs dangling over the edge like a pair of drop earrings. Even though it hadn't rained in weeks, the bricks felt slippery and she moved around with caution, knowing that if she fell down she could break a bone, and even if she didn't, Mother might just as easily do it for her.

When she had finished eating her treat, with the concentration of a circus performer on a tightrope, Leila inched her way towards the roof's far end, where she rarely ventured. She stopped halfway and was about to turn back when she picked up a sound – soft and muffled, like a moth against a lantern glass. Then the sound intensified. A thousand moths. Curious, she walked in that direction. And there, behind a pile of boxes, inside a large wire cage, were pigeons. Many, many pigeons. On both sides of the cage were bowls of fresh water and food. The newspapers spread underneath were marked with a few droppings but otherwise they seemed clean enough. Someone was taking good care of them.

Laughing, the child clapped her hands. A wave of tenderness welled up within her, caressing her throat like the carbonated bubbles of her favourite drink, gazoz. She felt protective towards her aunt, despite – or because of – her frailties. But this sentiment was soon overwhelmed by a sense of confusion. If Auntie Binnaz had been right about the pigeons, what else had she been right about? What if she really was her mother – they had the same blunt, upturned noses, and they both sneezed as soon as they woke, as if suffering from a mild allergy to the first light of the day. They also shared the strange habit of whistling as they spread butter and jam on toast, and spitting out the seeds when they ate grapes, or the skins when they ate tomatoes. She tried to consider what more they had in common, but the thought she kept returning to was this: all these years she had been scared of make-believe Gypsies who kidnapped small children and turned them into hollow-eyed beggars, but maybe the people she should be fearing were in her own home. Maybe it was they who had snatched her from her mother's arms.

For the first time she was able to stand back and regard herself and her family from a mental distance; and what she found out made her uncomfortable. She had always assumed they were a normal family, like any other in the world. Now she wasn't so sure. What if there was something different about them – something inherently wrong? Little did she yet understand that the end of childhood comes not when a child's body changes with puberty, but when her mind is finally able to see her life through the eyes of an outsider.

Leila began to panic. She loved Mother, and didn't want to think badly of her. She loved Baba too, though she was also scared of him sometimes. Hugging herself for comfort, sucking in lungfuls of air, she brooded on her predicament. She didn't know what to believe in any more, which direction to take; it was as if she were lost in a forest, the paths ahead jumping about and multiplying before her eyes. Who in the family was more reliable – her father, her mother or her aunt? Leila looked around as though in search of an answer. Everything was the same. And nothing would be from now on.

As the tastes of lemon and sugar melted on her tongue, so too her feelings dissolved into confusion. Years later, she would come to think of this moment as the first time she realized that things were not always what they seemed. Just as the sour could hide beneath the sweet, or vice versa, within every sane mind there was a trace of insanity, and within the depths of madness glimmered a seed of lucidity.

To this day she had been careful not to show her love for her mother when Auntie was around. From now on she would have to keep her love for her aunt a secret from Mother as well. Leila had come to understand that feelings of tenderness must always be hidden – that such things could only be revealed behind closed doors and never spoken about afterwards. This was the only form of affection she had learned from grown-ups, and the teaching would come with dire consequences.

Three Minutes

Three minutes had passed since Leila's heart had stopped, and now she remembered cardamom coffee – strong, intense, dark. A taste forever associated in her mind with the street of brothels in Istanbul. It was rather strange that this should follow on the heels of her recollections of childhood. But human memory resembles a late-night reveller who has had a few too many drinks: hard as it tries, it just cannot follow a straight line. It staggers through a maze of inversions, often moving in dizzying zigzags, immune to reason and liable to collapse altogether.

Hence Leila remembered: September 1967. A dead-end street down by the harbour, just a stone's throw from the port of Karaköy, near the Golden Horn, extending between rows of licensed brothels. There was an Armenian school nearby, a Greek church, a Sephardic synagogue, a Sufi lodge, a Russian Orthodox chapel – remnants of a past no longer remembered. The district, once a thriving commercial waterfront and home to prosperous Levantine and Jewish communities, and then the hub of Ottoman banking and shipping industries, nowadays witnessed transactions of a very different kind. Muted messages were conveyed through the wind, money changing hands as fast as it was acquired.

The area around the port was always so crowded that pedestrians had to move sideways like crabs. Young women in miniskirts walked arm in arm; drivers catcalled out of car windows; apprentices from coffeehouses scurried back and forth, carrying tea trays loaded with small glasses; tourists bent under the weight of their backpacks gazed around as if newly awake; shoe-shine boys rattled their brushes against their brass boxes, decorated with photos of actresses – modest ones on the front, nudes on the back. Vendors peeled salted cucumbers, squeezed fresh pickle juice, roasted

45

chickpeas and yelled over one another while motorists blasted their horns for no reason at all. Smells of tobacco, sweat, perfume, fried food and an occasional reefer – albeit illegal – mingled with the briny sea air.

The side streets and alleyways were rivers of paper. Socialist, communist and anarchist posters plastered the walls, inviting the proletariat and peasantry to join the upcoming revolution. Here and there, the posters had been slashed and defaced with far-right slogans and sprayed with their symbol: a howling wolf inside a crescent. Street cleaners with tattered brooms and weary looks picked up the litter, their energy sapped by the knowledge that new flyers would rain down as soon as they turned their backs.

A few minutes' walk away from the harbour, just off a steep avenue, was the street of brothels. An iron gate in need of a fresh coat of paint separated the place from the world outside. In front of it stood a few police officers on eight-hour shifts. Some of them visibly hated their job; they despised this street of ill repute and anyone who crossed its threshold: women and men alike. An unspoken reprimand in their brusque manners, they kept their unflinching gaze fixed on the men huddled by the gate, raring to get in but reluctant to queue. Whereas some officers took it as they would any other job, simply doing what they were asked to do, day in, day out, others secretly envied the punters, wishing they could trade places, if only for a few hours.

The brothel where Leila worked was among the oldest in the area. A single fluorescent tube flickered at the entrance with the force of a thousand tiny matches catching light and burning one after another. The air was thickened by the scent of cheap perfume, the taps encrusted with deposits of limescale and the ceiling coated with the sticky brown stains of nicotine and tar from years of tobacco smoke. An intricate lacework of cracks spread across the entire length of the foundation walls, as wispy as the veins of a bloodshot eye. Under the eaves, right outside Leila's window, dangled an empty wasps' nest – round, papery, mysterious. A hidden universe. Now and then she felt an urge to touch the nest, to break it open and reveal its perfect architecture, but each time she told herself that she had no right to disturb what nature had intended to remain intact, complete.

This was her second address on the same street. The first house had been so unbearable that before a year was up she had done something no one else had dared to do before or ever since: she had packed her few belongings, put on her one good coat and walked out to seek refuge in the brothel next door. The news had divided the community into two camps: some said she should immediately be returned to the previous place; otherwise, every mother's daughter would start doing the same thing, violating the unwritten code of work ethics, and the whole business would tumble into anarchy; others said that, according to the dictates of conscience, anyone who had been so desperate as to seek sanctuary should be provided with it. In the end, the madam of the second brothel, impressed by Leila's audacity as much as by the prospect of the fresh money she could bring in, had taken a shine to her and accepted her as one of her own. But not before paying a large sum to her colleague, extending her sincerest apologies and promising she would never let this happen again.

The new madam was a woman of ample proportions, resolute gait, and rouged cheeks that sagged like flaps of staked leather. She had a tendency to address every man who walked in, whether a regular or not, as 'my pasha'. Every few weeks she visited a hair-dressing salon named Split Ends where she had her hair dyed a different shade of blonde. Her wide-set, protuberant eyes gave her an expression of permanent surprise, although this she rarely was. A web of broken capillaries fanned out across the tip of her mighty nose, like streams threading their way down a mountainside. No one knew her real name. Both the prostitutes and the punters called her 'Sweet Ma' to her face and 'Bitter Ma' behind her back. She was all right as far as madams went, but she had a tendency to do everything to excess: she smoked too much, swore too much, shouted too much and was simply too much of a presence in their lives – a veritable maximum dose.

47

'We were founded way back in the nineteenth century,' Bitter Ma loved to boast, a proud lilt to her voice. 'And by none other than the great Sultan Abdülaziz.'

She used to keep a framed portrait of the Sultan behind her desk – until one day a client with ultra-nationalist leanings had reprimanded her about it in front of everyone. The man had told her in no uncertain terms not to tout such nonsense about 'our magnanimous ancestors and our glorious past'.

'Why would a sultan – the conqueror of three continents and five seas – allow a house of filth to open in Istanbul?' he had demanded to know.

Bitter Ma had stammered, nervously twisting her handkerchief. 'Well, I think it's because –'

'Who cares about what you think? Are you a historian or what are you?'

Bitter Ma had raised her freshly plucked eyebrows.

'Or maybe you are a professor!' The man had chuckled.

Bitter Ma's shoulders had drooped.

'An ignorant woman has no right to distort history,' the man had said, no longer laughing. 'You better get it straight. There were no licensed brothels in the Ottoman Empire. If a few ladies wished to ply their trade on the sly, they must have been Christians or Jews – or heathen Gypsies. Because I'm telling you, no proper Muslim woman would ever have agreed to such immorality. They'd rather have died of hunger than agreed to sell themselves. Until now, that is. Modern times, immodest times.'

After the lecture, Bitter Ma had quietly taken down the portrait of Sultan Abdülaziz and replaced it with a still life of yellow daffodils and citrus fruits. But since the second painting happened to be smaller than the first, the outline of the Sultan's frame remained visible on the wall, thin and pale like a map drawn in the sand.

As for the client, the next time he showed up, the madam, all smiles and bows, welcomed him with cordial sweetness, offering him a hot chick he was exceptionally lucky not to be missing out on:

'She's leaving us, my pasha. Going back to her village tomorrow morning. She managed to pay back her debts, this one. What can I do? Says she will be spending the rest of her days repenting. "Good for you," I said in the end. "You can pray for the rest of us too." '

It was a lie, a rather shameless one. The woman in question was leaving, but for a different reason altogether. On her latest visit to the hospital she had tested positive for both gonorrhoea and syphilis. Banned from working, she was obliged to stay away from the premises until completely free of infection. Bitter Ma did not mention this detail as she took the man's money and put it in the drawer. She had not forgotten how rude he had been to her. No one was to talk to her like that, especially not in front of her employees. For unlike Istanbul, a city of wilful amnesia, Bitter Ma had an excellent memory; she remembered every wrong that had ever been done to her, and when the right moment arrived, she took her revenge.

Inside the brothel the colours were dull: soulless brown, stale yellow and the insipid green of leftover soup. No sooner had the evening *ezan* reverberated over the city's leaden domes and swayback roofs than Bitter Ma would turn on the lights – a string of naked bulbs in shades of indigo, magenta, lilac and ruby – and the whole place would be bathed in the strangest glow, as if kissed by a demented pixie.

Next to the entrance was a large handwritten sign framed in metal that was the first thing anyone would see upon walking in. It read:

CITIZEN!

If you wish to protect yourself from syphilis and other sexually transmitted diseases, you must do the following:

1. *Before you go to a room with a woman, ask to see her health card. Check if she's healthy!*

2. *Use a sheath. Make sure you use a new one each time. You will not be overcharged for sheaths; ask the landlady and she will give you a fair price.*

3. *If you have any suspicion that you might have contracted a disease, do not hang around here, go straight to a doctor.*

4. *Sexually transmitted diseases can be prevented, if you are determined to protect yourself and to protect YOUR NATION!*

Working hours were from ten a.m. to eleven p.m. Twice a day Leila had a coffee break: half an hour in the afternoon and fifteen minutes at night. Bitter Ma did not approve of downtime in the evening, but Leila, insisting she got terrible migraines if she did not have her daily dose of cardamom coffee, stood her ground.

Every morning, as soon as the doors were opened, the women took their seats on the wooden chairs and low stools behind the glass panels at the entrance. Those who had recently joined the brothel could be told apart from the old-timers simply by the way they carried themselves. The newcomers sat with their hands in their laps, their gaze unfocused and distant like sleepwalkers who had just woken up in a strange place. Those who had been around for longer moved nonchalantly and freely across the room – cleaning under their fingernails, scratching itchy spots, fanning themselves, examining their complexions in the mirror, braiding each other's hair. Unafraid of making eye contact, they watched indifferently the men strolling along – in groups, pairs and alone.

A few of the women had suggested doing needlework or taking up knitting during these long hours of waiting, but Bitter Ma would hear none of it.

'Knitting – what a dopey idea! Do you want to remind these men of their boring wives? Or, worse, their mothers? Certainly not! We offer them what they have never seen at home, not more of the same.'

This being one of the fourteen brothels lined up along the same cul-de-sac, the clients had plenty of options. They would pace up and down, stop and leer, smoke and ponder, weighing up their choices. If they still needed time to think, they would stop by a street vendor and drink a shot of pickled-cucumber juice or eat a fried-dough pastry, known as *kerhane tatlisi*, 'bordello churro'. Experience had taught Leila that if a man did not make up his mind in the first three minutes, he would never do so. After three minutes her attention would shift to someone else.

Most of the prostitutes refrained from calling out to the punters, finding it sufficient to blow the occasional kiss or offer a wink, show some cleavage or uncross their legs. Bitter Ma did not approve of her girls appearing too eager. She said it cheapened the merchandise. Nor were they to act cold, as though they were unsure of their own quality. There had to be 'a fine sophisticated balance' – not that Bitter Ma herself was a well-balanced person, but she expected from her employees what she herself desperately lacked.

Leila's room was on the second floor, the first on the right. 'The best location in the house,' everyone said. Not because it offered any luxuries or a view of the Bosphorus but because, if anything were to go wrong, she could easily be heard from downstairs. The rooms at the other end of the corridor were the worst. Even if you screamed your head off, no one would come running.

In front of her door, Leila had placed a half-moon mat for the men to wipe their shoes on. The room was sparsely furnished: a double bed, covered with a floral-print bedspread and a matching ruffled valance, took up most of the space. Next to it was a cabinet with a locked drawer where she kept her letters and various objects that, though not at all precious, were of sentimental value to her. The curtains, tattered and faded from the sun, were the colour of sliced watermelon – and those black dots that resembled seeds were, in fact, cigarette burns. In one corner was a cracked sink; a gas cooker on which a brass *cezve* rested precariously; and, next to it, a pair of slippers – blue velvet with satin rosettes and beaded toes. They were the prettiest thing she owned. Pushed against the wall stood a walnut wardrobe that did not shut properly. Inside, underneath clothes on hangers, were a pile of magazines, a biscuit box full of condoms, and a musty-smelling blanket that had long gone unused. A mirror hung on the opposite wall, with postcards tucked into its frame: Brigitte Bardot smoking a slim cigar, Raquel Welch posing in an animal-hide bikini, the Beatles and their blonde girlfriends sitting on a carpet with an Indian yogi, and pictures of places – a capital city's river sparkling in the morning sun, a baroque square lightly dusted with snow, a boulevard bejewelled by the night-time lights – that Leila had never visited but yearned to explore one day: Berlin, London, Paris, Amsterdam, Rome, Tokyo . . .

It was a privileged room in many ways, one that revealed Leila's status. Most of the other girls had much less in the way of comfort. Bitter Ma was fond of Leila – partly because she was honest and hard-working; partly because she bore an uncanny resemblance to the sister Bitter Ma had left, decades ago, in the Balkans.

Leila was seventeen years old when she had been brought to this street – sold to the first brothel by a man and a woman, a couple of hustlers well known to the police. That was about three years ago, though it felt like another life already. She never talked about those days, just as she never talked about why she had run away from home or how she had arrived in Istanbul without a place to stay and with only five lira and twenty kurush. She regarded her memory as a graveyard; segments of her life were buried there, lying in separate graves, and she had no intention of reviving them.

The first months on this street had been so dark, the days like a rope mooring her to despair, that several times she had considered suicide. A fast, quiet death – it could be done. Back then, every detail had unsettled her; every sound had been a thunderclap to her ears. Even after she arrived in Bitter Ma's house, which was a slightly safer place, she did not think she could carry on. The stench from the toilets, the mouse droppings in the kitchen, the cockroaches in the basement, the sores in the mouth of a client, the warts on the hands of one of the other prostitutes, the food stains on the madam's blouse, the flies buzzing hither and thither – everything made her itch uncontrollably. At night, when she laid her head on the pillow, she picked up a faint, coppery smell in the air that she had come to identify as decaying flesh, and she feared that it was gathering under her fingernails, seeping into her bloodstream. She was sure she had caught some horrible disease. Invisible parasites were crawling under and over her skin. In the local hammam that the prostitutes visited once a week, she washed and scrubbed herself until her body burned red; and upon her return, she boiled her pillowcases and bedsheets. It was no use. The parasites kept coming back.

'It could be *sicologik*,' said Bitter Ma. 'I've seen it before. Look, I run a clean place here. If you don't like it, go back. But I'm telling you, it's all in your head. Tell me, was your mother also a hygiene freak?'

That made Leila stop cold. No more itching. The last thing she wanted was to be reminded of Auntie Binnaz or that big, lonely house in Van.

The only window in Leila's room overlooked the back premises: a small courtyard with a single birch tree, behind which stood a dilapidated building that remained unoccupied except for a furniture workshop on the ground floor. Inside, around forty men slogged away for thirteen hours a day, inhaling dust and varnish and chemicals they had no name for. Half of them were illegal immigrants. None of them had insurance. And most were no older than twenty-five. It wasn't a job one could do for long. The fumes from the resins destroyed their lungs.

The workers were supervised by a bearded foreman who seldom spoke and never smiled. On Fridays, as soon as he went to the mosque, a *takke* on his head, a rosary in his hand, the other men opened the windows and craned their necks, trying to spy on the whores. They couldn't see much since the curtains in the brothel were kept closed most of the time. But they did not give up, keen to catch a glimpse of curvy hip or bare thigh. Bragging to one another about tantalizing peeks, they chuckled; the dust that covered them from head to toe gave them wrinkles, greyed their hair, and made them look not so much like old men as like spectres stuck between two worlds. On the other side of the courtyard the women generally remained indifferent, but every now and then one of them, either out of curiosity or pity, it was hard to tell, would suddenly appear by the window and, leaning on the ledge, her breasts hanging heavy over her forearms, smoke quietly until the cigarette in her hand burned low.

A few of the labourers had a good voice, and they liked to sing, taking turns in leading. In a world they could neither fully under-stand nor prevail in, music was the only joy that was free of charge. Hence they sang copiously, passionately. In Kurdish, Turkish, Arabic, Farsi, Pashto, Georgian, Circassian and Baluchi they serenaded the women silhouetted in the windows, figures bathed in mystery, more shadow than flesh.

On one occasion, moved by the beauty of the voice she heard, Leila, who until then had always kept her curtains firmly closed, drew the drapes aside and glanced out at the furniture workshop. She saw a young man there, staring directly up at her as he kept singing the saddest ballad she had ever heard, about eloping lovers lost in a flood. His eyes were almond-shaped and the colour of burnished iron; his jawline was prominent and his chin was marked by a distinct cleft. It was the gentleness of his gaze that struck Leila. A gaze not clouded by greed. He smiled at her, revealing a set of perfect white teeth, and she couldn't help smil-ing back. This city always surprised her; moments of innocence were hidden in its darkest corners, moments so elusive that by the time she realized how pure they were, they would be gone.

'What's your name?' he shouted at her over the wind.

She told him. 'And what's yours?'

'Me? Don't have a name yet.'

54

'Everyone has a name.'

'Well, true . . . but I don't like mine. For now you can call me Hiç – "Nothing".'*

The following Friday, when she checked again, the young man wasn't there. Nor was he the week after. And so she assumed that he had gone forever, this stranger who had been composed of a head and a half-torso, framed by the window ledge like a painting from a different century, as if a product of someone else's imagination.

Yet Istanbul continued to surprise her. Exactly a year later she would meet him again – by a fluke. Except this time, Nothing was a woman.

By now, Bitter Ma had started sending Leila to her esteemed customers. Although the brothel was sanctioned by the government, and all transactions made on the premises remained legal, those outside the premises were unlicensed – and thereby tax-free. By delving into this new venture, Bitter Ma was taking a considerable risk – though a profitable one. If discovered, she would be prosecuted and, most probably, jailed. Yet she trusted Leila, knowing that even if she were caught, she would not tell the police who she was working for.

'You are a little clam, aren't you? Good girl.'

One night, the police raided dozens of nightclubs, bars and off-licences on both sides of the Bosphorus and scores of underage clubbers, drug users and sex workers were arrested. Leila found herself alone in a cell with a tall, well-built woman who, after giving her name as Nalan, threw herself down in a corner, humming distractedly and tapping out a rhythm on the wall with her long fingernails.

Leila would probably not have recognized her had it not been for the familiar song – that same old ballad. Her curiosity piqued, she studied the woman, taking in her bright, warm brown eyes, her square jaw, the cleft in her chin.

* *Hiç*: pronounced 'Heech'.

'Nothing?' Leila asked with an incredulous gasp. 'Do you remember me?'

The woman cocked her head to the side, her expression unreadable for a moment. Then, with a winsome smile that filled her face, she jumped up, narrowly avoiding bumping her head on the low ceiling.

'You are the girl from the brothel! What are you doing here?'

That night in custody, neither of them able to sleep on the dirt-smudged mattresses, they talked, at first in the darkness, then in the half-light of the dawn, keeping each other company. Nalan explained that, back when they had met, she had been only temporarily employed at the furniture workshop, saving money for sex-change treatment, which had proved to be more arduous and expensive than she had expected – *and her plastic surgeon was a complete arsehole.* But she tried not to complain, at least not too loudly, because, *damn it,* she was determined to go through with it. All her life she had been trapped in a body that felt as unfamiliar as a foreign word on the tongue. Born into a well-off family of farmers and sheep breeders in Central Anatolia, she had come to this city to correct the mistake that God the Almighty had so blatantly made.

In the morning, even though her back ached from sitting through the night, and her legs were as heavy as timbers, Leila felt as though some weight had been lifted from her – she had all but forgotten the sense of lightness that now suffused her being.

As soon as they were released, the two of them headed to a börek shop, urgently in need of a cup of tea. That one cup became many. After that day, they never lost touch, regularly meeting in the same corner shop. Realizing they had much to say to each other even when they were apart, they began to correspond. Nalan often sent Leila postcards with notes scrawled on the back in biro, full of spelling mistakes; whereas Leila preferred notepaper and used a fountain pen, her writing neat and careful, the way she had learned years ago at school in Van.

Now and then, she would put the pen down and think about

Auntie Binnaz, recalling her quiet dread of the alphabet. Leila had written to her family several times, but never heard back from them. She wondered what they did with her letters – did they keep them in a box away from all eyes or did they tear them up? Did the postman take them back, and if so, where? There had to be a place, some obscure address, for letters that remained unwelcome and unread.

Nalan lived in a dank basement flat – on the Street of Cauldron Makers, not far from Taksim Square – with sloping floorboards, crooked window frames and leaning walls; a flat so oddly arranged that it could only have been designed by an architect on a high. She shared this space with four other trans women, as well as a pair of turtles – Tutti and Frutti – that only she seemed able to tell apart. During every rainstorm it seemed that the pipes would burst or the toilets would overflow, though thankfully, Nalan observed, Tutti and Frutti were good swimmers.

'Nothing' not being an ideal nickname for a woman as assertive as Nalan, Leila decided to call her 'Nostalgia' instead – not because Nalan was dewy-eyed about the past, which she was clearly happy to leave behind, but because she was profoundly homesick in the city. She missed the countryside and its cornucopia of smells, yearning to fall asleep in the open air under a generous sky. There, she would not have to guard her back at all times.

Spirited and spunky, ferocious to her enemies, loyal to her dearest: Nostalgia Nalan – Leila's bravest friend.

Nostalgia Nalan, one of the five.

Nalan's Story

Once, and for a long time, Nalan was called Osman, the youngest son of a farming family in Anatolia. Redolent of freshly turned soil and the breath of wild herbs, his days were busy: ploughing the fields, raising the chickens, taking care of the dairy cows, making sure the honey bees survived the winter . . . A bee would work her entire brief life just to make enough honey to fill the tip of a teaspoon. Osman would wonder what he was going to create in his lifetime – the question both exciting and frightening him to the core. Night came early upon the village. After dark, as soon as his older siblings had gone to sleep, he would sit up in bed beside the wicker lamp. Slowly, bending his hands this way and that to a melody he alone could hear, he would form shadows that danced on the opposite wall. In the stories he invented, he would always take the main role – a Persian poetess, a Chinese princess or a Russian empress; the characters changed wildly, but one thing remained the same: in his mind, he was always a girl, never a boy.

At school, things couldn't have been more different. It wasn't a place for stories, the classroom. It was a place for rules and repetition. Struggling to spell certain words, memorize poems or recite prayers in Arabic, he found it hard to keep up with the other children. The teacher – a cold, dour man who paced up and down with a wooden ruler, which he would use to slap misbehaving students – had no patience with him.

Each term when they enacted patriotic plays, the popular students jostled for the roles of Turkish war heroes, while the rest of the class had to be the Greek army. Osman didn't mind being a Greek soldier though – all you had to do was die quickly and lie still on the floor for the rest of the play. But he *did* mind the constant teasing and bullying that he received every day. It had all started when one of the boys, catching him barefoot, noticed he had painted his toenails. *Osman is a sissy pants!* Once you had earned that label you might as well have walked into the class-room each morning with a bull's eye painted on your forehead.

Moneyed and propertied, his parents could have afforded to send their children to better schools, but his father, distrustful of the city and its people, preferred them to learn to work the land. Osman knew the names of plants and herbs the way his peers in the city knew the names of pop singers and film stars. Life was predictable and steady, a reliable chain of cause and effect: people's temper depended on the amount of cash earned, cash depended on the harvests, harvests depended on the seasons, and the seasons were in the hands of Allah, and Allah was in need of no one. The only time Osman stepped out of this cycle was when he went away to do his compulsory military service. In the army, he learned how to clean a rifle, how to load a gun, how to dig a trench, how to throw a grenade from a rooftop – skills he hoped he would never need again. Every night in the dormitory he shared with forty-three other soldiers, he longed to revive his old shadow plays, but there was neither an empty wall nor a charming oil lamp.

Upon his return he found his family exactly as he had left them. Yet he was not the same. He had always known he was a female inside, but the ordeal of the army had flattened his soul to such a degree that, strangely, he felt emboldened to live his own truth. By a fluke of fate, around that time his mother came up with the idea that he should now get married, and give her grandchildren, even though she had loads of them already. Despite his objections, she threw herself into finding him a suitable wife.

On the night of the wedding, while the guests clapped to the beat of the musicians' drums and the young bride waited in a room upstairs, her robe loosely belted, Osman sneaked out. Overhead he could hear the hoot of an eagle owl and the wailing of a stone-curlew, sounds as familiar to him as his own breathing. He trudged the twelve miles to the nearest station and jumped on the first train to Istanbul, never to return. At first he slept rough, working as a masseur in a hammam with poor hygiene and a worse reputation. Shortly after, he started cleaning the toilets in Haydarpaşa train station. It was in this last job that Osman formed most of his convictions about his fellow human beings. No one should try to philosophize on the nature of humanity until they had worked in a public toilet for a couple of weeks and seen the things that people did, simply because they could – destroying the water hose on the wall, breaking the door handle, drawing nasty graffiti everywhere, peeing on the hand towels, depositing every kind of filth and muck all over the place, knowing that someone else would have to clean it up.

This was not the city he had imagined, and surely these were not the people he wished to share the highways and byways with. But it was only here in Istanbul that he could outwardly transform himself into the person he really was inside, and so he stayed, and persevered.

Osman was no more. There was only Nalan, and no going back.

Four Minutes

Four minutes after her heart had stopped beating, a fleeting memory surfaced in Leila's mind, bringing with it the smell and taste of watermelon.

August 1953. The hottest summer in decades, that's what Mother had said. Leila mused on the idea of a decade: how long was it? Her grasp of time slipped through her fingers like silken ribbons. The month before, the Korean War had ended and Auntie's brother had safely returned to his village. Now Auntie had other things to worry about. Unlike the last, this pregnancy seemed to be progressing well, except she was feeling sick day and night. Seized by terrible bouts of nausea, she was having difficulty keeping down her food. The heat wasn't helping either. Baba suggested they all go on a holiday. Somewhere by the Mediterranean Sea; a change of air. He also invited his brother and his sister, along with their families.

Cramming into a minibus, they travelled to a fishing town on the south-east coast. There were twelve of them in all. Uncle, sitting next to the driver, sunlight flickering gaily across his face, told them funny stories about his student days, and when he ran out of stories he started singing patriotic anthems, urging everyone to join along. Even Baba did.

Uncle was trim and tall, with hair shaved close to the scalp and bluish-grey eyes with long lashes that curled at the ends. He was handsome, everyone said so, and one could see how hearing the same compliment all his life had affected his ways. He carried himself with an ease that other members of the family visibly lacked.

'Look at us, the mighty Akarsu family on the road! We could form our own football team,' Uncle was now saying.

Leila, sitting in the back with Mother, exclaimed, 'That's eleven players, not twelve.'

'Is that so?' Uncle said, looking at her over his shoulder. 'Then we'll be the players and you'll be the manager. Give us orders, make us do whatever you wish. We are at your service, ma'am.'

Leila beamed, delighted at the prospect of being the boss for once. During the rest of the journey, Uncle happily played along. At every pit stop, he opened the door for her, brought her drinks and biscuits and, after a little rain in the afternoon, carried her over a puddle in the road so that her shoes wouldn't get dirty.

'Is she a football manager or the Queen of Sheba?' said Baba, watching from the side.

Uncle said, 'She's the manager of our football team and the queen of my heart.'

And that made everyone smile.

It was a long, slow ride. The driver puffed on hand-rolled cigarettes, a thin smoke swirling around him, softly tracing unread, cursive messages above his head. Outside, the sun was beating down hard. Inside the bus, the air felt musty, stifling. Leila kept her hands under her legs to stop the hot vinyl from burning the backs of her thighs but, after a while, feeling tired, she gave up. She wished she had put on a long dress or a loose shalwar instead of cotton shorts. Thankfully, she had remembered to bring her straw hat with the bright red cherries on one side; they looked extremely appetizing.

'Let's swap hats,' said Uncle. He was wearing a narrow-brimmed white fedora that, though worse for wear, suited him well.

'Yes, let's!'

After dark, her new hat on her head, Leila stared out of the window at the blur of the motorway, the lights of the passing cars resembling the silvery, slimy trails that she had seen snails leave in the garden. Beyond the motorway glowed the street lamps of small towns, clusters of houses here and there, silhouettes of mosques and minarets. She wondered what kind of families inhabited those homes, and what kind of children, if any, were looking at their bus now, thinking about where they might be going. By the time they reached their destination, late in the evening, she had fallen asleep, hugging the fedora against her chest, her reflection in the window small and pale, floating past buildings.

Leila was surprised, and slightly disappointed, when she saw where they would be staying. Old, torn mosquito screens covered every window, splotches of mould crept up the walls, nettles and thorny weeds pushed their way through the stepping stones in the garden. But to her delight there was a wooden washtub in the yard, into which they could pump water. Up the road, a giant mulberry tree towered in the fields. When the wind came whirling down the mountain and slammed against the tree, it rained purple mulberries, staining their clothes and hands. It wasn't a comfortable house but it felt different, adventurous.

Her older cousins, all of them teenagers in various fits of the sulks, declared Leila too young to share a room with. Nor could she stay with Mother, who was given a room so small that it could scarcely accommodate her suitcases. So Leila had to sleep with the toddlers, some of whom wet their beds, and cried or chuckled in their sleep, depending on the content of their dreams.

Late at night, Leila lay awake, wide-eyed and very still, alert to every creak, every passing shadow. Judging by the droning of the mosquitoes, they must have got through the holes in the wire mesh. They swarmed around her head, buzzed inside her ears. They waited for the darkness to become complete and slipped into the room at the same time – both the mosquitoes and her uncle.

'Are you sleeping?' he asked the first time he came and sat on the edge of her bed. He kept his voice low, just above a whisper, careful not to wake up the toddlers.

'Yes . . . no, not really.'

'Hot, isn't it? I couldn't sleep either.'

Leila found it strange that he had not gone to the kitchen, where he could get himself a glass of cold water. There was a bowl of watermelon in the fridge, and it would have made a perfect midnight snack. Refreshing. Leila knew that some watermelons grew so large you could put a baby inside and still have room to spare. But she kept this information to herself.

Uncle nodded as if he had read her thoughts. 'I won't stay for long, just a little bit – if Your Highness would allow me?'

She tried to smile but her face felt stiff. 'Um, okay.'

He swiftly pulled aside the bedsheet and lay down next to her. She heard his heartbeat – loud and fast.

'Did you come to check on Tolga?' Leila asked after an awkward moment.

Tolga was Uncle's youngest son; he was sleeping in a cot by the window.

'I wanted to make sure everyone was okay. Let's not talk, though. We don't want to wake them up.'

Leila nodded. It made sense.

A rumbling rose from Uncle's stomach. He smiled, shyly. 'Oh, I must have had too much food.'

'Me too,' Leila said, although she hadn't.

'Really? Let me see how full your tummy is.' He pulled up her nightie. 'Can I put my hand here?'

Leila didn't say anything.

He started drawing circles around her belly button. 'Hmm. Are you ticklish?'

Leila shook her head. Most people were ticklish on their feet and their armpits. She was ticklish around her neck, but she was not going to tell him that. It seemed to her that if you told people your weakest spot they would definitely target it. She kept quiet.

At first the circles were small and light, but they grew larger, reaching her privates. She pulled away, embarrassed. Uncle inched

64

closer. He smelled of things she didn't like – chewed tobacco, alcohol, fried aubergine.

'You have always been my favourite,' he said. 'I'm sure you are aware of that.'

Was she his favourite? He had made her the manager of the football team, but still. Seeing her confusion, Uncle caressed her cheek with his other hand. 'Do you want to know why I love you the best?'

Leila waited, curious to hear the answer.

'Because you are not selfish like the others. A smart, sweet girl. Don't ever change. Promise me you won't change.'

Leila nodded, thinking how annoyed her older cousins would be if they heard him compliment her like that. What a pity they weren't here.

'Do you trust me?' His eyes were topaz crystals in the dark.

And there she was, nodding again. Much later in life, Leila would come to loathe this gesture of hers – an unconditional obedience to age and authority.

He said, 'When you are older, I'll protect you from boys. You don't know what they're like. I won't let them get close to you.'

He kissed her on her forehead, just like he had done every Eid when they visited them as a family and he gave her boiled sweets and pocket money. He kissed her the same way. And then he left. That first night.

The next evening, he didn't show up and Leila was ready to forget the whole incident. Yet the third night he was back. He smiled more broadly this time. A spicy scent lingered in the air; could it be that he had applied aftershave? As soon as she saw him coming, Leila closed her eyes, pretending to be asleep.

Quietly, he pulled aside the bedsheet, cuddled next to her. Again he put his hand on her belly, and this time the circles were bigger, persistent – searching, demanding what he already believed belonged to him.

'Yesterday I couldn't make it, your *yenge* was feeling poorly,' he said, as though apologizing for a missed appointment.

Down the corridor Leila could hear her mother snoring. Baba and Auntie had been given a large room upstairs, close to the bathroom. Leila had overheard them say that Auntie kept waking up at odd hours throughout the night, and it would be better if she slept alone. Did that mean she was no longer fighting her demons? Or perhaps it meant that the demons had finally won the war.

'Tolga wets the bed,' Leila blurted out, opening her eyes.

She didn't know why she said that. She had never seen the boy do such a thing.

If Uncle was taken aback, he didn't show it. 'I know, sweetheart. I'll take care of it, you shouldn't worry.'

His breath was warm against her neck. He had grown stubble; it made her skin prickle. Leila recalled the sandpaper Baba used to give a nice finish to the wooden cradle he was making for the baby on the way.

'Uncle –'

'Hush. We shouldn't disturb the others.'

We. They were a team.

'Hold it,' he said, and pushed her hand down the front of his pyjama shorts, towards a place between his legs. The child winced and drew her fingers back. Grabbing her wrist, he shoved her hand down again, sounding frustrated and furious. 'I said, hold it!'

Under her palm Leila felt his hardness. He squirmed, groaned, clenched his teeth. He moved back and forth, his breath quickening. She lay still, petrified. She wasn't even touching him any more, but she didn't think he was aware of that. He groaned one last time and stopped moving. He was panting heavily. There was a sharp smell in the air and the bedsheet was wet.

'Look what you've done to me,' he said when he found his voice.

Leila felt confused, embarrassed. She sensed instinctively that this was wrong and it should never have happened. It was her fault.

'You are a naughty girl,' Uncle said. He looked solemn, almost sad. 'You seem so sweet and innocent, but it is just a mask, isn't it?

66

Deep underneath, you're as dirty as all the others. Bad-mannered. How you have fooled me.'

A stab of guilt went through Leila, so sharp she could hardly move. Tears welled up in her eyes. She tried not to cry, but failed. Now she was sobbing.

He watched her for a moment. 'Okay, fine. I can't bear to see you cry.'

Almost at once, Leila's crying slowed, though she felt no better, only worse.

'I still love you.' His lips pressed on her mouth.

No one had kissed her on the mouth before. Her entire body went numb.

'Don't worry, I won't tell anyone,' he said taking her silence for compliance. 'But you must prove your trustworthiness.'

Such a long word. *Trustworthiness.* She wasn't even sure what it meant.

'It means you mustn't tell anyone,' said Uncle, a step ahead of her thoughts. 'It means this will be our secret. Only two people can know about it: you and I. No third person allowed. Now tell me, are you good at keeping secrets?'

But of course she was. She was holding too many secrets in her chest already; this would be yet another one.

Later on, growing up, Leila would ask herself over and again why he had chosen her. Theirs was a large family. There were others around. She wasn't the prettiest. She wasn't the smartest. In truth, she didn't think she was special in any way. She kept brooding on this, until one day she realized how awful the question was. Asking 'Why me?' was another way of saying, 'Why not someone else?' and she hated herself for that.

A holiday house with moss-green shutters and a split-rail fence that ended where the pebble beach began. The women were cooking the meals, sweeping the floors, washing the dishes; the men were playing cards, backgammon, dominoes; and the children ran around, unsupervised, throwing burrs at each other that stuck to everything they came into contact with. The ground was strewn with crushed mulberries and there were watermelon stains all over the upholstery.

A holiday house by the sea.

Leila was six years old; her uncle was forty-three.

The day they returned to Van, Leila came down with a fever. She had a metallic taste in her mouth, a knot of pain lodged deep in the pit of her stomach. Her temperature was so high that Binnaz and Suzan scooped her up and carried her between them to the bathroom, where they plunged her into cold water – to no avail. She was kept in bed, a vinegar-soaked towel on her forehead, an onion poultice on her chest, boiled cabbage leaves on her back and slices of potato all over her belly. Every few minutes they rubbed egg whites on the soles of her feet. The whole house stank like the fish market at the end of a summer's day. Nothing helped. Talking incoherently, grinding her teeth, the child slipped in and out of consciousness, sparkles of light dancing in front of her eyes.

Haroun called the local barber – a man who, among his many other duties, performed circumcisions, extracted teeth and gave enemas – but it turned out he was away on an emergency. So Haroun sent for the Lady Pharmacist instead – not an easy decision for him to take, since he had no liking for the woman, nor she for him.

No one knew her real name for sure. She was 'the Lady Pharmacist' to all and sundry, a strange woman by all accounts, but one with authority. A stout, bright-eyed widow sporting a bun as tight as her smile, she wore tailored suits and perky little hats and spoke with the confidence of those used to being heard. A champion of secularism, modernity and too many other things that came from the West. A staunch opponent of polygamy, she did not hide her dislike of a man with two wives; even the thought of it made her cringe. In her eyes, Haroun and his whole family, with their superstitions and stubborn refusal to adapt to a scientific age, were the very antithesis of the future she had in mind for this conflicted country.

Still, she came to help. She was accompanied by her son, Sinan. The boy was about the same age as Leila. An only child raised by a single working mother: it was unheard of. The people of this town often gossiped about them, sometimes with scorn, even ridicule, but trod with caution nevertheless. Despite their whispers, they still had a lot of respect for the Lady Pharmacist and had found themselves, at unexpected moments, in need of her help. Consequently, the mother and son lived on the edge of society, tolerated, though never quite accepted.

'How long has this been going on?' asked the Lady Pharmacist as soon as she arrived.

'Since last night . . . We've done everything we could think of,' said Suzan.

Binnaz, by her side, nodded.

'Yes, I can see what you've done – with your onions and potatoes,' scoffed the Lady Pharmacist.

Sighing, she opened her black leather bag, similar to the one carried by the local barber to boys' circumcision parties. She took out several silver boxes, a syringe, glass bottles, measuring spoons.

Meanwhile, half hiding behind his mother's skirts, the boy craned his head and stared at the shivering, sweating girl in the bed.

'Mama, is she going to die?'

'Shh, don't speak nonsense. She'll be fine,' said the Lady Pharmacist.

Only now turning her head to the side, trying to trace the sound, Leila looked at the woman and saw the needle she held in the air, the droplet on its tip glowing like a broken diamond. She began to cry.

'Don't worry, I'm not going to hurt you,' said the Lady Pharmacist.

Leila meant to say something but she lacked the strength. Her eyelids fluttered as her consciousness slipped away.

'Okay, can one of you two give me a hand? We need to turn her on her side,' said the Lady Pharmacist.

Binnaz volunteered instantly. Suzan, equally eager to help, searched around for a meaningful task and settled on pouring more vinegar into a bowl on the bedside table. A sharp smell filled the air.

'Go away,' Leila said to the silhouette by her bed. 'Uncle, go.'

'What's she saying?' Suzan asked with a puzzled frown.

The Lady Pharmacist shook her head. 'Nothing, she's hallucinating, poor darling. She'll be fine after the injection.'

Leila's crying turned raw – deep, rasping sobs.

'Mama, wait,' said the boy, his face etched with concern.

He approached the bed, leaning in close to Leila's head, and spoke softly in her ear. 'You need to hug something when you get injections. I have a stuffed owl at home, and a monkey, but the owl is the best.'

As he spoke, Leila's sobs ebbed away into a long, slow sigh and she fell silent.

'If you don't have a toy, you can squeeze my hand. I wouldn't mind.'

Gently, he took the girl's hand, light to the touch, almost lifeless. Yet to his surprise, just as the needle pushed in, she laced her fingers into his and did not let go.

Afterwards, Leila fell asleep immediately. A thick, heavy slumber. She found herself in a salt marsh, wading alone through a thicket of reeds, beyond which extended the vast ocean, the waves rough and choppy, crashing one after another. She saw her uncle calling from a fishing boat in the distance, rowing with ease despite the weather, approaching fast as a heartbeat. Alarmed, she tried to turn back, but she could barely move in the glutinous mud. It was then that she sensed a comforting presence beside her: the son of the Lady Pharmacist. He must have been standing there all along, carrying a duffel bag.

70

'Here, take this,' he said, as he pulled out of his bag a chocolate bar, wrapped in shiny tin foil. As she accepted the offer, despite her unease Leila felt herself start to relax.

When her temperature dropped and she opened her eyes, able at last to eat some yogurt soup, Leila immediately enquired about him, not knowing that they would meet again before long, and that this quietly intelligent, slightly awkward, kind-hearted and painfully shy boy would become her first true friend in life.

Sinan, her sheltering tree, her refuge, a witness to all that she was, all that she aspired to and, in the end, all that she could never be.

Sinan, one of the five.

Sinan's Story

Their home was above the pharmacy. A tiny flat that overlooked on one side a pasture where cattle and sheep grazed contentedly, and, on the other, an old, decrepit cemetery. In the morning his room was bathed in sunlight but turned gloomy after dusk – and that was when he returned from school. Every day he would open the door with the key he carried around his neck, and wait for his mother to come home from work. There would be food ready on the kitchen worktop; light meals, since his mother had no time for anything more complicated. She would put easy snacks in his school bag – cheese and bread, and way too often eggs, despite his protests. The boys in the classroom made fun of his lunch boxes, complaining about the smell. They called him Egg Tart. They themselves brought proper home-made dishes – grape-leaf sarma, stuffed sweet peppers, ground-meat börek . . . Their mothers were housewives. Everyone else's mother was a housewife in this town, it seemed to him. Everyone's but his.

All the other children had large families and talked about their cousins and aunts and brothers and sisters and grandparents, whereas in his house it was only him and his mother. Just the two of them, ever since his father had passed away last spring. A sudden heart attack. Mother still slept in the same room, *their* bedroom. Once he had seen her caressing the sheets on the other side of the bed with one hand, as if feeling for the body she used to snuggle up against, while touching her neck and her breasts with the other, driven by a longing Sinan had no understanding of. Her face was contorted and it took him a moment to realize she was crying. He felt a sizzle of pain in his stomach, a tremor of helplessness. It was the first time he had seen her cry.

Father had been a soldier, a member of the Turkish army. He

had believed in progress, reason, Westernization, enlightenment – words whose exact meaning the boy had not understood and yet felt comfortable with, so accustomed had he been to hearing them. Father had always said this country would one day become civilized and enlightened – on a par with European nations. *One cannot change geography*, he'd say, *but one can trick destiny*. Although most people in this eastern town were ignorant, crushed under the weight of religion and rigid convention, with the right kind of education they could be saved from their past. Father had believed in this. And Mother too. Together they had toiled away, an ideal couple of the new Republic, determined to build a bright future together. A soldier and a pharmacist, both strong-willed, stout-hearted. And he was their offspring, their only child, endowed with their best quality, their progressive spirit, though he feared he didn't resemble them much, not really, neither in character nor in appearance.

Father had been tall and lean, his hair slick as glass. So many times, standing in front of the mirror with grooming lotion and a comb, the boy had tried to emulate his father's hairstyle. He had used olive oil, lemon juice, shoe polish, and once a chunk of butter, which had caused an awful mess. Nothing had worked. Who would have believed that he, with his chubby features and clumsy ways, was the son of that soldier with the perfect smile and perfect posture? His father may have been gone but he was present in everything. The boy did not think he himself would leave such a big void if it were he who had gone. Now and then he caught his mother staring at him pensively, wearily, and it occurred to him that she might be wondering why he had not died instead of his father. It was in such moments that he felt so lonely and ugly that he could barely move. Then, just at his loneliest, his mother would come and hug him, brimful of tender love, and he would be embarrassed by his own thoughts, embarrassed and slightly relieved, but still with the nagging suspicion that, no matter how hard he tried and how much he changed, he would always fail her somehow.

He looked out of the window – a quick, furtive glance. The cemetery scared him. It had a strange, haunting smell, especially in autumn, when the world turned tawny. Generations of men in his family had died far too early. His father, his grandfather, his great-grandfather . . . However tenaciously he tried to control his emotions, the boy couldn't escape a feeling of foreboding that someday soon it would be his turn to be buried there. When his mother visited the cemetery, which she did often, to clean her husband's grave or plant flowers or, sometimes, just to sit there doing nothing, he spied on her from his window. He had never seen his mother without make-up or with a hair out of place, and watching her sitting there in the mud and dirt, with dead leaves clinging to her clothes, made him flinch, and fear her a little bit, as though she had turned into a stranger.

Everyone in the neighbourhood visited the pharmacy, old and young. Occasionally, women in black burqas came, pulling their children along behind them. Once he had heard a woman asking for a cure to stop her from having babies. She already had eleven kids, she had said. Mother had given her a small, square package and sent her off. A week later the woman had returned, complaining about severe stomach pain.

'You swallowed them?' Mother had exclaimed. 'The condoms?'

Upstairs the boy had gone still, listening.

'They weren't for you, they were for your husband!'

'I know that,' the woman had said, sounding tired. 'But I couldn't convince him to use them, so I thought I'd better take them myself. Maybe it will help, I thought.'

Mother was so enraged she kept mumbling to herself even after the woman had left.

'Ignorant, simple-minded peasants! They breed like rabbits! How can this poor country ever modernize if the uneducated continue to outnumber the educated? We make one child and raise him with care. Meanwhile they produce ten little brats, and if they can't look after them so what? They let them fend for themselves!'

Mother was gentle with the dead, less so with the living. But the boy thought one should be even gentler with the living than with the dead, because, after all, they were the ones struggling to make sense of this world, weren't they? He, with bits of butter stuck in his hair; that peasant woman, with condoms in her stomach . . . Everyone seemed a little lost, vulnerable and unsure of themselves, whether they were educated or not, modern or not, Eastern or not, grown up or a child. That's what he reckoned, this boy. He, for one, always felt more comfortable next to people who were not perfect in any way.

Five Minutes

Five minutes after her heart had stopped beating, Leila recalled her brother's birth. A memory that carried with it the taste and smell of spiced goat stew – cumin, fennel seeds, cloves, onions, tomatoes, tail fat and goat's meat.

She was seven years old when the baby arrived. Tarkan, the much-coveted son. Baba was on cloud nine. All these years he had been waiting for this moment. As soon as his second wife went into labour, he downed a glass of raqi and locked himself in a room where he remained sprawled on the sofa for hours, chewing at his lower lip, fingering his rosary beads, just like he had done on the day Leila was born.

Although the birth took place in the afternoon – on an unusually balmy day in March 1954 – Leila was not allowed to see the baby until later in the evening.

She ran her hand through her hair and approached the cradle, cautiously – her face set in an expression she had already decided on. How determined she was not to like this boy, an unwanted intruder in her life. But the very second her gaze landed on his rosebud face, doughy cheeks and knees dimpled like soft clay, she knew it was impossible for her not to love her brother. She waited, utterly still, as though she expected to hear a word of greeting from him. There was something extraordinary in his features. Just as a wayfarer, entranced by a sweet melody, might stop and listen intently for its source, so she tried to make sense of him. She was surprised to notice that, unlike anyone else in the family, her brother's nose seemed flattened and his eyes were slanted slightly upwards. He had the air of one who had travelled from afar to get to this place. This made her love him even more.

'Auntie, can I touch him?'

Sitting up in the wrought-iron, four-poster bed, Binnaz smiled. There were dark bags under her eyes and the delicate skin over her cheekbones seemed stretched tight. All throughout the afternoon she had been in the company of the midwife and the neighbours. Now that they were gone, she savoured this quiet moment with Leila and her son.

'Of course you may, my dear.'

The cradle, which Baba had carved out of cherrywood and painted sapphire blue, was decorated with evil-eye beads dangling from its handle. Every time a lorry passed outside, rattling the windows, the beads, caught in the glare of the headlights, slowly rotated like planets in a solar system of their own.

Leila held out her index finger to the baby, who instantly grasped it and pulled it towards his velvet mouth.

'Auntie, look! He doesn't want me to go.'

'That's because he loves you.'

'He does? But he doesn't even know me.'

Binnaz winked. 'He must have seen your picture in the school of heaven.'

'What?'

'Don't you know, up there in the seventh heaven there is a huge school with hundreds of classrooms.'

Leila smiled. For Auntie, whose own lack of formal education was a source of enduring regret, that must have been her idea of Paradise. Now that Leila had started school herself and had seen what it was like, she strongly disagreed.

'There, the students are unborn babies,' Binnaz carried on, unaware of the child's thoughts. 'Instead of desks, they have cradles facing a long blackboard. Do you know why?'

Blowing a strand of hair out of her eyes, Leila shook her head.

'Because on that blackboard are pictures of men, women, children . . . so many of them. Each baby chooses the family he'd like to join. As soon as your brother saw your face, he said to the angel on duty, "That's it! I want her to be my sister! Please send me to Van."'

Leila's smile grew wider. Out of the corner of her eye she glimpsed a feather drifting away – perhaps from a pigeon hiding on the roof or an angel flying overhead. Despite her reservations about school, she decided that she liked Auntie's version of Paradise.

Binnaz said, 'From now on, we'll be inseparable – you, me and the baby. Remember our secret?'

Leila drew a sharp breath. Since that waxing day last year, neither of them had brought up the subject.

'We'll tell your brother that I am your mother, not Suzan. Then the three of us will have one big secret.'

Leila considered this. In her experience, a secret was meant to stay between two people. She was still thinking about this when the sound of the doorbell reverberated through the house. She heard her mother open the door. Voices amplified in the corridor. Familiar voices. Uncle and his wife and their three sons had come to congratulate them.

No sooner had the guests entered the room than a shadow passed across Leila's face. She took a step back, extricating herself from her brother's silky grip. Her brows pulled into a frown. She fixed her gaze on the rows of fallow deer that walked clockwise around the border of the Persian carpet in perfect symmetry. They reminded her of the way she and the other children, clad in black uniforms and carrying satchels, marched in single file to their classrooms each morning.

Quietly, Leila sat down on the floor and pulled her legs up beneath her, studying the carpet. Upon closer inspection, she noticed that not all the deer were following the rules. Was one of them standing still, front hooves poised, head turned longingly backwards, tempted perhaps to set off in the opposite direction towards a wooded valley, rich in willows? She squinted at the wayward creature until her vision blurred, and the deer, as though magically animated, moved towards her, sunshine radiating through its majestic antlers. Inhaling the scent of the grassland, the child extended her hand towards the animal; if only she could jump on its back and ride off out of this room.

Meanwhile, no one was paying Leila any attention. They were all gathered around the baby.

'He's a bit chubby, isn't he?' said Uncle. Gently, he took Tarkan out of the cradle and lifted him up.

The baby seemed very floppy, and appeared to have a very short neck. Something was not right. But Uncle pretended not to have noticed it. 'He'll be a wrestler, my nephew.'

Baba raked his fingers through his copious hair. 'Oh, I wouldn't want him to be a wrestler. My son will be a minister!'

'Please, not a politician,' said Mother.

They laughed.

'Well, I told the midwife to take his umbilical cord to the mayor's office. If she can't get in, she promised to hide it in the garden. So don't be surprised if my son becomes the mayor of this town one day.'

'Look, he's smiling. I think he agrees,' said Uncle's wife, her lipstick a bright pink.

They all fawned over Tarkan, passing him around, making cooing sounds and uttering pleasantries that might not even have been words.

Baba's eyes fell on Leila. 'Why are you so silent?'

Uncle turned towards Leila with an inquisitive expression. 'Yes, why is my favourite niece not talking today?'

She did not answer.

'Come, join us.' Uncle fingered his chin, a gesture she had seen him make before when he was about to utter a witticism or launch into a funny story.

'I'm fine here . . .' Her voice trailed off.

Uncle's gaze shifted from curiosity to something that resembled suspicion.

Seeing him scrutinize her like that, Leila was overcome by a wave of anxiety. She felt ill to her stomach. Slowly, she stood up. She shifted her weight from one foot to the other and composed herself. Her hands, after straightening the front of her skirt, became perfectly still.

'May I go now, Baba? I've got homework.'

The grown-ups smiled at her knowingly.

'That's okay, dear,' said Baba. 'Go and study.'

As Leila walked out of the room, her footsteps muffled by the carpet where a lonely deer stood abandoned, she heard Uncle whisper behind her back, 'Oh, bless her! She's jealous of the baby, poor darling.'

The next morning Baba visited a glass-maker and ordered an evil-eye bead, bluer than the skies and larger than a prayer rug. On the fortieth day following Tarkan's birth, he sacrificed three goats and distributed their meat to the poor. And, for a while, he was a happy, proud man.

Months later, two grains of rice appeared in Tarkan's mouth. Now that he had his first teeth, it was time to determine the boy's future profession. All the neighbouring women were invited. And they came, dressed neither as conservatively as they would on a Qur'an reading day, nor as boldly as they would if it were leg-waxing day. Today their clothes were somewhere in between, signifying motherhood, domestic life.

A large, white umbrella was held open above Tarkan's head, on which they poured a potful of cooked wheat berries. The baby looked a little startled as he watched the wheat raining down on him, but to everyone's relief he did not cry. He had passed the first test. He would be a strong man.

Now he was made to sit on the carpet, surrounded by a range of objects: a wad of money, a stethoscope, a tie, a mirror, a rosary, a book, a pair of scissors. If he chose the money, he'd become a banker; if the stethoscope, a doctor; if the tie, a government official; if the mirror, a hairdresser; if the rosary, an imam; if the book, a teacher; and if he motioned towards the scissors instead, he was sure to follow in his father's footsteps, becoming a tailor.

Forming a semicircle, inching closer, the women waited, barely breathing. Auntie's face was pure concentration, her eyes slightly glazed and fixed on a single target, like a person about to swat a fly. Leila suppressed an urge to laugh. She glanced at her brother, who was sucking his thumb, unaware that he was at a critical crossroads – about to choose the course of his destiny.

'Come this way, darling,' said Auntie, gesturing towards the book. Wouldn't it be nice if her son became a teacher – or, even better, a headmaster? She would visit him every week, sauntering through the school gates with pride: welcome, at last, in a place she had longed to be part of as a child, but from which she had been excluded.

'No, this way,' said Mother, pointing at the rosary. As far as she was concerned, nothing was as prestigious as having an imam in the family – a good deed that would bring them all closer to God.

'Are you out of your minds?' piped up an elderly neighbour. 'Everyone needs a doctor.' With her chin she pointed towards the stethoscope while her eyes followed the baby and her voice trickled with honey. 'Come over here, dear child.'

'Well, I'd say lawyers earn more money than anyone,' said the woman sitting next to her. 'Clearly you've forgotten that. I don't see a copy of the constitution here.'

Meanwhile, Tarkan's puzzled eyes scanned the objects around him. Not interested in any of them, he turned his back to the guests. That was when he caught sight of Leila, who was standing silently behind him. Instantly, the baby's expression softened. He reached out towards his sister, pulled off Leila's bracelet – of brown leather braiding with a blue satin cord woven through it – and held it in the air.

'Hah! He doesn't want to be a teacher . . . or an imam,' said Leila with a chuckle. 'He wants to be me!'

And the girl's joy was so pure and spontaneous that the grown-ups, despite their disappointment, felt obliged to join her laughter.

A frail child with poor muscle tone and control, Tarkan often got sick. The slightest physical effort seemed to exhaust him. He was small for his age; his body did not seem to be growing in proportion. As time went by, anyone could see that he was different, though no one talked about it openly. It was only when he was two and a half years old that Baba agreed to take him to a hospital. Leila insisted on accompanying them.

It was raining in earnest when they reached the doctor's office. Baba placed Tarkan on a bed that had been covered with a sheet. The baby's eyes moved from him to Leila and back, his lower lip sagging, poised to cry, and for the thousandth time Leila felt a surge of love so strong and helpless that it almost hurt. Softly, she put her hand on the warm round of his belly and smiled.

'I see you have a problem here. I'm sorry about your son's condition – it happens,' the doctor said after he had examined Tarkan. 'These kids can't learn a thing, there's not much point in trying. They don't live long anyhow.'

'I don't understand.' Baba kept a tight rein on his voice.

'This baby is a *mongoloid*. You never heard of it?'

Baba stared off into space, silent and motionless, as if it were he who had asked a question and was now waiting for a reply.

The doctor removed his glasses and held them up to the light. He must have found them sufficiently clean, for he returned them to his nose. 'Your son is not normal. Surely you are aware of this by now. I mean, it's obvious. I don't even understand why you are so surprised. And where is your wife, may I ask?'

Baba cleared his throat. He was not going to tell this patronizing man that he did not approve of his young wife leaving the house unless strictly necessary. 'She's at home.'

'Well, she should have come with you. It's important that she is clear about the situation. You need to talk to her. In the West, there are institutions for these kids. They stay there their whole lives and don't bother anyone. But we don't have that kind of support here. Your wife will have to take care of him. It won't be easy. Tell her she should not get too attached. They usually die before they reach puberty.'

Leila, who had been listening to every word, her heart accelerating, scowled up at the man. 'Shut up, you stupid, bad man! Why are you saying horrible things?'

'Leyla . . . behave,' said Baba – though perhaps not as sternly as he would have at any other time.

The doctor turned to the girl with a bewildered look, as if he had forgotten she was in the room. 'Don't worry, child, your brother doesn't understand anything.'

'He does!' Leila yelled, her voice like shattered glass. 'He understands everything.'

Taken aback by her outburst, the doctor raised a hand to pat her on the head, but he must have thought better of it because he swiftly brought it down again.

Baba took Tarkan's condition personally, certain that he had done something terrible to draw God's ire. He was being punished for his sins, past and present. Allah was sending him a message, loud and clear, and if he still refused to receive it, worse things were to follow. All this time he had lived in vain, preoccupied with what *he* wanted of the Almighty, never thinking about what the Almighty wanted of him. Had he not sworn to stop drinking alcohol the day Leila was born, but then gone back on his word? His whole life was full of broken promises and incomplete tasks. Now that he managed to quieten the voice of his *nafs*, his ego, he was ready to redeem himself. After consulting with his sheikh, and upon his advice, he decided to stop making *alla franga* garments for women. No more skimpy dresses, no more short skirts. He would use his skills to better purpose. Whatever life he had left, he would dedicate it to spreading the fear of God because he bore witness to the blows that rained on humans when they stopped fearing Him.

His two wives could take care of his two children. Baba was done with marriage, and done with sex, which, he now realized, just like money, had a way of complicating things. He moved to a dimly lit bedroom at the back of the house, ordering all the furniture inside to be removed – except for a single mattress, a blanket, an oil lamp, a wooden chest, and a handful of books carefully chosen by his sheikh. His clothes and rosaries and ablution towels he kept inside the chest. All items of comfort, even a pillow, were to be relinquished. Like many a belated believer, Baba was keen to make up for what he regarded as his lost years. Yearning to bring everyone around him to God – *his* God – he wanted to have disciples, if not in the dozens, then at least a few. Or else, a single devoted follower. And who would fit this role better than his daughter, who was fast becoming a defiant youngster, her attitude increasingly rude and irreverent?

If Tarkan had not been born with severe Down's syndrome, as his condition came to be called years later, Baba might have distributed his expectations and frustrations more evenly between his children, but, as things stood, they were all placed on Leila. And, as the years went by, those expectations and frustrations multiplied.

13 April 1963. Age sixteen, Leila had fallen into the habit of following the world news closely – both because she was interested in what happened elsewhere and also because it helped her not to think too much about her own limited life. This afternoon, peering over the newspaper spread on the kitchen table, she read out the news for Auntie. Far away in America a brave black man had been arrested for protesting against the ill-treatment of his people. His crime: holding a march without a permit. There was a photo of him with a caption underneath that read, 'Martin Luther King sent to jail!' He wore a neat suit and a dark tie, his face tilted towards the camera. It was his hands that grabbed Leila's

attention. He held them gracefully in the air, his palms curved towards each other as though he were carrying an invisible crystal ball that, though it would not show him how the future would look, he had nevertheless promised himself never to drop.

Slowly, Leila turned the page to the domestic news. Hundreds of peasants in Anatolia had held a march against poverty and unemployment. Many had been arrested. The newspaper said the government in Ankara was determined to crush the mutiny and not to make the same mistake as the Shah in Iran, just next door. Shah Pahlavi had been distributing land to landless peasants in the hope of earning their loyalty and the plan did not seem to be working. Discontent was brewing in the land of pomegranates and Caspian tigers.

'Tut-tut, the world is running as fast as an Afghan hound,' Auntie said after Leila had finished reading the news. 'There's so much misery and violence everywhere.'

Auntie glanced out of the window, intimidated by the world far and beyond. It was one of the endless troubles of her life that, even after all this time, and even after she had had two children, her fear of being kicked out of this house had not abated in the slightest. She still did not feel secure. Tarkan, who was nine years old now but had the communication skills of a three-year-old, was sitting on the carpet by her feet, playing with a ball of wool. It was the best toy for him, without any sharp edges or unsafe bits. He had been feeling unwell the whole month, complaining of chest pains, weakened by a flu that never seemed to leave him. Although he had gained a lot of weight recently, his skin had the pale glow of the emaciated. Watching her brother with an anxious smile, Leila wondered if he understood that he would never be like other children. She hoped not. For his own good. It must be painful to be different and to know it deep within.

None of them was aware back then that this would be the last time Leila, or anyone in the family, would be reading the papers aloud. If the world was changing, so was Baba. After his sheikh had passed away, he had been looking for a new spiritual master.

Early in the spring, he started to attend *dhikr* ceremonies of a *tariqa* based on the outskirts of Van. The preacher there, a decade younger than him, was a stern man with eyes the colour of dry grass. Although the *tariqa* had historical roots in the time-honoured Sufi philosophies and mystical teachings of love, peace and self-effacement, it had nowadays become an axis of rigidity, zealotry and hubris. Jihad, once regarded as the lifelong struggle against one's own *nafs*, now meant only the war against infidels – and infidels were everywhere. 'How could the state and religion be separated when they are one and the same in Islam?' the preacher wanted to know. Maybe this artificial duality worked for Westerners, with their heavy drinking and loose morals, but not for the people here in the East, who liked to have God's guidance in everything they did. Secularism was another name for the reign of Sheitan. The *tariqa* members would fight against it with every fibre of their being, and one day put an end to this man-made regime by bringing back God-made sharia.

To this end, every member had to open the way for God's work, starting with their personal life, the preacher advised. They were obliged to make sure that their families – their wives and children – lived according to the holy teachings.

And this is how Baba waged a holy war in the house. First, he instituted a new set of rules. Leila was no longer allowed to go to the house of the Lady Pharmacist to watch TV. From now on she was to refrain from reading any publications, and to especially avoid *alla franga* ones, including the popular *Hayat* magazine, which featured a different actress on its cover each month. Singing contests, beauty pageants and sports competitions were immoral. Figure skaters with their skimpy skirts were all sinners. Swimmers and gymnasts in their skintight outfits were provoking lustful thoughts in pious menfolk.

'All those girls flipping in the air, naked!'

'But you used to enjoy sports,' Leila reminded him.

'I had gone astray,' Baba said. 'My eyes are open now. Allah did not want me to get lost in the wilderness.'

Leila did not know what wilderness her father was talking about. They lived in a city. Not a big one, but a city nonetheless.

'I'm doing you a favour. One day you'll appreciate it,' Baba would say as the two of them sat at the kitchen table with a pile of religious pamphlets between them.

Every few days, Mother, in the soft, plaintive voice she reserved for praying, reminded Leila that she should have already started covering her hair. The time had come and passed. They had to go to the bazaar together and choose the best fabrics, just as they had once agreed – except Leila no longer felt bound by this understanding. Not only did she refuse to wear a headscarf, but she treated her body as if it were a mannequin she could shape and dress and paint to her heart's content. She bleached her hair and eyebrows with lemon juice and chamomile tea, and when all the lemons and chamomile in the kitchen mysteriously disappeared, she turned to Mother's henna. If she couldn't be blonde, why not be a redhead? Quietly, Mother disposed of all the henna in the house.

On the way to school one day Leila saw a Kurdish woman with a traditional tattoo on her chin, and, inspired by her, the next week she had a black rose imprinted just above her right ankle. The ink for the tattoo was based on a centuries-old formula known to local tribes: wood-fire soot, gall-bladder liquid from a mountain goat, deer tallow and a few drops of breastmilk. With each push of the needle, she flinched a little but endured the pain, feeling strangely alive with hundreds of splinters under her skin.

Leila decorated her notebooks with pictures of famous singers, even though Baba had told her that music was *haram* and Western music even more so. Because he said this, leaving no room for compromise, Leila had of late been listening to Western music exclusively. It wasn't always easy to follow the European or

American singles charts in a place so remote and secluded, but she seized on whatever she could. She was especially fond of Elvis Presley, who, with his dark handsomeness, looked more Turkish than American, endearingly familiar.

Her body had been changing fast. Hair under her arms, a dark patch between her legs; new skin, new smells, new emotions. Her breasts had turned into strangers, a pair of snobs, holding the tips of their noses in the air. Every day she checked her face in the mirror with a curiosity that made her uneasy, as though half expecting to see someone else staring back. She applied make-up at every opportunity, kept her hair unbound instead of in neat braids, wore tight skirts whenever she could, and had recently, secretly, taken up smoking, stealing from Mother's tobacco pouches. She had no friends in the classroom. The other students found her either strange or scary, she couldn't tell which. In voices loud enough for her to hear, they gossiped about her, calling her a bad apple. That was all fine by Leila: she avoided them anyway, particularly the popular girls with their judgemental glares and sharp remarks. Her grades were low. Baba did not seem to mind. Soon she would get married and start her own family. He didn't expect her to be an exemplary student; he expected her to be a good girl, a modest girl.

Still to this day, her only friend at school was the son of the Lady Pharmacist. Their friendship had stood the test of time, like an olive tree that grows stronger as the years pass. By nature timid and taciturn, Sinan was a whizz with numbers and always got the highest grade in maths. He had no other friends either, unable to keep up with the assertive energy of most of his peers. Next to dominant personalities – the class teacher, the headmaster and, above all, his mother – he usually kept quiet and withdrew into himself. Not with Leila though. When they were together he wouldn't stop talking, his voice full of excitement. At every break and lunchtime at school, they sought each other out. Sitting in a corner by themselves – while other girls gathered in groups or jumped rope and other boys played football or marbles – they would chat endlessly, ignoring the reproving stares directed at them in a town where the sexes kept to their designated spaces.

Sinan had read everything he could find on the First and Second World Wars – the names of the battles, the dates of the bombing raids, the heroes of the resistance movement . . . He knew an awful lot of information about Zeppelins and the German Count that these airships had been named after. Leila loved to listen to him as he told her about them, speaking with such passion that she almost saw one drifting overhead, its massive, cylindrical shadow brushing over the minarets and domes as it floated towards the great lake.

'One day you too will invent something,' Leila said.

'Me?'

'Yes, and it'll be better than the German Count's invention because that killed people. Whereas yours will help others. I am sure you'll do something truly remarkable.'

She was the only one who thought him capable of doing extra-ordinary things.

Sinan was particularly curious about codes and code-breaking. His eyes glowed with delight when he talked about the secret transmissions of the resistance movement in wartime, which he called 'sabotage broadcasts'. Not that he cared much about the content; it was the power of the radio that fascinated him, the unwavering optimism of a voice in the dark speaking to an empty space, trusting there was someone out there willing to listen.

Unbeknownst to Baba, it was this boy who kept feeding Leila with books, magazines and newspapers – none of which she was able to read in her own house any more. Thus she learned that there had been a big freeze in England, women had gained the right to vote in Iran, and that the war was not going well for the Americans in Vietnam.

'Those clandestine radio broadcasts you keep telling me about,' said Leila as the two of them sat under the only tree in the play-ground. 'I was thinking, you are like that, aren't you? Thanks to you, I follow what's happening in the world.'

His face lit up. 'I am your sabotage radio!'

The bell rang, announcing it was time to go back to the classroom. As she stood up and dusted herself off, Leila said, 'Maybe I should call you Sabotage Sinan.'

'You serious? I'd love that!'

And so it was that the only child of the only woman pharmacist in town earned the nickname of Sabotage. The boy who one day, not long after Leila ran away from home, would follow her all the way from Van to Istanbul, the city where all the discontented and all the dreamers eventually ended up.

Six Minutes

Six minutes after her heart had stopped beating, Leila pulled from her archive the smell of a wood-burning stove. 2 June 1963. Uncle's oldest son was getting married. His fiancée came from a family that had earned its wealth through trade along the Silk Road, which, as many in the region knew but preferred not to mention when outsiders were around, was not all about silk and spice, but also about poppies. From Anatolia to Pakistan, from Afghanistan to Burma, poppies grew in their millions, swaying in the breeze, their bright colour rebellious against the arid landscape. The milky fluid oozed from the seed pods, drop by magical drop, and while the farmers remained poor, others made a fortune.

No one brought this up at the lavish party thrown in the grandest hotel in Van. The guests revelled until the early hours of the morning. There was so much tobacco smoke that it looked like the whole place was on fire. Baba watched with disapproving eyes anyone who stepped on to the dance floor, but his biggest scowl was reserved for the men and women who had locked arms in the traditional dance, halay, shaking their hips as if they had never heard of modesty. Still he did not make a comment – for his brother's sake. He was fond of him.

The next day, family members from both sides met at a photographer's studio. Against a series of changing vinyl backdrops – the Eiffel Tower, Big Ben, the Leaning Tower of Pisa, and a flock of flamingos rising towards the sunset – the newly-weds posed for posterity, sweltering in their expensive, new clothes.

Leila studied the happy couple from the side. The bride, a fine-boned, dark-haired young woman, fitted neatly into her pearly gown, a bouquet of white gardenias in her hand and around her waist a red belt, a symbol and declaration of chastity. In her presence Leila felt a gloom so heavy that it was as if she carried a rock in her chest. A thought came to her unbidden: she would never be able to wear a gown like that. She had heard all kinds of stories about brides who, on their wedding nights, had turned out not to be virgins – how their husbands marched them to hospitals for intimate examinations, their footsteps echoing emptily behind them across dark streets, neighbours peering out from behind lace curtains; how they were delivered back to their fathers' houses, where they were punished in whatever way their families saw fit; how they could never fully become part of society again, humiliated and disgraced, a hollow cast to their youthful features . . . She picked at a cuticle on her ring finger, pulling it until it bled. That familiar jolt in her gut calmed her down. She did this sometimes. She cut herself on her thighs and upper arms, where no one could see the marks, using the same knife with which she sliced an apple or an orange at home, the skin curling gently under the glint of the blade.

How proud Uncle was that day. He was dressed in a grey suit with a white silk waistcoat and a patterned tie. When it was time for the whole family to have their picture taken, he rested one hand on his son's shoulder while his other hand clasped Leila's waist. No one noticed.

On the way back from the studio, the Akarsus stopped at a bakery with a nice patio and tables in the shade. The tantalizing aroma of börek, fresh out of the oven, wafted through the window.

Uncle placed the order for everyone: a samovar of tea for the grown-ups, icy lemonades for the youngsters. Now that his son was married to the daughter of a rich family, Uncle took every opportunity to display his own wealth. Just the other week he had given a telephone to his brother's family so that they could all be in touch more often.

'Bring us something to nibble on too,' Uncle said to the waiter.

A few minutes later, the man appeared with their drinks and a generous plate of cinnamon rolls. If Tarkan were here, Leila thought, he would instantly grab one, his honest eyes bright with joy, his happiness pure, unmasked. Why wasn't he included in these family celebrations? Tarkan never travelled anywhere, not even to a fake Eiffel Tower; save for the doctor's visit made when he was just a small child, he had not so much as glimpsed the world beyond the garden fence. When neighbours came for a visit, he was kept in a room away from prying eyes. Because Tarkan stayed at home all the time, so did Auntie. They were not close any more, Leila and Auntie; each passing year seemed to pull them further apart.

Uncle poured the tea, held his glass towards the light. After taking one sip he shook his head. He signalled to the waiter, leaned forward and spoke very slowly, as though each word were an effort. 'Look at this colour, see? Not nearly dark enough. What did you put in it, eh? Banana leaves? It tastes like dishwater.'

Apologizing hastily, the waiter took the samovar away, spilling a few drops on the tablecloth.

'Clumsy, isn't he?' said Uncle. 'Doesn't know his right hand from his left.' He turned towards Leila, his voice suddenly conciliatory. 'So how's school? What's your favourite subject?'

'None,' Leila said with a shrug. She kept her gaze on the tea stains.

Baba knitted his brows. 'Is this how you talk to your elders? You have no manners.'

'Don't worry,' said Uncle. 'She's young.'

'Young? Her mother was married and working her fingers raw at her age.'

Mother straightened her back.

'It's a new generation,' said Uncle.

'Well, my sheikh says there are forty signs that Judgement Day is near. One is that young people get out of control. That's exactly what's happening nowadays, isn't it? All those boys with mop-top hair. What will they have next – long hair, like a girl's? I always

93

tell my daughter, be careful. There is so much moral decay in this world.'

'What are the other signs?' asked Uncle's wife.

'I can't remember all of them off the top of my head. There are thirty-nine more, obviously. For one thing, we'll see massive landslides. Oceans will surge. Oh, there will be more women in the world than men. I'll give you a book where it's all explained.'

Leila noticed, out of the corner of her eye, Uncle watching her intently. She turned her head aside, a little too sharply, and that was when she saw a family approaching. A happy family, they seemed to be. A woman with a smile as wide as the Euphrates River, a man with kind eyes, and two girls with satin bows in their hair. They were looking for a table, and settled on the one next to theirs. Leila noticed how the mother caressed the cheek of the younger girl, whispering something that made her chuckle. The older girl, meanwhile, was inspecting the menu with her father. They chose their pastries together, asking each other what they would like to have. Everyone's opinion seemed to be of value. They were close and inseparable, like stones mortared together. Watching them, Leila felt a pang so sudden and sharp that she had to lower her gaze, fearing her envy would show on her face.

By now the waiter had appeared with a new samovar and a clean set of glasses.

Uncle grabbed a glass, took a sip and curled up his lips in distaste. 'You have some nerve to call this tea. It's not even hot enough,' he blustered, savouring his new-found power over this decorous, meek man.

Shrinking like a nail under the hammer of Uncle's ire, the waiter apologized profusely and rushed back. After what felt like a long time, he appeared with a third samovar, so hot this time that it released endless curls of steam into the air.

Leila observed the man's bloodless face; he seemed so tired as he filled the glasses. Tired but also annoyingly passive. And that was when Leila recognized in his behaviour a familiar sense of helplessness, an unconditional surrender to Uncle's power and authority that she, more than anyone, was guilty of. With a sudden impulse, she stood up and grabbed a glass. 'I'd like some tea!'

Before anyone could say a word, she took a sip, scalding her tongue and the roof of her mouth so badly her eyes watered. Still she managed to swallow the liquid and gave the waiter a lopsided grin. 'Perfect!'

The man nervously glanced at Uncle, then back at Leila. He mumbled a quick 'thank you' and disappeared.

'What do you think you are doing?' Uncle said, more startled than upset.

Mother tried to soften the mood. 'Well, she was just –'

Baba interjected, 'Don't defend her. She's behaving like a crazy person.'

Leila felt her heart constrict. Here, in front of her eyes, was the reality she had quietly sensed all this time but told herself did not exist. Baba had sided with Uncle, not with her. It would always be like this, she now understood. Baba's first instinct would always be to help out his brother. She pursed her bottom lip, scabby from picking. Only later, much later, would she come to think of this moment in time, small and ordinary though it may have been, as a harbinger of what was to come. Never in her life had she felt as lonely as she did now.

Ever since Baba had stopped tailoring clothes for Westernized customers, money had been tight. The previous winter, they had been able to afford to heat only a few rooms in so large a house; but the kitchen was always warm. They spent a lot of time there all year round: Mother winnowed rice, soaked beans, and prepared meals on the wood-burning stove, while Auntie kept a close eye on Tarkan, who, if left unsupervised, ripped his clothes, suffered painful falls and swallowed things that almost choked him.

'You'd better get it straight, Leyla,' Baba said as Leila sat at the kitchen table with her books that August. 'When we die and we are alone in our graves, two angels will visit us: one blue, one black. They are called Munkar and Nakir, the Denied and the Denier. They will ask us to recite surahs from the Qur'an – down to the letter. If you fail three times, you'll be bound for hell.'

He pointed towards the cupboards, as if hell were between the jars of pickled cucumbers that lined the shelves.

Exams made Leila nervous. At school she had failed most of them. As she listened to Baba, she could not help wondering: how would the black and blue angels test her knowledge of religion when the moment arrived? Would the test be oral or written, interview-style or multiple choice? Would wrong answers lose her marks? Would she learn the results right away or would she have to wait until all the scores were in – and if that were the case, how long would the process take, and would a supreme authority make the announcement, the High Council of Just Deserts and Eternal Damnation?

'What about people in Canada or Korea or France?' Leila asked.

'What about them?'

'Well, you know . . . they are not Muslim, generally. What happens to them after they die? I mean, the angels can't ask them to recite *our* prayers.'

Baba said, 'Why not? Everyone gets the same questions.'

'But those people in other countries can't recite the Qur'an, can they?'

'Exactly. Anyone who is not a proper Muslim will fail the angels' exam. Straight to hell. That's why we must spread Allah's message to as many people as possible. That's how we'll save their souls.'

For a moment, they stood still listening to the spit and crackle of the wood burning in the stove, and it felt like it was telling them something urgent in its own language.

'Baba . . .' Leila sat up. 'What's the most dreadful thing about hell?'

She expected him to say it was the pits full of scorpions and snakes or the boiling waters that smelled of sulphur or the biting frost of Zamhareer. He could have said it was being forced to drink molten lead or feed off the Zaqqum Tree, whose branches bore heads of demons instead of luscious fruits. But after a slight pause, Baba replied, 'It's God's voice . . . This voice that never stops shouting, threatening, day in, day out. He tells sinners they were given a chance but they have let Him down, and now they must pay the price.'

Leila's mind was racing even as she grew still. 'God won't forgive?'

Baba shook his head. 'No – and even if He decides to forgive one day, it'll be long after every sinner has suffered the worst torments.'

Leila looked out of the window. The sky was turning a mottled grey. A lone goose was flying towards the lake, strangely soundless.

'What if . . .' Leila breathed in a lungful of air and let it out slowly. 'Let's say, what happens if you have done something wrong, and you know it's wrong, but you really didn't mean to do it?'

'That won't help. God will still punish you, but if it's just once, He might be more merciful.'

Leila picked at a hangnail, a tiny bead of blood pooling on her thumb. 'And if it's more than once?'

Baba shook his head, his brow furrowed. 'Then it's eternal damnation, there is no excuse. No getting away from hell. I might sound harsh to you now, but one day you'll thank me. It's my duty to teach you right from wrong. You need to learn all this while you are still young and sinless. Tomorrow it might be too late. As the twig is bent, so grows the tree.'

Leila closed her eyes, a hardness beginning to form in her chest. She was young, but she did not consider herself sinless. She had done something terrible, and not just once, not twice, but many times. Uncle continued to touch her. Every time the families got together, Uncle found a way to get close to her, but what had happened a couple of months ago – when Baba was having an operation to remove kidney stones and Mother had to stay in the hospital with him for about a week – was so unspeakable that even remembering it now made Leila feel sick again. Auntie had been staying with Tarkan in her room, and had not heard a thing. That whole week, Uncle had visited her every night. It hadn't bled after that first time, but it had always hurt. When she tried to keep him away, Uncle reminded her that it was she who had started this affair back in the holiday house that smelled of sliced watermelon.

I used to think to myself, Why, she's a sweet innocent girl, but it turns out you like to play games with men's minds . . . Remember how you behaved on the bus that day, giggling all the time to get my attention? Why were you wearing those tiny shorts? Why did you allow me to come to your bed at night? You could have told me to leave and I would have done so, but you didn't. You could have slept in your parents' room, but you didn't. Every night you waited for me. Did you ever ask yourself why? Well, I know why. And you know why.

She had filth in her, of this she was convinced. Filth that wouldn't wash away, like a crease in her palm. And now here was Baba telling her that Allah, who knew everything and saw everything, would not forgive her.

Shame and self-reproach had been Leila's constant companions for too long, twin shadows that followed her everywhere she went. Yet this was the first time she felt an anger she had never experienced before. Her mind was aflame, every muscle in her body taut with a burning rage she didn't know how to contain. She did not want to have anything to do with this God who invented copious ways of judging and punishing human beings but did so little to protect them when they needed Him.

She stood up, scraping her chair back noisily on the tiled floor.

'Where are you going?' Baba's eyes widened.

'I need to check on Tarkan.'

'We aren't done here yet. We are studying.'

Leila shrugged. 'Yeah, well, I don't want to study any more. I'm bored.'

Baba flinched. 'What did you say?'

'I said I'm borrred.' She stretched the word like chewing gum in her mouth. 'God, God, God! I've had enough of this crap.'

Baba lunged towards her, his right hand raised. Then, just as suddenly, he drew back, trembling, disappointment in his eyes. His face broke into fresh lines, cracking like dry clay. He knew, and she knew, that he had almost slapped her.

Baba never hit Leila. Neither before nor after. Though a man of several shortcomings, he never displayed physical aggression or uncontrolled wrath. So for bringing this impulse out in him, for rousing something so dark, so alien to his character, he would always hold her responsible.

She, too, blamed herself and would continue to do so for years to come. Back then she was used to that – everything she did and thought tended towards an all-pervasive guilt.

The memory of that afternoon would remain so deeply seared on her mind that even now, years later, inside a metal rubbish bin on the outskirts of Istanbul, as her brain continued to shut down, she still remembered the smell of the wood-burning stove with an intense, penetrating sadness.

Seven Minutes

As Leila's brain fought on, she remembered the taste of soil – dry, chalky, bitter.

In an old issue of *Hayat* magazine that she secretly borrowed from Sabotage Sinan, she had seen a blonde woman clad in a black swimsuit and black stilettos, happily swirling a plastic ring. A caption underneath the picture read, 'In Denver, American model Fay Shott spins a hula hoop around her slender waist.'

The picture had intrigued both children, though for different reasons. Sabotage wanted to know why anyone would wear high-heeled shoes and a swimsuit just to stand on a patch of green grass. Whereas Leila was drawn to the ring itself.

Her mind wandered back to the spring when she was ten years old. On the way to the bazaar with Mother, she had seen a group of boys chasing an old man. When they caught up with him, the boys, shouting and laughing, had drawn a circle around him with a piece of chalk.

'He is a Yazidi,' Mother had said, upon seeing Leila's surprise. 'He can't get out of there on his own. Someone must erase that circle for him.'

'Oh, let's help him then.'

Mother's expression was not so much one of annoyance as confusion. 'What for? Yazidis are evil.'

'How do you know?'

'How do I know what?'

'That they are evil?'

Mother had pulled her by the hand. 'Because they worship Satan.'

'How do you know?'

'Everyone knows that. They are cursed.'

'Who cursed them?'

'God, Leila.'

'But did God not create them?'

'Of course He did.'

'He created them as Yazidis and then He was angry at them for being Yazidis . . . that doesn't make sense.'

'Enough! Move!'

On the way back from the bazaar Leila had insisted on passing through the same street, just to check if the old man was still there. To her immense relief, he was nowhere to be seen, the circle partly erased. Maybe the whole thing was a made-up story and he had walked out of it easily. Maybe he had had to wait for someone to come and put an end to his confinement. Years later now, when Leila saw the circle around the waist of the blonde woman, she remembered that incident. How could the same shape that separated and trapped one human being become a symbol of ultimate freedom and sheer bliss for someone else?

'Stop calling it a *circle*,' said Sabotage Sinan, when she shared her thoughts with him. 'It's a hula hoop! And I've asked my mother to get me one from Istanbul. I begged her so much she ordered two in the end: one for her, one for you. They have just arrived.'

'For me?'

'Well, it was for me – but I want mine to be yours! It's bright orange.'

'Oh, thank you, but I cannot accept it.'

Sabotage was adamant. 'Please . . . can't you consider it a present . . . from me?'

'But what will you tell your mother?'

'It'll be fine. She knows how much I care about you.' A deep blush spread from his neck to his cheeks.

Leila yielded, even though she knew her father would not be happy.

It was no small feat bringing a hula hoop home without being noticed. It would fit neither in her bag nor inside her clothes. She thought about burying it under the leaves in the garden for a few days, but that wasn't a good plan. In the end, she rolled it through the kitchen door while no one was there and quickly ran with it to the bathroom. There, in front of the mirror, she tried twirling the plastic ring just like the American model did. It was harder than she thought. She would have to practise.

From the music box of her mind she chose a song by Elvis Presley, singing his love in a language utterly foreign to her. '*Trit-me-nayz. Don-kiz-me-wans-kiz-me-twayz.*' She didn't feel like dancing at first, but how could she reject Elvis in his pink jacket and yellow trousers – colours so unusual in this town, particularly for men, that they seemed defiant, like the flag of a rebel army.

She opened the cupboard where Mother and Auntie kept their few toiletries. There, among bottles of pills and tubes of cream, nestled a treasure: a lipstick. A vivid cerise. She applied it generously over her lips and cheeks. The girl in the mirror looked at her with the eyes of a stranger, as if through a frosted window. In the reflection she caught, for a fleeting moment, a simulacrum of her future self. She tried to see if she was happy, this woman, both familiar and beyond her grasp, but the image evaporated, leaving not a trace, like dew from a morning leaf.

Leila would never have been discovered had Auntie not been vacuuming the runner in the corridor. She would have heard Baba's footsteps, heavy as they were.

Baba shouted at her, the whole of his mouth pulled tight like a drawstring pouch. His voice bounced off the floor where seconds ago Elvis had been showing his signature dance moves. With a look of disappointment by now all too habitual, Baba glowered at her.

'What do you think you are doing? Tell me where you got this ring from!'

'It's a present.'

'From whom?'

'A friend, Baba. It's no big deal.'

'Really? Look at yourself, are you my daughter? I cannot

recognize you any more. We worked so hard to give you a decent upbringing. I can't believe you behave like a . . . *whore*! Is that what you want to become in the end? A damned whore?'

The coarse, rasping sound of the word as he expelled it into the room sent a cold shiver running through her body. She had never heard the term before.

After that day, Leila never saw the hula hoop again, and though she would wonder from time to time what Baba might have done with it, she could not bring herself to ask. Had he dumped it in the rubbish? Had he given it to someone else? Or had he buried it, perhaps, in the hope of turning it into yet another ghost, of which she increasingly suspected that this house already had too many?

The circle, the shape of captivity for an old Yazidi man, but a symbol of freedom for a young American model, thus became a sad memory for a girl in an Eastern town.

September 1963. After consulting his sheikh, Baba had decided that since Leila was getting out of control, it would be better if she stayed at home until the day she got married. The decision was made, despite her protests. Even though it was the beginning of a new term, and graduation day was now not far away, Leila was being pulled out of school.

Thursday afternoon, Leila and Sabotage walked back home together for the last time. The boy followed a few steps behind her, wearing a defeated look, his mouth contorted with despair, his hands thrust in his pockets. He kept kicking the pebbles in his path, his backpack swinging over his shoulders.

When they reached Leila's house, they stopped by the gate. For a moment neither of them spoke.

'We have to say goodbye now,' said Leila. She had gained some weight over the summer; there was a new roundness to her cheeks.

Sabotage rubbed his forehead. 'I'm going to ask my mother to talk to your father.'

'No, please. Baba wouldn't like that.'

'I don't care. It's so unfair what he is doing to you.' His voice broke.

Leila turned her face away, only because she couldn't bear to see him cry. 'If you are not going to school any more, then I'm not going either,' said Sabotage.

'Don't be silly. And please don't mention any of this to your mother. Baba wouldn't be happy to see her. You know they don't get along.'

'What if *I* talk to your parents?'

Leila smiled, mindful of how much willpower it must have taken her reticent friend to make such a suggestion. 'Believe me, it won't change anything. I appreciate it though . . . I really do.' A knot tightened in her gut, and for a moment she felt physically sick, shaky, as if whatever resolve had kept her going since early morning had deserted her. As she always did when she found herself emotionally cornered, she moved with urgent haste, not wanting to prolong things any further.

'Okay, I must go now. We'll see each other around.'

He shook his head. School was the only place unmarried young people of different sexes could interact. There was nowhere else.

'We'll find a way,' she said, sensing his doubt. She kissed him lightly on the cheek. 'Come on, cheer up. Take care!'

She sprinted away from him without so much as a second glance. Sabotage, who had had a growth spurt in the last few months and found it hard to adjust to his new height, stayed still for a long minute. Then, not knowing why he was doing it, he started filling his pockets with pebbles, then stones, the bigger the better, feeling heavier with each weight added.

Meanwhile, Leila had gone straight to the garden, where she sat under the apple tree that she and Auntie had once decorated with strips of silk and satin. *The ballerinas.* In the upper branches she could still see a thin piece of fabric fluttering in the breeze. She placed her hand on the warm earth and tried not to think about anything. She grabbed a handful of soil, took it to her mouth and chewed it slowly. Acid swelled in her throat. She grabbed more soil, and this time swallowed it faster.

A few minutes later, Leila entered the house. She tossed her backpack on a chair in the kitchen, not noticing that Auntie, who was boiling milk to make yogurt, was watching her intently.

'What have you been eating?' Auntie asked.

Inclining her head, Leila licked the corners of her mouth. With the tip of her tongue she touched the grains stuck between her teeth.

'Come here. Open your mouth. Let me see.'

Leila did as she was told.

Auntie's eyes narrowed, then grew wide. 'Is this . . . soil?'

Leila said nothing.

'Are you eating soil? My God, why would you do such a thing?'

Leila didn't know what to say. It was not a question she had asked herself before. But as she considered it now, a thought occurred to her. 'You once told me about this woman in your village, remember? You said she ate sand, broken glass . . . even gravel.'

'Yes, but that poor peasant woman, she was pregnant –' Auntie said haltingly. She squinted at Leila, the way she stared at the shirts she ironed, looking for errant creases.

Leila shrugged. A new kind of indifference seized her, a numbness she had no experience of previously; she felt as if nothing mattered much, and perhaps never really had. 'Maybe me too.'

The truth was she had no idea how pregnancy made itself known initially. That was one of the things about not having any girlfriends or older sisters. She had no one to ask. She had thought about consulting the Lady Pharmacist, and tried a couple of times to bring up the subject, but when a suitable moment came, she had not been able to muster the courage.

All the colour drained from Auntie's face. She chose to make light of things nonetheless. 'Honey, I can assure you, for that to happen, you need to get to know a man's body. One doesn't become pregnant by touching a tree.'

Leila gave a perfunctory nod. She poured herself a glass of water and rinsed her mouth out before drinking. She set the glass aside and then said in a low, emotionless voice, 'But I do . . . I know everything about a man's body.'

Auntie's eyebrows shot up. 'What are you talking about?'

'I mean, does Uncle count as a man?' Leila said, still talking to the glass.

Auntie stopped moving. Inside the copper pan, the milk rose slowly. Leila walked towards the stove and turned the flame off.

The next day Baba wanted to have a word with her. They sat in the kitchen, around the table where he had taught her prayers in Arabic and told her about the black and blue angels who would come to visit her in the grave.

'Your aunt tells me something very disturbing . . .' Baba paused.

Leila kept quiet, hiding her trembling hands under the table.

'You have been eating soil. Never do that again. You'll get worms, do you hear me?' Baba's jaw angled to one side, his teeth jammed together, as if he were crunching something invisible. 'And you shouldn't make things up.'

'I'm not making things up.'

In the ashen light from the window, Baba looked older and somehow smaller than usual. He contemplated her grimly. 'Sometimes our minds play tricks on us.'

'If you don't believe me, take me to a doctor.'

A look of despair crossed his face, replaced quickly by a new hardness. 'Doctor? So the whole town hears about it? Never. Do you understand? You are not to talk about this to strangers. Leave it to me.'

Then he added, too quickly, as if verbalizing an answer he had memorized earlier, 'This is a family problem and we'll find a solution together as a family.'

Two days later they were around the kitchen table again, Mother and Auntie joining them this time, crumpled tissues in their hands, eyes red and swollen from crying. In the morning, both women had quizzed Leila about her time of the month. Leila, who hadn't bled for the past two months, told them wearily, brokenly, that she had started bleeding the morning before, but there was something wrong with it this time: it was too heavy, too painful; every time she moved, a sharp needle jabbed deeper into her insides, leaving her breathless.

While Mother had seemed secretly relieved to hear this and quickly changed the subject, Auntie had stared at her with sorrowful eyes, recognizing in Leila's miscarriage one of her own. 'It will pass,' she had said in a soft murmur. 'It will be over soon.' It was the first time in years anyone had told Leila anything about the mysteries of the female body.

Then, in as few words as possible, Mother had told her that she no longer had any reason to fear pregnancy, and it was better this way, *a blessing in disguise*; they should all leave it behind and never talk about it again, except in their prayers, when they should thank God for His merciful intervention at the last possible minute.

'I spoke with my brother,' Baba said the next afternoon. 'He understands you're young . . . confused.'

'I'm not confused.' Leila studied the tablecloth, tracing its intricate embroidery with her finger.

'He told me about this boy you were seeing at school. We've been kept in the dark, apparently everyone has been talking about it. The pharmacist's son, my goodness! I never liked that sneaky, cold woman. I should've known. Like mother, like son.'

Leila felt her cheeks go red. 'You mean Sabotage . . . Sinan? Leave him out of this. He's my friend. My only friend. He's a kind boy. Uncle is lying!'

'Stop it. You need to learn to respect your elders.'

'Why don't you ever believe me – your own daughter?' She felt drained of energy.

Baba cleared his throat. 'Listen, let's all calm down now. We must deal with the situation wisely. We've had a family meeting. Your cousin Tolga is a good boy. He has agreed to marry you. You'll get engaged –'

'What?'

Tolga: the child who had been in the same room in that holiday house, sleeping in a cot while his father drew circles on her belly at nights. That boy had now been chosen by the family elders as her future husband.

Mother said, 'He is younger than you, we know, but that's fine. We'll announce the engagement, so that everyone knows you are committed to each other.'

'Yes, that will shut any nasty mouths,' Baba carried on. 'Then you'll have a religious wedding. In a few years you can have an official marriage too, if you wish. In the eyes of Allah, a religious marriage is enough.'

Leila said, in a voice far steadier than she felt, 'How do you manage to see with the eyes of Allah? I've always wondered.'

Baba placed a hand on her shoulder. 'I know you are worried. But you don't have to be any more.'

'And what if I refuse to marry Tolga?'

'You will do no such thing,' said Baba, his expression tighter.

Leila turned towards Auntie, her eyes wide. 'How about you? Do *you* believe me? Because I did believe you, remember?'

For a second Leila thought she was going to nod her head – the slightest of gestures would do – but Auntie did not. Instead she said, 'We all love you, Leyla-jim. We want our lives to go back to normal. Your father will fix this thing.'

'Fix this *thing*?'

'Don't be rude to your aunt,' said Baba.

'Which aunt? I thought she was my mother. Is she or is she not?'

No one answered.

'This house is full of lies and deceptions. Our lives have never been normal. We are not a normal family . . . Why are you always pretending?'

'Enough, Leyla!' Mother said, her frown deepening. 'We are all trying to help you here.'

Leila spoke slowly. 'I don't think so. I think you are trying to save Uncle.'

Her heart pushed against her chest. All these years, she had dreaded what would happen if she told her father what had been going on behind closed doors. She had been certain that he would never believe her, given how fond he was of his brother. But now she understood, with a sinking feeling, that Baba did believe her, in fact. That was why he had not marched to the Lady Pharmacist's house, trembling with outrage and indignation, and demanded her son marry his soiled daughter. That was why he was trying to keep things quiet, within the family. Baba knew who was telling the truth and who was lying.

November 1963. Towards the end of the month, Tarkan got very sick. His flu had deteriorated into pneumonia, but the doctor said it was primarily his heart that was failing him. The wedding plans were put on hold. Auntie was beside herself with worry. So was Leila, although the numbness that had taken hold of her had only deepened these days, and she found it increasingly hard to show her emotions.

Uncle's wife visited often, offering help, bringing home-made stews and trays of baklava as though to a house of mourning. At times Leila caught the woman staring at her with something akin to pity. Uncle himself did not show up. Leila would never know whether this was his decision or Baba's.

The day Tarkan died, they threw open all the windows in the house so that his soul could swap places with light, and his breath could turn into air, and whatever remained of him could fly away in peace. *Like a trapped butterfly*, thought Leila. That's what his brother had been in their midst. She feared they had all let this beautiful child down, one by one, including herself, mostly herself.

The same afternoon, in plain daylight, Leila left home. She had been planning this for a while, and when the moment came, she did everything hotfoot, thoughts running pell-mell through her mind, worried that if she hesitated, even for a second, she might lose heart. So she walked out – without a thought, without a blink. Not through the kitchen door. Everyone was there, family and neighbours, men and women, the only time that the sexes could freely mingle being either at weddings or funerals. The guests' voices dwindled as the imam started to recite the Surah al-Fatiha: '*Guide us to the straight path. The path of those upon whom You have bestowed favour, not of those who have evoked Your anger or of those who have been led astray.*'

Leila went instead to the front of the house and opened the main door, strong and solid with die-cast bolts and iron chains, though strangely light to the touch. In her bag she carried four hard-boiled eggs and about a dozen winter apples. She headed straight to the Lady Pharmacist's shop but did not dare go in. She wandered around outside, ambling through the old cemetery behind the shop, reading the names of the dead on the tombstones and wondering what kind of lives they might have led, as she waited for her friend to return from school.

The money that she needed for her bus fare Sabotage Sinan stole from his mother.

'Are you sure about this?' the boy kept asking as they walked together to the station. 'Istanbul is massive. You don't even know anybody there. Stay in Van.'

'Why? There is nothing here for me any more.'

A flicker of pain crossed his face, which Leila noticed, albeit too late. She touched his arm. 'I didn't mean you. I'm going to miss you so much.'

'I'll miss you too,' he said, a fuzz of hair shadowing his upper lip. Gone was the roly-poly boy; he had grown thinner lately, his round face had narrowed somewhat, his cheekbones had become more pronounced. For a second he seemed to be about to say something else, but he lost courage when he allowed his gaze to shift away from her face.

'Look, I'll write to you every week,' Leila promised. 'We'll see each other again.'

'Won't you be safer here?'

Although Leila did not say this aloud, somewhere in her soul echoed the words she had a feeling she had heard before: *Just because you think it's safe here, it doesn't mean this is the right place for you.*

The bus smelled of diesel exhaust, lemon cologne and fatigue. The passenger sitting in front of her was reading a newspaper. Leila's eyes widened when she saw the news on the front page: the President of America, a man with a sunny smile, had been assassinated. There were pictures of him and his pretty wife in her suit and pillbox hat as they rode in a motorcade, waving to the crowds, just minutes before the first shot. She wanted to read more but the lights were soon turned off. Out of her bag she took a hard-boiled egg, peeled it and ate it quietly. Then time slowed down and her eyelids closed.

So unsuspecting and uninformed was she back then, she thought she could handle Istanbul, beat the megalopolis at its own game. Yet she was no David; and Istanbul, no Goliath. There was no one praying for her to succeed, no one she could turn to if she didn't. Things had a way of disappearing easily around here – she learned this as soon as she arrived. While she was washing her face and hands in a toilet at the bus station, someone stole her bag. In a second she lost half her money, the remaining apples and her bracelet – the one her little brother had held up in the air on the day of his teeth-cutting ceremony.

As she sat on an empty crate outside the toilet, collecting her thoughts, an attendant carrying a bucket of car-wash soap and a sponge approached her. He seemed polite and considerate, and upon discovering her predicament he offered help. Leila could stay at his aunt's place for a few months. His aunt had recently retired from her job as a cashier in a shop, and she was old and lonely, in need of company.

'I'm sure she's a nice person, but I must find a place of my own,' said Leila.

'Sure, I get it,' said the young man, smiling. He gave her the name of a hostel nearby that was clean and safe, and wished her good luck.

As darkness descended, the sky drawing in around her, she finally made it to the hostel: a dilapidated building on a side street that didn't seem to have been painted or cleaned in years, if ever. She didn't realize that, as she had found her way to the address, he had been following her.

Once inside, she walked over to the corner of the room, past a couple of stained and chipped chairs, and a bulletin board plastered with scruffy, out-of-date notices, where a gaunt, taciturn man was seated at a wobbly trestle table that functioned as a reception desk, behind him several room keys hanging from numbered hooks on a mildewed wall.

Now upstairs in the room, feeling on edge, she pushed the chest of drawers behind the door. The sheets, yellowed like old newspaper, smelled musty. She spread her jacket over the bed and lay down in her clothes. Exhausted, she fell asleep faster than she thought. Late at night she woke up to a sound. Someone was outside in the corridor, turning the door handle, trying to get in.

'Who's there?' Leila yelled.

Footsteps in the corridor. Measured, unhurried. After that she slept not a wink, alert to every sound. In the morning she returned to the bus station, the only place she knew in the city. The young man was there, carrying water to the drivers with a long-limbed grace.

This time she accepted his offer.

The aunt – a middle-aged woman with a shrill voice and skin

so pale that one could see the veins beneath – gave her food and nice clothes, too nice, insisting she must 'enhance her assets' if she was planning to go to job interviews, starting next week.

Those first days passed in a glow of ease. Open and searching as it was, her heart was vulnerable, and, though she refused to admit it to herself, then or later, she fell under the spell of this young man and his studied charm. She was gripped by something akin to relief that she was able finally to talk to someone – otherwise she would have never told him about what had transpired in Van.

'You can't go back to your family, that's clear,' he said. 'Look, I have known girls like you – most were from shitty towns. Some did all right here, got places, but many didn't. Stick with me if you are clever enough, or Istanbul will crush you.'

Something in his tone made her wince, a controlled anger that she now understood was lodged inside his soul, hard and heavy as a millstone. She quietly resolved to herself to leave this place at once.

He sensed her discomfort. He was good at that, picking up on people's anxieties.

'We'll talk later,' he said. 'You mustn't worry too much.'

It was this same man and the woman – who was, in truth, not his aunt but his business partner – who sold Leila to a stranger the same night, and within a week to several others. Alcohol, there was always alcohol, in her blood, in her drinks, on her breath. They made her drink a lot so that she could remember little. What she failed to see earlier she saw now: the doors were padlocked, the windows sealed, and Istanbul was not a city of opportunities, but a city of scars. The descent, when it started, spiralled rapidly, like water sucked through a plug. The men who visited the house were from different age groups, held various low-skilled, low-paid jobs, and almost all had families of their own. They were fathers, husbands, brothers . . . Some had daughters her age.

The first time she managed to call home, she couldn't stop her hands from trembling. By now she had become so deeply engulfed in this new world that they let her walk on her own in the vicinity, confident that she had nowhere to go any more. The night before it had rained, and she saw snails out on the pavement, absorbing the same moist air that made her feel like she was suffocating. Standing in front of the post office, she fumbled for a cigarette, the lighter shaking in her grasp.

When she finally decided to go inside, she told the operator she wished to make a reverse-charge call, and hoped that her family would agree to pay. They did. Then she waited for Mother or Auntie to pick up the receiver, unsure which woman she would rather talk to first, trying to fathom what each might be doing at this moment. They answered – together. They cried when they heard her voice. And she did too. Somewhere in the background rose the ticking of the clock in the hall, an unwavering rhythm of stability, sharply at odds with the uncertainty surrounding them. Then, silence – deep, dank, dripping. A gooey liquid into which they sank lower and lower. It was clear that both Mother and Auntie wanted her to feel guilty, and Leila did – more than they could ever imagine. But she also understood that after she had left, Mother's heart had closed like a fist and, with Tarkan dead, Auntie was unwell again. When she hung up the phone, heavy with a sense of defeat, she knew she could never go back and this slow death that she found herself in was now her life.

Still, she continued to call them at every opportunity.

Once Baba, home early, answered the phone. Upon hearing her voice, he let out a gasp and fell quiet. Leila, acutely aware that this was the first time she had ever seen him vulnerable, fumbled for the right words.

'Baba,' she said, her voice betraying the strain she was under.

'Don't me call that.'

'Baba . . .' she repeated.

'You've brought us shame,' he said, his breathing laborious. 'Everyone is talking behind our backs. I can't go to the teahouse any more. I can't walk into the post office. Even at the mosque they won't talk to me. No one greets me on the street. It's as if I'm a ghost; they can't see me. I had always thought, "Maybe I don't have riches, maybe I couldn't find treasures, and I don't even have sons, but at least I have my honour." Not any more. I am a broken man. My sheikh says Allah will curse you and I will live to see the day. That will be my compensation.'

There were drops of condensation on the window. She touched one gently with her fingertip, held it for a second, and then let go, watching it roll down. A pain throbbed somewhere inside her body, in a place she was unable to locate.

'Don't phone us again,' he said. 'If you do, we'll tell the operator we are not accepting the call. We don't have a daughter called Leyla. Leyla Afife Kamile: you don't deserve those names.'

The first time Leila was arrested and tucked into a transport van with several other women she kept her palms pressed together, her eyes fixed on the chink of sky visible through the window bars. Worse than the treatment they were given at the police station was the follow-up examination at the Istanbul Venereal Diseases Hospital – a place she would visit regularly over the years. She was handed a new ID card – one on which the dates of her health check-ups were written in neat columns. If she missed a check-up, she was told, she would be detained on the spot. Then she would have to spend the rest of the night in jail, or go back to the hospital again to be tested for STDs.

To and fro, from the police station to the hospital and back again.

'Hooker's ping-pong', the prostitutes called it.

It was on one of those hospital visits that Leila met the woman who would become her first friend in Istanbul. A young, slim African named Jameelah. Her eyes were round and exceptionally bright, their lids almost translucent; her hair was woven in tight cornrows against her scalp; her wrists were painfully thin, scarred with red marks, which she tried to cover with multiple brace-lets and bangles. She was a foreigner and, like all foreigners, she carried with her the shadow of an elsewhere. They had seen each other several times before but never exchanged so much as a greet-ing. By now Leila had learned that the women rounded up in various corners of the city, whether natives or non-natives, belonged to invisible tribes. Members of different tribes were not supposed to interact.

On each shared visit, they would perch on the benches along a narrow corridor that smelled so strongly of antiseptic they could taste it on their tongues. The Turkish prostitutes were seated on one side and the foreigners on the other. Since the women were called into the examination room one by one, the waits were unbearably long. In the winter, they would keep their hands under their armpits and their voices low, saving their energy for the rest of the day. This section of the hospital, which other patients and most of the staff steered clear of, was never heated properly. In the summer, the women would stretch out languidly, picking scabs, slapping mosquitoes, carping about the heat. They would take off their shoes, massaging their tired feet, and a faint smell would per-meate the air, curdling around them. Occasionally, one of the Turkish prostitutes would make an acerbic remark about the doctors or the nurses, or those on the opposite bench, the foreigners, the invaders, and there would be laughter, not of a happy kind. In such a narrow space, enmity could surge and circulate with the speed of an electric charge, and die down equally fast. The locals particularly disliked Africans, whom they accused of stealing their jobs.

That evening, as Leila looked over at the young black woman sitting across from her, she did not see her foreignness. Instead she saw her braided bracelet and remembered the one she had lost; she saw the talisman she had sewn inside her cardigan, and remem-bered all the talismans that had failed to protect her; she saw the way she hugged her rucksack against her chest, as if expecting to be kicked out of this place, if not of this country, at any second, and recognized in her manner a familiar loneliness, a forlornness.

She had the odd feeling that she might as well be staring at her own reflection.

'That's a pretty bracelet you have.' Leila pointed at it with her chin.

Slowly, almost imperceptibly, the other woman lifted her head and surveyed Leila with a direct gaze. Although she said nothing in return, there was a stillness about her expression that made Leila want to keep talking to her.

'I had a bracelet just like that,' Leila said, leaning forward. 'I lost it when I came to Istanbul.'

In the ensuing silence, one of the local prostitutes made a lewd comment, and the others giggled. Leila, now beginning to regret having spoken in the first place, lowered her eyes and retreated into her thoughts.

'I make myself. . .' said the woman, just when everyone thought she would never speak. Her voice was a long, drawn-out whisper, slightly raspy, her Turkish broken. 'Different for everyone.'

'You choose different colours for each person?' asked Leila, now engaged. 'That's lovely, how do you decide?'

'I look.'

After that day, every time they met they exchanged just a few more words, shared just a little more, gestures filling the silences where words were unavailable. Then, one afternoon, months after that initial exchange, Jameelah reached out from the opposite bench, crossing an invisible wall, and dropped something light inside Leila's palm.

It was a braided bracelet in periwinkle and heather and dark cherry – shades of purple.

'For me?' Leila asked softly.

A nod. 'Yes, your colours.'

Jameelah, the woman who looked into people's souls and, only when she saw what she needed to see, decided whether to open up her heart to them.

Jameelah, one of the five.

Jameelah's Story

Jameelah was born in Somalia to a Muslim father and a Christian mother. Her early years had been blissfully free, though she would only realize this long after they were gone. Her mother had once told her that childhood was a big, blue wave that lifted you up, carried you forth and, just when you thought it would last forever, vanished from sight. You could neither run after it nor bring it back. But the wave, before it disappeared, left a gift behind – a conch shell on the shore. Inside the seashell were stored all the sounds of childhood. Even today, if Jameelah closed her eyes and listened intently, she could hear them: her younger siblings' peals of laughter, her father's doting words as he broke his fast with a few dates, her mother's singing while she prepared the food, the crackle of the evening fire, the rustling of the acacia tree outside . . .

Mogadishu, the White Pearl of the Indian Ocean. Under the clear sky, she would shield her eyes to look at the slum dwellings in the distance, their presence as precarious as the mud and driftwood they were built with. Poverty was not something she had to worry about back then. Days were uneventful, and dreaming was easy and as sweet as the honey she drizzled on her flatbread. But then the mother she adored died of cancer after a long, painful decline that did not dim her smile until the very end. Her father, now a shadow of the man he had been, finding himself alone with five children, was unprepared for the burden he had to shoulder. His face darkened and, gradually, so did his heart. The family elders urged him to marry again – this time someone from his own religion.

Jameelah's stepmother, a widow herself, was jealous of a ghost, determined to erase all traces of the woman she felt she was there to replace. Soon Jameelah – the eldest daughter – was clashing with her stepmother on nearly everything, from what she wore to what she ate and how she spoke. To restore some calm to her disconcerted spirit, she began to spend more time on the streets.

One afternoon, her feet took her to her mother's old church, the one she had stopped attending but had never completely forgotten. Without giving it much thought, she pushed open the tall wooden door and stepped in, inhaling the smell of candle wax and polished wood. By the altar was an aged priest, who spoke to her about the girl her mother had been, long before she became a wife and a mother, stories from another life.

Jameelah had no intention of visiting the church again, but, a week later, she did. By the age of seventeen she had joined the congregation at the cost of infuriating her father and breaking her siblings' hearts. As far as she was concerned, she hadn't made a choice between two Abrahamic religions; she was simply holding on to an invisible thread that connected her to her mother. No one else saw it that way. No one forgave her.

The priest said she should not be too sad since now she had found an even bigger family, a family of believers, but, hard as she tried, the peaceful fulfilment she was told would come, sooner or later, escaped her. Once again she found herself alone, without family or church.

She needed to find a job. There were none – except a few she wasn't qualified for. The slum she used to observe from a distance soon became her address. Meanwhile, the country was changing. All her friends, echoing the words of Mohamed Siad Barre – Mighty Mouth – went on about liberating Somalis living under the yoke of others. A Greater Somalia. They said they were ready to fight for it – and to die for it. It seemed to Jameelah that everyone, including herself, was trying to avoid the present moment; she, by longing to go back to her childhood; her friends, by aspiring to a future as uncertain as the shifting sands of a maritime desert.

Then things started to get ugly, and the streets were not safe any more. The smell of burning tyres, gunpowder. Opponents of the regime were arrested with Soviet-made weapons. Prisons – relics of the former British and Italian rule – were filling up fast. Schools, government buildings and military barracks were turned into temporary jails. Still there was not enough room to lock up all those arrested. Even parts of the presidential palace would have to be used as a jail.

Around this time, an acquaintance told her about some fering-hees who were looking for healthy, hard-working African women to take to Istanbul. For menial jobs – housekeeping, babysitting, cooking and the like. The acquaintance explained that Turkish families liked to have Somalian help at home. Jameelah saw an opportunity. Her life, like a door, had closed, and she was eager for another to open elsewhere. *He who has not travelled in the world has no eyes*, she thought.

Along with more than forty people, mostly women, she made the journey to Istanbul. Upon arrival they were lined up and separated into groups. Jameelah noticed that younger girls like herself were kept to one side. The rest were soon taken away. She would not see any of them again. By the time she understood it was a sham – a pretext to bring people in as cheap labour and for sexual exploitation – it was too late for her to escape.

The Africans in Istanbul came from all sides of the old continent – Tanganyika, Sudan, Uganda, Nigeria, Kenya, Upper Volta, Ethiopia – escaping civil war, religious violence, political insurgency. The number of asylum seekers had increased daily over the years. Among them were students, professionals, artists, journalists, scholars . . . But the only Africans mentioned in the newspapers were those who, like her, had been trafficked.

A house in Tarlabasi. Threadbare sofas, frayed bedsheets turned into curtains, the air filled with the smell of burnt potatoes and fried onions, and of something tart, like unripe walnuts. At night, several of the women would be summoned – they never knew which of them it would be. Every couple of weeks the police would pound on their door, round them up and take them to the Venereal Diseases Hospital for a check-up.

Those women who resisted their captors were locked up in a cellar underneath the house, so dark and small they could only fit if they crouched down. Worse than the hunger, and the pain in their legs, was the conflicted anxiety of worrying about their jailers, that something might happen to these men, the only people who knew their whereabouts – and the consequent fear that they might find themselves abandoned there forever.

'It's like breaking horses,' said one of the women. 'That's what they are doing to us. Once our spirits are broken, they know we won't go anywhere.'

But Jameelah had never stopped planning her escape. This was what she was deliberating the day she met Leila at the hospital. She was thinking, maybe she was only a half-broken horse, too frightened to bolt, too lame to dare, but still able to remember the sweet taste of, and therefore to yearn for, freedom.

Eight Minutes

Eight minutes had gone by, and the next memory that Leila pulled from her archive was the smell of sulphuric acid.

March 1966. On the street of brothels, upstairs in her room, Leila was reclining on her bed, flipping through a glossy magazine that had on its cover a picture of Sophia Loren. She wasn't really reading, distracted as she was by her own thoughts – until she heard Bitter Ma call her name.

Leila dropped the magazine. Slowly, she rose to her feet and stretched her limbs. She crossed the corridor as if in a daze, descending the stairs, her cheeks slightly flushed. A middle-aged client was standing next to Bitter Ma, his back half turned to her, inspecting the painting of yellow daffodils and citrus fruits. She recognized the cigar he was holding before she recognized his face. It was the man all the prostitutes tried to avoid. Cruel, mean and foul-mouthed, he had been so violent a couple of times that he had been banished from the premises. But today Bitter Ma seemed to have pardoned him – again. Leila's face closed.

He was wearing a khaki vest with several pockets. It was this detail that caught Leila's attention before anything else. Only a photojournalist would need such a thing, she thought – or someone with a lot to hide. Something in his manner made Leila think of a jellyfish; not out in the open sea, but in a bell jar, its translucent tentacles hanging in the confined space. It was as if there were nothing holding him up straight; his entire body was a flaccid mass, composed of a different kind of solidity, one that could, at any moment, liquefy.

Placing her palms on the desk and leaning forward with her enormous bulk, Bitter Ma gave the man a wink. 'Here she is, my pasha: Tequila Leila! She's one of my finest.'

'Is that her name? Why do you call her that?' He eyed Leila from head to toe.

'Because she's impatient, that one. She wants life to run fast. But she's resilient too; she can guzzle the sour and the bitter, like downing tequila shots. I gave her that name.'

The man laughed unhappily. 'Then she is perfect for me.'

Upstairs in the room where just a few minutes before she had been looking at Sophia Loren's perfect figure and white lace dress, Leila took off her clothes. The floral skirt, the bikini top – a pink frilly thing that she hated. She peeled off her stockings but kept her velvet slippers on, as though to feel more secure.

'Do you think the bitch is watching us?' the man said under his breath.

Leila glanced at him in surprise. 'What?'

'The madam downstairs. She could be spying on us.'

'Of course not.'

'Look, right there!' He pointed at a crack in the wall. 'See her eyeball? See how it moves? The devil!'

'There's nothing there.'

He squinted at her, his gaze clouded with an unmistakable hatred and spite. 'You work for her, why should I trust you? The devil's servant.'

Leila suddenly felt scared. She took a step back, a sick feeling growing in her stomach at the realization that she was alone in a room with a man who was mentally unstable.

'Spies are watching us.'

'Trust me, there is no one else here,' Leila said soothingly.

'Shut up! Stupid bitch, you don't know a thing,' he bawled, and then dropped his voice. 'They are recording our conversation. They have placed cameras everywhere.'

He was patting his pockets now, his words an incomprehensible murmur. He produced a little bottle. When he pulled out the cork, it made a sound like a suppressed groan.

Leila panicked. In her confusion, she moved towards him, trying to understand what the bottle contained, then changed her mind and backed away, heading towards the door. Were it not for those dainty slippers that she adored so much, she could have escaped faster. She tripped, lost her balance, and the liquid he had tossed at her only a second ago hit her in the back.

Sulphuric acid. He was planning to pour the rest on her face, but she managed to dash into the corridor, despite the acid burning into her flesh. The pain was unlike anything else. Out of breath and shaking, she leaned against the wall like an old, discarded broom. Her head spinning, she nevertheless dragged herself towards the stairs, and gripped the banister tight to keep herself from collapsing. When she was able to make a sound – a raw, feral sound – her voice broke, raining down on all the rooms inside the brothel.

A hole remained in the floorboard where the acid had spilled. After she was released from hospital, the scar on her back still tender and discoloured – the wound never fully healing – Leila often sat next to that spot. She would run a finger around it, feeling its amorphous shape, its rough edge, as though they shared a secret, she and the floorboard. If she looked at that dark hole long and hard enough, it would start to swirl, like eddies on the surface of cardamom coffee. Just as she had seen the deer on the carpet move when she was a child, now she watched an acid hole swirl.

'It could have been your face, you know. Count your lucky stars,' Bitter Ma said.

The clients echoed the sentiment. They told her how fortunate she was that the disfigurement had not prevented her from working. If anything she was more popular than before, in greater demand. She was a prostitute with a story, and men seemed to like that.

After the attack, the number of police officers on the street of brothels increased – for about two weeks. Throughout the spring of 1966, violence was escalating in every corner of the city, political factions clashed, blood was washed with blood, students were gunned down on university campuses, the posters on the streets had turned angrier, their tone more urgent, and soon the extra officers were deployed elsewhere.

For a long while after the attack, Leila avoided, as much as she could, the other women, most of whom were older than her and irritated her with their spiky words and sardonic humour. She fought back when she needed to; otherwise, she mostly kept to herself. Depression was common among the women on this street, tearing into their souls as fire tears into wood. No one used the word though. *Miserable*, was what they said. Not about themselves, but about everyone and everything else. *The food is miserable. The payment is miserable. My feet hurt, these shoes are miserable.*

There was only one woman that Leila liked to spend time with. An Arab woman of indeterminate age, she was so short that she had to buy her clothes from children's departments. Her name was Zaynab122, which, depending on her mood, she spelled as Zainab, Zeinab, Zayneb, Zeynep . . . She claimed she could write her name in 122 different ways. That number was also a reference to her height, which was exactly 122 centimetres. Dwarf, Pygmy or Thumbling – she had been called such names and worse. So fed up was she with people staring at her, and secretly or openly wondering how tall she was, that, in an act of defiance, she had added the measurement to her name. Her arms were out of proportion to her torso, her fingers were fat and stubby, and her neck was almost non-existent. A broad forehead, a cleft palate and wide-set, intelligent slate-grey eyes were the most prominent features in her face. Her Turkish was fluent, though spoken with a guttural accent that betrayed her roots.

Mopping the floors, scrubbing the toilets, vacuuming the rooms, Zaynab122 worked hard even as she assisted the prostitutes with their every need. None of this was easy, for she suffered not only from shortened limbs, but also from curvature of the spine, which made it hard for her to stand on her feet for long hours.

Zaynab122 was a fortune-teller in her spare time – but only for people she favoured. Twice a day without fail, she brewed coffee for Leila. After she had finished her drink, Zaynab122 would peer into the dark residue at the bottom of the cup. She preferred to talk about neither the past nor the future, only the present. Her predictions she kept to under a week or a few months at most. But one particular afternoon, Zaynab122 broke her own rule.

'Today your cup is full of surprises. I've never seen anything like it.'

They were sitting on the bed, side by side. Outside, somewhere down the road, a playful melody rose, reminding Leila of the ice-cream trucks she had heard as a child.

'Look! An eagle perched high on a mountaintop,' said Zaynab122, revolving the cup. 'There's a halo around its head. A good omen. But there's a raven down there.'

'And that's a bad omen?'

'Not necessarily. It's a sign of conflict.' Zaynab122 turned the cup one more time. 'Oh, my God, you need to see this!'

Curiously, Leila leaned forward and squinted into the cup. All she found in there was a jumble of brown stains.

'You'll meet someone. Tall, slender, handsome . . .' Zaynab122 spoke faster now, her words like sparks from a fire. 'Path of flowers, that means a great romance. He's holding a ring. Oh dear . . . you're going to get married.'

Leila straightened her back, studied her palm. Her eyes narrowed as though she were peering at a scorching sun in the distance or a future just as impossible to reach. When she spoke again, her voice was flat. 'You're making fun of me.'

'I swear I am not.'

Leila hesitated. Had it been anyone else saying such things she would have walked out of the room right away. But this was a woman who never said anything mean about others, although she was ridiculed by them all the time.

Zaynab122 tilted her head to the side like she did when she was searching for the right words in Turkish. 'Sorry if I sounded too excited, I couldn't help it. I mean . . . it's been years since I've come across a reading this hopeful. What I say is what I see.'

Leila shrugged. 'It's just coffee. Stupid coffee.'

Zaynab122 took off her glasses, wiped them with her handkerchief and put them on again. 'You don't believe me, that's fine.'

Leila grew still, her eyes focused somewhere outside the room. 'It's a serious thing to believe in someone,' she said. And for a moment she was a girl in Van again, standing in the kitchen, watching the woman who had given birth to her chop lettuce and earthworms. 'You can't just say it like that. It's a big commitment, to believe.'

Zaynab122 stared at her – a long, curious look. 'Well, on that we agree. So why not take my words seriously? One day, you'll leave this place in a wedding gown. Let this dream give you strength.'

'I don't need dreams.'

'That's the silliest thing I've ever heard from your lips,' said Zaynab122. 'We all need dreams, *habibi*. One day you are going to surprise everyone. They'll say, "Look at Leila, she moved mountains! First she walks out of one brothel to another; she has enough courage to leave an awful madam. Then she quits the street altogether. What a woman!" They will talk about you even long after you've gone. You'll give them hope.'

Leila drew in a breath to protest but said nothing.

'And when that day comes, I want you to take me with you. Let's go together. Besides, you'll need someone to hold your veil. It'll be a long one.'

In spite of herself, Leila could not resist the trace of a smile that played at the corners of her mouth. 'When I was in school . . . back in Van . . . I saw a picture of a princess bride. My God, she was beautiful. Her gown was the prettiest thing and her veil was two hundred and fifty feet long, imagine!'

Zaynab122 walked towards the sink. She rose on tiptoes and let the water run. This she had learned from her master. If the coffee grounds revealed exceptionally good news, they had to be washed off right away. Otherwise, Destiny could step in and mess things up, as was its wont. Gently, she dried the cup and put it on the windowsill.

Leila carried on: 'She looked like an angel, standing there in front of her palace. Sabotage cut out the picture and gave it to me to keep.'

'Who is Sabotage?' asked Zaynab122.

'Oh.' Leila's face darkened. 'A friend. He was a dear friend.'

'Well, about that bride . . .' Zaynab122 said. 'Her veil was two hundred and fifty feet, did you say? That's nothing, *habibi*. Because I'm telling you, Princess you might not be, but if what I've seen in your cup is true, your gown will be even prettier.'

Zaynab122, the diviner, the optimist, the believer; for whom the word 'faith' was synonymous with the word 'love' and for whom God, therefore, could only be Beloved.

Zaynab122, one of the five.

Zaynab's Story

Zaynab was born a thousand miles away from Istanbul, in an isolated mountain village in northern Lebanon. For generations the Sunni families in the area had only intermarried, and dwarfism was so common in the village that they often attracted curious visitors from the outside world – journalists, scientists and the like. Zaynab's brothers and sisters were average-sized and when the time came they would marry, one after another. Among her siblings she alone had inherited her parents' condition, both of them little people.

Zaynab's life changed the day a photographer from Istanbul knocked on their door, asking permission to take her picture. The young man was travelling through the region, documenting unknown lives in the Middle East. He was desperately looking for someone like her. 'Nothing beats female dwarfs,' he said with a coy smile. 'But Arab female dwarfs are a double mystery for Westerners. And I want this exhibition to be shown across Europe.'

Zaynab did not expect her father to agree to this, but he did – on the condition that the family's name and whereabouts were not mentioned. Day after day, she posed for the photographer. He was a talented artist, despite having no understanding of the human heart. He failed to notice the blush that spread on his model's cheeks every time he entered the room. After shooting over a hundred photos, he left satisfied, claiming that her face would be the centrepiece of his exhibition.

That same year Zaynab, due to her deteriorating health, travelled to Beirut with an older sister, and stayed in the capital for a while. It was here, in the shadow of Mount Sannine, in between successive hospital visits, that a master fortune-teller, taking a liking to her, taught her the ancient art of tasseography – divination based on reading tea leaves, wine dregs, coffee grounds. Zaynab sensed that for the first time in her life her unusual physique could work to her advantage. People seemed fascinated by the idea of having a dwarf predict their futures – as if by virtue of her size she had a special acquaintance with the uncanny. On the streets she might be taunted and pitied, but in the privacy of her reading room she was admired and revered. This she liked. She got better at her craft.

Thanks to her new métier, Zaynab was able to earn money. Not much, but enough to give her hope. Yet hope is a hazardous chemical capable of triggering a chain reaction in the human soul. Tired of people's intrusive gaze and with no prospects of getting married or finding a job, she had long carried her body like a curse. As soon as she saved enough money, she allowed herself to fantasize about leaving everything behind. She would go to a place where she could create herself anew. Hadn't every story she'd been told since she was a child carried the same message? You could traverse deserts, climb mountains, sail oceans and beat giants, so long as you had a crumb of hope in your pocket. The heroes in those tales were, without exception, male, and none was her size, but that didn't matter. If they had dared, so could she.

For weeks after her return home, she talked to her ageing parents, hoping to convince them to allow her to go away, find her own path. Being the dutiful daughter that she had been all her life, there was no way she could travel abroad, or anywhere, without their blessing, and if they'd refused, she would have stayed. Her brothers and sisters were fiercely against this dream of hers, which they saw as pure madness. But Zaynab was adamant. How could they possibly know how she felt deep within when Allah had created them so differently? What did they know about being a little person, clinging with your fingers to the edge of society?

In the end, once again, it was her father who understood her better than anyone.

'Your mother and I are getting old. I have been asking myself, what will you do on your own when we are gone? Of course, your sisters will take good care of you. But I know how proud you are. I always wanted you to marry someone your size; it didn't happen.'

She kissed his hand. If only she could explain to him that marriage was not her destiny; that many a night when she put her head on the pillow she saw the Travelling Angels, the *Dardail*, and could never be sure afterwards whether it was a dream or a vision; that perhaps her home was not where she was born but where she chose to die; that with what remained of her health, her years on earth, she wished to do what no one in the family had done to this day and become one of *the journeyers*.

Her father breathed deeply and angled his head, as though he had heard everything. He said, 'If you must leave, then you shall, *ya ruhi*. Make friends, good ones. Loyal ones. No one can survive alone – except the Almighty God. And remember, in the desert of life, the fool travels alone and the wise by caravan.'

April 1964. The day after a new constitution was promulgated, describing Syria as a 'Democratic Socialist Republic', Zaynab arrived in the town of Kessab. Helped through by an Armenian family, she crossed the border into Turkey. She was determined to go to Istanbul, though she was not sure why, save for a distant moment in time, a secret desire, the face of the photographer still at the back of her mind, tugging at her memory, the only man she had ever loved. She hid among cardboard boxes in the back of a lorry, plagued by the scariest thoughts. Every time the driver stepped on the brakes, Zaynab feared something awful would happen, but the journey was surprisingly uneventful.

Finding a job in Istanbul, however, was not easy. No one wanted to hire her. Without knowing the language she could not practise divination. After weeks of searching, she was hired at a hairdresser's named Split Ends. The work was onerous, the money barely enough, the owner unkind. Unable to stand on her feet for long hours each day, she suffered from excruciating back pain. Still she carried on. Months passed, and then a whole year.

One of the regular customers, a thickset woman who had her hair dyed a different shade of blonde every few weeks, was fond of Zaynab.

'Why don't you come and work for me?' said the woman one day.

'What kind of a place is it?' Zaynab enquired.

'Well, it's a brothel. And before you protest, or throw something at my head, let me make one thing clear: I run a decent place. Established, legal. We go way back to Ottoman times, just don't tell that to everyone. Some people don't want to hear it, apparently. Anyway, if you come work for me, I'll make sure you are treated properly. You'll do the same kind of job you are doing here – cleaning up, brewing coffee, washing the cups . . . Nothing more. But I'll pay you better.'

And this is how Zaynab122, having journeyed from the high mountains of northern Lebanon to the low hills of Istanbul, came into Tequila Leila's life.

Nine Minutes

In the ninth minute, Leila's memory simultaneously slowed down and spun out of control as fragments of her past whirled inside her head in an ecstatic dance, like passing bees. She now remembered D/Ali, and the thought of him brought along the taste of chocolate bonbons with surprise fillings inside – caramel, cherry paste, hazelnut praline . . .

July 1968. It had been a long, sweltering summer; the sun baked the asphalt and the air felt clammy. Not so much as a whiff of breeze, a quick shower of rain, not a single cloud in the sky. Seagulls stood still on the rooftops, their eyes fixed on the horizon, as if waiting for the ghosts of enemy armadas to return; magpies perched on the magnolia trees, surveying their surroundings for shiny trinkets, but they stole little in the end, too lazy to move in the heat. A week ago a pipe had burst and dirty water had run along the streets as far south as Tophane, forming puddles here and there on which children floated paper boats. Uncollected rubbish released a rancid odour. The prostitutes had been complaining about the stench and the flies. Not that they expected anyone to listen. No one thought the pipe would be fixed any time soon. They would have to wait, just like they waited for many other things in life. Yet to everyone's immense surprise, one morning they woke up to the sound of workmen drilling the road and mending the faulty pipe. Not only that, but the loose stones in the pavement had been repaired and the gate at the entrance to the street of brothels had been painted. It was now a dark, dull green, the colour of leftover lentils – a colour only a government official hurrying to get work done would ever choose.

It turned out the prostitutes were right to suspect that the authorities were behind this frenzy of activity. The reason soon became clear: Americans were coming. The Sixth Fleet was on its way to Istanbul. An aircraft carrier that weighed 27,000 tons was going to drop anchor in the Bosphorus to take part in NATO operations.

The news caused ripples of excitement throughout the street of brothels. Hundreds of sailors were soon to disembark with crisp dollars in their pockets, and many would no doubt be in need of a woman's touch after weeks away from home. Bitter Ma was beside herself with joy. She put a CLOSED sign on the front door and ordered everyone to roll up their sleeves. Leila and the other women grabbed mops, brooms, dust cloths, sponges . . . whatever cleaning object they could possibly find. They polished the door handles, scrubbed the walls, swept the floors, washed the windows, and repainted the door frames in an eggshell white. Bitter Ma wanted the whole building to be redone, but, reluctant to hire a professional painter, she had to settle for an amateur finish.

Meanwhile, there was another flurry of activity across the city. The municipality of Istanbul, determined to give the American visitors a proper taste of Turkish hospitality, festooned the streets with flowers. Thousands of flags were unfurled, and left hanging helter-skelter from car windows, balconies and front gardens. NATO IS SAFETY, NATO IS PEACE read a banner hung on the wall outside a luxurious hotel. When all the street lights, now repaired and renewed, were turned on, a golden glow reflected off the freshly swept asphalt.

On the day the Sixth Fleet arrived, a twenty-one-gun salute was fired. At about the same time, just to make double sure there would be no trouble, the police raided the campus of Istanbul University. Their aim was to round up leftist student leaders and keep them in custody until the fleet had left the city. Waving their batons, emboldened by their pistols, they descended on the canteens and the dorms, the sound of their boots regular as the chatter of cicadas. But the students did something quite unexpected: they resisted. The ensuing stand-off became violent and bloody – thirty students were arrested, fifty badly beaten, and one murdered.

That night Istanbul looked glamorous and beautiful, although deeply nervous – like a woman who had dressed up for a party she no longer wished to attend. There was a tension in the air that only increased as the hours went by. Many across the city slept in fits and starts, anxiously waiting for daylight, fearing the worst.

The next morning, dew still glistening on the flowers that had been planted for the Americans, thousands of protesters were on the streets. A surge of people began marching towards Taksim Square singing revolutionary anthems. In front of the Dolmabahçe Palace – home to six noted Ottoman sultans and nameless concubines – the procession came to an abrupt stop. For a fleeting moment, there was an awkward quiet, that interstice in a demonstration when the crowd holds its breath, waiting without knowing for what. Then, a student leader, grabbing a megaphone, shouted at the top of his voice in English, '*Yankee, Go Home!*'

The crowd, as though energized by a jolt of lightning, chanted in unison, '*Yankee, Go Home! Yankee, Go Home!*'

By now the American sailors, having disembarked from the ships early in the day, were milling around, ready to check out the historic city, take a few pictures, get some souvenirs. When they first heard the sounds in the distance they did not think much of it – until they rounded a corner and ran straight into the angry demonstrators.

Sandwiched between the protest march and the waters of the Bosphorus, the sailors opted for the latter, diving straight into the sea. Some swam away and were rescued by fishermen; others stayed close to the shore, and were pulled out by passers-by when the march had come to an end. Before the day was over, the commander of the Sixth Fleet, not finding it safe to linger, decided to leave Istanbul earlier than planned.

Meanwhile, in the brothel, Bitter Ma, who had bought bikini tops and grass skirts for all the women and prepared a sign in her pidgin English that read WELCOME JONS, was incandescent. She had always disliked lefties, and now she hated them all the more. Who the hell did they think they were, cutting off her business like that? All that painting, cleaning and waxing had been for nothing. As far as she was concerned, that's what communism amounted to: a monumental waste of decent, well-meaning people's hard work! She hadn't slogged away all her life so that a handful of misguided radicals could come and tell her she must now distribute her hard-earned money to gaggles of idlers and loafers and paupers. No sir, she would never do that. Resolving to donate money to every anti-communist cause in the city, however tenuous, she unleashed a curse under her breath and turned the sign on the door to OPEN.

Now that it was clear the American sailors would not be visiting the street of brothels, the prostitutes had slacked off. Upstairs in her room, Leila sat on her bed cross-legged, a ream of paper balanced on her lap, tapping the pen against her cheek. She was hoping to have some quiet time for herself. She wrote:

Dear Nalan,

I have been thinking about what you told me the other day regarding the intelligence of farm animals. You said that we kill them, we eat them, and we think we are smarter than them, but we never really understand them.

You said cows recognize people who have hurt them in the past. Sheep can identify faces as well. But I ask myself, what good does it do them to remember so much when they can't change a thing?

You said goats are different. Although they get upset easily, they also forgive quickly. Are we humans, just like sheep and goats, composed of two kinds: those who can never forget and those who can forgive . . .

Startled from her thoughts by a loud, piercing sound, Leila paused. Bitter Ma was shouting at someone. The madam, already outraged, sounded steamed up.

'What do you want, son?' Bitter Ma was saying. 'Just tell me what it is you're after!'

Leila left the room and went downstairs to check.

There was a young man at the door. His face was flushed, his long, dark hair dishevelled. He was panting slightly, like someone who had been running for dear life. One look at him and Leila sensed he might be one of the leftist protesters on the streets, probably a university student. When the police barricaded the roads, arresting people left, right and centre, he must have broken off from the procession and dashed into an alley, only to find himself in front of the street of brothels.

'I'm asking you one last time, don't try my patience.' Bitter Ma frowned. 'What the hell do you want? And if you don't want anything, fine, get out! You can't just stand there like a scarecrow. Speak up!'

The young man glanced around, his arms folded tight across his chest, as if hugging himself for comfort. It was that gesture that touched Leila's heart.

'Sweet Ma, I think he's here to see me,' said Leila from above the stairs.

Taken by surprise, he looked up and saw her. The softest smile upturned the corners of his mouth.

At the same time, Bitter Ma was observing the stranger from beneath her drooped lids, waiting to hear what he would say to that.

'Uhm, yes . . . that's right . . . I'm here to talk to the lady, actually. Thank you.'

Bitter Ma shook with laughter. '*Talk to the lady – actually? Thank you?* Right, son. What planet did you say you came from?'

The young man blinked, suddenly shy. He passed a palm across his temple, as though needing time to find the answer.

Bitter Ma was serious now, all business. 'So do you want her or not? You got money, my pasha? Because she's expensive. One of my best.'

The door opened just then and a client walked in. In the changing light pouring in from the street, Leila couldn't read the young man's expression for a moment. And then she saw: he was nodding his head, a look of calm spreading over his anxious face.

When he came upstairs to her room, he gazed around with interest, inspecting every detail – the cracks in the sink, the cupboard that did not shut properly, the curtains riddled with cigarette holes. Finally, he turned back and saw that Leila was slowly undressing.

'Oh, no, no. Stop!' He took a quick step back, his head at a tilt, his face in a scowl, chiselled by the reflected glare from the mirror. Embarrassed by his outburst he composed himself. 'I mean . . . please, keep your clothes on. I really am not here for that.'

'Then what do you want?'

He shrugged. 'How about we just sit and chat?'

'You want to *chat*?'

'Yes, I'd love to get to know you. Gosh, I don't even know your name. Mine is D/Ali – not my legal name, but who wants to keep that, right?'

Leila stared at him. In the furniture workshop across the yard, someone began singing – a song she couldn't recognize.

D/Ali fell back on to the bed and pulled his legs up, sliding easily into a cross-legged position, his cheek resting in the palm of his hand. 'And don't worry if you're not in the mood to talk, honestly. I could just as well roll a cigarette for us. We can smoke it in silence.'

D/Ali. His raven hair falling in waves down to his collar; his eyes a restless emerald that turned a brighter shade when he was thoughtful or confused. The son of immigrants, a child of forced displacements and diasporas. Turkey, Germany, Austria, back to Germany, and once again Turkey – traces of his past showed here and there, like a cardigan that had snagged on rogue nails along the way. Until she met him, Leila had never known anyone who had set up house in so many places and yet did not feel quite at home anywhere.

His real name, the one in his German passport, was Ali.

At school, year after year, he had been subjected to the sneers and, every now and then, to the slurs and fists of racist students. Then one of them had learned about his passion for art. That gave them even more reason to make fun of him each morning when he walked into the classroom. *Here comes a boy named Ali . . . what an idiot, he thinks he is Dali!* It had cut him to the core of his being, the endless jeering, the barbs. But one day, when a new teacher asked everyone in the class to introduce themselves, he leaped to his feet first, and said with a steady, confident smile: 'Hi, my name is Ali, but I like it better when people call me D/Ali.' From then on the snide comments had stopped, but he, headstrong and independent, had started using, and even enjoying, what was once a hurtful nickname.

His parents, both from a village by the Aegean Sea, had moved to Germany from Turkey in the early 1960s as *Gastarbeiter*, 'guest workers' – invited to come and work, and when no longer needed, expected to pack their bags and leave. His father had moved there first, in 1961, sharing a hostel room with ten other workers, half of whom could neither read nor write. At night, by the dim light of a lamp, those who were literate would write letters for those who were not. Within a month of living in such a cramped space, everyone had learned everything about each other, from family secrets to blocked bowels.

A year later, the father was joined by his wife, with D/Ali and their twin daughters in tow. At first, things did not work out quite as they had hoped. After a failed attempt to relocate themselves in Austria, the family returned to Germany. The Ford factory in Cologne needed workers, and they settled in a neighbourhood where the streets smelled of asphalt when it rained, the houses all looked the same, and the old lady downstairs called the police at the slightest noise from their flat. Mother bought fluffy slippers for everyone and they got used to speaking in hushed tones. They watched TV with the volume down and did not play music or flush the toilet in the evenings: these were not tolerated either. D/Ali's younger brother was born here, and this was where they all grew up, lulled to sleep by the murmuring waters of the Rhine.

D/Ali's father, whose dark hair and square jaw he had inherited, often talked about moving back to Turkey. When they had saved enough money, and were done with this cold, arrogant country, they would up and leave. He was having a house built back in his village. A large house with a pool and an orchard at the rear. At night they would listen to the hum of the valley and the occasional whistle of a pigeon and they would not have to wear fluffy slippers or speak quietly any more. The more years that went by, the more fastidiously he planned their return. No one else in the family took him seriously. Germany was home. Germany was the *fatherland* – even if the father of the family could not accept this fact.

By the time D/Ali reached secondary school it was clear to all his teachers and classmates that he was destined to become an artist. Yet his passion for art had never been encouraged in the family. Even when his favourite teacher came to talk to them, his parents failed to understand. D/Ali would never forget the shame he felt that afternoon: Mrs Krieger, a heavily built woman, perched on a chair, a small tea glass balanced daintily in her hand, trying to explain to his parents that their son was *really* talented and could win a place at an art and design school if only he could be tutored and mentored. D/Ali watched his father: he was listening with a smile that did not reach his eyes, pitying this German woman with salmon-pink skin and cropped blonde hair, telling him what to do with his own son.

When D/Ali was eighteen, his sisters attended a party at a friend's house. Something went terribly wrong that night. One of the twins did not come back home, even though she had permission to stay only until eight o'clock. The next morning, she was found by the highway, unconscious. Rushed to the hospital in an ambulance, she was treated for hypoglycaemic coma due to excessive alcohol consumption. They pumped her stomach until she felt like her soul had been emptied out. D/Ali's mother hid the incident from her husband, who was working a late shift that night.

Rumours travel fast in a village, and every immigrant community, no matter its size, is a village at heart. Soon the scandal had reached their father's ears. Like a storm unleashing its fury over the length and breadth of a valley, he punished his entire family. This was it, the last straw. His children would return to Turkey. All of them. The parents would stay in Germany until retirement, but the younger ones would, from now on, live with their relatives in Istanbul. Europe was no place to raise a daughter, much less two daughters. D/Ali was to attend a university in Istanbul and keep a sharp eye on his siblings. If anything untoward were to happen, he would be held responsible.

And so he arrived there, at the age of nineteen, with his broken Turkish and his irreparably German ways. He was used to feeling like an outsider in Germany, but until he started living in Istanbul he had never thought he would feel the same way in Turkey, if not even more so. It wasn't only his accent and the way he involuntarily sprinkled a *ja* or an *ach so!* at the end of his sentences that made him stand out. It was the expression on his face, as if he were perpetually dissatisfied or disenchanted with what he saw, what he heard, what he couldn't bring himself to be part of.

Anger. Those first months in the city, he was often seized by a sudden excess of anger, not so much at Germany or Turkey as at the order of things, at the capitalist regime that tore families apart, at the bourgeois class that fed on workers' sweat and pain, at a lopsided system that did not allow him to belong anywhere. He had read extensively about Marxism when he was in secondary school, and had always admired Rosa Luxemburg, brave and brilliant woman that she was, murdered in Berlin by the Freikorps and dumped in a canal – a canal that flowed placidly through Kreuzberg, a place D/Ali had visited several times and once, secretly, dropped a flower into. A rose for Rosa. Yet it was only when he started at Istanbul University that he would fall in with a diehard leftist group. His new comrades wanted to demolish the status quo, and build everything anew, as did D/Ali.

So when D/Ali showed up at Leila's door in July 1968, running away from the police breaking up the demonstration against the

Sixth Fleet, he brought with him the smell of tear gas along with his radical ideas, complicated past and soulful smile.

'How did you end up here?' men always asked.

And each time Leila told them a different story, depending on whatever she thought they might like to hear — a tale customized to client requirements. It was a talent she had learned from Bitter Ma.

But she wouldn't do that with D/Ali, and he never asked the question anyhow. Instead he wanted to know other things about her — what did breakfasts taste like when she was a child in Van, what were the aromas that she remembered most vividly from winters long gone, and if she were to give every city a scent, what would be the scent of Istanbul? If 'freedom' were a type of food, he wondered, how did she think she would experience it on the tongue? And how about 'fatherland'? D/Ali seemed to perceive the world through flavours and scents, even the abstract things in life, such as love and happiness. Over time it became a game they played together, a currency of their own: they took memories and moments, and converted them into tastes and smells.

Savouring the cadence of his voice, she could listen to him for hours and never get bored. In his presence she felt a sense of lightness that she had not experienced in a long while. A trickle of hope, such as she had imagined herself incapable of feeling any more, swept through her veins and made her heart beat faster. It reminded her of the way she had felt when, as a little girl, she used to sit on the roof of their house in Van and watch the landscape like there was no tomorrow.

What puzzled Leila the most about D/Ali was how, from the very beginning, he treated her as his equal, as if the brothel were just another classroom in the university he attended and she a student he kept running into along the dimly lit corridors. It was this, more than anything, that put Leila off guard — this unexpected

142

sense of equality. An illusion, surely, but one that she treasured. As she walked in this unfamiliar territory, discovering him, she was also rediscovering herself. Anyone could see how her eyes lit up when she saw him, but few knew that the excitement was accompanied by a surge of guilt.

'You shouldn't come here any more,' Leila said one day. 'It's not good for you. This place is full of misery, don't you see? It contaminates people's souls. And don't think you're above it, because it'll suck you in; it's a swamp. We're not normal, none of us is. Nothing here is natural. I don't want you to spend time with me any more. And why do you come here so often when you don't even –'

She didn't complete the sentence, worried that he might think she was upset on account of his still not having slept with her, for the truth was she liked and respected that about him. She had been holding on to it, like a precious gift he had given her. Strangely, though, it was only in the absence of sex that she allowed herself to think of him in that way, to the point that, every now and then, she caught herself wondering what it would be like to touch his neck, kiss that tiny scar to the side of his chin.

'I come because I like seeing you, it's as simple as that,' D/Ali said in a subdued tone. 'And I don't know who's *normal* in a system so crooked.'

D/Ali said that, as a rule, people who overused the word 'natural' did not know much about the ways of Mother Nature. If you told them how snails, worms and black sea bass were hermaphrodites, or male seahorses could give birth, or male clownfish turned female halfway through their lives, or male cuttlefish were transvestites, they would be surprised. Anyone who studied nature closely would think twice before using the word 'natural'.

'Fine, but you pay so much money. Bitter Ma charges you by the hour.'

'Oh, she does,' D/Ali said unhappily. 'But let's imagine for a moment that we were dating, and I could take you out or you could take me out. What would we do? We'd go to a movie, and then to a fancy restaurant and a ballroom . . .'

143

'A fancy restaurant! A ballroom!' Leila echoed with a smile.

'My point is, we'd be spending money.'

'That's different. Your parents would be horrified if they knew you were wasting their hard-won cash in a place like this.'

'Hey, I don't get money from my parents.'

'Really? But I thought . . . Then how do you afford *this*?'

'I work.' He winked.

'Where?'

'Here and there and everywhere.'

'For whom?'

'For the revolution!'

She looked away, unsettled. And, once again in her life, she was torn between her gut and her heart. Her gut warned her that there was more to him than the considerate, gentle young man she saw and she had to be very careful. But her heart pushed her forward – just like it had done when, as a newborn baby, she had lain motionless under a blanket of salt.

So she stopped objecting to his visits. Some weeks he would come every day, other times only over the weekends. She sensed, with a lurching heart, that on many a night he was out with his comrades, their long, dark shadows cast before them on empty streets, but what they might be doing with their time she chose not to ask.

'Yours is back!' Bitter Ma would yell from downstairs every time he showed up, and if Leila had a customer with her, D/Ali would have to wait on a chair by the entrance. Those were the moments when Leila felt so ashamed she could die: when she invited him afterwards into a room that smelled of another man. But if D/Ali was disturbed by any of this he never commented on it. A hushed concentration permeated his movements, and his eyes watched her intently, oblivious to everything else, as though she was, and had always been, the centre of the world. His kindness was spontaneous, uncalculated. Every time he said goodbye and left, after exactly an hour, a void spread into every corner of the room, swallowing her whole.

D/Ali never forgot to bring her a little present – a notebook for her to write in, a velvet ribbon for her hair, a ring in the shape of a serpent eating its own tail, and, at times, chocolate bonbons with surprise fillings – caramel, cherry paste, hazelnut praline . . . They would sit on the bed, open the box, taking their time to decide which bonbon to eat first, and, for a full hour, talk and talk. Once, he touched the scar on her back, left from the acid attack. Tenderly he traced the wound, which, like a prophet parting the sea, broke her skin apart.

'I want to paint you,' he said. 'May I?'

'A painting of me?' Leila blushed a little and lowered her gaze. When she looked at him again she found him smiling at her, just as she had known he would.

The next time he appeared carrying an easel and a wooden box full of bristle brushes, oil paints, palette knives, sketchpads and linseed oil. She posed for him, sitting on the bed in her short crimson crêpe skirt and matching beaded bikini top, her hair pulled up into a soft bun, her face slightly turned from the door as if willing it to stay shut forever. He would keep the canvas in the wardrobe until his next visit. When he had finished, after about a week, she was surprised to see that where her acid scar lay he had painted a tiny white butterfly.

'Be careful,' said Zaynab122. 'He's an artist, and artists are selfish. As soon as he gets what he wants, he'll vanish.'

Yet, to everyone's surprise, D/Ali kept coming back. The whores made fun of him, saying he was clearly incapable of getting an erection and incapable of fucking, and when they ran out of jokes they complained about the smells of turpentine. Knowing they were jealous, Leila paid them no heed. But when Bitter Ma, too, started to grumble, mentioning repeatedly that she did not want any lefties around, Leila began to worry that she would not be able to see him any more.

On one of those days, D/Ali approached Bitter Ma with an unexpected offer.

'That still life on the wall . . . I mean, no offence, but those daffodils and lemons seem a bit shoddy. Have you ever considered having a portrait up there?'

'Actually, I had one,' said Bitter Ma, though she refrained from telling him it was of Sultan Abdülaziz. 'But I had to give it away.'

'Ach so, that's a shame. Maybe you need a new portrait then. Why don't I paint you – for free?'

Bitter Ma laughed hoarsely, the rolls of fat around her waist quivering in amusement. 'Don't be silly. I'm not a beauty. Go find someone else.' She paused, suddenly serious. 'You're not kidding?'

That same week, Bitter Ma began to pose for D/Ali, holding her knitting up against her chest both to show her skill and to hide her double chin.

When D/Ali had finished the painting, the woman on the canvas looked like a happier, younger and thinner version of the original model. Now all the prostitutes wanted to pose for him, and this time it was Leila who was jealous.

The world is no longer the same for the one who has fallen in love, the one who is at its very centre; it can only spin faster from now on.

Ten Minutes

As time ticked away, Leila's mind happily recollected the taste of her favourite street food: deep-fried mussels – flour, egg yolks, bicarbonate of soda, pepper, salt, and mussels fresh from the Black Sea.

October 1973. The Bosphorus Bridge, the world's fourth longest, finally completed after three years of work, was opened to traffic following a spectacular public ceremony. At one end of the bridge, a large sign was erected: *Welcome to the Asian Continent*. At the other end, another sign read, *Welcome to the European Continent*.

Early in the morning, on both sides of the bridge, crowds had gathered for the occasion. In the afternoon the President gave an emotional speech; army heroes, some of whom were so old that they had fought in the Balkan Wars, the First World War and the War of Independence, stood to attention in dignified silence; foreign dignitaries sat on a high platform alongside political grandees and provincial governors; red-and-white flags fluttered in the wind for as far as the eye could see; a band played the national anthem and everyone sang at the tops of their voices; thousands of balloons were released into the air; and Zeybek dancers swirled in circles, their arms held spread at shoulder height, like eagles aloft.

Later on, when the bridge was opened to pedestrians, people were able to walk from one continent to the other. Surprisingly, though, so many citizens chose this picturesque location for their suicides that in the end the authorities decided to ban pedestrian access altogether. That all came later, however. Now it was a time of optimism.

The day before had been the fiftieth anniversary of the Republic of Turkey. That had been a massive event in itself. And today Istanbulites were celebrating this feat of engineering, over five thousand feet long – the offspring of Turkish workers and developers and British engineers from the Cleveland Bridge and Engineering Company. The Bosphorus Strait, slender and narrow, had always been called 'the neckline of Istanbul', and here was a bridge decorating it like an incandescent necklace. High above the city the necklace glowed, dangling over the waters where the Black Sea blended with the Sea of Marmara on one side and the Aegean ran to meet the Mediterranean on the other.

The whole week there had been such an intense, shared sense of jubilation in the air that even the beggars in the city smiled as if their stomachs were full. Now that Asian Turkey was permanently connected to European Turkey, a bright future awaited the entire country. The bridge heralded the beginning of a new era. Turkey was now technically *in* Europe – whether people over there agreed or not.

At night, fireworks exploded overhead, illuminating the dark autumn sky. On the street of brothels, the girls stood in groups along the pavement, watching and smoking. Bitter Ma, who considered herself a true patriot, was teary-eyed.

'What an amazing bridge – it's massive,' said Zaynab122, looking up at the fireworks.

'Birds are so lucky,' said Leila. 'Imagine, they can perch on it whenever they like. Seagulls, pigeons, magpies . . . And fish can swim underneath. Dolphins, bonitos. What a privilege. Wouldn't you like to end your life like that?'

'Of course I wouldn't,' said Zaynab122.

'Well, I would,' said Leila doggedly.

'How can you be so romantic, honey?' Nostalgia Nalan, clearly amused, gave an exaggerated sigh. She came to visit Leila from time to time, but her presence made Bitter Ma nervous. The law was clear about it: transvestites could not be employed in brothels – and since they could not get a job anywhere else either, they had to work on the streets. 'Do you have any idea how much that giant construction has cost? And who's paying for it – we, the people!'

Leila smiled. 'You sound like D/Ali sometimes.'

'Speaking of whom . . .' Nalan gestured to her left with her head.

Turning aside now, Leila saw D/Ali approaching, his jacket crumpled, his boots clopping heavily, a large canvas bag on his shoulder and in his hand a paper cone full of fried mussels.

'For you,' he said, as he handed her the mussels. He knew how much she loved them.

D/Ali did not speak again until they were upstairs and the door was firmly closed. He planted himself down on the bed, rubbing his forehead.

'Are you all right?' Leila asked.

'Sorry. I'm in a bit of a state. They almost got me this time.'

'Who? The police?'

'No, the Grey Wolves. The fascists. There's this group that's in charge of the area.'

'Fascists are in charge of *this* area?'

His eyes bored into her. 'Every neighbourhood in Istanbul has two competing groups: one from them and one from us. Unfortunately, around here they've managed to outnumber us. But we fight back.'

'Tell me what happened.'

'I rounded a corner and there they were in a huddle, shouting and laughing. I think they were celebrating the bridge. Then they saw me —'

'They know you?'

'Well, we all kind of recognize each other by now, and even if we don't, we can easily make a guess about someone based on the way they look.'

Clothes were political. And so was facial hair – particularly the moustache. The nationalists wore theirs pointing downwards, in the shape of a crescent moon. The Islamists kept theirs clipped, small and neat. The Stalinists preferred walrus-like moustaches that looked as if they had never seen a razor. D/Ali himself was always clean-shaven. Leila didn't know if this gave off a political message, and, if so, of what kind exactly. She found herself studying his lips – straight and rose-coloured. She never looked at men's lips, deliberately avoiding that, and catching herself doing this now troubled her.

'They chased me so hard,' D/Ali was saying, unaware of her thoughts. 'I could have run faster if I hadn't been carrying this.'

Leila eyed the bag. 'What's in it?'

He showed her. Inside the bag there were hundreds, if not thousands, of flyers. She pulled one out and studied it. A drawing covered half the page. Factory workers in blue smocks under a patch of light streaming from the ceiling. Men and women, side by side. They looked confident and otherworldly, almost angelic. She grabbed another flyer: coal miners with bright blue overalls, their features etched with soot, their eyes big and wise under their helmets. Quickly, she sifted through the other flyers. The people in them all had set jaws and strong muscles; they were not pale and weary like the workers she saw every day at the furniture workshop. In D/Ali's communist world, everyone was sturdy and muscular and bursting with health. She thought of her brother and her heart twisted in her chest.

'You don't like the pictures?' he said, observing her.

'I do. Did *you* draw them?'

He nodded. A flash of pride lit his features. His paintings, printed on an underground press, were distributed all over the city.

'We leave them everywhere – cafes, restaurants, bookstores, cinemas . . . But now I'm a bit worried. If the fascists catch me with the flyers, they'll beat the hell out of me.'

'Why don't you leave the bag here?' Leila said. 'I'll hide it under the bed.'

'I can't, it might put you in danger.'

She laughed softly. 'Who is going to search this place, darling? Don't worry, I'll keep an eye on the revolution for you.'

That night, after the doors of the brothel were locked, and the whole place was plunged into silence, Leila took out the flyers. Most of the prostitutes went to their homes to sleep; they had elderly parents to look after or children to take care of, but a few stayed in the building. Somewhere down the corridor a woman was snoring loudly, while another was talking in her sleep, her voice pleading and frail, although it was hard to make out what she said. Leila sat back in bed and began to read: *Comrades Be Vigilant. US Get Out of Vietnam Now! The Revolution Has Begun. The Dictatorship of the Proletariat.*

She studied the words, frustrated at how their full power, their true meaning, kept eluding her. She remembered Auntie's silent panic each time she looked at a piece of writing. A stab of regret went through her. Why had it never occurred to her, when she was young, to teach her mother how to read and write?

'I've been meaning to ask you something,' Leila said the next day, when D/Ali was back. 'Will there be any prostitution after the revolution?'

He gave her a blank look. 'Where did that come from?'

'I've been wondering what will happen to us if you guys win.'

'Nothing bad will happen to you – or to your friends. Look, none of this is your fault. It's capitalism that's to blame. The inhuman system that creates profits for the moribund imperialist bourgeoisie and their conspirators by abusing the weak and exploiting the working class. The revolution will defend your rights. You are a proletarian too, a member of the working class, don't forget.'

'But are you going to close this place or keep it open? What about Bitter Ma?'

'The madam is nothing more than an exploitative capitalist, no better than a champagne-swilling plutocrat.'

Leila said nothing.

'Look, that woman makes a profit from your body. Yours and many others. After the revolution she will have to be punished – fairly, of course. But we will shut down all the brothels and clean up the red-light districts. They'll become factories. Prostitutes and streetwalkers will all be factory workers – or peasants.'

'Oh, some of my friends might not like that,' said Leila, her eyes narrowing, as if squinting into a future in which Nostalgia Nalan were running away in a skimpy dress and heels from whatever cornfield she had been forced to work in.

D/Ali seemed to be thinking the same thing. He had met Nalan several times and was impressed by her willpower. He didn't know what Marx would have made of people like her. Or Trotsky, for that matter. He didn't remember reading anything, in all the books he'd studied, about transvestites who no longer wished to be peasants. 'I'm sure we'll find the right work for your friends.'

Leila smiled, secretly enjoying listening to his passionate speech, but the words that came out of her mouth did not reflect that. 'How can you believe in all this? It sounds like a fantasy to me.'

'This is not a fantasy. Nor a dream. It is the flow of history.' He sulked, looking hurt. 'Can you make a river run the other way? You can't. History is moving, inexorably and logically, towards communism. Sooner or later, it'll come, that big day.'

Seeing him get upset so easily, Leila felt a rush of affection for him. Her hand landed gently on his shoulder, settling in there like a nesting sparrow.

'But I do have a dream, if you are wondering.' D/Ali squeezed his eyes tight shut, not wanting to see her face when she heard what he was about to say. 'It's about you, actually.'

'Oh yeah? What is it?'

'I want you to marry me.'

The silence that followed was so deep that Leila, keeping her gaze steadily on D/Ali, could hear the low murmur of the waves in the harbour, and the sound of a fishing boat's engine in the slap of water. She drew in a breath but somehow it felt like the air didn't reach her lungs, her chest was so full. Then the alarm clock went off, making them both flinch. Bitter Ma had recently placed a clock in every room, so that when their hour was over, no customer would overstay.

Leila straightened up. 'Do me a favour, please. Don't say such things to me again.'

D/Ali opened his eyes. 'Are you angry? Don't be.'

'Look, there are things you should never say in this place. Even if you mean well, and I have no doubt that you mean well. But I need to make it clear: I don't like this kind of talk. I find it very . . . disturbing.'

For a moment he looked lost. 'I'm just surprised that you haven't noticed it yet.'

'Noticed what?' Leila pulled her hand away as though from fire.

'That I love you,' he said. 'Ever since I saw you for the first time . . . on the stairs . . . the day the Sixth Fleet came . . . remember?'

Leila felt her cheeks go red. Her face was burning. She wanted him to leave, without another word, and never come back. Sweet though it might have been for years, it was apparent to her now that this relationship would hurt them.

After he had gone, she walked to the window and, despite Bitter Ma's strict orders, opened the curtains. She flattened her cheek against the pane, through which she could see the lonely birch tree and the furniture workshop, smoke spewing from its heating vent. She imagined D/Ali striding towards the harbour, his gait fast and urgent as usual, and in her mind she watched him loyally, lovingly, until he disappeared into a dark alley under a cascade of fireworks.

That whole week, galvanized by the upbeat mood, *gazinos* and nightclubs were full to bursting. On Friday, after the evening prayer, Bitter Ma sent Leila to a stag party at a *konak* by the Bosphorus. All night long, thinking about D/Ali and what he had said to her, she was assailed by a gloom she couldn't overcome, unable to pretend and play along, her whole manner painfully slow, sluggish, as if dredged from a lake. She sensed the hosts were unhappy with her performance and would later complain to the madam. Clowns and prostitutes, she thought bitterly, who wants them around when they are sad?

On the way back, she trudged wearily, her feet throbbing from standing in high heels for hours on end. She was starving, not having eaten since lunch the day before. No one thought about offering her food on such nights, and she never asked.

The sun was rising over the red-tiled rooftops and lead-covered domes. The air had a fresh feel, the scent of a promise. She passed by apartment buildings still asleep. A few paces ahead she noticed a basket, tied to a rope that was hanging from a window on an upper floor. Inside were what looked like potatoes and onions. Someone must have ordered them from the grocer's nearby and forgotten to haul the basket up.

A sound made her stop in her tracks. She grew still, straining to hear. A few seconds later, she caught a whimper so feeble that at first she thought she might have imagined it, courtesy of her sleep-deprived brain. Then she glimpsed a shapeless silhouette on the pavement, a heap of flesh and fur. A wounded cat.

Simultaneously, someone else had seen the animal and was approaching from the opposite side of the road. A woman. With her soft brown eyes that crinkled at the corners, pointy nose and stout frame, she resembled a bird – a bird that a child might have drawn, bubbly and round.

'Is the cat okay?' the woman asked.

They both leaned forward and saw it in the same instant: its intestines spilled out, its breathing slow and laboured, the animal was horribly injured.

Leila took off her scarf and wrapped it around the cat. Gently, she lifted it, cradling it in one arm. 'We need to find a vet.'

'At this hour?'

'Well, we don't have much choice, do we?'

They began to walk together.

'My name is Leila, by the way. With an "i" in the middle, not a "y". I've changed the spelling.'

'I'm Humeyra. Spelled the normal way. I work in a *gazino* down by the wharf.'

'What do you do there?'

154

'Me and my band, we are on stage every night,' she said, and added more forcefully, and not without a trace of pride, 'I'm a singer.'

'Oh, do you sing any Elvis?'

'No. We do old songs, ballads, some new stuff too, mostly arabesque.'

The vet, when they were able to find one, was irritated at being woken up at this hour, but thankfully he did not turn them away.

'In all my years, I've never seen anything like this,' the man said. 'Broken ribs, a punctured lung, smashed pelvis, fractured skull, missing teeth . . . It must have been run over by a car or a truck. I'm sorry, I really doubt we can save this poor animal.'

'But you doubt,' said Leila slowly.

The vet's eyes became slits behind his glasses. 'Sorry?'

'I mean you are not a hundred per cent sure, right? You *doubt*, which means there is a chance she could survive.'

'Look, I understand you want to help, but, believe me, it's better to put her to sleep. This animal has already suffered too much.'

'We'll find another vet then.' Leila turned to Humeyra. 'We will, right?'

The other woman hesitated – only for a second. She nodded her support. 'Right.'

'Fine, if you're that adamant, I'll try to help,' said the vet. 'But I make no promises. And I must tell you, it's not going to be cheap.'

Three operations and months of painful treatment were to follow. Leila covered most of the costs, and Humeyra chipped in as best she could.

In the end, time proved Leila right. The cat, with her cracked claws and missing teeth, clung to life with might and main. Given that her recovery was nothing short of a miracle, they called her Sekiz – 'Eight', for clearly a creature that could endure so much pain had to have nine lives, eight of which must have been spent.

The two women took turns to look after her – gradually building a steady friendship.

A few years later Sekiz, after a wild phase of nightly escapades, got pregnant. Ten weeks on, she gave birth to five kittens with highly distinct personalities. One of the kittens was black with a tiny patch of white, and he was stone deaf. Together, Leila and Humeyra named him Mr Chaplin.

Hollywood Humeyra, the woman who knew by heart the most beautiful ballads of Mesopotamia, and whose life resembled somewhat the sad stories many of them told.

Hollywood Humeyra, one of the five.

Humeyra's Story

Humeyra was born in Mardin, not far from the Monastery of St Gabriel on the limestone plateaus of Mesopotamia. Serpentine streets, stone houses. Growing up in a land so ancient and troubled, she was surrounded on all sides by remnants of history. Ruins upon ruins. New graves inside old graves. Listening to the endless legends of heroism and tales of love had made her homesick for a place that no longer existed. Strange as it was, it seemed to her that the border – where Turkey came to an end and Syria began – was not a fixed dividing line, but a living, breathing thing, a nocturnal creature. It shifted while people on both sides were sound asleep. In the mornings, it adjusted itself again, ever so slightly, to the left or the right. Smugglers travelled across the border, back and forth, holding their breaths as they crossed fields full of landmines. Sometimes in the stillness an explosion would be heard and the villagers would pray that it was a mule torn to pieces, and not the smuggler it carried.

The vast landscape stretched from the foot of Tur Abdin – 'Mountain of the Servants of God' – towards a flat land that turned a pale sandy fawn in summer. Yet the region's inhabitants often behaved like islanders. They were different from the neighbouring tribes and they felt it in their bones. The past closed in over them like deep, dark waters, and they swam, not alone, never alone, but accompanied by the ghosts of their ancestors.

Mor Gabriel was the oldest Syriac Orthodox monastery in the world. Like a hermit who sustains himself on water and meagre morsels of food, the monastery had managed to survive on faith and grains of grace. Throughout its long history it had seen bloodshed, genocide and persecution, the monks tyrannized by every invader who had traversed the region. While its fortified stone walls, light as milk, had survived, its spectacular library had not. Of the thousands of books and manuscripts it had once proudly housed, not a single page remained. Inside the crypt, hundreds of saints were buried – martyrs too. Outside, olive trees and orchards extended down the road, giving their distinctive scents to the air. A calm prevailed throughout that those who did not know history might easily mistake for peace.

Humeyra, similar to many children in the region, had been raised with songs and ballads and lullabies in various languages: Turkish, Kurdish, Arabic, Persian, Armenian, Syriac-Aramaic. She had heard stories about the monastery and seen tourists, journalists, clergymen and clergywomen come and go. It was the nuns who intrigued her the most. Like them, she was determined never to marry. But the spring she turned fifteen she was abruptly pulled out of school and betrothed to a man her father had been doing business with. By the age of sixteen she was already a wife. Her husband was an unambitious man, taciturn and easily frightened. Humeyra, knowing he had not wanted this marriage, suspected he had a sweetheart somewhere whom he could not forget. Time and again, she caught him watching her with resentment, as though he blamed her for his own regrets.

The first year together she tried, over and again, to understand him and his needs. Her own were unimportant. But he was never happy, the frown lines on his forehead reappearing fast, like a window that steamed over as soon as it was wiped. Soon after, his business hit hard times. They had to move to the house of his family.

Living with her in-laws broke Humeyra's spirit. Every day, all day, she was treated like a servant – a servant without a name. *Bride, go and bring the tea. Bride, go and cook the rice. Bride, go and wash the sheets.* Always being sent somewhere, never able to stay put, she had the bizarre feeling that they wanted her both to remain within reach and to disappear completely. Still, she might have endured it all if it hadn't been for the beatings. Once her husband broke a wooden coat hanger on her back. Another time he hit her on the legs with a pair of iron tongs that left a claret-coloured mark on the side of her left knee.

Going back to her parents' house was out of the question. So was staying in this place of misery. One early morning, while everyone was asleep, she stole the golden bracelets her mother-in-law kept in a biscuit box on her bedside table. Her father-in-law's dentures, soaking in a glass of water beside the box, smiled conspiratorially. She would not get much for the bracelets at the pawnbroker's, but it would be enough to buy a bus ticket to Istanbul.

In the city, she learned fast – how to walk in stilettos, how to iron her hair straight, how to apply make-up that looked dazzling under the neon lights. She changed her childhood name to Humeyra, got herself a fake ID. That she had a rich voice and knew hundreds of Anatolian songs by heart helped her to find a job in a nightclub. The first time on stage she shook like a leaf, but thankfully her voice held. She rented the cheapest room she could find in Karaköy, just off the street of brothels, and that's where, one night after work, she met Leila.

They supported each other with the kind of loyalty that only those with few to rely on could muster. Upon Leila's advice, she dyed her hair blonde, put in turquoise contact lenses, and had a nose job and a total change of wardrobe. She did all these things and more, because she received word that her husband was in Istanbul, looking for her. Awake or asleep, Humeyra was terrified she might become a victim of an honour killing. She couldn't help imagining the moment of her murder, each time envisioning a worse end. Women accused of indecency weren't always killed, she knew; sometimes they were just persuaded to kill themselves. The number of forced suicides, particularly in small towns in south-east Anatolia, had escalated to such a degree that there were articles about it in the foreign press. In Batman, not far from where she was born, suicide was the leading cause of mortality for young women.

But Leila always told Humeyra to set her mind at ease. She assured her friend that she was one of the lucky ones, the resilient ones, and, like the walls of the monastery she had grown up looking at, like the cat they had saved together that fortuitous night, she was, despite all the odds stacked against her, destined to survive.

Ten Minutes Twenty Seconds

In the final seconds before her brain completely shut down, Leila remembered a wedding cake – three tiered, all white, layered with buttercream icing. Neatly perched on top of it was a ball of red wool with tiny knitting needles at its side, all made in sugar. A nod to Bitter Ma. If the madam had not sanctioned it, Leila would never have been able to leave.

Upstairs in her room she looked at her face in the cracked mirror. In the reflection she thought she saw, for a fleeting moment, her past self. The girl she had been back in Van stared at her with wide-open eyes, an orange hula hoop in her hand. Slowly, compassionately, she smiled at that girl, finally making peace with her.

Her wedding gown was simple but elegant with delicate lace sleeves and a fitted silhouette that accentuated her waistline.

A knock on the door broke her reverie.

'Did you keep that veil short on purpose?' asked Zaynab122, entering the room. A squelching sound came from her padded insoles as she crossed the bare floor. 'Remember, I predicted it was going to be much longer. Now you are making me question my skills.'

'Don't be silly. You were right about everything. I just wanted to keep things simple, that's all.'

Zaynab122 walked towards the coffee cups they kept in the corner. Empty though it was, she glanced at one of the cups, sighing.

There was an uneasy moment before Leila spoke again. 'I still cannot believe Bitter Ma is letting me go.'

'It's because of the acid attack, I think. She still feels guilty, as well she should. I mean, she knew that man was off his nut, but she took his money and offered you up – like a lamb to the slaughter. He could have killed you, that beast.'

But it wasn't out of sheer kindness or an admission of some uncon-
fessed guilt that Bitter Ma had given her much-needed blessing.
D/Ali had paid her a hefty sum – an amount unheard of on the street
of brothels. Later on, when Leila would pressure him about where he
had got the money from, he would say his comrades had chipped in.
The revolution, he claimed, was all for love and for lovers.

The sight of a prostitute getting out of a brothel in a wedding
gown – not something that happened very often – drew a knot of
spectators. Bitter Ma had decided that if an employee of hers was
going to leave for good, she would be given a proper bash. She had
hired two Romani musicians, brothers by the look of them, one of
whom was banging a drum while the other played a clarinet, his
cheeks bulging, his eyes dancing to a lively tune. Everyone had
poured on to the street, cheering, clapping, stamping, whistling,
ululating, waving handkerchiefs, watching with rapt attention.
Even the police officers, having abandoned their posts by the gate,
had come to see what the fuss was about.

Leila knew that by now D/Ali's family had heard about what
they regarded as a scandal. His father, having flown in from Germany on the earliest flight, had tried to knock sense into his
son – firstly quite literally, by threatening to hit him (though he
was too old for that), next by threatening to cut him off from the
family fortune (not that there was much of a fortune), and lastly by
threatening him with outright rejection (that had hurt more than
anything). But D/Ali, ever since he was a boy, had a way of hardening in the face of aggression and his father's attitude had only
strengthened his resolve. His sisters kept calling to report that
their mother was crying all the time, grieving, as though he were
dead and buried. Leila knew D/Ali did not relay everything so as
not to upset her, and secretly she was grateful for this.

Even so, a few times she had tried to bring up her worries, not
quite able to believe that the past, her past, wouldn't form a wall
between them and grow in size, in impenetrability. 'Does it not
bother you? And even if it doesn't now, won't it in the future?
Knowing who I am, what I have been doing . . .'

'I don't follow what you're saying.'

'Yes, you do.' Her voice, which had roughened with strain, softened. 'You know exactly what I'm talking about.'

'Fine, and I'm telling you, in almost every language we use different words to talk about past and present, and for good reason. So, that was your *past* and this is your *present*. It'd bother me tremendously if you held another man's hand today. Just so you know, I'd be super jealous.'

'But . . .'

He kissed her gently, his eyes aglow with warmth. He guided her fingers towards the tiny scar on the side of his chin. 'See this? It happened when I fell from a wall. Primary school. And this one, here on my ankle, when I toppled off my bike trying to cycle one-handed. The one on my forehead is the deepest. A present from my beloved mother. She got so upset at me she threw a plate at the wall, missing badly, of course. It could have hit me in the eye. She cried more than I did. Another mark to carry for life. Does it bother you that I have so many scars?'

'Of course not! I love you just as you are!'

'Exactly.'

Together they rented a flat on Hairy Kafka Street. Number 70. The top floor. The apartment had been neglected and the area was still rough, with tanneries and leather manufacturers scattered around, but they were both confident that they could handle the challenge. In the mornings, as Leila lay back beneath the cotton sheets, she would inhale the smells of the neighbourhood, each day a different combination, and life would feel unusually sweet, heaven-sent.

They each had their favourite spot by the same window, where they would sip their tea in the evenings and watch the city extending before them, mile after mile of concrete. They would look at Istanbul with curious eyes, as if they were not part of it, as if they were alone in the world, and all those cars and ferry boats and red-brick houses were only background decoration, details in a painting for their eyes only. They could hear the sound of seagulls overhead, and the occasional police helicopter, another emergency somewhere. Nothing affected them. Nothing disturbed their peace. In the mornings, whoever woke up first would put the kettle on the stove and prepare the breakfast. Toasted bread, salted peppers, and simit bought from a passing vendor on the street, served with white cubes of cheese drizzled with olive oil, and two sprigs of rosemary – one for her, one for him.

Invariably after breakfast, D/Ali would grab a book, light a cigarette and start reading aloud passages from it. Leila knew that he wanted her to feel as passionately as he did about communism. He wanted them to be members of the same club, citizens of the same nation, dreamers of the same dream. This worried her deeply. Just as she had failed once before in believing in her father's God, she worried that she might fail this time to believe in her husband's revolution. Maybe it was her. Maybe she just didn't have enough faith inside.

Yet D/Ali thought it was only a matter of time. One day she too would join the ranks. So he kept feeding her with all the information he could to this end.

'Do you know how Trotsky was killed?'

'No, darling, tell me.' Leila ran the tips of her fingers back and forth over the tight black curls on his chest.

'It was with an ice pick,' D/Ali said grimly. 'Stalin's orders. He sent an assassin all the way to Mexico. Stalin was intimidated by Trotsky and his internationalist vision, you see. They were political rivals. I need to tell you about Trotsky's Theory of Permanent Revolution. You're going to love it.'

Can anything be permanent in this life, Leila wondered, but thought it best to keep her doubts to herself. 'Yes, darling, tell me.'

Expelled twice due to low grades and even poorer attendance, readmitted twice thanks to two separate amnesties for failed students, D/Ali still went to university, but Leila had no expectation that he would take his education seriously. The revolution was his priority, not this *bourgeois brainwashing* that some insisted on calling education. Every few nights he met with his friends to put up posters or distribute flyers. It had to be done in the dark, as quietly and swiftly as possible. *Like golden eagles*, he said. *We alight, we take off.* Once he came back with a black eye; the fascists had ambushed them. Another night he didn't show up at all, and she spent the night worried sick. But overall, she knew, and he knew, they were a happy couple.

1 May 1977. Early in the day, D/Ali and Leila left their small apartment to join the march. Leila was nervous, a gnawing tightness in her stomach. She was worried that someone might recognize her. What would she do if a man she walked next to turned out to be an old client of hers? D/Ali sensed her fears but insisted they should go together. He said she belonged in the revolution and should not allow anyone to tell her that she did not have a place in that fair society of the future. The more she hesitated, the more adamant he became that she, even more than he and his friends, had a right to take part in International Workers' Day. They were lapsed students, after all; she was the real proletarian.

Once convinced, Leila took a long time to decide what to wear. Trousers seemed to be a good choice, but how tight and what fabric and which colour? And for the top, she guessed it would be sensible to go for the kind of casual shirt favoured by many socialist women, loose and unrevealing – though she wanted to look pretty too. And feminine. Was that a bad thing? A bourgeois thing? In the end she decided on a powder-blue dress with a lace collar, a red bag across her chest, a white cardigan and red flat shoes. Nothing flashy, but she hoped not completely unfashionable. Next to D/Ali she still looked like a rainbow, of course. He had chosen dark jeans, a black button-down shirt and black shoes.

When they joined the march they were surprised to find how massive it was. Leila had never seen so many people together. Hundreds of thousands had gathered – students, factory workers, peasants, teachers – stepping in tandem, their faces locked in concentration. An endless stream of sounds flowed forth as slogans were chanted and anthems were sung. Far ahead, someone was playing a drum, but as hard as she tried Leila couldn't see who it was. Her eyes, apprehensive till now, brightened with renewed energy. For the first time in her life she felt part of something bigger than herself.

There were banners and posters everywhere, a swarm of words scattered in all directions. *Fight against Imperialism*; *Neither Washington Nor Moscow, but International Socialism*; *Workers of the World, Unite!*; *The Boss Needs You, You Don't Need the Boss*; *Eat the Rich . . .* She saw a sign that said, *We Were There: We Drove the Americans into the Sea*. A blush crept over her cheekbones. She, too, had been there on that day in July 1968, working in the brothel. She remembered how Bitter Ma had made everyone tidy up the place, and how disappointed she was when the Americans did not show up.

Every few minutes D/Ali turned his acute gaze on Leila to see how she was doing. He never let go of her hand. The day was scented with the perfume of the Judas trees, imbuing everything with fresh hope and renewed courage. But now that she felt buoyant, as if she finally belonged somewhere, and now that she had allowed herself this rare moment of lightness, Leila was seized by that familiar wariness, the need to be guarded. She began noticing details she had failed at first to see. Underneath the sweet fragrance, she picked out the odour of bodies sweating, of tobacco, stale breath and rage – a rage so strong it was almost palpable. Leila watched each group carrying their own banner, each slightly separate from the next. As the procession moved on, she heard some of the protesters shout and curse at others. That surprised her immensely. Until then she had not understood how divided the revolutionaries were among themselves. Maoists despised Leninists, and the Leninists loathed the anarchists. Leila knew that her beloved was destined to follow a different path altogether: that of Trotsky and his Permanent Revolution. She wondered whether, just as too many cooks spoiled the broth, too many revolutionaries could ruin a revolution, but once again she kept her thoughts to herself. After hours of footslogging, they reached the area around the Intercontinental Hotel in Taksim Square. The crowd had ballooned further, and the air was horribly humid. The bronze light of sunset washed over the protesters. In a corner, a street lamp came on, a bit too early, pale as a whisper. Far in the distance, standing on top of a bus, a union leader was giving a fiery speech, his voice mechanical and powerful through the megaphone. Leila felt tired. She wished she could sit down, if only for a moment. Out of the corner of her eye she observed D/Ali, the set of his jaw, the slant of his cheekbones, the tension in his shoulders. His profile was strikingly handsome against the thousands of faces around them, and the glow from the setting sun that painted his lips the colour of wine. She wanted to kiss him, taste him, feel him inside her. She lowered her gaze, perturbed by the thought that he would be disappointed if he only knew what had crossed her mind, trivial and vain, when she should have been thinking about more important things.

'Are you okay?' he asked.

'Oh, sure!' Leila piped with what she hoped was just the right tone, so as not to betray her tepid enthusiasm for the march. 'Do you have a cigarette?'

'Here, my love.' He pulled out a pack, offered her one, taking another for himself. With his silver Zippo he tried to light hers, but somehow it wouldn't catch.

'Let me do it.' Leila took the lighter from him.

That was when she heard the sounds – a series of rattles from all sides and above, as if God were running a stick over a railing in the sky. An eerie quiet descended on the square. It was as if no one were moving, no one were breathing, so pure was the stillness. Then came another bang. Leila recognized it this time for what it was. Her gut clenched in fear.

Beyond the pavements, behind protective walls, snipers had been positioned on the higher floors of the Intercontinental Hotel. Snipers with automatic weapons were shooting – aiming directly at the crowd. A scream shattered the protesters' startled silence. A woman was crying; someone else was yelling, telling people to run. And they did, without knowing which way to go. To their left was the Street of Cauldron Makers – the street where Nalan lived with her room-mates and turtles.

They headed off in that direction, thousands of bodies, like a river bursting its banks. Pushing, shouldering, shouting, running, tripping over each other . . .

Down the street an armoured police vehicle appeared out of nowhere, blocking the way. Now the protesters realized they were caught between the risk of snipers behind and the certainty of arrest and torture ahead. Then the shooting, which had momentarily slowed down, escalated to a continuous crackle. A great roar arose as thousands of mouths opened at once, a deep primal cry of horror and panic. Squeezed together, those at the back kept forging ahead, crushing those in front, like stones grinding against each other. A young woman in a pale floral dress slipped and slid under the armoured vehicle. Leila yelled at the top of her voice, the thud of her own heart pounding in her ears. Suddenly she was not holding D/Ali's hand any more. Had she let go of him or had he let go of her? She would never know. One second she could feel his breath on her cheek, and the next he was gone.

For a fleeting moment she was able to see him, about eight or ten feet away; she called out his name, over and again, but the crowd swept her away from him, like a rogue wave that carried away everything in its path. She heard the sound of bullets but could not tell any more where they were coming from; they could just as well have been fired from out of the ground. Next to her, a heavyset man lost his balance and toppled over, hit in the neck. She would never forget the expression on his face, one of incredulity more than pain. A few minutes earlier they had been at the helm of history, changing the world, demolishing the system – and now they were being hunted down without even a chance to see the faces of their assassins.

The next day, 2 May, over two thousand bullets were collected in the area surrounding Taksim Square. More than a hundred and thirty people were reported to have been severely injured.

Leila phoned every public hospital and private doctor in the area. When she could no longer find the strength to talk to strangers, one of her friends would take over the search. Each time, they were careful to provide D/Ali's legal name, for, like Leila, life had given him an alias along the way.

There were many Alis in the hospitals they called; some were being treated in beds, others were in the morgue, but there was no trace of her Ali. Two days later, Nostalgia Nalan tried one last place, a clinic in Galata that she knew from before. And they confirmed that D/Ali had been brought there. He was one of the thirty-four fatalities, most of them trampled to death in the stampede on the Street of Cauldron Makers.

Ten Minutes Thirty Seconds

In the final seconds before her brain surrendered, Tequila Leila recalled the taste of single malt whisky. It was the last thing that had passed her lips on the night she died.

November 1990. It had been an ordinary day. In the afternoon she made a bowl of popcorn for herself and Jameelah, who was staying with her. Special recipe – butter, sugar, popcorn, salt, rosemary. They had barely started eating when the phone rang. Bitter Ma was on the line.

'Are you tired?' In the background a soft, mystical melody played, not the kind of thing Bitter Ma would normally listen to.

'Would it make any difference?'

Bitter Ma pretended not to hear that. They had known each other for so long that they simply ignored the things they couldn't be bothered to take on board.

'Listen, I've got this fabulous client. He reminds me of that famous actor, the one who drives the talking car.'

'You mean the Knight Rider on TV?'

'Yes, bingo! The guy looks just like him. Anyway, his family is stupidly rich.'

'So what's the catch?' Leila asked, a little sharply. 'Deep pockets, young, handsome: a man like that doesn't need a hooker.'

Bitter Ma chuckled. 'The family is, how shall I put it . . . muchly, hopelessly conservative. Like, extreme. The father is a tyrant and a bully. He wants his son to take over his business.'

'You still haven't told me what the catch is.'

'Patience is a virtue. The young man is getting married next week. But the father is deeply concerned.'

'Why?'

'Two reasons. One, the son doesn't want to get married. He doesn't like his fiancée. My sources tell me he can't even stand to be in the same room as her at the moment. Two, and this is a bigger problem – I mean, not in my eyes, but in the eyes of the father –'

'Spit it out, Sweet Ma.'

'This boy isn't into women,' said Bitter Ma sighing, as if the ways of the world tired her. 'He has a long-term boyfriend. The father knows about it. The man knows everything. He believes marriage will cure his son of his deviant ways. So he found him a bride, planned his wedding and decided on their guest list, I guess.'

'What a father! He sounds like a jerk to me.'

'Yes, but he's no small jerk.'

'Ha, Jerk Pasha.'

'Right, and Jerk Pasha wants a kind, sophisticated, experienced woman to show his son the ropes before the wedding night.'

'Kind, sophisticated, experienced . . .' Leila repeated slowly, savouring each word. Bitter Ma seldom praised her, if ever.

'I could have called one of the other girls,' Bitter Ma said impatiently. 'You're getting old, for sure. But I know you need the money. Are you still taking care of that African girl?'

'Yes, she's with me.' Leila lowered her voice. 'All right then, where?'

'The Intercontinental.'

Leila's face closed. 'You know I don't go there.'

Bitter Ma cleared her throat. 'Well, that's the address. Up to you. But you need to learn to move on. Your D/Ali has been gone for a long time. What difference does it make, this hotel or that motel?'

Leila did not say anything.

'So? I can't wait all day.'

'Fine, I'll go,' Leila said.

'Good girl. Grand Deluxe Bosphorus Suite. Penthouse. Be there at quarter to ten. Oh, one more thing . . . You must wear a dress: long sleeves, low cut, gold, glittery – mini, needless to say. It's a special request.'

'Is this the son's request or the father's?'

Bitter Ma laughed. 'The father's. He says his son likes gold and anything shimmery. He thinks it might help.'

'Tell you what. Forget the son, send me to Jerk Pasha. I'd love to meet him – for real. It might do him good to loosen up a bit.'

'Don't be silly. The old man would shoot us both.'

'All right then . . . but I don't have a dress like that.'

'Then go and buy one,' Bitter Ma hissed. 'Don't piss me off.'

Leila pretended not to hear that. 'Are you sure the son is okay with this?'

'He isn't. He's had four girls before – apparently didn't even touch them. It's your job to make him change his mind. Capeesh?'

She hung up.

Towards the evening, Leila headed to Istiklal Avenue, a route she avoided unless necessary. The main drag of shops was always packed. Too many elbows, too many eyes. Teetering in her high heels, low-cut blouse and red leather miniskirt, she joined the throng of pedestrians. They all took small, synchronized steps, their bodies moulded together. From one end of the avenue to the other the crowd flowed, leaking out into the night like ink from a broken fountain pen.

Women glared, men leered at her. She watched wives linking arms with their husbands, some owning them, others happy to be owned. She watched mothers pushing buggies on their way home from family visits, young women with eyes cast down, unmarried couples holding hands furtively. People behaved as if they were above their surroundings, confident in the knowledge that the city would be here for them the next day, and every day thereafter. Then, fleetingly, she saw herself in a shop window – looking more tired and more distracted than her mental image of herself. She entered the store. The sales assistant – a gentle, softly spoken woman with a headscarf tied at the back of her head – recognized her from previous visits. She helped Leila to find just the right dress. 'Oh, it looks great on you, it really complements your complexion,' she said brightly as Leila stepped out of the fitting room. Words that had been said to countless other women, no matter what they put on. Leila smiled nonetheless, for the sales assistant had betrayed not a hint of prejudice. She paid the money and kept the dress on. Her old clothes she left there, tucked in a plastic bag. She'd pick them up later.

She checked her watch. Seeing she had a bit of time to kill, she headed to Karavan. The aromas of street food wafted along the road – döner kebab, rice with chickpeas, grilled sheep intestines.

In Karavan she found Nalan having a drink with a Swedish gay couple cycling from Gothenburg to Karachi – 4,855 miles. They would cross Turkey from one end to the other, then cycle through Iran. Last month they had stopped in Berlin, watched the West German flag being raised in front of the Reichstagsgebäude on the stroke of midnight. Now they were showing photos to Nalan, who seemed to be enjoying the exchange despite having no language in common. Leila sat with them for a while, happy to observe silently.

There was a newspaper on the table. She read the news first, and then her horoscope. *You believe you are a victim of circumstances beyond your control. Today is the day you can change that*, her horoscope said. *The astral alignment puts you in unusually high spirits. Expect an exciting encounter soon, but only if you take the initiative. Clear your head, don't keep your feelings locked up inside any more, go for a walk and be the master of your life. It's time to know yourself.*

Shaking her head, she lit a cigarette and placed the Zippo on the table. How wonderful that sounded: *Know yourself.* The ancients had been so fond of the motto, they had engraved it on their temple walls. And while Leila could see its truth, she thought the teaching was incomplete. It needed to be: *Know yourself and know*

173

an arsehole when you see one. Knowledge of self and knowledge of arseholes had to go hand in hand. Still, if she wasn't too tired at the end of tonight, she would walk back home, try to clear her head and be the master of her life, whatever that was supposed to mean.

At the agreed-upon hour, clad in her new dress and slingback stilettos, Leila walked towards the Intercontinental Hotel, its tall, solid frame outlined against the night sky. She felt her back tense, half expecting to hear the rumble of an armoured vehicle behind a corner, the sound of a bullet as it flew past her head, the screams and cries multiplying. Empty though the parking area in front of the building was, she felt the presence of hundreds of bodies pressing in from all sides. Her throat tightened up. Slowly, she released the pent-up air in her aching lungs.

A moment later, she entered through the glass doors and looked around, her expression composed. Custom-made chandeliers, polished brass lamps, marble floors: the same gaudy interior found in similar establishments everywhere. No signs of collective memory. No shared knowledge of history. The entire place had been decorated anew, the windows covered with silvery curtains, the past replaced by glitz and glam.

There was a walk-through metal detector and a conveyor belt at the entrance, and next to it three hefty guards. Security levels had been raised across the city since terrorist attacks targeting high-end hotels in the Middle East. Leila placed her handbag on the conveyor belt and passed through the metal detector, swaying her hips. The guards leered at her, each an open book. As she picked up her handbag from the opposite end of the belt she leaned over to give them a full view of her cleavage.

Behind the reception desk stood a young woman with a genuine tan and a fake smile. A flicker of bemusement crossed her face as Leila approached. For a split second, she was unsure whether

Leila was what she thought she was, or a foreign guest bent on having a wild night out in Istanbul, looking for an unforgettable memory to share with friends back home. If the latter, she'd keep smiling; if the former, she'd start frowning.

As soon as Leila spoke, the woman's expression changed from polite curiosity to outright contempt.

'Good evening, darling,' Leila said cheerily.

'How can I assist you?' The receptionist's voice was as cold as her gaze.

Tapping her fingernails on the glass countertop, Leila gave the room number.

'Whom shall I say is calling?'

'Say it's the lady he's been waiting for his whole life.'

The receptionist's eyes narrowed but she said nothing. Quickly, she dialled the number. A short conversation ensued between her and the man at the end of the line. She hung up, and said, without looking at Leila, 'He's expecting you.'

'Merci, darling.'

Leila sauntered towards the lifts and pressed the up button. An elderly American couple, going to their room, also got on and greeted her in that relaxed way Americans of a certain generation had. For them the night was ending. For Leila, it was just beginning.

Seventh floor. Long, well-lit corridors, harlequin-patterned carpets. Leila stood outside the penthouse apartment, took a deep breath and knocked on the door. A man opened it. He did indeed look like the actor in the talking car. There was a hint of redness around his eyes, which were blinking too fast, and she wondered if he had been crying. In his hand he held a phone, clutching it tightly as if he were afraid of letting it go. He had been speaking with someone. Was it his sweetheart? Her gut told her it must have been – only not the person he was about to marry.

'Oh, hi . . . I was expecting you. Come in, please.'

He was slurring a bit. A half-empty bottle of whisky sat on the walnut table, confirming Leila's suspicion.

He nodded towards the sofa. 'Do sit down. What can I offer you?'

She took off her scarf and tossed it on the bed. 'Do you have tequila, darling?'

'Tequila? No, but I can call room service if you'd like.'

How polite he was – and how broken. He didn't have the courage to stand up to his father, nor did he want to forgo the comforts he was accustomed to, and for this he probably hated himself, and would do so for the rest of his life.

She waved her hand. 'No need. I'll have whatever you're having.'

Half turning his back to her, he brought the phone to his lips and said, 'She's here. I'll call you later. Yes, of course. Don't worry.'

Whoever he was talking to had been listening to them all along.

'Wait.' Leila put out a hand.

He stared at her, unsure.

'Don't mind me. Keep talking,' she said. 'I'll have a smoke on the balcony.'

Without giving him time to object, Leila stepped outside. The view was quite something. Soft lights spilled from the last ferry boats, a cruise ship passed in the distance, and down by the wharf she could see a boat with a large illuminated sign announcing it was selling köfte and mackerel. How she wished she could be there now, perched on one of those tiny stools, tucking into a filled pitta, instead of being up here, on the seventh floor of a luxury hotel, in the company of despair.

About ten minutes later the double doors opened and he joined her, carrying two glasses of whisky. He handed one to her. They sat next to each other on a chaise longue, their knees touching, and sipped their drinks. It was top-notch single malt whisky.

'I heard your father was quite religious. Does he know you drink?' Leila asked.

He frowned. 'My father knows jackshit about me!'

He drank slowly, but with determination. If he kept going at this rate he was in for a terrible hangover in the morning.

'You know it's the fifth time he's done this in a month. He keeps arranging women for me, sending me to a different hotel each time. He covers the expenses. And then I have to receive these poor girls and spend the night with them. It's embarrassing.' He swallowed. 'My father waits a few days, realizes I'm not *cured*, and organizes another rendezvous. It will go on like this until the wedding, I guess.'

'What if you say no?'

'I lose everything,' he said, narrowing his eyes at the thought.

Leila downed her drink. She stood up, took the glass from his hand, put it on the floor next to hers. He stared at her – nervous.

'Look, darling. I understand you don't want to do this. I also understand there's someone you love and you'd rather be with that *person*.' She stressed the last word, avoiding mention of gender. 'Give that person another call now, and invite them here. Spend the night together in this gorgeous room, talk it through, and try to find a solution.'

'What about you?'

'I'm leaving. But you shouldn't tell anyone. Neither your father nor my fixer can know. We'll say we had a hot night. You were amazing, number-one love machine. I'll get my money, you'll get a bit of peace . . . but you need to figure things out. I'm sorry to say this, this wedding seems insane. It's not right to rope your fiancée into this mess.'

'Oh, she'd be happy, no matter what. She and her entire family are vultures, preying on our money.' He halted, realizing he might have said too much. Leaning forward, he kissed her hand. 'Thank you. I owe you one.'

'You are welcome,' Leila said as she headed towards the door. 'By the way, tell your father I was wearing a gold-sequinned dress. For some reason, it's important.'

Leila walked out of the hotel quietly, hiding behind a group of Spanish tourists. The receptionist, busy checking in new guests, didn't see her leave.

Back on the streets, she took a lungful of air. The moon was a waxing crescent, pale as ash. She realized she had left her scarf upstairs. For a moment she considered going back, but she didn't want to disturb him. She loved that scarf, dammit, it was pure silk.

She placed a cigarette between her lips, fumbled in her bag for the lighter. It wasn't there. D/Ali's Zippo was missing.

'Do you need a light?'

She lifted her head. A car had drawn up to the kerb and stopped just ahead of her. A silver Mercedes. Its rear windows were tinted, its lights turned off. Through the half-open window a man was watching her, a lighter in his hand.

She walked towards him, slowly.

'Good evening, angel.'

'Good evening to you.'

He lit her cigarette, his gaze lingering on her breasts. He wore a jade velvet jacket and, underneath it, a turtleneck in a darker green.

'Merci, darling.'

The other door opened and the driver stepped out. He was thinner than his friend, the shoulders of his jacket hanging loose. Bald-headed, cheeks sunken and sallow. Both men had the same arched eyebrows above close-set, small, dark brown eyes. They must be related, Leila thought. Cousins, perhaps. But her more immediate impression had been of how unhappy they seemed – especially for men so young.

'Hi,' said the driver curtly. 'That's a pretty dress.'

Something seemed to pass between the two men, a flicker of acknowledgement, as if they recognized her, even though she was certain they were total strangers. While Leila could forget names, she always remembered faces.

178

'We were wondering if you'd like a ride with us,' said the driver.

'A ride?'

'Yes, you know . . .'

'Depends.'

He offered her a price.

'Both of you? No way.'

'Only my friend,' said the driver. 'It's his birthday today, my present to him.'

Leila thought that was a bit odd, but she had seen odder things in this city and didn't mind. 'You sure you're not in?'

'No, I don't like . . .' He left the sentence unfinished. Leila wondered what it was exactly that he didn't like. Women in general or just her? She asked for twice the sum.

The driver looked away. 'Fine.'

Leila was surprised that he didn't try to haggle. It was rare for a transaction to be completed in this city without a round of bargaining.

'You coming?' the other man asked, opening the door from inside.

She hesitated. If Bitter Ma found out, she would be incandescent with rage. Leila rarely, if ever, accepted a job without her knowledge. But the money seemed too good to turn down, especially now that the bills were mounting for Jameelah, who had been diagnosed with lupus and was suffering from a flare-up. In a single night Leila would get two hefty payments, one from the father of the young man in the hotel, and now this.

'One hour, no more. And I'll tell you where to pull over.'

'Deal.'

She got into the car, planting herself into the back seat. She rolled down the window, breathing in the crisp, clean air. There were moments when the city felt fresh, as though washed by a bucketful of water thrown at it by a helpful hand.

She saw a cigar box on the dashboard and, on top of it, three porcelain angels with long gowns. She watched them for a moment, distracted.

179

The car was speeding now.

'Take the next right,' Leila said.

The man glanced at her in the rear-view mirror, something at once frightening and unbearably sad in his eyes.

A shiver ran down her spine. She sensed, too late, that he would not listen to her.

Remaining Eight Seconds

The last thing Leila remembered was the taste of home-made strawberry cake.

When she was growing up in Van, celebrations had been reserved for two revered causes: the nation and the religion. Her parents had commemorated the birth of the Prophet Mohammed and the birth of the Turkish Republic, but did not consider the birth of an ordinary human being sufficient cause for festivity every year. Leila had never asked them why that was. It was only after she had left home for Istanbul and discovered that other people seemed to have received a cake or a gift on their special days that the question hit her. Since then, on every 6 January she had done her best to have fun, no matter what. And if ever she came across someone partying too wildly, she did not judge them; who knew – just like her, they too might be overcompensating for a childhood deprived of party hats.

Every year on her birthday her friends had thrown a party for her, with cupcakes, swirling decorations and lots of balloons. The five of them: Sabotage Sinan, Nostalgia Nalan, Jameelah, Zaynab122 and Hollywood Humeyra.

Leila did not think one could expect to have more than five friends. Just one was a stroke of luck. If you were blessed, then two or three, and if you were born under a sky filled with the brightest stars, then a quintet – more than enough for a lifetime. It wasn't wise to hunt for more, lest in doing so you jeopardize those you counted on.

She had often thought five was a special number. The Torah contained five books. Jesus had suffered five fatal wounds. Islam had five pillars of faith. King David had killed Goliath with five pebbles. In Buddhism there were five paths, while Shiva revealed five faces, looking out in five different directions. Chinese philosophy revolved around five elements: water, fire, wood, metal, earth. There were five universally accepted tastes: sweet, salty, sour, bitter and umami. Human perception depended on five basic senses: hearing, sight, touch, smell, taste; even though scientists claimed there were more, each with a baffling name, it was the original five that everyone knew.

On what was to be her last birthday, her friends had settled on a rich menu: lamb stew with aubergine puree, börek with spinach and feta cheese, kidney beans with spicy pastrami, stuffed green peppers and a little jar of fresh caviar. The cake was a surprise, supposedly, but Leila had overheard them discussing it; the walls in the flat were thinner than the slices of pastrami, and, after decades of heavy smoking and even heavier drinking, Nalan rasped when she whispered, her voice husky like sandpaper scraping on metal.

Strawberry cream with fluffy, fairy-tale-pink icing. That's what they had planned. Leila was not a fan of pink. She liked fuchsia better – a colour with personality. Even the name melted on the tongue, mouth-wateringly sweet and punchy. Pink was fuchsia without grit; pale and lifeless as a bedsheet worn thin from too much washing. Maybe she should ask for a fuchsia cake.

'So how many candles are we putting on it?' Hollywood Humeyra asked.

'Thirty-one, darling,' Leila said.

'Sure, thirty-one my arse.' Nostalgia Nalan chuckled.

If friendship meant rituals, they had them by the truckload. In addition to birthdays, they celebrated Victory Day, Atatürk Commemoration, Youth and Sports Day, National Sovereignty and Children's Day, Republic Day, Cabotage Day, St Valentine's Day, New Year's Eve ... at every opportunity, they would dine together, feasting on delicacies they could barely afford. Nostalgia Nalan prepared her favourite drink, Pata Pata Boom Boom – a cocktail she had learned to mix while flirting with the barman in Karavan. Pomegranate juice, lime juice, vodka, crushed mint, cardamom seeds and a generous splash of whisky. Those of them who consumed alcohol got nicely sloshed, their cheeks turning a vivid red. The strict teetotallers drank Fanta orange instead. They spent the rest of the night watching black-and-white movies. Squeezing on to the sofa, they watched one film after another, utterly engrossed and silent, except for the occasional sigh and gasp. Those old Hollywood stars and those old Turkish stars were masters at captivating an audience. Leila and her friends knew their lines by heart.

She had never told her friends this, not in so many words, but they were her safety net. Every time she stumbled or keeled over, they were there for her, supporting her or softening the impact of the fall. On nights when she was mistreated by a client, she would still find the strength to hold herself up, knowing that her friends, with their very presence, would come with ointment for her scrapes and bruises; and on days when she wallowed in self-pity, her chest cracking open, they would gently pull her up and breathe life into her lungs.

Now, as her brain came to a standstill, and all memories dissolved into a wall of fog, thick as sorrow, the very last thing she saw in her mind was the bright pink birthday cake. They had spent that evening chatting and laughing, as if nothing could ever pull them apart and life were merely a spectacle, exciting and unsettling, but without any real danger involved, like being invited to someone else's dream. On TV, Rita Hayworth had tossed her hair and wiggled her hips, her gown falling to the floor in a silken rustle. Tilting her head towards the camera, she had given that famous smile of hers, the smile many around the world had mistaken for lust. But not them. Dear old Rita could not fool them. They never failed to recognize a sad woman when they saw one.

PART TWO

The Body

The Morgue

The morgue was located at the rear of the hospital, in the north-eastern corner of the basement. The corridor leading to it was painted a pale Prozac green and was noticeably colder than the rest of the building, as though exposed to draughts day and night. Inside, the acrid smell of chemicals hovered in the air. Around here there was little colour – chalk white, steel grey, ice blue and the dark, rusty red of congealed blood.

Wiping his palms on the sides of his coat, the medical examiner – a gaunt man with a slight stoop, a high domed forehead and obsidian-black eyes – glanced at the latest arrival. Another homicide victim. An expression of insouciance crossed his face. Over the years he had seen far too many of them – young and old, rich and poor, those accidentally hit by a stray bullet and those gunned down in cold blood. Every day new bodies arrived. He knew precisely when in the year casualties would soar and when they would tail off. There were more killings in the summer than in the winter; May to August was peak season for aggravated sexual assault and attempted murder in Istanbul. Come October, along with the temperature, crime dropped dramatically.

He had his own theory as to why, and was convinced it all had to do with people's dietary patterns. In autumn, shoals of bonito headed south from the Black Sea towards the Aegean, swimming so close to the surface one might think they were exhausted from the forced migration and the constant threat of trawlers, and just wanted to be caught once and for all. In restaurants, hotels, work-place cafeterias and homes, serotonin levels rose and stress levels plummeted as people consumed this delicious fatty fish. The outcome was fewer violations of law. But the lovely bonito could only do so much; soon crime rates would surge again. In a land where justice often came late, if it came at all, many citizens sought their own revenge, reciprocating hurt with bigger hurt. *Two eyes for an eye, a jaw for a tooth.* Not that all crime was planned – most was committed on the spur of the moment, in fact. A glance perceived as dirty could be grounds for manslaughter. A word misunderstood could be an excuse for bloodshed. Istanbul made killing easy, and dying even easier.

The medical examiner had inspected the body, drained the fluids and cut open the chest, making an incision from each collarbone to the breastbone. He had spent a long time examining the injuries and had noted the tattoo above the woman's right ankle and identified the patch of discoloured skin on her back – scarring clearly caused by a chemical burn from a caustic substance, most likely an acid. He guessed it was a couple of decades old. He wondered how it had happened. Had she been attacked from behind, or was it a freak accident – and if that were the case, why would she have had this type of acid in her possession?

A complete internal analysis not being required, he finally sat down to write a cursory report. For any further details, he consulted the police account attached to the file.

Name/Surname: Leyla Akarsu
Middle Names: Afife Kamile
Address: Hairy Kafka Street, 70/8. Pera, Istanbul.

The body is that of a well-developed, well-nourished Caucasian woman, measuring five feet seven and weighing 135 pounds. Age appears to be inconsistent with that stated on her ID of 32. It is likely she is somewhere between 40 and 45. An examination has been performed to determine the cause and manner of death.

Clothing: a gold-sequinned dress (torn), high-heeled shoes, lace underwear. A clutch bag containing an ID card, a lipstick, a notebook, a fountain pen and house keys. No money, no jewellery (might have been stolen).

The time of death is estimated to be between 3.30 a.m. and 5.30 a.m. No sign of sexual intercourse detected. The victim was beaten with a heavy (blunt) instrument and strangled to death after being knocked unconscious.

He paused his typing. The marks on the woman's neck troubled him. Next to the imprints of the murderer's fingers, there was a reddish stripe that seemed to have been made post-mortem. He wondered if she had worn a necklace that had been yanked off. Not that it mattered any more. Like all the unclaimed dead, she, too, would be consigned to the Cemetery of the Companionless.

No Islamic burial rituals would be performed for this woman. Nor of any other religion, for that matter. Her body would not be washed by the next of kin; her hair would not be braided into three separate braids; her hands would not be placed gently over her heart in a gesture of eternal peace; her eyelids would not be closed to make sure that from now on her gaze was turned inward. In the graveyard, there would be no pall-bearers or mourners, no imam leading the prayers and not one professional weeper hired to cry and wail louder than everyone else. She would be buried the way all the undesirables were – silently and swiftly.

Afterwards, she would probably have no visitors. Perhaps an old neighbour or a niece – one distant enough not to mind the shame brought upon the family – would show up a few times, but eventually the visits would cease. In just a few months' time, with no marker or stone, the woman's grave would fully blend in with its surroundings. In less than a decade, no one would be able to locate her whereabouts. She would become yet another number in the Cemetery of the Companionless, yet another pitiable soul whose life echoed the opening of every Anatolian tale: *Once there was, once there wasn't . . .*

The medical examiner hunched over his desk, his brow furrowed in concentration. He had no desire to learn who this woman was or what kind of a life she may have led. Even when he was new to the job, the stories of the victims were of little concern to him. What really interested him was death itself. Not as a theological concept or a philosophical question but as a subject of scientific enquiry. It never ceased to amaze him how little progress humanity had made with regards to funerary rites. A species that had dreamed up digital wristwatches, discovered DNA and developed MRI machines stalled miserably when it came to taking care of their dead. Things were hardly more advanced today than they had been a thousand years ago. True, those rolling in money and imagination seemed to have a few more choices than the rest; they could blast their ashes into outer space, if they so wished. Or freeze themselves – in the hope that a hundred years from now they would be revived. But for the majority of people the options were pretty limited: to be buried or cremated. That was about it. If there was a God up there, He must be laughing His head off at a human race capable of making atomic bombs and building artificial intelligence, but still uncomfortable with their own mortality and unable to sort out what to do with their dead. How pathetic it was to try to relegate death to the periphery of life when death was at the centre of everything.

He had worked with cadavers for so long, preferring their silent company to the endless chatter of the living. Yet the more bodies he inspected, the more intrigued he was by the process of death. When exactly did a living being turn into a corpse? As a young graduate fresh out of medical school, he had had a clear answer, but he wasn't so sure these days. It seemed to him now that, just as a stone dropped into a pond sent ripples out in concentric circles, the cessation of life generated a series of changes, both material and immaterial, and death should only be acknowledged when the final changes had been completed. In the medical journals he had been following fastidiously he had come across ground-breaking research that had excited him. Researchers at various world-renowned institutions had observed persistent brain activity in people who had just died; in some cases this had lasted for only a few minutes. In others, for as much as ten minutes and thirty-eight seconds. What happened during that time? Did the dead remember the past, and, if so, which parts of it, and in what order? How could the mind condense an entire life into the time it took to boil a kettle?

Successive research had also shown that more than a thousand genes continued to function in cadavers days after the person had been pronounced dead. All these findings fascinated him. Perhaps a person's thoughts survived longer than his heart, his dreams longer than his pancreas, his wishes longer than his gall-bladder . . . If that were true, shouldn't human beings be considered *semi-alive* as long as the memories that shaped them were still rippling, still part of this world? Though he might not know the answers, not yet, he valued the quest for them. He would never tell this to anyone, because they wouldn't understand, but he took great pleasure in working in the morgue.

A knock at the door jolted him from his thoughts.

'Come in.'

The orderly, Kameel Effendi, walked in, limping slightly. He was a good-natured, gentle soul, and after all these years a permanent fixture in the hospital. Although initially hired to do basic menial work, he performed whatever task was needed on any given day, including stitching up the odd patient when the emergency room was short of a surgeon.

'*Selamün aleyküm*, doctor.'

'*Aleyküm selam*, Kameel Effendi.'

'Is this the prostitute the nurses were whispering about?'

'Yes, it is. They brought her in just before noon.'

'Poor thing, may Allah forgive whatever sin she might have committed.'

The medical examiner smiled a smile that didn't quite reach his eyes. '*Might?* That's a funny thing to say, considering who she was. Her entire life was full of sin.'

'Well, perhaps that's so . . . but who knows who deserves heaven more – this unlucky woman or the zealot who thinks he is the only chosen of God.'

'Well, well, well, Kameel Effendi! I didn't know you had a soft spot for whores. You'd better watch out, though. I don't mind, but there are plenty of people out there who'd be ready to give you a good hiding if they heard you talk like that.'

The old man stood still, silent. He looked at the corpse with forlorn eyes, as though he had known her once. She seemed to be at peace. Most of the dead bodies he had come across over the years had been this way, and he often wondered whether they were relieved to be done with the struggles and misunderstandings of the world.

'Any family, doctor?'

'Nope. Her parents are in Van. They have been informed, but they refuse to claim her. Typical.'

'Any siblings?'

The medical examiner consulted his notes. 'She doesn't seem to have any . . . oh, I see, one brother, dead.'

'There's no one else?'

'Apparently there's an aunt who's unwell . . . so she won't do. And, hmm, there is an another aunt and an uncle —'

'Maybe one of them would help?'

'Not a chance. They both said they don't want to have anything to do with her.'

Stroking his moustache, Kameel Effendi shifted on his feet.

'Okay, I'm almost done here,' said the medical examiner. 'You can take her to the cemetery, the usual one.'

'Doctor, I was thinking about that . . . There's a group of people in the courtyard. They've been waiting for hours. They seem devastated.'

'Who are they?'

'Her friends.'

'Friends,' the medical examiner repeated, as if the word were new to him. He had little interest in them. The friends of a streetwalker could only be other streetwalkers, people he would probably see here one day, lying on the same steel table.

Kameel Effendi coughed faintly. 'I wish we could give the body to them.'

At this the other man frowned, a hard gleam in his eyes. 'You know perfectly well we are not authorized to do that. We can release bodies only to their immediate family.'

'I know, but —' Kameel Effendi paused. 'If there's no family, why not let the friends sort out the funeral?'

'Our state does not permit that, and for good reason. We'd never be able to trace who is who. There are all kinds of lunatics out there: organ thieves, psychopaths . . . it would be pandemonium.' He checked the old man's face, not trusting he understood the meaning of the last word.

'Yes, but in cases like this, what's the harm?'

'Look, we didn't make the rules. We just follow them. *Don't try to bring new customs to an old village.* It's hard enough to run this place as it is.'

The old man raised his chin in acknowledgement. 'All right, I understand. I'll give the cemetery a call. Just to make sure they've got space.'

'Yes, good idea, check with them.' The medical examiner pulled out a pile of documents from a folder, grabbed a pen and tapped it against his cheek. He stamped and signed each page. 'Tell them you'll send the body this afternoon.'

It was a formality, though. They both knew that while other graveyards in the city might be fully booked years in advance, there was always space available in the Cemetery of the Companionless – the loneliest graveyard in Istanbul.

The Five

Outside in the courtyard, five figures sat squeezed side by side on a wooden bench. Their shadows stretched across the paving stones in contrasting shapes and sizes. Having arrived just past noon, one after the other, they had been waiting here for hours. Now the sun was slowly descending and the light streamed slantwise through the chestnut trees. Every few minutes, one of them stood up and trudged wearily towards the building to speak to a manager or a doctor or a nurse – whomever they could get hold of. It was of no use. No matter how much they insisted, they had not been able to get permission to see their friend's body – let alone bury it.

Still they refused to leave. Their expressions carved by grief, as stiff as seasoned wood, they continued to wait. The other people in the courtyard, visitors and staff, shot questioning glances in their direction, whispering among themselves. A teenager sitting next to her mother watched their every move with a curiosity that was half contemptuous. An elderly headscarved woman scowled at them with the disdain she reserved for all oddballs and outsiders. Leila's friends were out of place here, but then again they didn't seem to belong anywhere.

Just as the evening prayer rose from a nearby mosque, a woman with a short, neat hairstyle and a peculiarly upright gait marched briskly out of the building towards them. She was wearing a khaki pencil skirt that fell below the knee, a matching pinstripe jacket and a large brooch in the shape of an orchid. She was the director of patient care services.

'There's no need for you to be here,' the director said without looking anyone in the eye. 'Your friend . . . the doctor has examined the body and written an official report. You may ask for a copy, if you wish. It'll be ready in about a week. But now you must leave – please. You are making everyone uncomfortable.'

'Don't waste your breath. We are not going anywhere,' said Nostalgia Nalan and, unlike the others, who had stood up when they saw the director, she remained seated as though to prove her point. Her eyes were a warm brown and almond-shaped – but that's not what people usually noticed when they looked at her. They saw her long polished nails, broad shoulders, leather trousers, silicone-implanted breasts. They saw a brazen transsexual staring back at them. Just as the director did now.

'Excuse me?' said the woman, sounding annoyed.

Gingerly, Nalan opened her handbag and took out a cigarette from a silver case, but, despite desperately needing one, she did not light it. 'What I'm saying is, we won't leave until we see our Leila. We'll camp out here if we have to.'

The director arched her brows. 'I think you may have misheard me, so let me be clear: there's no need for you to wait – and there's nothing you can do for your friend. You are not family.'

'We were closer to her than family,' Sabotage Sinan said, a tremble in his voice.

Nalan swallowed. There was a lump in her throat that wouldn't go away. Since she heard the news of Leila's murder she had not shed a single tear. Something blocked the pain – an anger hardening the edges of her every gesture and every word.

'Look, that has nothing to do with my institution,' the director said. 'The point is, your friend has been transferred to a cemetery. She has probably been buried already.'

'Wha . . . What did you just say?' Nalan rose to her feet slowly, as if waking from a dream. 'Why didn't you tell us?'

'Legally, we have no obligation to –'

'Legally? What about *humanly*? We could have gone with her if we'd known. And where did you self-loathing idiots take her, exactly?'

The director winced, her eyes widening for a second. 'First of all, you cannot talk to me like that. Secondly, I'm not authorized to reveal –'

'Then go and bring someone who is fucking authorized.'

'I will not be spoken to in this manner,' the director said, her jaw visibly quivering. 'I'm afraid I'm going to have to ask security to remove you from the premises.'

'I'm afraid I'm going to have to smack you in the face,' Nalan said, but the others held her hands and pulled her back.

'We need to be calm,' whispered Jameelah to Nalan – though it was not clear whether she heard the warning.

The director turned sharply on her kitten heels. She was about to walk off when she stopped and gave them a sidelong scowl. 'There are cemeteries reserved for such people. I'm surprised that you didn't already know that.'

'Bitch,' Nalan murmured under her breath. Her voice, raspy and thick, nevertheless carried – and of course she had wanted the director to hear what she thought of her.

A few minutes later, Leila's friends were escorted by security guards out of the hospital grounds. A crowd had gathered on the pavement, watching the incident with riveted eyes and amused smiles, proving once again that Istanbul was, and would always remain, a city of impromptu spectacles and ready-made, eager spectators. Meanwhile, no one paid any attention to the old man following the group a few feet behind.

After the unruly five had been left by the security guards at a corner far away from the hospital, Kameel Effendi approached them. 'Forgive me for intruding. May I have a word with you?'

One by one, Leila's friends turned their heads and stared at the old man.

'What do you want, *amca*?' said Zaynab122.

Her tone was suspicious, though not altogether unkind. Behind her tortoiseshell-framed glasses her eyes were red and swollen.

'I work at the hospital,' said the orderly, leaning in close. 'I saw you waiting there . . . my condolences for your loss.'

Not expecting to hear any words of sympathy from a stranger, Leila's friends stood motionless for a moment.

'Tell us, have you seen the body?' asked Zaynab122. Her voice dropped as she added, 'Do you think she . . . suffered a lot?'

'I saw her, yes. I believe it was a quick death.' Kameel Effendi nodded, trying to convince himself as much as the others. 'I'm the one who arranged for her to be taken to the cemetery. The one in Kilyos – I'm not sure whether you've heard of it, not many people have. They call it the Cemetery of the Companionless. Not a nice name, if you ask me. There are no headstones there, just wooden planks with numbers. But I can tell you where she's buried. You have a right to know.'

So saying, the old man produced a piece of paper and a pen. The backs of his hands were covered with bulging veins and age spots. Hurriedly, he scribbled a number in his sloppy writing.

'Here, keep this. Go and visit your friend's grave. Plant nice flowers. Pray for her soul. I heard she was from Van. So was my late wife. She died in the earthquake, back in 1976. For days we dug through the rubble, but we couldn't find her. After two full months, bulldozers flattened the whole area. People used to say to me, *Don't be so sad, Kameel Effendi. What difference does it make in the end? She's buried, aren't we all going to join her six feet under someday?* Maybe they meant well, but God knows how I hated them for saying such things. Funerals are for the living, that's for sure. It's important to organize a decent burial. Otherwise you can never heal inside, don't you think? Anyway, don't mind me, I'm just blabbering. I guess . . . I wanted to tell you, I know what it feels like not to be able to say goodbye to a loved one.'

'That must have been very hard for you,' said Hollywood Humeyra. Normally extremely talkative, she seemed to have run out of words.

'Grief is a swallow,' he said. 'One day you wake up and you think it's gone, but it's only migrated to some other place,

197

warming its feathers. Sooner or later, it will return and perch in your heart again.'

One by one the orderly shook their hands and wished them well. Leila's friends watched him limp away until he rounded the corner of the hospital building and disappeared through the large gate. Only then did Nostalgia Nalan, this big-boned and broad-shouldered six-foot-two-inch-tall woman, sit down on the edge of the pavement, pull her legs up to her chest and weep like a child abandoned in a foreign land.

No one spoke.

After a while, Humeyra placed her hand on the small of Nalan's back. 'Come on, my dear. Let's get out of here. We need to sort through Leila's things. We must feed Mr Chaplin. Leila would be terribly upset if we didn't take care of her cat. The poor animal must be starving.'

Biting her lower lip, Nalan quickly wiped her eyes with the back of her hand. She stood up, towering over the others, though her legs felt weak, rubbery. There was a dull, pounding ache in her temples. She gestured to her friends to go ahead without her.

'You sure?' Zaynab122 looked up with concern.

Nalan nodded. 'Sure, honey. I'll catch up with you later.'

They listened to her – as they always did.

Left alone, Nalan lit the cigarette she had been craving since early afternoon but had stopped herself from having because of Humeyra's asthma. She took a deep drag and held it in her lungs before exhaling a spiral of smoke. *You are not family*, the director had said. What did she know? Goddamn nothing. She knew not a single thing about Leila or any of them.

Nostalgia Nalan believed there were two kinds of families in this world: relatives formed the blood family; and friends, the water family. If your blood family happened to be nice and caring, you could count your lucky stars and make the most of it; and if not, there was still hope; things could take a turn for the better once you were old enough to leave your home sour home.

As for the water family, this was formed much later in life, and was, to a large extent, of your own making. While it was true that nothing could take the place of a loving, happy blood family, in the absence of one, a good water family could wash away the hurt and pain collected inside like black soot. It was therefore possible for your friends to have a treasured place in your heart, and occupy a bigger space than all your kin combined. But those who had never experienced what it felt like to be spurned by their own relatives would not understand this truth in a million years. They would never know that there were times when water ran thicker than blood.

Nalan turned around and looked at the hospital one last time. The morgue could not be seen from this far, but she shivered as if she could feel the chill of it in her bones. It wasn't that death scared her. Nor did she believe in an afterlife where the wrongs of this world would be miraculously righted. The only professed atheist among Leila's friends, Nalan saw the flesh – and not some abstract concept of the soul – as eternal. Molecules mixed with soil, providing nutrition for plants, those plants were then devoured by animals, and animals by humans, and so, contrary to the assumptions of the majority, the human body was immortal, on a never-ending journey through the cycles of nature. What more could one possibly want from the hereafter?

But Nalan had always assumed that she would die first. In every group of old and tested friends there was one person who knew instinctively that they would leave before the others. And Nalan had been certain that that person was her. All those oestrogen supplements and testosterone-blocking treatments and post-op painkillers, not to mention long years of heavy smoking, unhealthy eating and excessive drinking . . . It had to be her. Not Leila, who was full of life and compassion. It was a source of endless surprise – and slight annoyance – to Nalan that Istanbul had not hardened Leila into cynicism and bitterness the way she knew it had hardened her.

A chilly wind was blowing from the north-east, working its way inland, stirring the sewage fumes. She held herself tense against the cold. The ache in her temples had shifted, spreading across her chest and drilling into her ribcage, as if a hand were squeezing her heart. Far ahead the rush-hour traffic was clogging the arteries of the city, a city which now resembled an ailing giant animal, its breathing painfully slow and ragged. In contrast, Nalan's breathing was fast and furious, her features shaped by a burning indignation. What deepened Nalan's sense of helplessness was not only Leila's sudden death, or the brutal and horrific way it had happened, but the absolute lack of justice in everything. Life was unfair, and now she realized death was even more so.

Ever since childhood Nalan's blood had boiled to witness someone — anyone — being treated cruelly or unfairly. She wasn't naive enough to expect fairness from a world so *crooked*, as D/Ali used to say, but she believed that everyone had a right to a certain share of dignity. And inside your dignity, as if it were a patch of soil that belonged to no one else, you would sow a seed of hope. A tiny germ that one day, somehow, might sprout and blossom. As far as Nostalgia Nalan was concerned, that small seed was all there was worth fighting for.

She took out the piece of paper the old man had given them and read his scrawled note: *Kilyos. Kimsesizler Mezarliği, 705–*. The final number, a scrawly 2 upon closer inspection, crammed on to the bottom of the page, was barely legible. The handwriting was not the neatest. With the fountain pen she carried in her clutch bag, Nalan went over the whole thing. Then she carefully folded the piece of paper and put it back in her pocket.

It was not fair that they had dumped Leila in the Cemetery of the Companionless when she wasn't companionless at all. Leila had friends. Lifelong, loyal, loving friends. She might not have had much else, but this she surely had.

'The old man was right,' Nalan thought. 'Leila deserves a decent burial.'

She flicked the cigarette stub on to the pavement and crushed the burning end under her boot. A slow fog was creeping up from the harbour, obscuring the shisha cafes and bars at the edge of the waterfront. Somewhere in this city of millions Leila's murderer was having supper or watching TV, empty of conscience, human only in name.

Nalan wiped her eyes, but the tears kept returning. Her mascara was running down her cheeks. Two women passed by, each pushing a buggy. They gave her a surprised, pitying look and turned their heads away. Almost instantly Nalan's face took on a pinched expression. She was used to being shunned and despised simply because of how she looked and who she was. That was fine, but she couldn't bear for anyone to pity her or her friends.

As she set off at a brisk pace, Nalan had already made up her mind. She would fight back, the way she had always done. Against social conventions, judgements, prejudices . . . against silent hatred, which filled the lives of these people like an odourless gas, she would fight. No one had the right to cast aside Leila's body as though she didn't matter and never had. She, Nostalgia Nalan, would make sure her old friend was treated properly and with dignity.

This was not over. Not yet. Tonight she would talk to the others and together they would find a way to give Leila a funeral — and not just any funeral, but the finest funeral this manic old city had ever seen.

This Manic Old City

Istanbul was an illusion. A magician's trick gone wrong.

Istanbul was a dream that existed solely in the minds of hashish eaters. In truth, there was no Istanbul. There were multiple *Istanbuls* – struggling, competing, clashing, each perceiving that, in the end, only one could survive.

There was, for instance, an ancient Istanbul designed to be crossed on foot or by boat – the city of itinerant dervishes, fortune-tellers, matchmakers, seafarers, cotton fluffers, rug beaters and porters with wicker baskets on their backs . . . There was modern Istanbul – an urban sprawl overrun with cars and motorcycles whizzing back and forth, construction trucks laden with building materials for more shopping centres, skyscrapers, industrial sites . . . Imperial Istanbul versus plebeian Istanbul; global Istanbul versus parochial Istanbul; cosmopolitan Istanbul versus philistine Istanbul; heretical Istanbul versus pious Istanbul; macho Istanbul versus a feminine Istanbul that adopted Aphrodite – goddess of desire and also of strife – as its symbol and protector . . . Then there was the Istanbul of those who had left long ago, sailing to faraway ports. For them this city would always be a metropolis made of memories, myths and messianic longings, forever elusive like a lover's face receding in the mist.

All these Istanbuls lived and breathed inside one another, like matryoshka dolls that had come to life. But even if a wicked wizard managed to separate them and put them side by side, nowhere in this vast line-up would he find a part of the city more desired, demonized and denounced than one particular neighbourhood: Pera. A hub of commotion and chaos, for centuries this area was associated with liberalism, debauchery and Westernization – the three forces that led young Turkish men astray. Its name, from the

Greek, meant 'on the further side', or simply 'across' or 'beyond'. Across the Golden Horn. Beyond established norms. This, as it once was known, was Peran en Sykais – 'On the Opposite Shore'. And it was where, until the day before, Tequila Leila had made her home.

After D/Ali's death, Leila had refused to move out of the flat. Every corner was full of his laughter, his voice. The rent was high but she just about managed it. Late at night, back from work, she would wash herself under the rusted shower head that never delivered enough hot water, scrubbing her skin hard. Then, red and raw as a newborn, she would sit in a chair by the window and watch the morning break over the city. D/Ali's memory would envelop her, soft and comforting like a blanket. Many afternoons she would wake up, cramped and sore, having fallen asleep in this way, with Mr Chaplin curled up by her feet.

Hairy Kafka Street ran down between dilapidated buildings and small, dingy shops specializing in lighting fixtures. In the evenings, when all the lamps were turned on, the area acquired a sepia glow, as though it belonged to another century. Once, this place had been called Fur-Lined Kaftan Street – although a group of historians insisted it had been Fair-Haired Concubine Street. Either way, when the municipality, as part of an ambitious gentrification project, decided to renew the street signs in the area, the officer in charge, finding the name too clunky, shortened it to Kaftan Street. And so it was known until one morning, after a night of gale-force winds, a letter fell off and it became Kafta Street. But that, too, didn't stick for long. A literature student, with the help of a permanent marker, changed *Kafta* to *Kafka*. Fans of the author hailed the new moniker; others had no idea what it meant but embraced it nonetheless, liking its sound.

A month later, an ultra-nationalist newspaper published a story about secret foreign influence in Istanbul, claiming that this clear homage to a Jewish writer was part of a sinister plan to eradicate local Muslim culture. A petition was circulated to return the street's name to its original, despite the unresolved debate as to what that might have been. A banner was hung between two balconies and it read: *Love It or Leave It: One Great Nation*. Washed by the rain and bleached by the sun, the banner flapped in Istanbul's *lodos* – south-western wind – until one afternoon it snapped its strings and flew off, an angry kite in the sky.

By then the reactionaries had moved on to other battles. The campaign was forgotten as swiftly as it had materialized. In time, as with all else in this schizophrenic city, the old and the new, the factual and the fictitious, the real and the surreal amalgamated, and the place has come to be known as Hairy Kafka Street.

In the midst of this street, wedged between an old hammam and a new mosque, stood an apartment building that had once been modern and majestic and was now anything but. An amateur burglar had smashed the window of the main doorway and, scared by the noise, had run off without stealing anything. As none of the residents agreed to fork out the money to replace the glass, ever since then it had been held together with brown tape, the sort used by removal companies.

In front of that door Mr Chaplin was sitting now, his tail curled about him. He had a coal-black coat and jade eyes flecked with gold. One of his paws was white, as if he had dipped it in a bucket of lime and instantly changed his mind. His collar, adorned with tiny silver bells, tinkled each time he moved. He never heard the sound. Nothing disturbed the silence in his universe.

He had sneaked out the previous evening when Tequila Leila had left for work. This wasn't unusual, as Mr Chaplin was a nocturnal *flâneur*. He would always get back before dawn, thirsty and tired, knowing that his owner would have left the door ajar for him. But this time he was surprised to find the door closed. Since then he had been waiting patiently.

Another hour went by. Cars passed, honking their horns with abandon; street vendors shouted their wares; the school around the corner played the national anthem on loudspeakers and hundreds of pupils sang in unison. When they finished singing they took the collective oath: *May my existence be a gift to the Turkish existence*. Far in the distance, near a construction site where a worker had recently plunged to his death, a bulldozer rumbled, shaking the earth. Istanbul's babel of sounds filled the skies, but the cat didn't hear them either.

Mr Chaplin longed for a comforting pat on the head. He longed to be upstairs in his flat with a bowl full of mackerel-and-potato pâté – his favourite food. As he stretched and arched his back, he wondered where on earth his owner was, and why Tequila Leila was so unusually late today.

Grief

As dusk was falling, Leila's friends – apart from Nostalgia Nalan, who had still not caught up with them – arrived at the apartment building on Hairy Kafka Street. Letting themselves in would not be a problem since they each had a spare key.

A look of hesitation crossed Sabotage's features as they approached the main door. He realized, with a sudden tightening in his chest, that he was not ready to go into Leila's flat and face the painful void left by her absence. He felt a strong urge to walk away, even from those so dear to him. He needed to be alone, at least for a while.

'Maybe I should check back in at the office first. I left so abruptly earlier.'

This morning, when Sabotage had heard the news, he had grabbed his jacket and run out of the door, informing his boss on his way out that one of his children had come down with food poisoning. 'Mushrooms, it must be the mushrooms at dinner!' It wasn't the smartest excuse, but he hadn't been able to come up with anything better. There was no way he could have told his colleagues the truth. None of them knew about his friendship with Leila. But now it occurred to him that his wife might have called the office, exposing his lie, and he could be in deep trouble.

'Are you sure?' Jameelah asked. 'Isn't it late?'

'I'll just pop in, see if everything is okay and come straight back.'

'Fine, don't take too long,' said Humeyra.

'It's rush hour . . . I'll do my best.'

Sabotage hated cars, but since he was claustrophobic and couldn't stand being jammed inside a packed bus or ferry boat – and all buses and ferry boats were packed at this time of the day – he was painfully dependent on them.

The three women stood on the pavement and watched him walk away, his gait a little unsteady, his gaze fixed on the cobblestones, as if he could no longer trust the firmness of the ground. His shoulders stooped and his head bent at a painful angle, he seemed drained of all vitality. Leila's death had shaken him to his very core. Turning up his jacket collar against the quickening wind, he disappeared in a sea of people.

Zaynab122 discreetly wiped away a tear and pushed up her glasses. She turned to the other two and said, 'You girls go ahead. I'll nip into the grocer's. I need to make halva for Leila's soul.'

'All right, honey,' said Humeyra. 'I'll leave the main door open for Mr Chaplin.'

Nodding, Zaynab122 crossed the road, right foot first. '*Bismillah ar-Rahman ar-Rahim.*' Her body, deformed by the genetic disorder that had taken hold of her since she was a baby, aged faster than normal – as if life were a race it had to finish at full speed. But she rarely complained, and when she did it was only for God's ears.

Unlike the others in the group, Zaynab122 was deeply religious. A believer through and through. She prayed five times a day, refrained from alcohol and fasted the entire month of Ramadan. She had studied the Qur'an back in Beirut, comparing its numerous translations. She could recite whole chapters from memory. But religion for her was less a scripture frozen in time than an organic, breathing being. A fusion. She blended the written word with oral customs, adding into the mix a pinch of superstition and folklore. And there were things she had to do now to help Leila's soul on its eternal journey. She didn't have much time. Souls moved fast. She had to buy sandalwood paste, camphor, rosewater . . . and she definitely had to make that halva – which she then would distribute to strangers and neighbours alike. Everything had to be ready, even though she knew some of her friends might not appreciate her efforts – particularly Nostalgia Nalan.

There being no time to spare, Zaynab122 headed to the nearest store. Normally she wouldn't go there. Leila had never liked its owner.

The grocer's was a dimly lit store with floor-to-ceiling shelves displaying tinned and packaged products. Inside, the man known to the locals as 'the chauvinist grocer' stood leaning against a wooden counter worn smooth by time. Pulling at his long, curly beard, he pored over a page in an evening paper, his lips moving as he kept reading. A portrait of Tequila Leila stared out at him. 'Fourth Mysterious Murder in a Month', the caption read. 'Istanbul's Streetwalkers on High Alert'.

> Official enquiries established that the woman had gone back to working on the streets after leaving a licensed brothel at least a decade ago. The police believe she was robbed during the assault, given that no money or jewellery was found at the scene. Her case is now being linked to those of three other prostitutes who were murdered in the past month, all of them strangled. Their deaths shed light on the little-known fact that the homicide rate for Istanbul's sex workers is eighteen times higher than for other women, and most prostitute murders remain unsolved – in part due to the fact that few in the industry are willing to come forward to provide critical information. However, the law enforcement agencies are following up a number of important leads. The Deputy Police Chief told the press . . .

As soon as he saw Zaynab122 approach, the grocer folded the newspaper and stuffed it in a drawer. It took him a beat too long to compose himself.

'*Selamün aleyküm!*' the man said, unnecessarily loud.

'*Ya aleyküm selam,*' Zaynab122 responded as she stood next to a sack of beans that was taller than her.

'My condolences.' He craned his neck and jutted out his chin to get a better look at his customer. 'It was on TV, did you watch the afternoon news?'

'No, I didn't,' Zaynab122 said curtly.

'*Inshallah* they'll catch that maniac soon. I wouldn't be surprised if the murderer turns out to be a gang member.' He nodded in agreement with himself. 'They'd do anything for money, those looters. Too many Kurds, Arabs, Gypsies and whatnots in this city. Ever since they moved here the quality of life has vanished – poof!'

'I am an Arab.'

He smiled. 'Oh, but I didn't mean *you*.'

Zaynab122 studied the beans. *If Leila were here*, she thought, *she would put this odious man in his place*. But Leila was gone and Zaynab122, deeply averse to conflict, never quite knew how to deal with people who irritated her.

When she looked up again she saw that the grocer was waiting for her to speak. 'Sorry, my mind was elsewhere.'

The man gave a knowing nod. 'This is the fourth victim in a month, isn't it? Nobody deserves to die like that, even a fallen woman. I'm not judging anyone, don't get me wrong. I always say to myself, Allah will punish everyone as He sees fit. He won't let a single sin slide.'

Zaynab122 touched her forehead. She felt a headache coming on. Strange. She never had migraines. It was Leila who usually suffered from them.

'So when is the funeral? Did her family make arrangements?'

Zaynab122 flinched at the questions. The last thing she wanted to tell this nosy parker was that Leila was buried in the Cemetery of the Companionless because her family had refused to claim her body. 'Sorry, I'm in a hurry. Can I get a bottle of milk and a packet of butter, please? Oh, semolina flour too.'

'Sure, are you going to make halva? That's nice. Don't forget to bring me some. And don't worry, this one's on me.'

'No thanks, I can't accept that.' Standing on her tiptoes Zaynab122 placed the money on the counter and took a step back.

Her stomach rumbled – she remembered she hadn't eaten anything all day long.

'Um, one more thing: do you, by any chance, sell rosewater, sandalwood paste, camphor?'

The grocer gave her a curious look. 'Of course, sister, right away. My store has everything you need. I never understood why Leila didn't shop here more often.'

The Apartment

Back from his stroll, Mr Chaplin was pleased to find the main door ajar. He crawled into the apartment building and, once inside, whizzed up the stairs, the bells on his collar tinkling wildly.

As the cat approached Leila's flat, the door opened from the inside and Hollywood Humeyra appeared with a rubbish bag in her hand. She set the bag down outside the entrance. The caretaker would collect it later that evening. She was about to go back inside when she noticed the cat. She stepped into the hallway, her wide hips blocking the light.

'Mr Chaplin! We were wondering where you were.'

The cat brushed against the woman's legs, which were thick and sturdy, and covered in blue-green veins bulging through her skin.

'Oh, you cheeky creature. Come inside.' And Humeyra smiled for the first time in hours.

Deftly, Mr Chaplin made a beeline for the dining room, which also served as the living room and the guest room. He jumped into a basket cushioned with a fleece blanket. Keeping one eye open, one eye closed, he scanned the place, as though committing every single detail to memory, making sure nothing had changed while he was away.

Although in need of some repair, the flat was improbably charming, with its pastel colours, south-facing windows, high ceilings, a fireplace whose purpose seemed more aesthetic than practical, golden-blue wallpaper peeling at the edges, low-hanging crystal chandeliers, and uneven, cracked, but freshly scrubbed oak floorboards. On every wall there were framed paintings in an array of sizes. All of them were by D/Ali.

The two large front windows overlooked the roof of the old Galata Tower, which glared up at the apartment blocks and sky-scrapers in the distance as though reminding them that, hard though it might be to believe, it had once been the tallest building in the city.

Humeyra now entered Leila's bedroom and began sifting through boxes of curios, absent-mindedly humming to herself. A traditional melody. She didn't know what made her choose it. Her voice was tired but full and rich. For years she had sung in Istanbul's seedy nightclubs and acted in low-budget Turkish films, including a few X-rated ones that still caused her embarrassment. She'd had a good figure back then, and no varicose veins. It had been a dangerous existence. Once she had been injured in the crossfire between two rival mafia clans, and another time she had been shot in the knee by a demented fan. Now she was too old for that kind of life. Breathing in all that secondary smoke, night after night, had exacerbated her asthma and she carried an inhaler in her pocket that she used frequently. She had gained a lot of weight over the years – one of the many side effects of the kaleidoscope of pills she had been popping like sweets over the decades. Sleeping tablets, antidepressants, antipsychotics . . .

Humeyra believed there was something markedly similar about the experience of being overweight and being prone to melancholy. In both cases society blamed the sufferer. No other medical condition was regarded this way. People with any other illness received at least a degree of sympathy and moral support. Not the obese or the depressed. *You could have controlled your appetite . . . You could have controlled your thoughts . . .* But Humeyra knew neither her weight nor her habitual despondency was really a personal choice. Leila had understood this.

'Why are you trying to fight depression?'

'Because that's what I'm supposed to do . . . everyone says.'

'My mother – I used to call her Auntie – she often felt the same way, maybe worse. People always told her to fight depression. But I have a feeling that as soon as we see something as our enemy we make it stronger. Like a boomerang. You hurl it away, it comes back and hits you with equal force. Maybe what you need is to *befriend* your depression.'

'What a funny thing to say, honey. How am I to do that?'

'Well, think about it: a friend is someone you can walk with in the dark and learn lots of things from. But you also know you are different people – you and your friend. You are not your depression. You are much more than what your mood is today or tomorrow.'

Leila had urged her to cut down on the pills and take up a hobby, start exercising or volunteering in a women's shelter, helping those with stories similar to hers. But Humeyra found it incredibly hard to be around people to whom life had been unfairly harsh. When she'd tried before, all her best efforts and well-meaning words just seemed to turn into empty puffs of air. How could she give others hope and good cheer when she herself was constantly assailed by fears and worries?

Leila had also bought her books on Sufism, Indian philosophy and yoga – all of which she had become interested in after D/Ali's death. But, though Humeyra had flipped through these books many times, she had made little progress in that direction. It seemed to her that all these things, easy and handy though they claimed to be, were essentially designed for people who were healthier, happier or simply luckier than her. How could meditation help you to quieten your mind when you needed to quieten your mind in order to meditate? She lived with an endless commotion inside.

Now that Leila was gone, a pitch-black fear darted about in Humeyra's head like a trapped fly. She had taken a Xanax after leaving the hospital, but it didn't seem to be working. Her mind was tormented by gory images of violence. Cruelty. Butchery. A senseless, meaningless, baseless evil. Silver cars flashed in front of her eyes like knives in the night. Shuddering, Humeyra cracked her tired knuckles and forced herself to plough on, heedless of the fact that her massive chignon was coming undone, wisps of hair falling free across the nape of her neck. She found a stack of old photos under the bed, but it was too painful to look at them. This was what she was thinking about when she noticed the fuchsia chiffon dress draped over the back of a chair. As she picked it up, her face crumpled. It was Leila's favourite.

Normal Female Citizens

A bag full of groceries in each hand, Zaynab122 walked into the flat, puffing a little. 'Oh, those stairs are killing me.'

'What took you so long?' asked Hollywood Humeyra.

'I had to chat with that awful man.'

'Who?'

'The chauvinist grocer. Leila never liked him.'

'True, she didn't,' Humeyra said thoughtfully.

For a moment the two women were silent, each absorbed in her own thoughts.

'We must give Leila's clothes away,' said Zaynab122. 'And her silk scarves – my God, she had so many.'

'Don't you think we should keep them?'

'We must follow the custom. When someone dies their clothes are distributed to the poor. The blessings of the poor help the dead cross the bridge to the next world. The timing is important. We must act fast. Leila's soul is about to start its journey. The Bridge of Siraat is sharper than a sword, thinner than a hair . . .'

'Oh, here we go again. Give me a bloody break!' A husky voice rose from behind. Simultaneously, the door was pushed open, making the two women and the cat almost jump out of their skins.

Nostalgia Nalan stood by the entrance, frowning.

'You scared the life out of us,' said Humeyra, putting her hand on her racing heart.

'Good. It serves you right. You were too absorbed in your religious gobbledegook.'

Zaynab122 clasped her hands in her lap. 'I don't see any harm in helping the poor.'

'Well, it's not exactly that, is it? It's more a trade-off. *Here, you poor lot, take these hand-me-downs, give us your blessings. And here, dear*

God, take these blessing-coupons, give us a sunny corner in heaven. No offence, but religion is plain commerce. Give-and-take.'

'That's so . . . unfair,' Zaynab122 said, pouting. It wasn't exactly anger that she felt when people made light of her beliefs. It was sadness. And the sadness was heavier if the people in question happened to be her friends.

'Whatever. Forget what I said.' Nalan plonked herself down on the sofa. 'Where's Jameelah?'

'In the other room. She said she needed to lie down.' A shadow crossed Humeyra's face. 'She doesn't talk much. She hasn't eaten anything. I'm worried. You know her health . . .'

Nalan dropped her gaze. 'I'll talk to her. And where's Sabotage?'

'He had to rush to the office,' replied Zaynab122. 'He must be on his way back now, probably stuck in traffic.'

'Fine, we'll wait,' said Nalan. 'Now tell me, why was this door left open?'

The two other women exchanged a quick glance.

'Your best friend has been killed in cold blood, and here you are in her flat with the door wide open. Have you lost your minds?'

'Come on,' said Humeyra, drawing a deep, shuddering breath. 'It wasn't like anyone broke into this flat. Leila-jim was out on the street late at night. Witnesses saw her getting into a car – a silver Mercedes. All the victims were killed the same way, you know that.'

'So? Does that mean you're out of harm's way? Or do you assume that just because one of you happens to be small and the other –'

'Fat?' Humeyra blushed. She took out her inhaler and held it inside her palm. Experience had shown her that she used the inhaler more often when Nalan was around.

Zaynab122 shrugged. 'I'm fine with whatever word you use.'

'I was going to say *retired and depressed.*' Nalan waved a manicured hand. 'My point is, if you ladies assume that Leila's murderer is the only psycho in this city, good luck! Leave your door open. Actually, why not just put out a doormat: *Willkommen Psychopathen?*'

'I wish you'd stop taking everything to extremes.' Humeyra scowled.

Nalan considered this for a moment. 'Is it me or this city? I wish *Istanbul* would stop taking everything to extremes.'

Zaynab122 pulled at a loose thread on her cardigan and rolled it into a ball. 'I only nipped out to buy a few things and –'

'Well, it only takes a few seconds,' said Nalan. 'To get attacked, I mean.'

'Please stop saying horrible things . . .' Humeyra's voice trailed off as she decided to take another Xanax. Maybe two.

'She's right,' Zaynab122 agreed. 'It's disrespectful to the dead.'

Nalan held her head erect. 'You want to know what's disrespectful to the dead?' With a quick jerk of her hand, she unfastened her clutch bag and took out an evening newspaper. Opening it to the page where Leila's picture jumped out amid local and national press reports, she began to read aloud:

The Deputy Police Chief told the press, 'Rest assured we will find the perpetrator in no time. We have employed a special unit to deal with this case. At this stage, we ask the public to share with law enforcement any suspicious activity they may have seen or heard. However, citizens, especially women, do not need to be alarmed. These murders were not randomly committed. One particular group, without exception, was targeted. All the victims were streetwalkers. Normal female citizens have no need to worry about their safety.'

Nalan refolded the newspaper along its creases and clucked her tongue as she always did when in a temper. 'Normal female citizens! What this jackass is saying is, *All you goody-goody ladies, do not worry. You're safe. The only ones butchered on the streets are whores.* Now that's what I call being disrespectful to the dead.'

A feeling of defeat settled on the room, acrid and thick, like a sulphurous smoke that clung to everything it touched. Humeyra held her inhaler up to her mouth and took a puff. She waited for her breathing to slow down; it didn't. Closing her eyes, she willed herself to sleep. A deep, drugged slumber of forgetfulness. Zaynab122 sat ramrod straight, her headache getting worse. She would soon begin to pray and prepare the concoction that would help Leila's soul on its next journey. Not yet though. She lacked the strength right now and perhaps, just a little, she lacked even the faith. And Nalan, shoulders stiff inside her jacket, stayed silent, a hollowness to her features.

In a corner Mr Chaplin, having finished his last delicacy, licked himself clean.

The Silver Mercedes

Every evening a red-and-green boat called *Güney* – 'the South' – could be found moored on the shore of the Golden Horn, opposite the road from the Intercontinental Hotel.

The vessel had been named in honour of the Kurdish film director Yilmaz Güney, and had featured in one of his movies. The present owner didn't know this, and even had he known he wouldn't have cared. He had bought it years ago from a fisherman who no longer went to sea. The new owner had built a tiny galley and installed an iron grill to make köfte sandwiches. Soon grilled mackerel joined the menu, garnished with shredded onions and sliced tomatoes. In Istanbul, success for a street-food vendor depended not so much on what you sold as when and where you sold it. Night-time, though risky in other respects, was more profitable, not because customers were more generous but because they were hungrier. They poured out from the clubs and bars, alcohol coursing through their veins. Not quite ready to throw the towel in, they stopped at the boat stall, bent on one last indulgence before heading home. Ladies in shiny dresses and men in dark suits perched on stools by the dock and tucked into their sandwiches, tearing away at the coarse white pitta that in daylight they would have turned up their noses at.

This evening, the first customers appeared at seven o'clock – much earlier than usual. That's what the vendor thought when he saw a Mercedes-Benz pull up at the pier. He yelled at his apprentice, his nephew, the laziest boy in the city, who was slumped in the corner, watching a TV series as he cracked roasted sunflower seeds between his teeth with utter abandon. Beside him on the table was a growing pile of empty shells.

'Move your butt. We've got customers. Go and see what they want.'

The boy stood up, stretched his legs and filled his lungs with the salt-tanged breeze blowing in from the sea. After a lingering look at the waves lapping against the side of the boat, he grimaced, as though he had been set on solving some mystery but had now given up. Mumbling to himself, he stepped on to the pier and dragged his feet towards the Mercedes.

Under the street lamp the car glowed with polished confidence. It had tinted windows, a sleek, custom-made spoiler and grey-and-red chrome wheels. The boy, a fervent admirer of luxury automobiles since childhood, whistled in admiration. He himself would rather drive a Firebird – a steel-blue Pontiac Firebird. Now that was a car! He wouldn't drive it, he would fly it at a speed of –

'Hey, lad! Are you going to take our order or what?' said the man in the driver's seat, leaning out of the partly opened window.

Jerked out of his reverie, the boy took his time to reply: 'Yeah, okay. What would you like?'

'First off, some politeness.'

Only then did the boy lift his head and take a proper look at the two customers. The one who had been speaking was raw-boned and bald. He had an angular jaw and a pinched face pitted with acne scars. The other man was almost the opposite: pudgy and ruddy-cheeked. And yet they looked somehow related . . . perhaps it was the eyes.

Curious, the boy edged even closer to the car. The interior was as impressive as the exterior. Beige leather seats, beige leather steering wheel, beige leather dashboard . . . But what he saw next made him gasp. The colour drained from his face. He took the order and rushed back to the boat, walking as swiftly as his feet allowed, his heart thumping frantically in his ribcage.

'So? What do they want? Köfte or mackerel?' asked the vendor.

'Oh, köfte. And ayran to drink, too. But . . .'

'But what?'

'I don't want to serve them. They're *weird.*'

'What do you mean, *weird*?'

Even as he posed the question the vendor sensed he would not get an answer. He sighed with a shake of his head. The boy had become the breadwinner in his family ever since his father, a construction worker, had plunged to his death from a scaffolding tower. The man had been given no proper training, no safety equipment, and the scaffolding, it was later revealed, had not been erected correctly. The family had sued the construction company but nothing was likely to come of it. There were too many cases for the courts to deal with. As areas in Istanbul saw rapid gentrification and steep rises in real estate, the demand for luxury apartments soared, leading to a staggering number of accidents on building sites.

So the boy, still in school, had to work nights, whether he liked it or not. Yet he was too sensitive, too taciturn and too stubborn, clearly not suitable for hard labour – or for Istanbul, which in the end amounted to the same thing.

'Useless lad,' said the vendor, loud enough for his apprentice to hear.

Ignoring the remark, the boy placed the meatballs on the grill and started to prepare the order.

'Leave it!' said the vendor with a grunt of dissatisfaction. 'How many times do I need to tell you to oil the grill first?'

Snatching the tongs from the boy's hand, the vendor waved him away. Come tomorrow he was going to get rid of him – a decision he had postponed to this day out of pity, but enough was enough. He was not the Red Crescent. He had his own family to take care of, and a business to protect.

With a swift and agile hand, the vendor raked the glowing embers, kindled the fire, grilled eight pieces of köfte and stuffed them into half pittas with some sliced tomatoes. Grabbing two bottles of ayran, he placed everything on a tray and headed towards the car.

'Good evening, sirs,' the vendor said, his voice oozing politeness.

'Where's that lazy apprentice of yours?' asked the man in the driver's seat.

'Lazy, yes. You got that right, sir. My humble apologies if he has done anything wrong. I'm going to kick him out any day now.'

'Not a moment too soon, if you ask me.'

Nodding, the vendor handed the tray through the half-open window. He sneaked a glance at the inside of the car.

On the dashboard were four figurines. Angels with halos and harps, their skins splashed with blobs of reddish-brown paint, their heads bobbing almost imperceptibly now that the car was still.

'Keep the change,' said the man.

'Much appreciated.'

Even as he pocketed the money, the vendor was unable to tear his gaze from the angels. He began to feel sick. Slowly, almost despite himself, it dawned on him what his apprentice must have noticed right away: the stains on the dolls, the stains on the dashboard . . . those reddish-brown spots were not paint. They were dried blood.

The driver, as if he had read the vendor's mind, said, 'We had an accident the other night. I bumped my nose, it bled like hell.'

The vendor smiled in sympathy. 'Oh, that's too bad. *Geçmiş olsun.*'

'We need to have it cleaned but haven't had a chance.'

Nodding, the vendor took back his tray and was about to say goodbye when the car door on the opposite side opened. The passenger, who had remained silent until now, stepped out, the pitta in his hand. He said, 'Your köfte is delicious.'

The vendor glanced at the man, noticing the marks on his chin. It looked like someone had scratched his face. *A woman,* he thought, but that was none of his business. Trying to quell his thoughts, he said, his voice pitched higher than usual, 'Well, we're pretty well known. I have customers coming in from other cities.'

'Good . . . I take it you are not feeding us donkey meat,' said the man, laughing at his own joke.

'Of course not. Only beef. Top grade.'

'Excellent! Make us happy and you'll be sure to see us again.'

'Any time,' said the vendor, pressing his lips into a thin line. He felt content, almost grateful, despite his unease. If these men were dangerous, that was someone else's problem, not his.

'Tell me, do you always work at night?' the driver asked.

'Always.'

'You must be getting all kinds of customers. Any immoral ones? Prostitutes? Perverts?'

In the background, the boat bobbed up and down, disturbed by waves from a passing ship.

'My customers are decent people. Respectable and decent.'

'That's nice,' said the passenger, getting back into his seat. 'We don't want indecent people here, do we? This city has changed so much. It's so filthy now.'

'Yes, filthy,' said the vendor, only because he did not know what else to say.

When he returned to the boat he found his nephew waiting with his arms akimbo, his face taut and troubled. 'So? How did it go?'

'Fine. You should have served them. Why am I doing your job?'

'But didn't you see?'

'See what?'

The boy squinted at his uncle as if the man were shrinking in front of his eyes. 'Inside the car . . . there's blood on the steering wheel . . . on the dolls . . . it's everywhere. Shouldn't we call the police?'

'Hey, no police around here. I've a business to protect.'

'Oh right, your *business*!'

'What's wrong with you?' snapped the vendor. 'Don't you know there are hundreds out there who'd die to have your job?'

'Then give it to them. I don't care about your stupid köfte. I hate the smell anyhow. It's horse meat.'

'How dare you?' said the vendor, his cheeks aflame.

But the boy was not listening. His attention had swung back to the Mercedes-Benz, a cold and imposing form under the darkening sky that now hung low over the dock. He murmured, 'Those two men . . .'

The vendor's expression softened. 'Forget them, son. You're too young. Don't be so curious. That's my advice for you.'

'Uncle, aren't you curious yourself? Even a bit? What if they've done something wrong? What if they've killed someone? Then we'll be accomplices in the eyes of the law.'

'That's it.' The vendor banged down the empty tray. 'You watch far too much TV. All those half-baked American thrillers, and now you think you're quite the detective! Tomorrow morning, I'm going to talk to your mother. We'll find you a new job – and from now on, no more TV.'

'Yeah, whatever.'

And then there was nothing left to say. Neither of them spoke again for a while, a sense of lethargy washing over them. Beside the red-and-green fishing boat called *Güney*, the sea roiled and frothed, crashing with all its might against the boulders that edged the twisting road from Istanbul all the way to Kilyos.

The View from Above

Inside an elegant office occupying an entire floor of a new high-rise and overlooking the city's fast-growing commercial district, a young man sat in the waiting room, bouncing his leg nervously up and down. The secretary, behind a glass partition, craned her head to glance at him every now and then, a trace of an apologetic smile on her lips. Like him, she found it difficult to understand why his father had kept him waiting for the last forty minutes. But that was his father, always out to make a point and teach him a lesson he had neither the need nor the time for. The young man checked his watch again.

Finally, the door opened and another secretary announced he could come in.

His father was sitting behind his desk. An antique walnut piece with brass handles, claw feet and a sculpted top. Beautiful, but too grand for a room so modern.

Without a word the young man strode towards the desk and placed on it the newspaper he had brought with him. On the page it was opened to, Leila's face peered out from the text.

'What is this?'

'Father, read it. Please.'

The older man gave the newspaper a cursory glance, his gaze sweeping over the headline: *Slain Prostitute Found in City Waste Bin*. He frowned. 'Why are you showing me this?'

'Because I know this woman.'

'Oh!' His face brightened. 'Good to know you have lady friends.'

'Don't you understand? She's the woman you sent me. And she's dead. Murdered.'

The silence diffused outwards into the air; spreading and

congealing into an ugly and uneven thickness, stagnant like algae forming on a late-summer pond. He looked past his father towards the city beyond the window, the sprawl of houses fanning out under a fine haze, the streets densely crowded and the hills rolling into the distance. The view from high above was spectacular, if strangely lifeless.

'It's all in the report,' the young man said, struggling to control his tone. 'Three more women were killed this month . . . all of them in the same horrific way. And guess what? I know them, too. All of them. They are the women you sent me. Isn't that too much of a coincidence?'

'I thought we had arranged five for you.'

He paused, feeling embarrassed in a way only his father could make him feel. 'Yes, there were five, and four of them are dead. So I'm asking you again: isn't that too much of a coincidence?'

His father's eyes gave nothing away. 'What are you trying to say?'

The young man winced, unsure of how to proceed, a familiar fear kicking in, a trepidation that went way back, and all at once he was a boy again, sweating in the heat of his father's gaze. But then, just as suddenly, he remembered the women, the victims, particularly the last one. He recalled the exchange they'd had on the balcony, their knees touching slightly, the smell of whisky on their breaths. *Look, darling. I understand you don't want to do this. I also understand there's someone you love and you'd rather be with that person.*

Tears welled in his eyes. His lover said he suffered only because he had a good heart. He had a conscience, not something everyone could claim. But that was little consolation. Had those four women died because of him? How could that be? He feared he might be losing his mind.

'Is this your way of *correcting* me?' He realized, belatedly, he had raised his voice – almost to a shout.

His father pushed the newspaper away, his features hardening. 'Enough! I've nothing to do with this stupidity. Frankly, I'm surprised that you'd even think I'd go on the streets chasing whores.'

'Father, I am not accusing *you*. But maybe it was someone around you. There must be an explanation. Tell me, how did you arrange these meetings? Did someone make the appointments, the calls?'

'Of course.' His father mentioned the name of one of his right-hand men.

'Where is he now?'

'Why, he's still working for me.'

'You need to interrogate that man. Promise me you will.'

'Look, you mind your own business and I will mind mine.'

The young man raised his chin. The taut expression receded from his face as he struggled to say the next words. 'Father, I'm leaving. I need to get out of this city. I'm going to Italy – for a few years. I've been accepted on to a PhD programme in Milan.'

'Stop speaking nonsense. Your wedding is coming up. We have already sent out the invitations.'

'I'm sorry. You'll have to deal with that. I won't be here.'

His father stood up, his voice cracking for the first time. 'You cannot shame me!'

'I've made up my mind.' The young man's eyes fell on the carpet. 'Those four women –'

'Oh, stop that nonsense! I told you I had nothing to do with it.'

He stared at his father, studying his stern features as though to memorize what he refused to become. He had thought about going to the police, but his father was well connected and the case would be closed as soon as it was opened. He just wanted to go away – with his beloved.

'I won't send you a single cheque, you hear me? You'll come back to me on your knees, begging.'

'Goodbye, Father.'

Before he turned his back, he reached out, grabbed the newspaper, folded it and put it in his pocket. He didn't want to leave Leila's picture in this cold office. He still had her scarf.

227

The thinner one had been celibate his entire life. He often talked about the inconsequence of the flesh. He was a man of ideas, universal theories. When the big boss had asked him to arrange prostitutes for his son, he had been honoured to be entrusted with a job so secretive and sensitive. The first time he had waited outside the hotel, just to make sure the woman arrived and behaved well and everything went seamlessly. That same night, as he was sitting inside the car, smoking, he had an idea. It occurred to him that maybe this was no ordinary job. Maybe there was something else he was expected to do. A mission. The thought hit him with a jolt. He felt important, infinitely alive.

He broached the idea to his cousin: a coarse, simple-minded man with a quick temper and a quicker left fist. Not a thinker like him, but loyal, practical and capable of performing difficult tasks. The perfect partner.

To make sure they got the right woman they came up with a plan. Each time, they would ask the fixer to tell the prostitute to wear a particular outfit. That way they could easily recognize the woman when she left the hotel. The last time it was a gold-sequinned, tight-fitting minidress. After each murder, they added another porcelain doll to their collection of angels. For that is what they did, he believed. They turned whores into angels.

Not once had he touched any of the women. He took pride in that – being beyond the needs of the flesh. Cold as steel, each time he had watched from the side, until the very end. The fourth woman, unexpectedly, had fought back so hard, resisting with every ounce of her strength, that for a few minutes he feared he might have to get involved. But his cousin was strong, physically advantaged, and he kept a crowbar hidden on the floor.

The Plan

'I need a smoke,' said Nalan as she opened the balcony door and stepped out.

She glanced at the street down below. The neighbourhood was changing. Nothing felt familiar any more. Tenants came, tenants left – the new replaced the old. Areas of the city exchanged their residents like schoolboys trading football cards.

She placed a cigarette between her lips and lit it. As she inhaled the first puff, she studied Leila's Zippo. She flicked it open, snapped it shut, flicked it open, snapped it shut.

There was an engraving in English on one side of the lighter: *Vietnam: You Never Really Lived Until You Nearly Died.*

It occurred to Nalan that this antique Zippo was not the simple object it seemed to be, but a perpetual wanderer. It travelled from one person to another, outliving each of its owners. Before Leila, it had belonged to D/Ali, and before D/Ali, to an American soldier, who had been unfortunate enough to come to Istanbul with the Sixth Fleet in July 1968. The soldier, while running away from the young, angry, leftist protesters, had dropped the lighter in his hand, the cap on his head. D/Ali had picked up the former, and a comrade of his, the latter. In the ensuing commotion they were not able to see the soldier again, and even if they had, they were not sure they would have returned the items. Over the years, D/Ali had cleaned and polished the Zippo countless times. When it was broken, he took it to a repairer in a passageway in Taksim who mended watches and miscellaneous articles. But a part of him had always wondered what kind of horrors and carnage this little object might have witnessed in war. Had it watched the killings on both sides, seen at close hand the cruelties humans were capable of inflicting on fellow humans? Had it been present at the My Lai

Massacre, heard the screams of unarmed civilians – women and children?

After D/Ali's death, Leila had kept the Zippo, carrying it with her everywhere. Except for yesterday, when, slightly distracted and unusually quiet, she had left it on the table in Karavan. Nalan had been planning to give it to her today. *How could you forget your precious thingy? You're getting old, honey*, Nalan would have said. And Leila would have laughed. *Me, old? No way, darling. It's the Zippo that must have been confused.*

Nalan pulled a tissue out of her pocket and wiped her nose.

'You all right there?' asked Humeyra, poking her head around the balcony door.

'Yes, sure. I'll be back in a minute.'

Humeyra nodded, though she didn't seem convinced. Without another word, she left.

Nalan took a pull on her cigarette, releasing no more than a faint streak of smoke. The next puff she sent off towards the Galata Tower, the masterpiece of Genoese stonemasons and woodworkers. How many people in this city were doing the same thing just now, she marvelled, staring at the ancient cylindrical tower as though it held the answer to all their troubles.

On the street below a young man looked up and caught sight of her. His gaze grew intense. He yelled – an obscene comment.

Nalan leaned over the balcony railing. 'Was that for me?'

The man grinned. 'You bet. I'm into ladies like you.'

Frowning, Nalan straightened her back. She turned sideways, and asked the other women in her quietest voice, 'Is there an ashtray somewhere?'

'Um . . . Leila kept one on the coffee table,' said Zaynab122. 'Here.'

Nalan grabbed the ashtray, weighed it on her palm. Then, all of a sudden, she hurled it over the railing. It shattered on the pavement below. The man, having managed to spring back and dodge the blow, gawped, his face pale, his jaw tight.

230

'Idiot!' yelled Nalan. 'Do I whistle at your hairy legs, huh? Do I hassle you? How dare you talk to me like that?'

The man opened his mouth, then closed it. Briskly, he marched off, followed by an eruption of sniggers from a teahouse nearby.

'Get inside, please,' said Humeyra. 'You can't stand on the balcony and throw things at strangers. This is a house in mourning.'

Turning on her heels, Nalan entered the room, the cigarette still in her hand. 'I don't want to mourn. I want to *do* something.'

'What can we do, *hayati*?' said Zaynab122. 'Nothing.'

Humeyra looked concerned – and slightly drowsy, having taken two more pills on the sly. 'I hope you're not planning to go out and look for Leila's killer.'

'No, we'll leave that to the police, not that I trust them.' Nalan exhaled a plume of smoke through her nose and guiltily tried to fan it away from Humeyra, with little success.

Zaynab122 said, 'Why don't you pray to help her soul – yours too?'

Nalan scrunched her forehead. 'Why pray when God is no good at listening? It's called Divine Deafness. That's what they have in common, Mr Chaplin and God.'

'*Tövbe, tövbe*,' said Zaynab122, as she always did when she heard the Lord's name being uttered in vain.

Nalan found an empty coffee cup and stubbed out the cigarette. 'Look, you do the praying. I don't want to offend anyone's feelings. Leila deserved a great life and she didn't get it. At the very least she deserves a proper burial. We can't let her rot in the Cemetery of the Companionless. She doesn't belong there.'

'You must learn to accept things, *habibi*,' said Zaynab122. 'There is nothing any of us can do.'

In the background the Galata Tower wrapped itself in purple-and-crimson gossamer against the setting sun. Over seven hills and almost a thousand neighbourhoods, small and large, the city extended as far as the eye could see; a city prophesied to remain unconquered until the end of the world. Far in the distance, the Bosphorus whirled, mixing saltwater with freshwater as easily as it mixed reality and dream.

'But maybe there is,' said Nalan after a brief pause. 'Maybe there is one last thing we can do for Tequila Leila.'

Sabotage

By the time Sabotage arrived in Hairy Kafka Street, the inky gauze of the evening had settled upon the hills in the distance. He watched the last ray of light drift from the skyline and the day come to its end, filling him with a sense of abandonment. Normally he would be sweaty and irritable from all that time spent in traffic, fuming at the stupidities of drivers and pedestrians alike, but now he just felt drained. In his hands, he carried a box, wrapped in red foil and tied with a golden bow. Using his own key, he entered the building and climbed the stairs.

Sabotage was in his early forties now, of medium height and stocky build. He had a protruding Adam's apple, grey eyes that almost disappeared when he smiled, and a recently grown moustache that didn't suit his round face. He had been balding prematurely for years – it was especially premature given that he believed his life, his real life, had not yet started.

A man with secrets. This is what he had become when he followed Leila to Istanbul a year after she had gone. Leaving Van and his mother behind had not been easy for him, but he had done it, for two reasons, one clear, one hidden: to continue with his education (he was able to earn a place at a top university) and to find his childhood friend. All he had from her was a pile of postcards and an address no longer in use. She had written a few times, not saying much about her new life, and then, suddenly, the postcards had stopped coming. Sabotage sensed something had happened to her, something she did not wish to talk about, and he knew he had to find her no matter what. He had looked for her everywhere – in cinemas, restaurants, theatres, hotels, cafes, and then, when those places yielded nothing, in discotheques, bars, gambling parlours and, finally, with a heavy heart, in nightclubs and houses of ill repute. It was after a long, relentless search that he was able to locate her, thanks to a sheer coincidence. A boy he had been sharing a room with had become a regular in the street of brothels, and Sabotage overheard him tell another student about a woman with a rose tattoo on her ankle.

'I wish you hadn't found me. I have no desire to see you,' Leila had said when they met again for the first time in so long.

Her coldness had stabbed him in the heart. In her eyes there was a glow of anger and little else. But he sensed that, beneath the stern expression, what prevailed was shame. Worried and wilful, he kept coming back. Now that he had found her he was not going to let go of her again. Since he couldn't bear that notorious street with its sour smells, he often waited at its entrance, in the dappled shade of ageing oaks, sometimes for hours. Occasionally, when Leila walked out to buy herself something, or to get Bitter Ma her haemorrhoid cream, she saw him there, sitting on the pavement, reading a book or scratching his chin over a maths equation.

'Why do you keep coming here, Sabotage?'

'Because I miss you.'

Those were the years when half the students were busy boycotting classes and the other half boycotting the dissident students. Almost every day something happened on university campuses in the country: bomb squads arrived to detonate packages, students clashed in the cafeteria, professors were verbally abused, physically attacked. Despite it all, Sabotage managed to pass his exams, graduating with high honours. He found a job at a national bank and, save for a few company outings that he went on out of social obligation, he spurned all invitations that came his way. Whatever free time he had he tried to spend with Leila.

The year Leila married D/Ali, Sabotage quietly asked a colleague on a date. A month later he proposed to her. Though his marriage was not a particularly happy one, fatherhood was the best thing that would happen to him. For a while his career advanced rapidly and with conviction, but just when it looked like he might make it to the highest levels, he pulled back. Despite his brains, he was too shy, too withdrawn, to become a major player in any institution. The first time he gave a presentation he forgot his lines and broke into a terrible sweat. Silence swept across the conference room, punctured only by awkward coughs. He kept glancing at the door, as if he'd had second thoughts and longed to run away. He often felt that way. And so he chose to content himself with a mediocre position and settled into a passable life – as a good citizen, a good employee, a good father. But at no stage in this journey did he give up on his friendship with Leila.

'I used to call you my sabotage radio,' Leila would say. 'Look at you now. You are sabotaging your reputation, darling. What would your wife and colleagues say if they knew you were friends with someone like me?'

'They don't have to know.'

'How long do you think you can keep it from them?'

And Sabotage would say, 'For as long as is needed.'

His co-workers, his wife, his neighbours, his relatives, his mother, long retired from the pharmacy – none of them were aware that he had another life, that with Leila and the girls he was a different man altogether.

Sabotage spent his days with his head buried in balance sheets, conversing with no one unless absolutely necessary. Come twilight, he would leave the office, hop into his car, much as he hated driving, and head to Karavan – a nightclub that was popular with the unpopular. Here he relaxed, he smoked, and sometimes he danced. To cover for his lengthy absences, he told his wife that his piddling salary required him to work night shifts as a security guard in a factory.

'They produce powdered formula, for babies,' he had told her, only because he thought it would make it sound more innocent, the mention of babies.

Fortunately, his wife did not ask questions. If anything, she seemed almost relieved to see him leave the house every evening. It troubled him sometimes, simmered in the cauldron of his mind – did she want him out of her way? Still, it wasn't so much her that Sabotage worried about, but her large family. His wife came from a proud line of imams and hodjas. He would never dare tell them the truth. Besides, he loved his children. He was a doting father. Should his wife divorce him on grounds of his night life with tarts and transvestites, the courts would never give him custody of his children. They probably wouldn't even allow him to see them again. Truth could be corrosive, a mercurial liquor. It could eat holes in the bulwarks of daily life, destroying entire edifices. If the family elders learned his secret, all hell would break loose. He could almost hear their voices hammering inside his head – bawling, insulting, threatening.

Some mornings while shaving, Sabotage practised his defence speech in front of the mirror. The speech he would give if he were caught by his family one day and put through the wringer.

Are you sleeping with that woman? his wife would ask, her relatives at her side. *Oh, I rue the day I married you – what kind of a man wastes his children's allowance on a whore!*

No! No! It's nothing like that.

Really? You mean she's sleeping with you free of charge?

Please don't say such things! he would plead. *She is my friend. My oldest friend – from school.*

No one would believe him.

'I tried to come earlier but the traffic was an absolute nightmare,' Sabotage said as he sat back on a chair, tired and thirsty.

'Would you like a cup of tea?' Zaynab122 asked.

'No, thanks.'

'What's that?' asked Humeyra, pointing to the box in Sabotage's lap.

'Oh, this . . . a gift for Leila. It was in the office. I had been planning to give it to her tonight.' He pulled off the bow, opened the box. There was a scarf inside. 'Pure silk. She would have loved it.'

A lump came to his throat. Unable to swallow it down, he

gasped. All the sorrow he had tried to suppress now burst out. His eyes pricked and before he knew it he was crying.

Humeyra dashed to the kitchen and returned with a glass of water and a bottle of lemon cologne. The latter she sprinkled into the water, which she handed to Sabotage. 'Drink. This'll make you feel better.

'What is it?' Sabotage asked.

'My mother's remedy for sadness – and other things. She always kept some cologne handy.'

'Wait a second,' Nalan demurred. 'You're not going to give him that, are you? Your mum's remedy could ruin a man with no alcohol tolerance.'

'But it's just cologne . . .' Humeyra muttered, suddenly unsure.

'I'm fine,' said Sabotage. He returned the glass, embarrassed at being the centre of attention.

It was a well-known fact that Sabotage could not handle his liquor. A quarter of a glass of wine was enough to destroy him. On several occasions, having drained a few tankards of beer in an effort to keep up with the others, he had blacked out. On such nights he had adventures of which he had no recollection the next morning. People would tell him in painstaking detail how he had climbed up on a roof to watch the seagulls, or had conversed with a mannequin in a window, or had leaped on to the bar in Karavan and thrown himself at the dancers, assuming they would catch him and hoist him on to their shoulders, only to plummet to the floor instead. The stories he heard were so mortifying he would pretend to have nothing to do with the awkward figure at their centre. But of course he knew. He knew he could not tolerate alcohol. Perhaps he lacked the proper enzyme or had a dysfunctional liver. Or perhaps the hodjas and imams in his wife's family had put a curse on him to ensure he never strayed from the straight and narrow.

In striking contrast to Sabotage, Nalan was a legend in Istanbul's underground circles. She had got into the habit of downing shots after she had her first sex reassignment surgery. Though she had happily ditched her old blue identification (given to male citizens) for a new pink one (for female citizens), the post-operation pain had been so excruciating that she could only endure it with help from the bottle. Later, there had been further operations, each more elaborate and expensive. No one had warned her about any of this. It was a subject not many even in the trans community wished to talk about, and when they did it was in hushed tones. Sometimes the wounds became infected, tissue refused to heal, acute pain turned chronic. And while her body had been fighting against all these unexpected complications, her debts had piled up. Nalan had looked for a job everywhere. Anything would have done. When too many doors had been closed in her face, she even tried the furniture workshop where she had worked before. But no one would employ her.

The only professions open to trans women were hairdressing and the sex industry. And there were too many hairdressers in Istanbul already, with a salon seemingly down every alleyway and in every basement. Trans women were not allowed in licensed brothels either. Otherwise the customers felt cheated and complained. Eventually, like many others before and after her, she began working on the streets. It was dark, exhausting and dangerous; every car that stopped for her left an imprint on her desensitized soul, like tyres on the desert sand. With an invisible blade, she divided herself into two Nalans. One of them watched passively over the other, observed every detail and thought a lot, while the second Nalan did everything she was supposed to do and thought absolutely nothing. Insulted by passers-by, arbitrarily arrested by police, abused by clients, she suffered one humiliation after another. Most of the men who picked up trans women were of a particular kind, lurching unpredictably between desire and contempt. Nalan had been in the business long enough to know that the two emotions, unlike oil and water, mixed easily. Those who loathed you, would, unexpectedly, reveal an urgent lust, and those who seemed to like you could turn spiteful and violent as soon as they got what they wanted.

Each time there was a state occasion or a major international conference in Istanbul, as black cars carrying foreign delegates wove their way through the traffic from the airport to the five-star hotels scattered across the city, some police chief would decide to clean up the streets on their routes. On such occasions, all transvestites would be taken into custody overnight, swept away like so much litter. Once, after one of these clean-up operations, Nalan was kept in a detention centre where her hair was shaved in random patches and her clothes stripped. They had made her wait in a cell, naked and alone, every half hour or so coming to check how she was doing and to throw another bucket of dirty water over her head. One of the police officers – a quiet young man with fine features – seemed uncomfortable with the way his colleagues treated her. Nalan still remembered the look of hurt and helplessness on the man's face, and for a moment she was sorry for him, as if it were he, not she, who was confined in a small space, locked up in an invisible cell of his own. In the morning it was the same officer who had returned her clothes, and offered her a glass of tea with a sugar cube. Nalan knew that others had had it worse that night, and after the conference was over and she was released she had not told anyone what had transpired.

It was safer working in the nightclubs, provided she could find a way in, and time and again she had. As the club owners were delighted to discover, Nalan had a surprising talent. She could drink and drink, and not get even slightly tipsy. She would sit at a customer's table and engage in small talk, her eyes flashing like coins in the sun. Meanwhile, she would encourage her new-found companion to order the priciest drinks on the menu. Whisky, cognac, champagne and vodka would flow like the mighty Euphrates. Once the customer was sufficiently hammered, Nalan would move on to the next table, where she would start the same process all over again. The club owners adored her. She was a money-making machine.

Now Nalan stood up, filled a glass with water and offered it to Sabotage. 'That scarf you bought for Leila is so pretty.'

'Thank you. She'd have liked it, I think.'

'Oh, I'm sure she would.' Nalan touched him comfortingly, her fingertips lightly resting on his shoulder. 'I'll tell you what – why don't you put it in your pocket? You can give it to Leila tonight.'

Sabotage blinked. 'Say again?'

'Don't worry. Let me explain . . .' Nalan paused, suddenly distracted by a sound. She fixed her eyes on the closed door in the hallway. 'Are you girls sure that Jameelah is sleeping?'

Humeyra shrugged. 'She promised she'd come out as soon as she woke up.'

With quick, deliberate steps, Nalan strode to the door and turned the handle. It was locked from the inside. 'Jameelah, are you sleeping or are you crying your heart out? And, just maybe, eavesdropping on us?'

No answer.

Nalan said to the keyhole, 'I have a hunch you've been awake the whole time, feeling miserable and missing Leila. Since we all feel the same way, why not come out?'

Slowly, the door opened. Jameelah emerged.

Her large, dark eyes were swollen and bloodshot.

'Oh, love.' Nalan spoke gently with Jameelah, as she did with no one else, each word a sweet apple that had to be polished before being offered. 'Look at you. You must not cry. You need to take care of yourself.'

'I'm fine,' said Jameelah.

'Nalan is right – for once,' said Humeyra. 'Think about it this way: it would have made Leila terribly sad to see you in such a state.'

'That's true.' Zaynab122 smiled soothingly. 'Why don't you and I go to the kitchen? Let's check if the halva is ready.'

'We must also order some food,' said Humeyra. 'No one has eaten anything since this morning.'

Sabotage stood up. 'I'll help you, girls.'

'Great idea, go and check, and order food.' Nalan clasped her hands behind her and began pacing the length of the room, like a general inspecting her troops before the final battle. Under the light of the chandelier her fingernails glowed a bright shade of purple.

Standing by the window she glanced outside, her face reflected in the glass. A storm was brewing in the distance, rain clouds rolling towards the north-east, the area just around Kilyos. Her eyes, which had been doleful and pensive throughout the evening, now acquired a determined gleam. Her friends might not have heard about the Cemetery of the Companionless until this afternoon, but she already knew all she needed to know about that awful place. In the past she had met a number of people whose fate it was to be buried there, and she could easily imagine what had happened to their graves later on. The misery that was the cemetery's trademark had opened up like a hungry mouth, and swallowed them in one gulp.

Later, when they all sat around the table, and everyone had a little food in their belly, Nostalgia Nalan would tell her friends about her plan. She had to explain this as carefully and gently as possible, for she knew they would, at first, be scared.

Karma

Half an hour later, they all sat around the dining table. A pile of lahmacun – ground-meat flatbread, ordered from a local restaurant – stood in the middle, barely touched. No one had much of an appetite, though they pressed Jameelah to eat. She seemed so weak, her delicate face even more gaunt than usual.

At first they made desultory conversation. But talking, like eating, seemed too much of an effort. It felt strange sitting here in Leila's home without her popping her head round the kitchen door to offer them drinks or snacks, strands of her hair falling from behind her ear. Their eyes panned the room, lingering on every item, small and big, as though discovering them for the first time. What would happen to this flat now? It occurred to each of them that if the furniture, the paintings and the ornaments were all to be moved out, Leila might in some way disappear too.

In a little while, Zaynab122 went to the kitchen and returned with a bowl of sliced apples and a plate of the freshly made halva – for Leila's soul. Its sweetness filled the room.

'We should have put a candle on the halva,' said Sabotage. 'Leila was always looking for an excuse to turn dinners into celebrations. She loved parties.'

'Especially birthday parties,' Humeyra drawled, suppressing a yawn. She regretted taking three tranquillizers in quick succession. To dispel the drowsiness she had made a cup of coffee for herself and now she stirred the sugar, clinking her spoon noisily against the porcelain.

Nalan cleared her throat. 'Oh, how she lied about her age. I once told her, "Sweetheart, if you're going to tell tall tales, you'd better remember them. Just write it down somewhere. You can't be thirty-three years old one year, and twenty-eight the next!"'

They laughed, and then they caught themselves laughing and somehow it felt wrong, a transgression, and they stopped.

'Okay, I need to tell you something important,' Nalan announced. 'But please hear me through before you object.'

'Oh dear. This is not going to end well,' said Humeyra lackadaisically.

'Don't be negative,' said Nalan, and turned to Sabotage. 'Remember that truck of yours, where is it?'

'I don't have a truck!'

'Don't your in-laws have one?'

'You mean my father-in-law's dusty Chevrolet? It's been ages since he last used that heap of metal. Why are you asking?'

'That's fine, so long as it does its job. We're going to need a few more things: shovels, spades, maybe a wheelbarrow.'

'Am I the only one who has no idea what she's talking about?' said Sabotage.

Humeyra rubbed the inner corners of her eyes with her fingertips. 'Don't worry, none of us has a clue.'

Nalan sat back, her chest heaving. She felt her heart begin to beat faster under the strain of what she was about to say. 'I propose we all go to the cemetery tonight.'

'What?!' Sabotage rasped.

Slowly, it all came back to him now: his childhood in Van, the cramped little flat above the pharmacy, the room overlooking an ancient graveyard, the sound of rustling under the eaves that could have been the swallows or the wind or maybe something else. Shutting the memory out, he focused on Nalan.

'Give me a chance to explain. Don't react before you've heard me out.' In her eagerness, Nalan's words spilled out in a deluge. 'It makes me so mad. How can a person who has built wonderful friendships all her life be buried in the Cemetery of the Companionless? How can that be her address for eternity? It's unfair!'

A fruit fly appeared out of nowhere, hovering above the apples, and for a second they all sat still, watching, grateful for the distraction.

'We all loved Leila-jim.' Zaynab122 picked her words carefully. 'She's the one who brought us together. But she is no longer in this world. We must pray for her soul and let her rest in peace.'

Nalan said, 'How can she *rest in peace* if she's in an awful place?'

'Don't forget, *habibi*, it's only her body. Her soul is not there,' said Zaynab122.

'How do you know that?' Nalan snapped. 'Look, maybe for believers like you the body is trivial . . . temporary. But not for me. And you know what? I've fought so hard for my body! For these' – she pointed to her breasts – 'for my cheekbones . . .' She stopped. 'Sorry if that sounds frivolous. I reckon all you care about is this thing you call "the soul", and maybe there is one, what do I know? But I need you to see that the body matters too. It's not like it's nothing.'

'Carry on.' Humeyra breathed in the aroma of coffee before taking another sip.

'Remember the old man? He still blames himself for not giving his wife a proper funeral – even after all these years. Do you want to feel the same way all your lives? Each time we remember Leila, we'll have this guilt burning inside, knowing we haven't done our duty as friends.' Nalan cocked an eyebrow towards Zaynab122. 'Please don't be offended, but I just don't give a damn about the next world. Maybe you are right and Leila's already up there in heaven, teaching angels make-up techniques and waxing their wings. If that's the case, great. But what about the way she was mistreated here on earth? Are we going to be okay with that?'

'Of course not, tell us what to do!' Sabotage said impulsively, and instantly halted, the most extraordinary thought now occurring to him. 'Hang on. You are not about to suggest we go and dig her up, are you?'

They expected Nalan to wave her hand and roll her eyes to the heaven she did not believe in, as she always did when confronted with an absurd comment. When she mentioned going to the cemetery they had all assumed that what she had in mind was giving Leila a proper funeral, a last farewell. But now it dawned on them that Nalan might be making a more radical suggestion. A disturbing silence descended. It was one of those moments when everyone wanted to protest, but no one wished to be the first to do so.

Nalan said, 'I believe we should do this. Not only for Leila, but also for ourselves. Have you ever wondered what will happen to us when we die? Clearly, we'll all get the same five-star treatment.' She pointed a finger at Humeyra. 'You have run away, my love, abandoning your husband, shaming your family and your tribe. What else is on your CV? Singing in sleazy clubs. As if that's not bad enough, you've got a few tasteless films under your belt.'

Humeyra blushed. 'I was young. I had no —'

'I know, but *they* won't understand. Don't expect sympathy. Sorry, honey, you'll be going straight to the Cemetery of the Companionless. Probably Sabotage, too, if they find out that he's been living a double life.'

'Okay, enough,' Zaynab122 interjected, sensing she would be next in line. 'You're upsetting everyone.'

'I'm speaking the truth,' said Nalan. 'We all have baggage, shall we say. And no one more than me. It kills me, this hypocrisy. Everyone loves watching camp singers on TV. But the same people would go berserk if their own sons or daughters turned out the same way. I saw it with my own eyes, this woman, just outside Hagia Sophia, was holding a sign: *The End Is Nigh, Earthquakes Will Be Upon Us: A City Full of Whores and Trans Deserves Allah's Wrath!* Let's face it, I'm a magnet for hatred. When I die, I'll be dumped in the Cemetery of the Companionless.'

'Don't say that,' Jameelah pleaded.

'Maybe you don't realize, but this is no ordinary cemetery we are talking about. It's . . . it's pure misery over there.'

'How do you know?' Zaynab122 asked.

Nalan twisted one of her rings around. 'I've acquaintances who were buried there.' She did not have to tell them that almost everyone in the trans community ended up at this final address. 'We must get Leila out of that place.'

'It's like the Karmic cycle.' Humeyra cradled her mug between her hands. 'We're being tested every day. If you say you are a true friend, there'll come a time when your dedication will be tested. Cosmic forces will ask you to prove how much you really care. It was in one of the books Leila gave me.'

'I have no idea what you're saying, but I agree,' said Nalan. 'Karma, Buddha, yoga . . . whatever moves you. My point is, Leila saved my life. I'll never forget that night. It was just the two of us. These shitheads appeared out of nowhere and started throwing punches. The bastards stabbed me in the ribs. Blood everywhere. I'm telling you, I was bleeding like a slaughtered lamb. I thought I was dying, no kidding. Supergirl descended on me, Clark Kent's cousin, remember? She took me by my arms and pulled me up. That's when I opened my eyes. It was no Supergirl, it was Leila. She could have run away. But she stayed . . . for me. She got us out of there – I still don't know how she managed it. She took me to a doctor. A quack doctor, but still. He sewed me up. I owe Leila.' Nalan took a breath, and released it slowly. 'I don't want to force anyone. If you don't want to come, I'll understand, honestly. I'll do this alone if I have to.'

'I'll come with you,' Humeyra heard herself say. She knocked back what remained of her coffee, perkier now.

'You sure?' Nalan looked surprised, knowing of her friend's anxieties and panic attacks.

But the tranquillizers she had taken this evening seemed to be shielding Humeyra from fear – until their effect wore off. 'Yes! You're going to need a hand. But first I'll have to brew more coffee. Maybe I should make up a Thermos and take it with me.'

'I am coming too,' said Sabotage.

'You don't like cemeteries,' said Humeyra.

'I don't . . . but as the only man in the group I feel I have a responsibility to protect you from yourselves,' said Sabotage. 'Besides, you can't get hold of that truck without me.'

Zaynab122's eyes grew wide. 'Wait, wait everyone. We can't do this. It's a sin to exhume the dead! And where, may I ask, are you planning to take her afterwards?'

Nalan shifted in her chair, only now realizing she hadn't given enough thought to the second part of her plan. 'We'll take her to a nice, decent resting place. We'll visit her often, bring flowers. We might even manage to commission a headstone. A marble one, shiny and smooth. With a black rose and a poem by one of D/Ali's favourite poets. Who was that Latin American guy he liked so much?'

'Pablo Neruda,' said Sabotage, his eyes sliding to a painting on the wall. It was of Leila sitting on a bed, dressed in a short crimson skirt, her breasts spilling from a bikini top, her hair pulled high, her face slightly turned towards the viewer. She was so beautiful, unreachable. Sabotage knew that D/Ali had painted this in the brothel.

'Yes, Neruda!' said Nalan. 'They have a peculiar way of mixing sex and sorrow, those Latin Americans. Most nations do one or the other better, but the Latinos triumph at both.'

'Or a poem by Nâzim Hikmet,' said Sabotage. 'Both D/Ali and Leila loved him.'

'Right, great, so we've got the headstone sorted.' Nalan nodded her approval.

'What headstone? Do you know how crazy you sound? You don't even know where you're going to bury her!' said Zaynab122, throwing up her hands.

Nalan frowned. 'I'll come up with something, okay?'

'I think we should lay her to rest next to D/Ali,' said Sabotage. All eyes turned to him.

'Yes, why didn't I think of that?' Nalan huffed. 'He's in that sunny graveyard in Bebek – fabulous location, great view. Lots of poets and musicians are buried there. Leila will be in good company.'

'She'll be with the love of her life,' Sabotage said without looking at anyone.

Zaynab122 sighed. 'Can you all come back to your senses? D/Ali is in a well-protected cemetery. We can't just go there and start digging. We'll have to get an official permit.'

'Official permit!' Nalan scoffed. 'Who's going to check it in the middle of the night?'

Heading towards the kitchen, Humeyra gave Zaynab122 an appeasing nod. 'You don't have to come, it's all right.'

'I have no choice,' Zaynab122 said, her voice quavering with emotion. 'Someone needs to stand at your side, pray the right prayers. Otherwise you're all going to end up cursed for the rest of your lives.' She lifted her head, looked at Nalan and squared her shoulders. 'Promise me you won't swear on cemetery ground. No profanities.'

'Promise,' said Nalan blithely. 'I'll be nice to your djinn.'

While the others had been debating, Jameelah had quietly left the table. She was now standing by the door, having put on a jacket, and was busy tying her shoelaces.

'Where are you going?' Nalan asked.

'I'm getting ready,' Jameelah said, calmly.

'Not you, my love. You must stay at home, make yourself a nice cup of tea, keep an eye on Mr Chaplin and wait for us.'

'Why? If you're going, I'm going.' Jameelah's eyes narrowed, her nostrils flaring slightly. 'If this is *your* duty as a friend, it's also my duty.'

Nalan shook her head. 'Sorry, but we must consider your health. I can't take you to a cemetery in the middle of the night. Leila would have skinned me alive.'

Jameelah threw her head back. 'Will you all please stop treating me as if I'm dying! Not yet, okay? I'm not dying yet.'

Rage was so rare an emotion for her that they fell quiet.

A gust of wind blew in from the balcony, fluttering the curtains. For an instant, it was almost as if there was a new presence in the room. A barely perceptible tickle, like a stray hair on the back of one's neck. But it grew stronger, and now they could all feel its power, its pull. Either they had stepped into some invisible realm, or another realm was seeping into theirs. As the clock on the wall ticked off the seconds, they all waited for midnight to arrive – the paintings on the walls, the rumbling flat, the deaf cat, the fruit fly and the five old friends of Tequila Leila.

The Road

On the corner of the Büyükdere Road, across from a kebab restaurant, there was a speed trap that had ensnared many careless drivers and was certain to ensnare many more. Time and again a patrol car would lurk unseen behind a thick clump of shrubs and catch unsuspecting vehicles racing through the intersection.

From the drivers' point of view, what made the trap unpredictable was the hours it was manned. Sometimes traffic police were there with the dawn, sometimes only in the afternoon. There were days when they were nowhere to be seen, and one might think they had packed up and gone. But then there were days when a blue-and-white car sat constantly in wait, like a panther biding its time before the fatal attack.

From the officers' point of view, this was one of the worst spots in Istanbul. Not because there were no drivers to stop and fine, but because there were simply too many. And much as handing out piles of tickets generated revenue for the state, it was not as if the state was disposed to showing gratitude. So the officers had to ask themselves what good it did to be vigilant. Besides, the job was fraught with pitfalls. Every now and then the car they pulled over turned out to belong to the son or nephew or wife or mistress of a top government official, top businessman, top judge or top army general. And then the policemen would get in top trouble.

It had happened to a colleague – an earnest, decent fellow. He had stopped a young man in a steel-blue Porsche for reckless driving (eating pizza, his hands off the wheel) and running a red light – violations that were, to be honest, committed by scores of drivers every day in Istanbul. If Paris was the city of love, Jerusalem the city of God, and Las Vegas the city of sin, Istanbul was the city of multitasking. But the policeman had stopped the Porsche, all the same.

'You ran a red light and –'

'Really?' The driver had cut him off. 'Do you know who my uncle is?'

That was a hint any sharp officer would have heeded. Thousands of citizens in all echelons of society heard similar insinuations every day and would instantly get the message. They understood that fines could be tweaked, rules could be bent, exceptions could be made. They knew that a government employee's eyes could be blinded temporarily and ears could be deafened for as long as needed. But this particular policeman, though not new to the job, suffered from an incurable malady: idealism. Upon hearing the driver's words, instead of backing off, he had said, 'I don't care who your uncle is. Rules are rules.'

Even children knew this was not true. Rules were *sometimes* rules. At other times, depending on the circumstances, they were empty words, absurd phrases or jokes without a punchline. Rules were sieves with holes so large that all sorts of things could pass through; rules were sticks of chewing gum that had long lost their taste but could not be spat out; rules in this country, and across the entire Middle East, were anything but rules. Forgetting this had cost the officer his job. The driver's uncle – a top minister – had made sure he was posted to a dreary little town on the eastern border where there were no cars for miles around.

So tonight, when two patrolmen positioned themselves at the infamous spot, they were reluctant to write any tickets. Sitting back, they listened to a football match on the radio – second league, nothing major. The younger of the two started talking about his fiancée. He did that incessantly. The other officer could not understand what compelled a man to do that; he himself was eager to keep his mind off his wife as much as possible, certainly for the few blissful hours he was at work. Excusing himself to have a smoke, he stepped out of the car and lit a cigarette, his eyes on the empty road. He hated his job. This was new to him.

Boredom he had felt before, fatigue too, but hatred was not something he was used to, and he struggled with the intensity of the emotion.

His eyebrows rose as he looked up and saw a solid wall of cloud in the distance. A thunderstorm was gathering. He felt a twinge of apprehension. Just as he reflected on whether the rainwater might flood the basements across the city, like it did the last time, he was startled by a loud, screeching noise. The hairs on his neck stood on end. The squeal of tyres on asphalt sent a chill down his spine. He caught a movement out of the corner of his eye even before he had the chance to turn. Then he saw the vehicle: a monster hurtling down the road, a metallic racehorse galloping towards an invisible finish line.

It was a pickup truck – a 1982 Chevrolet Silverado. The kind one rarely came across in Istanbul, more suited as it was to wider roads in Australia or America. It looked like it had once been goldfinch yellow, bright and cheery, but now it was covered in patches of dirt and rust. It was the figure at the wheel that really caught the police officer's attention though. In the driver's seat sat a hefty woman, her bright red hair flying in all directions, a cigarette dangling from her mouth.

As the truck flashed by, the officer caught a glimpse of the people huddled in the back. They were holding on to one another tightly against the wind. And though it was hard to make out each of their faces, from the way they were crouching their discomfort was clear. In their hands, they held what appeared to be spades and shovels and pickaxes. Suddenly, the truck veered to the left and then to the right, and would surely have caused an accident had there been another vehicle on the road. An overweight woman in the back shrieked and lost her balance, letting go of the pickaxe she had been holding. The tool tumbled out on to the road with a thud. Then they all disappeared – the truck, the driver, the passengers.

The police officer tossed his cigarette to the ground, stomped it out and swallowed, taking a moment to process what he had just witnessed. His hands trembled as he opened the door and extracted the car radio.

His colleague was also staring at the road. His voice was full of excitement when he spoke. 'Oh my God, did you see that? Is that a pickaxe?'

'Looks like it,' said the older officer, doing his best to sound calm and in control. 'Go pick it up. We may need it as evidence, and it can't be left there.'

'What do you think is going on?'

'My gut tells me that truck is not just trying to get somewhere fast . . . there's something fishy here.' With that he turned on the car radio. 'Two-three-six on duty to dispatch. Are you receiving?'

'Go ahead, Two-three-six.'

'Chevrolet pickup. Speeding driver. Could be dangerous.'

'Any other passengers?'

'Positive.' His voice caught in his throat. 'Suspicious cargo — four individuals in the back. They're heading towards Kilyos.'

'Kilyos? Confirm.'

The policeman repeated the description and location, then waited for the dispatcher to relay the information to other police units in the area.

When the crackle of static on the car radio had faded away, the young officer said, 'Why Kilyos? There's nothing there at this time of night. Sleepy old town.'

'Unless they're going to the beach. Who knows, maybe there's a moonlight party.'

'Moonlight party . . .' echoed the young officer, his voice betraying a twinge of envy.

'Or maybe they are heading to that wretched cemetery.'

'What cemetery?'

'Oh, you wouldn't know. Strange, spooky place by the sea. Near the old fortress,' the older officer mused in reply. 'Late one night, many years ago, we were on the heels of this thug and the bastard ran into the cemetery. I followed him — God, I was naive. My foot tripped over something in the dark. Was it a tree root or a thighbone? I didn't dare look. I just stumbled on. I heard something ahead of me – a deep, low moan. I was sure it wasn't human, but it didn't sound like an animal either. I turned around and ran back the way I came. Then – I swear on the Qur'an – the sound started to follow me! There was this weird, rancid smell in the air. I've never been so scared in my life. I managed to get out, but the next day my wife said, "What were you doing last night? Your clothes smell awful!"'

'Wow, that's creepy. I never knew.'

Nodding, the older officer said, 'Yeah, well, consider yourself lucky. It's one of those places better not to know. Only the damned end up in the Cemetery of the Companionless. Only the doomed.'

The Doomed

About an hour's drive from Istanbul's city centre, on the shores of
the Black Sea, sat an old Greek fishing village called Kilyos, famous for its powdery beaches, small hotels, sharp cliffs, and a
medieval fortress that had not once succeeded in repelling an
invading army. Over the centuries, many had come and many had
gone, leaving their songs, prayers and curses behind: the Byzan-
tines, the Crusaders, the Genoese, the corsairs, the Ottomans, the
Don Cossacks and, for a brief period, the Russians.

Not a soul remembered any of this today. The sand that gave
the area its Greek name – Kilia – covered and erased everything,
replacing the remnants of the past with smooth oblivion. Nowadays the entire coastal stretch was a popular holiday destination
for tourists, expats and locals. It was a place full of contrasts: private and public beaches; women in bikinis and women in hijabs;
picnicking families on blankets and cyclists whizzing by; rows of
expensive villas crammed against low-cost housing; thick strips of
oak, pine and beech trees, and concrete car parks.

The sea was pretty rough in Kilyos. Riptides and strong waves
drowned a few people each year, their bodies hauled from the
water by coastguards in rubber boats. It was impossible to say
whether the victims had swum outside the buoys, recklessly self-
confident, or whether the undercurrent had pulled them into its
embrace like a sweet lullaby. From the water's edge, holidaymakers watched as each tragic incident unfolded. Shielding their eyes
from the sun, peering through their binoculars, they stared in a
single direction, as though transfixed by a spell. When they started
talking again they did so animatedly; companions sharing an
adventure, if only for a few minutes. Finally, they returned to
their sunloungers and hammocks. For a while their faces remained

blank and they seemed to consider going elsewhere – another beach where the sand was just as golden, the wind probably calmer and the sea less crazy. Yet this was a fine location in so many other ways, with its affordable prices, good restaurants, clement weather and breath-taking views, and God knew how badly they were in need of some rest. Although they would never voice it out loud, and may not even have admitted it to themselves, a part of them resented the dead for having the nerve to drown in a holiday resort. It seemed like an act of extreme selfishness. They had worked hard all year round, saved money, put up with the whims of their bosses, swallowed their pride and restrained their anger and, in their moments of despair, dreamed of lazy days in the sun. So the holidaymakers remained. When they wished to cool off, they took a quick dip, pushing aside the nagging thought that only moments before, in the same waters, some unfortunate soul had met their end.

Every now and then, a boat full of asylum seekers capsized in these waters. Their bodies were pulled from the sea and placed side by side, journalists gathering around to write their reports. Then the bodies were loaded into refrigerated vans designed to carry ice cream and frozen fish, and driven to a special graveyard – the Cemetery of the Companionless. Afghans, Syrians, Iraqis, Somalis, Eritreans, Sudanese, Nigerians, Libyans, Iranians, Pakistanis – they were buried so far from where they were born, laid to rest haphazardly wherever space was available. Around them, on all sides, were Turkish citizens who, though neither asylum seekers nor undocumented migrants, had, in all likelihood, felt equally unwelcome in their own homeland. So it was that, unbeknownst to tourists and even many locals, there was a burial ground in Kilyos – one of a kind. It was reserved for three types of dead: the unwanted, the unworthy and the unidentified.

Covered with clumps of sagebrush, nettles and knapweed, and enclosed by a wooden fence with missing posts and sagging wires, this was the most peculiar cemetery in Istanbul. It had few, if any, visitors. Even veteran grave-robbers gave it a wide berth, dreading the curse of the accursed. Disturbing the dead was fraught with danger, but to disturb those who were both doomed and dead was an open invitation to disaster.

Almost everyone interred in the Cemetery of the Companionless was, in some way or another, an outcast. Many had been shunned by their family or village or society at large. Crack addicts, alcoholics, gamblers, small-time criminals, rough sleepers, runaways, throwaways, missing citizens, the mentally ill, derelicts, unwed mothers, prostitutes, pimps, transvestites, AIDS patients . . . The undesirables. Social pariahs. Cultural lepers.

Among the residents of the graveyard were also cold-blooded murderers, serial killers, suicide bombers and sexual predators, and, as baffling as it may be, their innocent victims. The evil and the good, the cruel and the merciful, had been planted six feet under, side by side, in row after godforsaken row. Most of them did not have even the simplest of tombstones. Neither a name nor a date of birth. Only a coarsely hewn wooden board with a number and sometimes not even that, just a rusty tin placard. And somewhere in this unholy mess, among the hundreds and hundreds of untended graves, there was one freshly dug.

This is where Tequila Leila was buried.

Number 7053.

Number 7054, the grave to her right, belonged to a songwriter who had taken his own life. People still sung his songs everywhere, without knowing that the man who had written those poignant lyrics lay in a forgotten grave. There were many suicide victims in the Cemetery of the Companionless. Often they came from small towns and villages where the imams had refused to give them funerals, and their bereaved families, out of shame or sorrow, had agreed to have them buried far away.

Number 7063, the grave to Leila's north, belonged to a murderer. On a jealous rampage, he had shot his wife, then charged to the house of the man he suspected his wife had been having an affair with, and shot him as well. Having one bullet and no targets left, he had aimed the gun at his temple, missed, taken off the side of his head, slid into a coma and died a couple of days later. No one had claimed his body.

Number 7052, the neighbour to Leila's left, was another dark soul. A fanatic. He had resolved to walk into a nightclub and shoot down every sinner who was dancing and drinking, but he hadn't been able to procure the guns. Frustrated, he had decided to make a bomb instead, using a pressure cooker filled with nails dipped in rat poison. He had planned everything down to the last detail – except he had blown up his own house while preparing the lethal device. One of the nails flying in all directions had hit him straight in the heart. This had happened only two days ago and now he was here.

Number 7043, the neighbour to Leila's south, was a Zen Buddhist (the only one in the cemetery). She had been flying from Nepal to New York to visit her grandchildren when she suffered a brain haemorrhage. The plane had made an emergency landing. She had died in Istanbul, a city she had never set foot in before. Her family had wanted her body to be burned and her ashes returned to Nepal. According to their belief, her funeral pyre needed to be set alight where she had exhaled her last breath. But as cremation was illegal in Turkey, she had to be buried instead, and buried fast, as required by Islamic law.

There were no Buddhist graveyards in the city. There were various graveyards – historical and modern; Muslim (Sunni, Alevi and Sufi), Roman Catholic, Greek Orthodox, Armenian Apostolic, Armenian Catholic, Jewish – but nothing specifically for Buddhists. In the end, the grandmother was brought to the Cemetery of the Companionless. Her family had given their consent, saying she wouldn't have minded as she was at peace even among strangers.

Other graves near Leila's were occupied by revolutionaries who had died in police custody. *Committed suicide*, it said in official records, *found in his cell with a rope* [or a necktie or a bedsheet or a shoelace] *around his neck*. The bruises and the burns on the corpses told a different story, one of severe torture in police custody. A number of Kurdish insurgents were also buried here, carried from the other end of the country all the way to this graveyard. The state did not want them to turn into martyrs in the eyes of their people, so the bodies were carefully packaged, as if made of glass, and transferred.

The youngest residents of the graveyard were the abandoned babies. Wrapped bundles deposited in mosque courtyards, sun-drenched playgrounds or dimly lit cinemas. Those who were lucky enough were rescued by passers-by and handed to police officers, who kindly fed and dressed them, and gave them a name – something cheerful like Felicity, Joy or Hope to counter their dismal beginnings. But every now and then there would be babies who were not as fortunate. One night out in the cold was enough to kill them.

On average fifty-five thousand people died in Istanbul every year – and only about one hundred and twenty of them ended up here in Kilyos.

Visitors

In the depth of the night, silhouetted against a sky sliced by flashes of lightning, a Chevrolet pickup truck zoomed past the old fortress, kicking up billows of dust. It rattled forward, skidded its way over a kerb, swerving violently towards the outcrop of rocks that separated the land from the sea, but managing to swing back on to the road at the last second. A few yards on, it finally jerked to a halt. For a moment there was no sound — either inside or outside the vehicle. Even the wind, which had been blowing hard since late afternoon, seemed to have died down.

The driver's door opened with a screech and Nostalgia Nalan jumped out. Her hair glowed in the moonlight, a halo of fire. She took a few steps, her gaze fixed on the cemetery spreading out in front of her. Carefully, she surveyed the scene. With its rusty iron gate, rows of decrepit graves, wooden boards passing for markers, broken fence offering not a speck of protection from hoodlums, and gnarled cypress trees, the place looked eerie and uninviting. Just as she thought it would. Inhaling a lungful of air, she glanced over her shoulder and announced, 'We're here!'

Only then did the four shadows, huddled against each other in the back of the truck, dare to budge. One by one they raised their heads and sniffed the air, like deer checking whether there were any hunters about.

The first to stand up was Hollywood Humeyra. As soon as she scrambled out, a rucksack on her back, she patted the top of her head and checked her chignon, which stuck out at an odd angle.

'Oh, God, my hair is a mess. I can't feel my face. It's frozen.'

'It's the wind, you wimp. There's a storm tonight. I told you to cover your heads. But oh no, you never listen to me.'

'It wasn't the wind, it was your driving,' Zaynab122 said, lowering herself with difficulty from the back of the pickup.

'You call that *driving*?' Sabotage jumped down and then helped Jameelah.

Sabotage's sparse hair stood in quills. He regretted not wearing a woolly hat, but that was nothing next to the regret he was beginning to feel for having agreed to visit this wretched place in the dead of night.

'How on earth did you get your licence anyway?' asked Zaynab122.

'Slept with the instructor, I bet,' Humeyra muttered under her breath.

'Oh, shut up, all of you.' Nalan frowned. 'Didn't you see the road? Thanks to me, we've at least arrived safe and sound.'

'Safe!' said Humeyra.

'Sound!' said Sabotage.

'Bastards!' Swift and purposeful, Nalan stomped towards the back of the truck.

Zaynab122 sighed. 'Um, could you watch your language? We made a deal. No yelling and no swearing in the cemetery.' She pulled her rosary out of her pocket and began to finger it. Something told her that it was not going to be easy, this night-time venture, and she would need all the help she could get from the good spirits.

Meanwhile, Nalan had pulled down the tailgate and started taking out the tools – a wheelbarrow, a digging hoe, a mattock, a shovel, a spade, a torch, a coil of rope. She placed them on the ground and scratched her head. 'We're missing a pickaxe.'

'Oh, that,' said Humeyra. 'I . . . I might have dropped it.'

'What do you mean, you might have *dropped* it? It's a pickaxe, not a hanky.'

'I couldn't hold on to it. Blame yourself. You were driving like a maniac.'

Nalan gave her a cold glare, which went unnoticed in the dark. 'Okay, enough chit-chat. Let's get a move on. We don't have much time.' She took hold of the spade and the torch. 'Everyone grab a tool!'

One by one, they followed her lead. Somewhere in the distance the sea roared and crashed to the shore with enormous force. The wind picked up again, carrying with it the smell of brine. In the background, the old fortress waited patiently – as it had for decades – and the shadow of an animal scurried past its gates, a rat perhaps, or a hedgehog, running for shelter before the storm.

Silently, they pushed the cemetery gate open and went in. Five intruders, five friends, looking for the one they had lost. As though on cue, the moon disappeared behind a cloud, plunging the entire landscape into shades of black, and, for a passing moment, this lonely site in Kilyos could have been anywhere in the world.

The Night

Night-time in the cemetery was not like night-time in the city. Around here, darkness was less an absence of light than a presence of its own – a living, breathing entity. It followed them like a curious creature, whether to warn them of a danger lying ahead or to shove them towards it when the moment came, they could not tell.

Onward, against the fierce wind, they walked. At first they moved briskly, with an eagerness sparked by discomfort, if not plain fear. They proceeded in single file with Nalan leading the way, spade in one hand, torch in the other. Behind her, each with their own tools, were Jameelah and Sabotage, then Humeyra, pushing the empty wheelbarrow. As for Zaynab122, she brought up the rear, not only because her legs were shorter, but also because she was busy sprinkling salt flakes and poppy seeds to ward off evil spirits.

A pungent smell rose from the ground – of damp earth, wet stone, wild thistles, rotting leaves, and things they did not wish to name. A heavy, musky smell of decay. They saw rocks and tree trunks covered with green lichen, its leaf-like scales bright and ghostly in the dark. In places, an ivory mist hovered before their eyes. Once they heard a rustle that sounded as if it rose from below the earth. Nalan stopped and panned her torch around. Only then did they grasp the vastness of the cemetery and the size of their task.

For as long as they could, they stuck to a single path, undeterred by its narrowness and slippery surface, for it seemed to be taking them in the right direction. But soon the path disappeared and they found themselves trudging up a trackless hill among the graves. There were hundreds and hundreds of them, most marked with boards that bore a number, though quite a few seemed to have lost theirs. In the anaemic light of the moon they looked spectral.

Occasionally, they came across graves privileged with a limestone slab, and once they found an inscription:

Assumest not that thou art alive but I am gone.
Nothing is what it seems in this forgotten land . . .

Y. V.

'That's it, I'm going back,' said Sabotage, his hand closed around his shovel.

Nalan removed a bramble from her sleeve. 'Don't be daft. It's just a silly poem.'

'Silly poem? This man is threatening us.'

'You don't know it's a man. There are only initials.'

Sabotage shook his head. 'Doesn't matter. Whoever's buried here is warning us not to go any further.'

'Just like in the movies,' murmured Humeyra.

Sabotage nodded. 'Yeah, when a group of visitors enter a haunted house and by the end of the night, they're all dead! And you know what the audience think? *Well, they had it coming, really* – which is what the newspapers will say about us tomorrow morning.'

'Tomorrow morning's papers have already gone to press,' said Nalan.

'Oh, great then.' Sabotage tried to smile. And for a brief moment it felt as if they were in Leila's flat on Hairy Kafka Street, all six of them, chatting and teasing each other, their voices tinkling like glass chimes.

Another flash of lightning, this time so close the earth glowed as though illuminated from below. It was followed almost instantly by a crack of thunder. Sabotage stopped and removed a tobacco pouch from his pocket. He rolled himself a joint but struggled with the match. The wind was too strong. Finally, he managed to light it and took a deep drag.

'What are you doing?' asked Nalan.

'For my nerves. My poor, frayed nerves. I'm going to have a heart attack in this place. The men on my father's side of the family have all died before hitting forty-three. My father had a heart attack when he was forty-two. Guess how old I am! I swear it's a health hazard for me to be here.'

'Come on, if you get stoned, what good will you be?' Nalan arched an eyebrow. 'Besides, a cigarette can be spotted from miles away. Why do you think soldiers on the battlefield are banned from smoking?'

'Good grief, we're not in a war! And what about your torch? Can the *enemy* see the tip of my joint but not that glaring beam of yours?'

'I'm aiming it at the ground,' said Nalan, shining the torch on a grave nearby to make her point. Disturbed, a bat flew off, flapping over their heads.

Sabotage flicked away his joint. 'Fine. Happy now?'

They zigzagged around wooden planks and gnarled trees, sweating in spite of the cold; tense and irritable like the unwanted visitors they knew they were. Ferns and thistles brushed against their legs; autumn leaves scrunched underfoot.

Nalan's boot got stuck on a tree root. She staggered to regain her balance. 'Oh, shit!'

'No profanities,' warned Zaynab122. 'The djinn might hear you. They live in tunnels underneath graves.'

'Maybe now is not the right time to tell us,' said Humeyra.

'I wasn't trying to scare you.' Zaynab122 surveyed her mournfully. 'Would you even know what to do if you came across a djinn? Don't panic, that's rule number one. Don't run, number two – they're faster than us. Number three: don't scorn him – or her, female djinn have the worst tempers.'

'That I can totally relate to,' said Nalan.

'Is there a rule number four?' asked Jameelah.

'Yes: do not let them charm you. The djinn are masters of disguise.'

Nalan snorted, and then caught herself. 'Sorry.'

'It's true,' Zaynab122 pressed on. 'If you had read the Qur'an, you'd know. The djinn can take the form of anything they want: human, animal, plant, mineral . . . See that tree? You *think* it's a tree, but it could be a spirit.'

Humeyra, Jameelah and Sabotage stole sideways glances at the beech tree. It seemed old and ordinary, with a knotty trunk, and branches that appeared as lifeless as the corpses underground. But now that they were staring at it closely, perhaps it did exude an uncanny energy, an unearthly aura.

Nalan, who had carried on unperturbed, slowed down and glanced back over her shoulder. 'Enough! Stop freaking them out.'

'I'm trying to help,' said Zaynab122 defiantly.

Even if all that nonsense were true, why load people with information they wouldn't know what to do with? Nalan wanted to say, but refrained. In her view, human beings resembled peregrine falcons: they had the power and the ability to soar up to the skies, free and ethereal and unrestrained, but sometimes they would also, either under duress or of their own free will, accept captivity.

Back in Anatolia, Nalan had seen at close hand how falcons would perch on their captors' shoulders, obediently waiting for the next treat or command. The falconer's whistle, the call that ended freedom. She had also observed how a hood would be put on these noble raptors to make sure they would not panic. Seeing was knowing, and knowing was frightening. Every falconer knew that the less it saw the calmer the bird.

But underneath that hood where there were no directions, and the sky and the land melted into a swathe of black linen, though comforted, the falcon would still feel nervous, as if in preparation for a blow that could come at any moment. Years later now, it seemed to Nalan that religion – and power and money and ideology and politics – acted like a hood too. All these superstitions and predictions and beliefs deprived human beings of sight, keeping them under control, but deep within weakening their self-esteem to such a point that they now feared anything, everything.

Not her though. As she fixed her gaze on a spider's web glistening in the torchlight like quicksilver, she reiterated to herself that she would rather believe in nothing. No religion, no ideology. She, Nostalgia Nalan, would never be blindfolded.

Vodka

Having arrived at a corner where the path started up again, the band of friends came to a halt. Here the grave numbers seemed haphazard, out of sequence. In the passing light of her torch, Nostalgia Nalan read aloud: 'Seven thousand and forty, seven thousand and twenty-four, seven thousand and forty-eight . . .'

She frowned, as if suspecting someone was mocking her. She had never been good at maths. Or at any other subject, really. To this day, one of her recurring dreams involved her being back at school. She saw herself as a little boy clad in an ugly uniform, hair cropped painfully short, beaten by the teacher in front of the whole class for poor spelling and poorer grammar. Back then the word 'dyslexia' had not yet entered the Dictionary of Daily Life in the village, and neither the teacher nor the headmaster had shown Nalan any sympathy.

'You okay?' asked Zaynab122.

'Sure!' Nalan pulled herself together.

'These markers are so weird,' muttered Humeyra. 'Which way do we go now?'

'Why don't you all stay here? I'll go and check,' said Nalan.

'Maybe one of us should come with you?' Jameelah looked concerned.

Nalan waved her hand. She needed to be alone for a brief moment and collect her thoughts. Taking out a flask from the inside of her jacket, she drank a hefty glug to fortify herself. Then she handed the flask to Humeyra, the only other person in the group who could consume alcohol: 'Try it, but be careful.'

So saying, she disappeared.

Now without a torch, and with the moon hiding momentarily behind a cloud, the four of them were left in the darkness. They inched closer together.

'You realize this is how it begins,' Humeyra murmured. 'In the movies, I mean. One of them leaves the others, and is brutally killed. It happens only a few yards from the group but they don't know it, of course. Then another walks off and meets the same end . . .'

'Relax, we're not going to die,' said Zaynab122.

If Humeyra, despite the tranquillizers she had taken, was becoming nervous, Sabotage was feeling worse. He said, 'That liquor she gave you . . . Why don't we have a sip?'

Humeyra hesitated. 'You know it's a disaster when you drink.'

'But that's on a normal day. We are in a state of emergency tonight. I told you girls about the men in my family. I'm not scared of this *place* exactly. It's death that makes my blood run cold.'

'Why don't you smoke your joint?' Jameelah suggested helpfully.

'Don't have any left. How am I going to walk in this state? Or dig up a grave?!'

Humeyra and Zaynab122 glanced at each other. Jameelah shrugged her shoulders.

'Fine,' said Humeyra. 'I need a sip myself, to be honest.'

Grabbing the flask from her, Sabotage guzzled an impressive draught. Then another.

'That's enough,' Humeyra said. She, too, knocked back a slug. An arrow of fire shot down her throat. She screwed up her face and hunched over. 'What . . . argh . . . What was that?!'

'I don't know, but I liked it,' said Sabotage, and snatched the flask for another quick gulp. It felt good, and in a flash he downed another slurp.

'Hey, stop it.' Humeyra took back the flask and put the lid on. 'That's strong stuff. I've never –'

'Okay, let's go! It's this way,' rose a voice from the shadows. Nalan was coming back.

'Your liquor,' said Humeyra walking towards her. 'What kind of a poison is it?'

'Oh, did you try it? It's special. They call it Spirytus Magnanimus.

Polish vodka – or Ukrainian, Russian or Slovak. We fight over who invented baklava, was it the Turks or the Lebanese or the Syrians or the Greeks . . . and those Slavs have their own vodka wars.'

'So that was *vodka*?' Humeyra asked incredulously.

Nalan beamed. 'You bet! But no other vodka comes close. Ninety-seven per cent alcohol. Functional, practical. Dentists give it to their patients before they extract teeth. Doctors use it for surgery. They even make perfume with it. But in Poland, they drink it at funerals – to toast the dead. So I thought it'd be appropriate.'

'You brought a lethal vodka to a cemetery?' said Zaynab122, and shook her head.

'Well, I'm not expecting you to appreciate it,' said Nalan, sounding offended.

'And were you able to find Leila's grave?' Jameelah enquired, changing the subject to dispel the tension.

'Yes, yes! It's on the other side. Ready, everyone?'

Without waiting for an answer, Nostalgia Nalan pointed her torch to the path on their left and marched on, failing to notice the strange smile that had descended on Sabotage's face and the glaze that had settled in his eyes.

To Err is Human

Finally, they had made it. Leaning in towards one another, they stared at a particular grave as if it were a riddle they needed to decode. Like most of the other graves, this one, too, had just a number on it. Neither 'Tequila' nor 'Leila' was engraved on her headstone. She did not have a headstone. Nor a well-tended plot with a neat border of flowers. All she had was a wooden board scrawled on by some cemetery worker.

Disturbed by their presence, a lizard scurried from beneath a rock and ran for cover, disappearing into the tangle of bushes ahead. Dropping her voice to a whisper, Humeyra asked, 'Is this where Leila-jim is buried?'

Nalan stood with a quiet intensity. 'Yes, let's dig.'

'Not so fast.' Zaynab122 raised a hand. 'We must pray first. You cannot exhume a body without a proper ritual.'

'Fine,' said Nalan. 'Just make it short, please. We need to hurry.'

Zaynab122 produced a jar from her bag and sprinkled around the grave the mixture she had prepared earlier: rock salt, rose-water, sandalwood paste, cardamom seeds and camphor. With eyes closed and palms turned upwards, she recited the Surah al-Fatiha. Humeyra joined her. Sabotage, feeling dizzy, had to sit down before he could say his prayers. Jameelah crossed herself three times, her lips moving silently.

The ensuing silence was imbued with sadness.

'All right, time to move on,' said Nalan.

Using her full weight, Nalan drove her spade deep into the earth, pressing hard on the top of the blade with her boot. Earlier she had been worried that the ground would be frozen, but it was fairly soft and wet, and she quickly set to work, falling into a rhythmic motion. Soon she was surrounded by the familiar, comforting smell and feel of the soil.

An image flashed through Nalan's mind. She remembered the first time she saw Leila — at first she was just another face in the windows of the brothel, her breath misting the glass. She moved with a quiet grace that almost belied her surroundings. With her hair falling over her shoulders, and her large, dark, expressive eyes, Leila resembled the woman on a coin that Nalan had once found while ploughing the fields. Like that Byzantine empress, there was something elusive in her expression, defying time and place. She remembered how they used to meet in the börek shop, trusting and confiding in each other.

'Have you ever wondered what happened to her?' Leila had asked out of the blue one day. 'That young bride of yours . . . you left her in that room — alone.'

'Well, I'm sure she got married to someone else. She must have a troop of kids by now.'

'That's not the point, darling. You send me postcards, no? You should write her a letter. Explain what happened and apologize.'

'Are you serious? I was forced into a sham marriage. It would have killed me. I ran away to save myself. Would you rather I'd stayed and lived a lie my entire life?'

'Not at all. We must do what we can to mend our lives, we owe that to ourselves — but we need to be careful not to break others while achieving that.'

'Oh, God!'

Leila had looked at him in that patient, knowing way she had.

Nalan had thrown her hands up. 'Okay, fine . . . I'll write to my dear *wife*.'

'Promise?'

As Nalan continued to dig up Leila's grave, her thoughts flicked involuntarily to that long-ago forgotten exchange. She heard Leila's voice inside her head and she also remembered that she had never written that promised letter.

Sabotage now stood on the edge of the grave, watching Nalan with a wonder tinged with admiration. He had never been good at manual labour; at home, whenever a tap needed fixing or a shelf had to be put up, they would call a neighbour. Everyone in the family saw him as a man absorbed in boring subjects, such as numbers and tax returns, whereas Sabotage preferred to think of himself as having a creative mind. A neglected artist. Or an unappreciated scientist. A wasted talent. He had never told Leila how he had envied D/Ali. What else had he not told her? Memories raced through his mind, each a separate and distinct piece of the jigsaw puzzle that was his long relationship with Leila, a picture full of irreparable cracks and missing pieces.

Speeded up by the vodka coursing through his system, blood pounded in his ears. He almost closed his ears, trying to shut out the sound. He waited. When the impulse did not pass, he threw his head back as if hoping to find consolation in the sky. Up there he noticed the strangest thing; his expression went slack. A face was staring down at him from the surface of the moon. It was surprisingly familiar. He squinted until his eyes became slits. It was his own face! Somebody had drawn him on the moon! Stunned, Sabotage let out a gasp of disbelief, loud and wheezy like a samovar hissing before coming to the boil. He pursed his lips and bit at the inside of his mouth, trying to control himself, but to no avail.

'Did you see the moon? I'm up there!' Sabotage said, his cheeks aflame.

Nalan stopped digging. 'What's wrong with him?'

Sabotage rolled his eyes. 'What's wrong with me? Absolutely nothing. Why do you always assume something's wrong with me?'

With a sharp intake of breath, Nalan dropped the spade and strode over to him. She held him by the shoulders and inspected his pupils, noticing they were dilated.

Swiftly, Nalan turned to the others. 'Did he have a drink?'

Humeyra swallowed. 'He wasn't feeling well.'

Nalan clenched her jaw. 'I see. And what exactly did he have?'

'Your . . . vodka,' said Zaynab122.

'What? Are you out of your minds? Even I'm cautious with that. Who is going to take care of him now?'

'I will,' said Sabotage. 'I can take care of myself!'

Nalan grabbed the spade again. 'Make sure you keep him away from me. I mean it!'

'Come, stay by my side,' Humeyra said as she gently pulled Sabotage towards her.

Sabotage sighed with a weary exasperation. Once again he was seized by that all-too-familiar feeling of being misunderstood by the people closest to him. He had never set great store by words, expecting the people he loved to read him through his silences. When he had to talk openly, he often hinted at things; when he had to disclose his emotions, he concealed them even more. Perhaps death was scary for everyone, but more so for the one who knew, deep within, that he had lived a life of pretences and obligations, a life shaped by the needs and demands of other people. Now that he had reached the age his father had died – leaving him and his mother all alone in a parochial, gossipy neighbourhood in Van – he had every right to ask himself what would remain of him when he, too, was gone.

'Didn't anyone else see me on the moon?' Sabotage asked, rocking on his heels, his entire body swaying like a raft on choppy waters.

'Hush, my love,' said Humeyra.

'But have you seen?'

Zaynab122 said, 'Yes, yes. We did.'

'It's gone now,' said Sabotage, eyes cast down, despondency settling into his features. 'Poof! No more. Is that what happens when you die?'

'You're here with us.' Humeyra opened her Thermos and offered him some coffee.

Sabotage took a few sips, but did not seem comforted. 'I wasn't exactly telling the truth when I said I wasn't scared of this place. It gives me the creeps.'

'Me too,' said Humeyra quietly. 'I was feeling brave when we set off, but not any more. I'm sure I'm going to have nightmares for a long time.'

Although they felt ashamed for not helping Nalan, the four of them stood helplessly side by side, watching lumps of soil being scooped out of the ground, one after another, destroying what little order and peace there was in this strange place.

Now that the grave was opened, Sabotage and the girls clustered around the mound of earth, not daring to look down into the dark pit. Not yet.

Nalan climbed out of the hole she had dug, panting and covered in mud. She wiped the sweat off her brow, not realizing she had smudged dirt across her forehead. She said, 'Thanks for the help, lazy bastards.'

The others did not respond. They were too scared to talk. Agreeing to this crazy plan and hopping into the truck had felt like an adventure, and the right thing to do for Leila. But now, all of a sudden, they were seized by a raw, primordial fear; the vows they had taken earlier had little bearing when faced with a corpse in the middle of the night.

'Come on. Let's get her out.' Nalan panned her torch around the inside of the grave.

A few tree roots became visible in the light, wriggling like snakes. At the bottom of the hole was the shroud, speckled with clods of earth.

'How come there's no coffin?' asked Jameelah when she managed to inch closer and glance down.

Zaynab122 shook her head. 'Christians do that. In Islam we bury our dead with a simple shroud. Nothing else. It makes us all equal in death. What did your people do back home?'

'I never saw a dead person before,' said Jameelah, her voice catching. 'Except my mother. She was a Christian but converted to Islam after she got married . . . though . . . there were disagreements about her funeral. My father wanted a Muslim burial; my aunt, a Christian one. They got into a big fight. Things got ugly.'

Zaynab122 nodded as a cloak of sadness engulfed her. Religion for her had always been a source of hope, resilience and love – a lift that carried her up from the basement of darkness into a spiritual light. It pained her that the same lift could just as easily take others all the way down. The teachings that warmed her heart and brought her close to all humanity, regardless of creed, colour or nationality, could be interpreted in such a way that they divided, confused and separated human beings, sowing seeds of enmity and bloodshed. If she were summoned by God one day, and had a chance to sit in His presence, she would love to ask Him just one simple question: 'Why did you allow Yourself to be so widely misunderstood, my beautiful and merciful God?'

Slowly, her gaze wandered down. What she saw there jolted her out of her thoughts. She said, 'There should have been wooden planks over Leila's shroud. Why wasn't her body protected?'

'I guess the gravediggers just didn't care.' Nalan dusted off her hands and turned to Zaynab122. 'Okay, jump in!'

'What? Me?'

'I need to stay here and pull the rope. Someone has to get in. You are the smallest.'

'Precisely, I can't go down there. If I do, I won't be able to get out.'

Nalan gave this some thought. She glanced at Humeyra – too fat; then at Sabotage – too drunk; and finally at Jameelah – too weak. She sighed. 'Fine, I'll do it. I've been down there long enough already, I suppose.'

Putting her spade aside, she moved closer and peered over the edge. A wave of sorrow rose in her chest. Down there was her best friend – the woman with whom she had shared more than two decades of her life – good times, bad times and terrible times.

'Okay, here is what we're going to do,' Nalan announced. 'I'll crawl down, you'll throw me the rope, and I'll tie it around Leila. At the count of three, you pull her up, got it?'

'Got it!' Humeyra rasped.

'How are we going to pull? Let me see,' Sabotage said and, before anyone could stop him, he had pushed his way forward.

Under the influence of the knock-out vodka, his normally bloodless complexion had flushed a shade of red reminiscent of a butcher's block. He was sweating profusely, although he had taken off his jacket. He craned his head as far as he could and squinted into the grave. He paled.

A few minutes earlier, he had seen his face on the moon. That had been a shock. But now there was a ghostly imprint of his face on the shroud below. It was an intimation from Death. His friends might not get it, but he knew that Azrael was telling him that he would be next. His head began to spin. Feeling queasy, he staggered forth half-blind, losing his balance. His feet shot out from under him; sliding down, he tumbled straight into the grave.

It all happened so fast that the others had no time to react – apart from Jameelah, who let out a scream.

'Now look at you!' Nalan stood with her legs wide apart, hands on her hips, surveying Sabotage's predicament. 'How could you be so careless?'

'Oh dear, are you all right?' Humeyra peeked cautiously over the edge.

Down in the pit, Sabotage stood perfectly still but for his trembling jaw.

'Are you even alive?' asked Nalan.

Finding his voice, Sabotage said, 'I feel . . . I think . . . I'm inside a grave.'

'Yes, we can tell,' said Nalan.

'Don't panic, my dear,' said Zaynab122. 'Think about it this way. You're facing your fear, it's good for you.'

'Get me out. Please!' Sabotage was in no state to appreciate any counsel. Careful not to step on the shroud, he moved aside, but instantly shifted again, fearing unseen creatures in the pitch-black recesses of the grave.

'Come on, Nalan, you must help him,' said Humeyra.

Nalan heaved her shoulders in a shrug. 'Why should I? Maybe it would be good for him to stay there and learn a lesson.'

'What did she say?' Sabotage's voice came out in a gurgle, as though a solid substance were stuck in his throat.

Jameelah broke in: 'She's just teasing. We're going to save you.'

'That's true, don't worry,' said Zaynab122. 'I'll teach you a prayer to help –'

Sabotage's breathing accelerated. Against the darkness of the grave's side walls, his face had taken on a ghastly pallor. He placed a hand on his heart.

'Oh, my God! I think he's having a heart attack – just like his father,' said Humeyra. 'Do something, quick!'

Nalan sighed. 'Okay, fine.'

No sooner had Nalan jumped down into the pit and landed next to him than Sabotage wrapped his arms around her. Never in his life had he been so relieved to see her.

'Um, can you take your hands off me? I can't move.'

Reluctantly, Sabotage loosened his arms. Time and again in his life he had been castigated and whittled down to the nub by others: at his childhood home by a strong, loving but strict mother; at school by his teachers; in the army by his superiors; in the office by almost everyone. Years of browbeating had crushed his soul, leaving a pulp where courage might otherwise have bloomed.

Regretting her tone, Nalan leaned forward and knitted her hands together. 'Come on. Up you go!'

'You sure? I don't want to hurt you.'

'Don't worry about that. Just get on with it, honey.'

Sabotage put a foot in Nalan's hands, a knee on Nalan's shoulder, and his other foot on Nalan's head, clambering his way up. Humeyra, with a bit of help from Zaynab122 and Jameelah, reached down and hauled him out.

'Thank you, God!' Sabotage said as soon as he reached ground level.

'Yeah, I do the hard work, God gets the credit,' grumbled Nalan from down in the pit.

'Thank you, Nalan,' said Sabotage.

'You're welcome. Now can somebody *please* throw me the rope?'

They did. Grabbing the rope, Nalan tied it around the body. 'Pull!'

At first the corpse refused to budge, determined, it seemed, to stay where it was. Then, inch by inch, they were able to lift it up. When it was high enough, carrying it carefully, Humeyra and Zaynab122 placed the corpse on the ground, as gently as they could manage.

Finally, Nalan scrambled up, her hands and knees covered with scratches and cuts. 'Phew. I'm exhausted.'

But no one heard her. The others were all staring at the shroud, eyes wide with disbelief. While being hoisted up, a part of the fabric had been ripped open and a face was now partly visible.

'This person has a beard,' said Sabotage.

Zaynab122 looked up at Nalan in horror as the truth dawned on her. 'Allah have mercy on us. We exhumed the wrong grave.'

'How could we make such a mistake?' asked Jameelah, after they had reburied the bearded man and smoothed over his grave.

'It's because of the old man at the hospital.' A tinge of embarrassment in her voice, Nalan took out the piece of paper from her pocket. 'He's got the worst handwriting. I wasn't sure whether this was seven thousand and fifty-two or seven thousand and fifty-three. How was I to know? It's not my fault.'

'It's fine,' Zaynab122 said tenderly.

'Come on.' Humeyra composed herself. 'Let's dig up the right grave. We'll help you this time.'

'I don't need help.' Nalan, back to her assertive self, grabbed her spade. 'Just keep an eye on him.' She pointed a finger at Sabotage.

Sabotage frowned. He hated being seen as a weakling. Like so many timid people, he secretly believed there was, and always had been, a hero within him, itching to come out and show the whole world who he really was.

Meanwhile, Nalan had already started digging, despite the burning ache between her shoulder blades. Her arms and the rest of her body felt sore too. She glanced furtively at her palms, worrying that she might be getting calluses. During her long, arduous transition from the outward appearance of a man to the woman inside that she already was, it had been her hands that had frustrated her the most. Ears and hands, they were the hardest parts to change, her surgeon had explained. Hair could be transplanted, a nose could be reshaped, breasts could be made bigger, and fat could be removed and injected elsewhere – it was amazing how you could become an entirely new person – only there wasn't much to be done about the size or shape of your hands. No number of manicures could compensate for that. And she had the strong, solid hands of a farmer, which she had been ashamed of all these years. But tonight she was grateful for them. Leila would have been proud of her.

She excavated slowly and deliberately this time. Humeyra, Jameelah, Zaynab122 and even Sabotage worked silently by her side, removing small amounts of soil at a time. Again the grave was unearthed, again Nalan jumped in, and again the rope was tossed in.

Compared to the previous attempt, the body felt lighter as they hoisted it up and out. Gently, they placed it on the ground. Afraid of what they might see this time around, they cautiously lifted up a corner of the shroud.

'It's her,' said Humeyra, her voice breaking.

Zaynab122 took off her glasses and wiped at her eyes with the palms of her hands.

Nalan brushed away the strands of hair stuck to her sweaty forehead. 'All right then. Let's take her back to her love.'

Carefully, they placed their friend's body in the wheelbarrow. Nalan held the torso in place, balancing it against her legs. Before setting off, she opened the vodka and took a hefty gulp. The liquid coursed down her gullet towards her belly, burning on its way down, nice and warm, like a friendly campfire.

Another bolt of lightning pierced the sky and hit the ground about a hundred feet away, momentarily illuminating the entire grave-yard. Caught mid-hiccup, Sabotage flinched. He let out a strange sound. Then the sound became a growl.

'Stop making that noise,' said Nalan.

'It's not me!'

He was telling the truth. A pack of dogs had materialized out of nowhere. There were about ten of them, maybe more. A large, black mongrel stood at the head of the group, ears flattened, eyes flashing yellow, teeth bared. They were closing in.

'Dogs!' Sabotage swallowed hard, his Adam's apple bobbing in his throat.

Zaynab122 whispered, 'Or maybe djinn.'

'You'll know which when they bite your arse,' said Nalan. Slowly, she inched closer to Jameelah, shielding her.

'What if they're rabid?' asked Humeyra.

Nalan shook her head. 'See their ears, they're clipped. These dogs aren't feral. They've been neutered. Probably vaccinated too. Stay calm, everyone. If you don't make a move, they won't attack.' She paused, as a new idea occurred to her. 'Have you got any food with you, Humeyra?'

'Why are you asking me?'

'Open that bag. What do you have in there?'

'Just coffee,' Humeyra said at first, but then sighed. 'Okay, I've got a bit of food too.'

Out of her rucksack came the leftovers from dinner.

'I can't believe you've brought all this,' said Zaynab122. 'What were you thinking?'

Nalan said, 'Why, a nice midnight picnic in the graveyard, of course.'

'I just thought we might get hungry.' Humeyra pouted. 'It sounded like it was going to be a long night.'

They tossed the food to the dogs. In thirty seconds it was gone – but those thirty seconds were all that were needed to create a rift in the pack. The food not being enough for each and every dog, fights broke out. A minute ago they had been a team. Now they were rivals. Nalan grabbed a stick, dipped it in the meat sauce and hurled it as far as she could. The dogs bolted after it, snarling at each other.

'They're gone!' Jameelah said.

'For now,' Nalan warned. 'We must hurry. Just make sure you stay close to each other. Walk fast, but no sudden moves. Nothing to provoke them, understood?'

Fired with a new sense of purpose, she pushed the wheelbarrow forward. Dragging their tired feet and carrying their tools, the group marched towards the truck, back the way they had come. Despite the wind, there was a very slight odour emanating from the corpse. Even if it had been stronger, no one would have mentioned it, not wanting to offend Leila. She had always been fond of her perfumes.

The Return

The rain, when it finally arrived, came down in torrents. Trudging through the mud and clambering out of ruts, Nalan struggled to manoeuvre the wheelbarrow. Sabotage plodded along wearily beside Jameelah, holding their only umbrella over the young woman's head. Soaked to the skin, he seemed more sober now. At their heels came Humeyra, breathing hard, unused to such physical exertion, her fingers curled around her inhaler. She knew without having to look down that her stockings were in tatters and her ankles were scratched and bleeding. At the back tottered Zaynab122, sliding about in her squishy wet shoes as she tried to keep pace with people taller and stronger than her.

Nalan jutted out her chin and stopped for no apparent reason. She turned off the torch.

'Why'd you do that?' said Humeyra. 'We can't see a thing.'

It wasn't exactly true – the moonlight, however dim, illuminated the narrow path.

'Be quiet, honey.' A look of concern flashed across Nalan's face. Her whole body had gone rigid.

'What's going on?' murmured Jameelah.

Nalan tilted her head at an odd angle, listening to a sound in the distance. 'See those blue lights over there? There's a police car behind those bushes.'

When they looked in that direction, about sixty feet beyond the cemetery gates, they saw the parked car.

'Oh, no! It's over. We're busted,' said Humeyra.

'What shall we do?' Zaynab122 had only now caught up with them.

Nalan had no idea. But she had always assumed that half the job of being a leader was acting like one. 'I'll tell you what,' she said without losing a beat. 'We'll leave the wheelbarrow here, it's too noisy – even in this fucking rain. I'll carry Leila and we'll keep walking. When we get to the truck, climb into the front with me – all of you. Leila will go in the back. I'll cover her with a blanket. We'll inch our way silently out of here. Once we hit the main road, I'll step on the gas, and that's it. Free as birds!'

'They won't see us?' asked Sabotage.

'Not at first, it's too dark. They will eventually, but it will be too late by then. We'll race past. There's no traffic at this hour. Seriously, it'll be okay.'

Another crazy plan to which, once again, they agreed in unison, no better options presenting themselves.

Nalan lifted Leila's body in her arms, and hauled it over her shoulder.

Now we're even, she thought, remembering the night they were attacked by thugs.

That was long after D/Ali had died. While she had been married to him, Leila had never thought she would have to go back on the streets one day. That part of her life was over, she had told everyone, and most of all herself, as if the past were a ring one could take off on a whim. But back then anything seemed possible. Love danced a fast tango with youth. Leila was happy; she had all she needed. And then D/Ali was gone, just as unexpectedly as he had come into her life, leaving Leila with a hole in her heart that would never heal and a growing pile of debts. It had turned out that D/Ali had borrowed the money he had paid to Bitter Ma, and not from his comrades, as he had once claimed, but from loan sharks.

Nalan now remembered an evening in a restaurant in Asmalimescit where they often dined, the three of them. Stuffed vine leaves and fried mussels (D/Ali had ordered them for everyone, though mostly for Leila), pistachio baklava and quince with clotted cream (Leila had ordered them for everyone, though mostly for

D/Ali), a bottle of raqi (Nalan had ordered it for everyone, though mostly for herself). By the end of the night D/Ali had got wonderfully inebriated, which rarely happened because he had what he liked to call *the discipline of a revolutionary*. Nalan had not met any of his comrades yet. Nor had Leila, which was strange given that they had been married for over a year by then. D/Ali had never said this openly, and would probably have denied it if asked, but it was clear from his behaviour that he was worried his comrades might not approve of his wife and her quirky friends.

Whenever Nalan tried to bring this up, Leila would look daggers at her and find a way to change the subject. These were harrowing times, Leila would remind Nalan afterwards. Innocent civilians were being killed, every day a bomb exploded somewhere, universities had turned into battlegrounds, fascist militia were on the streets and there was systematic torture in prisons. Revolution, to some, might have been merely a word, yet to others it was a matter of life and death. When things were so dire and millions suffered so badly, it was foolish to feel offended by a group of young people for still not having met them in person. Nalan respectfully disagreed. She wanted to understand what kind of a revolution would have no room in its vast embrace for her and her newly enlarged breasts.

That evening, Nalan had been determined to ask D/Ali about it. They were sitting at a table by the window, where a breeze brought in the scent of honeysuckle and jasmine, mingled with the smells of tobacco, fried food and aniseed.

'I need to ask you something,' Nalan said while trying to avoid Leila's gaze.

At once D/Ali straightened. 'Great, I have a question for you too.'

'Oh! Then you first, honey.'

'No, you first.'

'I insist.'

'Fine. If I were to ask you what the biggest difference is between Western European cities and our cities, what would you say?'

Nalan took a swig of her raqi before responding. 'Well, over here we women often need to carry a safety pin on the bus, in case someone molests us and we need to prick the jerk. I don't think it's the same in a big Western city. There are always exceptions, no doubt, but as a rule of thumb I'd say the telling sign between "here" and "there" is in the number of safety pins used on public buses.'

D/Ali smiled. 'Yes, maybe that too. But I think the most important difference is in our cemeteries.'

Leila gave him a curious glance. 'Cemeteries?'

'Yes, sweetheart.' D/Ali pointed at the untouched baklava in front of her. 'Are you not going to eat that?'

Knowing he had the sweet tooth of a schoolboy, Leila pushed the plate towards him.

D/Ali said that in major European cities burial grounds were carefully laid out and neatly kept, and so green they could pass for royal gardens. Not so in Istanbul, where the graveyards were as messy as the lives led above ground. But it was not all a matter of tidiness. At some point in history, Europeans had the brilliant idea of sending the dead to the outskirts of their towns. It wasn't exactly 'out of sight, out of mind', but it was definitely 'out of sight, out of urban life'. Graveyards were built beyond city walls; ghosts were separated from the living. It was all done quickly and efficiently, like removing the yolks from the whites. The new arrangement had proved highly beneficial. When they no longer had to see tombstones – those ghastly reminders of life's brevity and God's severity – European citizens were galvanized into action. Having pushed death out of their daily routines, they could focus on other things: composing arias, inventing the guillotine and then the steam locomotive, colonizing the rest of the world and carving up the Middle East . . . You could do all that and much more if only you could take your mind off the disturbing thought of being a mere mortal.

'What about Istanbul?' Leila asked.

Scooping up the last bit of baklava, D/Ali replied, 'It's different over here. This city belongs to the dead. Not to us.'

In Istanbul it was the living who were the temporary occupants, the unbidden guests, here today and gone tomorrow, and deep down everyone knew it. White headstones met citizens at every turn – alongside highways, shopping malls, car parks or football fields – scattered in every nook, like a broken string of pearls. D/Ali said that if millions of Istanbulites had only lived up to a fraction of their potential it was because of the unnerving proximity of the graves. One lost one's appetite for innovation when constantly reminded that the Grim Reaper was just round the corner, his scythe shining red in the setting sun. That was why renovation projects came to nought, the infrastructure failed and the collective memory was as flimsy as tissue paper. Why insist on designing the future or remembering the past when we were all slipping and sliding our way to the final exit? Democracy, human rights, freedom of speech – what was the point, if we were all about to die anyhow? The way the cemeteries were organized and the dead were treated, D/Ali concluded, was the most striking difference between civilizations.

The three of them had then lapsed into silence, listening to the clatter of cutlery and clanging of plates in the background. Nalan still didn't know why she had said what she said next. The words had spilled out of her mouth as though they had a will of their own.

'I'll be the first to snuff it, you'll see. I want both of you to dance around my grave, no tears. Smoke, drink, kiss and dance – that's my will.'

Leila frowned, upset at her for saying such things. She raised her face towards the fluorescent lamp flickering above, her beautiful eyes now the colour of rain. D/Ali, however, had just smiled – a gentle, sorrowful smile, as if he knew, deep within, that whatever Nalan claimed, he would be the first among them to leave.

'So what were *you* going to ask?' D/Ali said.

And suddenly Nalan had a change of heart: it didn't matter any more, the question of why they were not meeting his comrades and of what the revolution was going to be like in that bright future that might or might not come. Perhaps nothing was worth worrying about in a city where everything was constantly shifting and dissolving, and the only thing they could ever rely on was this moment in time, which was already half gone.

Sopping wet and exhausted, the friends reached the Chevrolet. They all climbed into the front seat – except for the driver. Nalan was busy in the back, securing Leila's body, passing ropes around her and fastening them to the truck's sides to make sure she wouldn't roll around. Satisfied, she joined the others, softly closed her door and released the breath she had been holding.

'All right. Everyone ready?'

'Ready,' said Humeyra into a stretch of silence.

'Now let's be super quiet. The hardest part is over. We can do this.'

Nalan placed the key in the ignition, giving it a gentle twist. The engine came to life and, a second later, music blared out. Whitney Houston poured into the night, asking where do broken hearts go.

'Fuck!' said Nalan.

She slammed a hand to the tape player – too late. The two police officers, out stretching their legs, were staring in their direction, stupefied.

Nalan glanced in the rear-view mirror and watched the officers sprint to their car. Throwing back her shoulders, she said, 'Okay, change of plan. Hold on tight!'

Back to the City*

Its tyres spinning on the rain-slick road, the 1982 Chevrolet accelerated down the hill and through the woods, splattering mud in all directions. There were weather-beaten posters and billboards on both sides of the route. One, peeling along its edges and only just legible, read: *Come to Kilyos . . . your dream vacation . . . just around the corner.*

Nalan floored the accelerator. She could hear the sirens of the police car blaring, though still far behind, the small Škoda struggling to speed up without sliding on the mud and skidding out of control. And suddenly Nalan was grateful for the mud, for the rain, for the storm and, yes, for the old Chevrolet. Once they reached the city it would be harder to outpace the police car; then she would have to trust herself. She knew the back streets well.

Off to the right, where the road forked and tall firs formed a copse in the middle, a deer froze in the glare of the headlights. Looking at the animal, Nalan had a sudden idea. She aligned the axle parallel to the kerb, hoped the bottom of the truck was high enough and drove straight towards the copse, where she instantly turned off the headlights. It all happened so fast, no one dared to breathe a word. They waited, trusting fate, or God, trusting forces beyond their control and power. A minute later, the police car whizzed by without seeing them and headed towards Istanbul, ten miles away.

By the time they were back on the road theirs was the only vehicle in sight. At the first intersection, a traffic light swinging in the wind on overhead wires turned from green to red. The truck careered on at top speed. Far in the distance the city rose, and

* 'Istanbul' derives from *eis ten polin* in Medieval Greek, meaning 'to the city'.

above its outline a streak of orange pierced the dark sky. Soon it would be dawn.

'I hope you know what you're doing,' said Zaynab122, having by now run out of prayers. There being not enough space, she was half sitting on Humeyra's lap.

'Don't worry,' said Nalan, gripping the wheel tighter.

'Yes, why worry?' said Humeyra. 'If she keeps on driving like this we won't be in this world for much longer anyway.'

Nalan shook her head. 'Come on, stop stressing, everyone. Once we're in the city, we won't be so exposed. I'll find a side street, and we'll make ourselves invisible!'

Sabotage looked out of the window. The effects of the vodka had hit him in three stages: first came excitement, then fear and apprehension, and finally melancholy. He wound down the glass. The wind rushed in and filled the cramped space. Try as he might to stay calm, he couldn't see how they could possibly shake off the police. And if he were caught with a dead body and a bunch of dodgy-looking women, what would he tell his wife and his ultra-conservative in-laws?

He sat back, closed his eyes. In the darkness stretching ahead, Leila appeared, not as a grown woman, but as a young girl. She was wearing her school uniform, white socks and red shoes, the toes slightly scuffed. Briskly, she sprinted towards a tree in the garden, knelt down, grabbed a handful of soil, tucked it into her mouth and chewed.

Sabotage had never told her that he had seen her doing that. It had come as a shock to him: why would anyone eat dirt? Not long after, he had noticed the cuts on the inside of her arms, and he guessed there might be more of them on her legs and thighs. Worried, he had pressed her about it, but she had just shrugged. *It's okay, I know when to stop.* The confession, because that's what it was, had only deepened Sabotage's concern. He, before anyone, and more than anyone, had seen through her pain. A heavy and dense sorrow had settled in him; a fist had closed around his heart. A sorrow he'd kept hidden from everyone, and nourished all these years, because what was love if it wasn't nursing someone else's pain as if it were your own? He reached out his hand, and the girl in front of his eyes disappeared, like a vision.

Sabotage Sinan had many, many regrets in life, but nothing compared to the regret he felt for never having told Leila that since they were children in Van, walking together to school every morning as the sky above them cleared to blue, finding each other during break times, skipping stones on the edge of the great lake in summer, cradling mugs of steaming salep in winter as they sat side by side on a garden wall and studied pictures of American artists, ever since those long-lost days, he had been in love with her.

Unlike the road from Kilyos, the streets of Istanbul, even at this ungodly hour, were anything but empty. The Chevrolet rattled past one apartment block after another, their windows dark and empty like missing teeth or hollowed-out eyes. Every now and then something unexpected appeared in front of the truck: a stray cat; a factory worker back from a night shift; a homeless man looking for cigarette butts in front of an upmarket restaurant; a lonely umbrella blowing around in the wind; a junkie standing in the middle of the road, grinning at a vision only he could see. All the more vigilant, Nalan leaned forward, ready to swerve at any point. She grumbled to herself, 'What's wrong with these people? They should all be in bed at this hour.'

'I bet that's exactly what they're thinking about us,' Humeyra said.

'Well, we have a mission.' Nalan glanced in the rear-view mirror.

In addition to dyslexia, Nalan had mild dyspraxia. It hadn't been easy for her to get a driving licence, and while Humeyra's insinuation earlier had been crude, it wasn't altogether untrue. She had flirted with the driving instructor. Just a bit. Yet in all the years since, she had never had an accident. That was no small feat in a city where there were more road hogs per square yard than buried Byzantine treasures. She had always thought that, in a way, driving was like sex. To enjoy it to the fullest, one needed not to rush and always to consider the other side. *Respect the journey, go with the flow, do not compete and never try to dominate.* But this city was full of maniacs speeding through red lights and cutting into emergency lanes as if they were tired of living. Sometimes, just for a lark, Nalan would tailgate their vehicles, flashing her headlights and blasting her horn, inches from their rear bumpers. She would get so dangerously close that she could see the eyes of the drivers in their rear-view mirrors — just above the dangling air fresheners, football pennants and gemstone rosaries — and watch their horrified expressions as they realized they were being chased by a woman, and the woman in question might be a *travesti*.

Upon approaching Bebek, they noticed a police car parked at the corner of the steep road which led to the old Ottoman cemetery and then, further up, to Bosphorus University. Was it waiting for them or was it just another patrol car on a break? Either way, they could not risk being seen. Shifting gear, Nalan made a quick U-turn and stamped on the accelerator, sending the speedometer needle shooting into the red.

'What shall we do?' asked Jameelah. There were beads of sweat on her forehead. The trauma of the day and the exertion of the night were now taking their toll on her weary body.

'We'll find another cemetery,' said Nalan, her voice stripped of its usual commanding tone.

They had lost too much time. Before long it would be morning and they would be left with a corpse in the back of the truck with nowhere to house it.

'But it's going to be light soon,' objected Humeyra.

Watching Nalan struggle to find the right words, seeming finally to have lost control of the situation, Zaynab122 lowered her eyes. Ever since they had left the cemetery she had been troubled by pangs of conscience. She felt terrible about exhuming Leila's body and was worried that they might have committed a sin in the eyes of Allah. Yet now, as she observed Nalan's uncharacteristic confusion, another thought struck her with the force of a revelation. Maybe the five of them, just like the people in a miniature painting, were stronger and brighter, and far more alive, when they complemented each other. Maybe she had to relax and let go of her own way of doing things because this was, after all, Leila's burial.

'How are we going to find another cemetery at this hour?' Sabotage asked, pulling at his moustache.

'Maybe there is no need,' Zaynab122 said so quietly that they all strained to hear. 'Maybe we don't have to bury her.'

Nalan screwed up her face in a puzzled frown. 'Say that again?'

'Leila didn't want to be buried,' said Zaynab122. 'We talked about it once or twice, back in the brothel. I remember telling her about the four saints who protect this city. I said to her, "I hope one day I'll be buried next to a saint's shrine." And Leila said, "That's nice, I hope you will. But not for me. If I had a choice I'd never want to be buried six feet under." I was a bit irritated at the time, because our religion is clear on this. I told her not to say such things. But Leila insisted.'

'What do you mean? She asked to be cremated?' bellowed Sabotage.

'Oh, God, no.' Zaynab122 pushed her glasses back. 'She meant the sea. She said she had been told that the day she was born, someone in their house had freed the fish they kept in a glass bowl. She seemed to like that idea very much. She said that when she died she would go and find that fish, even though she couldn't swim.'

'Are you telling us that Leila wanted to be thrown into the sea?' asked Humeyra.

'Well, I'm not sure she wanted to be *thrown* exactly, and it's not like she left a will or anything, but, yes, she said she'd rather be in the water than under the earth.'

Nalan scowled without taking her eyes off the road. 'Why didn't you tell us before?'

'Why would I? It's one of those conversations you don't really take seriously. Besides, it's a sin.'

Nalan turned to Zaynab122. 'Then why are you telling us now?'

'Because suddenly it makes sense,' said Zaynab122. 'I understand her choices might not match mine, but I still respect them.'

They were all thinking now.

'So what shall we do?' asked Humeyra.

'Let's take her to the sea,' said Jameelah, and the way she said it, with such lightness and certainty in her voice, made the others feel like it had been the right thing to do all along.

And just like that the Chevrolet Silverado zoomed towards the Bosphorus Bridge. The very bridge whose opening Leila had celebrated with thousands of fellow Istanbulites once upon a time.

PART THREE

The Soul

The Bridge

'Humeyra?'

'Hmmm?'

'You okay, honey?' asked Nalan, hands tight on the wheel.

Through half-closed eyelids Humeyra replied, 'I feel a bit sleepy, sorry.'

'Have you taken anything this evening?'

'Maybe a little something.' Humeyra smiled weakly. Her head rolled on to Jameelah's shoulder, and just like that she fell asleep.

Nalan sighed. 'Oh, great!'

Jameelah inched closer, repositioning herself to make Humeyra more comfortable.

As soon as her eyes had closed, Humeyra tumbled into a velvety slumber. She saw herself as a child in Mardin, scooped up in her oldest sister's arms. Her favourite sister. Then her other siblings joined them and now they were whirling in a circle, laughing. In the distance the half-reaped fields stretched flat and the windows of the Monastery of St Gabriel caught the sunlight. Leaving her siblings behind, she walked towards the ancient building, listening to the sough of the wind through the crevices in the stones. It looked different somehow. As she approached, she saw the reason why: the monastery was constructed out of pills instead of bricks. All the pills she had ever swallowed – with water, with whisky, with Coke, with tea, dry. Her face distorted. She sobbed.

'Shhh, it's just a dream,' said Jameelah.

Humeyra fell quiet. Unaffected by the clamour of the truck, her expression turned serene. Her hair came loose, its roots stubbornly black under the pile of intense yellow.

Jameelah began to sing a lullaby in her mother tongue, her voice as clear and penetrating as an African sky. Listening to her,

Nalan, Sabotage and Zaynab122 all felt the warmth of the song without having to understand a single word. There was something strangely comforting in the way different cultures had arrived at similar customs and melodies, and in how, all around the world, people were being rocked in the arms of loved ones in their moments of distress.

As the Chevrolet sped on to the Bosphorus Bridge, dawn broke in all its glory. A full day had passed since Leila's body had been found inside a metal rubbish bin.

Hair clinging damp to her neck, Nalan revved the engine. The truck made a coughing sound and shuddered, and for a second she feared it was about to let them down, but it forged on, grumbling. She held the wheel tighter with one hand and patted it with the other as she murmured, 'I know, love. You're tired, I understand.'

'Are you talking to vehicles now?' asked Zaynab122 with a smile. 'You talk to everything – except God.'

'You know what? I promise, if this thing ends well, I'll say hello to Him.'

'Look.' Zaynab122 pointed out of the window. 'I think He's saying hello to you.'

Outside, the strip of sky along the horizon had turned the luminous violet of an oyster's inner shell, delicate and iridescent. The vast expanse of the sea was dotted with ships and fishing boats. The city looked silky and soft, as if it didn't have any edges.

As they headed towards the Asian shore, luxurious mansions came into view, and behind those the solid villas of the middle class, and further up in the hills, row upon row of ramshackle sheds. Scattered between the buildings were the graveyards and saints' shrines, their pale old stones like white sails, as though they might float off.

Out of the corner of her eye, Nalan checked on Humeyra and lit a cigarette, feeling less guilty about it than she would normally, as if asthma were a condition that didn't affect those in deep sleep. She did try to blow the smoke out through the open window, but the wind brought it all back in.

She was about to throw the cigarette out when Sabotage piped up from his corner, 'Wait. Let me take a puff first.'

He smoked quietly, growing pensive. He wondered what his children were doing right now. It broke his heart that they had never met Leila. He had always assumed that one day they would all get together over a nice breakfast or lunch, and the children would instantly adore her, just like he did. Now it was too late. It seemed to him that he had always been too late for everything. He had to stop hiding, pretending, separating his life into compartments, and find a way to bring his many realities together. He should introduce his friends to his family and his family to his friends, and if his family did not accept his friends, he should do his best to make them understand. If only it weren't so difficult to do that.

He threw away the cigarette, closed the window and pressed his forehead against the glass. Something in him was shifting, gathering power.

In the rear-view mirror Nalan saw two police cars enter the road, far behind them, leading to the bridge. Her eyes grew wide. She hadn't expected them to catch up so soon. 'There's two of them! They're behind us.'

'Maybe one of us should get out and try to distract them?' said Sabotage.

'I can do that,' said Zaynab122 quickly. 'I may not be able to give you a hand with the body. But I can do this. I could pretend to be injured or something. They'll have to stop for me.'

'You sure?' asked Nalan.

'Yes,' said Zaynab122 firmly. 'Positive.'

Nalan screeched the truck to a halt and helped Zaynab122 to get out, then hopped back in immediately. Humeyra, disturbed by the commotion, opened her eyes slightly, shifted in her seat and went back to sleep.

'Good luck, honey. Be careful,' said Nalan through the open window.

Then they whizzed off, leaving Zaynab122 on the pavement, her small shadow standing between her and the rest of the city.

Halfway across the bridge, Nalan hit the brakes and turned the wheel sharply to the left. Pulling over, she skidded to a stop.

'Okay, I need help,' Nalan said, something she rarely admitted.

Sabotage nodded and squared his shoulders. 'I'm ready.'

The two of them darted round to the back of the truck and unfastened the ropes holding Leila. Swiftly, Sabotage took the scarf out of his pocket and tucked it into the folds of the shroud. 'I shouldn't forget her present.'

Together, they hoisted Leila's body up on to their shoulders and, sharing the weight, shuffled over towards the knee-high barriers. Carefully, they swung their legs over the barriers and kept walking. When they reached the outer railing they lowered the body to rest on the metal surface. As they caught their breath, looking suddenly small under the massive zigzagging steel cables that hung overhead, they glanced at each other.

'Come on,' said Sabotage, his face set into hard lines.

They pushed the body further across the railing, gently and tentatively at first, as if encouraging a child to enter a classroom on her first day.

'Hey, you two!'

Nalan and Sabotage both froze — a man's voice tore the air, the sound of screeching tyres, the smell of burning rubber.

'Stop!'

'Don't move!'

An officer ran out from a police car, yelling commands, and then another.

'They've killed someone. They're trying to get rid of the body!'

Sabotage paled. 'Oh, no! She was already dead.'

'Shut up!'

'Put him on the ground. Slowly.'

'*Her*,' Nalan couldn't help saying. 'Look, let us explain please –'

'Silence! Don't make another move. This is a warning, I'll shoot!'

Another police car pulled up. Sitting on the back seat was Zaynab122, her eyes full of fear, her face ashen. She had not been able to distract them for long. Nothing was going according to plan.

Two more officers got out.

On the opposite lane of the bridge, traffic was building. Cars passed slowly, curious faces peering from the windows: a private car carrying a family returning from holiday, suitcases piled up in the back; a city bus already half packed with early risers – cleaning ladies, shop assistants, street vendors – now they were all gawking.

'I said, put that body down!' an officer repeated.

Nalan lowered her eyes, a flush of realization crossing her face. Leila's body would be seized by the authorities and once again buried in the Cemetery of the Companionless. There was nothing they could do. They had tried. They had failed.

'I'm sorry,' whispered Nalan, half turning to Sabotage. 'It's all my fault. I made a botch of everything.'

'No sudden moves. And keep your hands up!'

Even as she kept hold of the body with one arm, Nalan took a small step towards the officers, her free hand raised in surrender.

'Put the body down!'

Nalan bent her knees, ready to pull the body back down gently on to the pavement, but she paused, having noticed that Sabotage was not doing the same thing. She glanced at him, puzzled.

Sabotage stood still, as though he had not heard a single word of what the officers had said. As he almost closed his eyes, all the colour leached from the sky and the sea and the entire city, and for a moment everything was as black and white as Leila's favourite films, except for a single hula hoop swirling, drawing circles in a bright, assertive orange, full of life. How he wished he could have

301

turned back time just like that. How he wished, instead of giving Leila the money for the bus journey that would take her away from him, he had asked her to stay in Van and marry him. Why had he been such a coward? And why was the price of not saying the right words at the right time so high?

With a sudden force, Sabotage lurched forward and shoved the body over the barrier, the breeze in his face laced with salt, tasting like his tears.

'Stop!!!'

Sounds dissolved in the air. The squawk of a seagull. The pull of a trigger. A bullet struck Sabotage in the shoulder. The pain was excruciating but strangely bearable. He caught sight of the sky. Infinite, fearless, forgiving.

Back in the truck, Jameelah screamed.

Leila descended into the void. She dropped over two hundred feet, fast and straight. Beneath her the sea shimmered blue and bright like an Olympic pool. As she fell down, a few folds of her shroud came undone, floating around and above her, like the pigeons her mother had raised on the roof. Except these were free. There were no cages to confine them.

Into the water she plummeted.

Away from this madness.

The Blue Betta Fish

Leila feared she might land on the head of a lonely fisherman in a rowboat. Or a homesick sailor taking in the view as his ship glided under the bridge. Or a chef preparing breakfast for his employers on the deck of a luxury yacht. That'd be just her luck. But none of these things happened. Instead she dropped down amidst the chatter of the seagulls, the swish of the wind. The sun was rising over the horizon; the grid of houses and streets on the opposite shore seemed aflame.

Above her was a clear sky, beaming an apology for the storm of the previous night. Below her were the crests of waves, the flecks of white spattered as though from a painter's brush. Far away on all sides, cluttered and chaotic, hurt and hurtful, but beautiful as always, was the old city herself.

She felt light. She felt content. And with every yard she dropped, she shed another negative feeling: anger, sadness, longing, pain, regret, resentment, and its cousin, jealousy. She jettisoned them all, one by one. Then with a jolt that shook her entire being she broke the surface of the sea. Water parted around her and the world came alive. It was unlike anything she had experienced before. Soundless. Boundless. Leila looked around, taking it all in, despite its immensity. Ahead of her she caught sight of a tiny shadow.

It was the blue betta fish. The very one that had been released into the creek in Van on the day she was born.

'Nice to see you, finally,' said the fish. 'What took you so long?'

Leila did not know what to say. Could she speak under the water?

Smiling at her confusion, the blue betta fish said, 'Follow me.'

Now finding her voice, Leila said, with a shyness she could not conceal, 'I don't know how to swim. I never learned.'

'Don't worry about that. You know everything you need to know. Come with me.'

She swam – slowly and clumsily at first, and then smoothly and assuredly, gradually increasing the tempo. But she was not trying to get anywhere. There was no reason to rush any more and nothing to run away from. A shoal of bream swirled in and around her hair. Bonitos and mackerels tickled her toes. Dolphins escorted her, flipping and splashing above the waves.

Leila surveyed the panorama, a universe in Technicolor, each direction in the water a new pool of light, seemingly flowing into the other. She saw the rusting skeletons of sunken passenger boats. She saw lost treasures, surveillance vessels, imperial cannons, abandoned cars, ancient shipwrecks, concubines who had been thrust out of palace windows inside sacks and then dropped into the blue, their jewels now tangled with the weeds, their eyes still searching for a meaning in a world that had brought them so cruel an end. She found poets and writers and rebels from the Ottoman and Byzantine times, each cast into the deep for their treacherous words or contentious beliefs. The ghastly and the graceful – everything was present around her, in rich abundance.

Everything but pain. There was no pain down here.

Her mind had fully shut down, her body was already decomposing and her soul was chasing a betta fish. She was relieved to have left the Cemetery of the Companionless. She was happy to be part of this vibrant realm, this comforting harmony that she had never thought possible, and this vast blue, bright as the birth of a new flame.

Free at last.

Epilogue

The flat on Hairy Kafka Street was decorated with balloons, streamers and banners. Today would have been Leila's birthday.

'Where is Sabotage?' asked Nalan.

They had fresh justification for calling him that, now that he had finally, and fully, sabotaged his life. After being shot while pushing the dead body of a prostitute off the Bosphorus Bridge, accompanied by dubious friends, he had been all over the newspapers. Within the same week he had lost his job, his marriage, his house. He had learned only belatedly that his wife had been having a long-term affair, and that is why she had always been happy to see him leave in the evenings. That had given him some leverage during the divorce settlement. As for his wife's family, they no longer talked to him, though thankfully his children did, and he was allowed to see them every weekend, which was all that mattered. He now had a small stall near the Grand Bazaar, selling knock-off merchandise. He was making half the money he used to earn, but he did not complain.

'Stuck in traffic,' said Humeyra.

Nalan waved a newly manicured hand. Between her fingers she held an unlit cigarette and D/Ali's Zippo. 'I thought he didn't have a car any more. What's his excuse this time?'

'That he doesn't have a car. He has to take the bus.'

'He'll be here soon, give him some time,' said Jameelah soothingly.

Nodding, Nalan stepped out on to the balcony, pulled up a chair and sat down. Looking down the street, she saw Zaynab122 leaving the grocer's with a plastic bag in her hand, walking with some difficulty.

Nalan clutched her side, seized with a sudden cough, a smoker's hack. Her chest hurt. She was getting old. She had no pensions or savings, nothing to sustain her. It had been the wisest thing for the five of them to start living together in Leila's flat and share the costs. They were more vulnerable on their own; together, they were stronger.

Far in the distance, beyond the roofs and domes, was the sea, shimmering like glass, and deep in the water, somewhere and everywhere, was Leila – a thousand little Leilas stuck to fish fins and seaweed, laughing from inside clam shells.

Istanbul was a liquid city. Nothing was permanent here. Nothing felt settled. It all must have begun thousands of years ago when the ice sheets melted, the sea levels rose, the floodwaters surged, and all known ways of life were destroyed. The pessimists were the first to flee the area, probably; the optimists would have chosen to wait and see how things would turn out. Nalan thought that one of the endless tragedies of human history was that pessimists were better at surviving than optimists, which meant that, logically speaking, humanity carried the genes of people who did not believe in humanity.

When the floods arrived, they burst in from all sides, drowning everything in their path – animals, plants, humans. In this way the Black Sea was formed, and the Golden Horn, and the Bosphorus, and the Sea of Marmara. As the waters flowed all around, together they created a patch of dry land, on which someday a mighty metropolis was built.

It still had not solidified, this motherland of theirs. When she closed her eyes, Nalan could hear the water roiling under their feet. Shifting, whirling, searching.

Still in flux.

Note to the Reader

Many things in this book are true and everything is fiction.

The Cemetery of the Companionless in Kilyos is a real place. It is growing fast. Lately, an increasing number of refugees who drowned in the Aegean Sea while trying to cross to Europe have been buried here. Like all the other graves, theirs have only numbers, rarely names.

The residents of the cemetery mentioned in this book were inspired by newspaper clippings and factual stories about people buried there – including the Zen Buddhist grandmother who was travelling from Nepal to New York.

The street of brothels is real too. And so are the historical events mentioned in the story, including the My Lai Massacre in Vietnam in 1968 and the massacre in Istanbul on International Workers' Day in 1977. The Intercontinental Hotel from which snipers opened fire on the crowds has now become the Marmara Hotel.

Until the year 1990, Article 438 of the Turkish Penal Code was used to reduce the sentence given to rapists by one-third if they could prove that their victim was a prostitute. Legislators defended the article with the argument that 'a prostitute's mental or physical health could not be negatively affected by rape'. In 1990, in the face of an increasing number of attacks against sex workers, passionate protests were held in different parts of the country. Owing to this strong reaction from civil society, Article 438 was repealed. But there have been few, if any, legal amendments in the country since then towards gender equality, or specifically towards improving the conditions of sex workers.

And finally, although the five friends are products of my imagination, they have been inspired by actual people – natives and latecomers and foreigners — I have met in Istanbul. While Leila and her friends are entirely fictional characters, the friendships described in this novel, at least in my eyes, are as real as this beguiling old city.

Glossary

agha: honorific title in the Ottoman Empire

amca: traditional address for an old man

ayran: yoghurt drink

börek: filled pastry

cezve: coffee pot

darbuka: goblet drum

dhikr: form of devotion where the name of God or His attributes are repeated; associated with Sufi brotherhoods

ezan: call to prayer

feringhee: foreigner

gazino: Turkish music hall

geçmiş olsun: get well soon

grape-leaf sarma: stuffed grape leaves

habibi: my love

haram: forbidden by Islamic law

hayati: my life

hodja: Muslim headmaster

kader: destiny

konak: mansion

nafs: ego

nazar: evil eye

nine: grandmother

salep: hot milk with cinnamon and wild orchid

Sheitan: Satan

simit: type of bagel with sesame seeds

takke: skullcap

tariqa: Sufi order or school

tövbe: repent

ya ruhi: my soul

yenge: aunt-in-law (or sister-in-law)

Zamhareer: part of hell that is extremely cold

Zaqqum Tree: tree that grows in hell

Zeybek: a form of folk dance in Western Turkey

Cemetery of the Companionless, Turkey
Photo credit © Tufan Hamarat

Acknowledgements

There are some special people who helped me during the writing of this novel. I am deeply grateful to them.

My heartfelt thanks to my wonderful editor, Venetia Butterfield. It is a true blessing for a novelist to work with an editor who understands her like no one else does, and guides and encourages her with faith, love and determination. Thank you, dear Venetia. I owe a big thank you to my agent, Jonny Geller, who listens, analyses and sees. Every conversation we have opens a new window in my mind.

Many thanks to those people who patiently read earlier versions of this book and provided me with advice. Stephen Barber, what an amazing friend, a generous soul, you are! Thank you, Jason Goodwin, Rowan Routh and dear Lorna Owen for being with me all the way through. Thank you so much, Caroline Pretty: you've been most thoughtful and helpful. Thank you, Nick Barley, who read the first chapters and told me to keep going without a doubt, without looking back. Huge thanks to Patrick Sielemann and Peter Haag, who have stood by me from the very beginning. How can I forget your valuable support?

I want to express my gratitude to Joanna Prior, Isabel Wall, Sapphire Rees, Anna Ridley and Ellie Smith at Penguin UK, and Daisy Meyrick, Lucy Talbot and Ciara Finan at Curtis Brown. Thanks also to Sara Mercurio, who sends me the loveliest emails from LA, and Anton Mueller for words of wisdom from New York. And to the editors and friends at Doğan Kitap – a beautiful and brave team swimming against the current, guided by nothing other than a love of books. My gratitude, too, to beloved Zelda and Emir Zahir, and dear Eyup, and to my mother, Shafak, the woman whose name I adopted as my surname long, long ago.

My grandmother passed away shortly before I started writing this novel. I didn't go to her funeral, as I didn't feel comfortable travelling to my motherland at a time when writers, journalists, intellectuals, academics, friends and colleagues were being arrested on the most baseless charges. My mother told me not to worry about not visiting Grandma's grave. But I did worry and I felt guilty. I was very close to Grandma. She was the one who raised me.

The night I finished the novel there was a waxing moon in the sky. I thought about Tequila Leila and I thought about Grandma, and though the former is a fictional character and the latter as real as my own blood, somehow it felt to me that they had met and become good friends, *sister-outsiders*. After all, boundaries of the mind mean nothing for women who continue to sing songs of freedom under the moonlight . . .